THE WEB

by J. J. Johnstone

L. J. J. Johnstone

DORRANCE
PUBLISHING CO
EST. 1920
PITTSBURGH, PENNSYLVANIA 15222

Dorrance Publishing Co
701 Smithfield Street
Pittsburgh, PA 15222
Visit our website at *www.dorrancebookstore.com*

ISBN: 978-1-4809-1938-9
eISBN 978-1-4809-2053-8

ACKNOWLEDGMENTS

This is an important page in this book. Without the loving help and support of the following people mentioned, this book may never have been written and published.

Adrian and Natalia, how do I say thanks for all of your encouragement and support?

Laura and Dave, who has always been there and I know always will be.

Doug, even though you are gone now, your encouragement and love made me stronger.

Bev and Don, friends that are as close as family. Your encouraging words mean a lot.

Art and Phyllis, who have helped me to believe in people.

Frank, your support has meant a lot.

Daniel, over the years you have been a strong supporter.

Chris, I know you will always be just a call away.

And last but certainly not least, John. Your understanding, patience, love, and support while this book was being written is greatly appreciated.

My kids have been my reason for living, loving, and surviving. Even when they were young, I got strength from just being in their presence.

Each one has amazed me as to who they have grown up to be. They have become such strong-minded and successful individuals. I am so proud of them.

God gave me a gift, to be able to see what was important in life, even when there are trials and hurdles I had to overcome. He blessed me with three fantastic children. Throughout my journey, God has allowed my life to be touched by people who have left their mark with me, making me a stronger individual. Each one has helped to mold me to who I am today. Thank you to all of you.

Love you all.

All artwork in this book was done by me.

I heard the sounds of shattering glass as I fell through the top of the coffee table. The light coming through the living room window glistened on the broken and shattered glass, making the hundreds of pieces now lying on the floor look like sparkling diamonds on the carpet. It was only moments before this that I had been dusting this coffee table as I had heard the front door open and had turned to see my husband quickly walking up to me, and then, without realizing what was happening, I felt a sharp impact hit my face the sensation of falling and not being able to stop myself. Dazed, I looked up and saw his fist coming my way again. I tried to move out of the way of his swinging hand, but I felt the sting of another strike again, this time making my head buzz, and I felt disoriented. I was only able to move a few inches, and I could feel the broken glass cutting into my hands. I could taste blood, and my head was throbbing.

I closed my eyes as I felt the pain ringing through my head. The room was spinning, and I was sure there were bells tolling somewhere far off. I could feel darkness starting to fall over me, but I knew I had to fight the urge to faint. I took a big breath and pushed on the ground, trying to get my legs under me to stand. My heart was beating fast, and I felt sick to my stomach as I tried to clear my thoughts and figure out what had upset Jim.

Jim yelled, "Stay down, you bitch. Why do you make me do this? Do you think I really want to come home and just start beating up my wife? How many beatings do I have to give you before you become a decent person? I tried calling you, and you didn't answer, so I know you went out somewhere."

I tried to speak, but I found that my head was hurting so much it made it hard to talk. I spoke slowly and choose my words carefully, trying not to agitate him any more than he already was. "It was so hot in here that I couldn't take it anymore, and I just wanted to sit in the shade out back and cool off. Jay took his little truck outside and was playing under the tree. He had been too hot all day, and he couldn't sleep during his afternoon nap."

Jim roughly pulled me to my feet and tossed me roughly onto the sofa, saying, "You could have sat on the balcony."

"The sun was on the balcony, and it just made it even hotter in here," I tried to explain.

"Look at this mess you've created here in our new home," he said angrily. "Get this place cleaned up. I'm going out to a restaurant to eat, as I can see you didn't bother to make dinner either. I guess you didn't have enough time to bother cooking since you had to be outside."

"I didn't know you would be home today. I thought you were out of town for the week." I said as I struggled to get up off the sofa and then quickly sat back down again when I realized how dizzy I was.

He had already turned and was opening the door to leave. "I come and go as I please," he said. He stopped and shot me an angry look over his shoulder and then he left.

I sat on the sofa, looking at all the broken glass and the blood that was splattered over everything. It seemed like every time I blinked a sharp pain went through my head.

I felt a tear roll down my cheek. It was another episode of feeling like I was totally alone in the world, and I feared what he would be like when he came home again.

In 1976 we had purchased a three-bedroom condo in a rather nice apartment building. The apartment we bought had been used as the model apartment for the building, so it was fully decorated with expensive wallpaper and plush carpets in all the rooms, except the kitchen, where it was tiled flooring. All the rooms were large, with an L-shaped living and dining room that were both decorated in yellow and silver; the kitchen was also decorated in yellows and silvers as well. There was a large laundry room that could have been used as another bedroom, and then there were three nicely decorated bedrooms. The first two bedrooms going up the hallway were done in neutral colors, and the master bedroom with an in-suite washroom was all done in deep purples with white trim and looked very stunning with our white bedroom furniture.

It was an attractive apartment and seemed very spacious. We had the end unit which was nice as the apartment had windows facing the back of the building as well as the end of the building.

At the back of the building, there was a park-like setting with old maple trees, and many large evergreen trees overlooking a ravine that had a nice creek running through it. At the end of the building we could see the playground where the children in the building loved to go and play. When Jim was home sometimes we would take Jay out to play on the swings and slide.

Jim's work was industrial flooring, and he worked for a very busy company that got a lot of jobs out of town. If they didn't offer the out-of-town jobs to Jim, then he would go and ask to be sent on the out-of-town jobs. That left Jay and I on our own throughout the week, and then Jim would usually be home on the weekends. Jim would never leave any money for us in case we ran out of anything or if we needed something. His view was that if I ran out of something I could wait until he got back. When he came home from out of town he would be moody and would spend a lot of his time at a pool hall in downtown Toronto that he had enjoyed going to for years. His father even offered to purchase the pool hall for Jim so that he could be home with his family more. When Jim's father mentioned it to him, Jim's reply was that he preferred to be out of town so that he could live more freely and not have to deal with a wife and kid. In reality we did not have a good relationship. In fact, we barely had a relationship at all.

I got up from the sofa to get myself to the bathroom and wash the blood off my face. Surprisingly, I only had a few red marks on my face. Most of the damage seemed to be at the back of my head where I guess I hit the glass of the coffee table as I went down. At least it won't be too noticeable, I thought to myself. My hands were cut, and I pulled a couple of pieces of broken glass out of my left hand and figured they would heal quickly. I pulled up my blouse to find that there were several cuts on my right rib cage and back. My right arm had two long scratches and one deep cut that I washed off and bandaged.

I took the towel I had just used and threw it into the sink with some water to soak the blood out. I then I made my way back to the living room and began to pick up the splintered and large pieces of glass. I thought to myself that I was lucky Jay had slept through the noise and was still sleeping as I cleaned the mess up. He had enjoyed his day playing outside, and the fresh air always made him tired. I walked up the hallway after I had cleaned up most of the debris. I peeked in on him as he lay there with an angelic look on his face. I hoped to myself that he would always sleep in such peace as I turned around and went back to the living room to finish cleaning up.

I heaved a big sigh of relief as I finished cleaning up. I took the chrome legs of the coffee table and sat them in the laundry room where they would be out of the way.

I checked in on Jay, and he was still sleeping soundly. I decided to take a bath, so I filled the tub with water and removed my clothes to climb in and was shocked to see the many bruises I had forming all over my back and legs as well as the cuts I had not discovered before. I crawled into the tub and just sat there and soaked. I wished I could soak away the pain that was mental, but nothing seemed to ever wipe away that pain. I laid in the tub for about half an hour, and then I thought I should get out and get dressed.

I prepared dinner for Jay and me, and then I went into his room to wake him up.

"Hey, how is my little man? Are you going to wake up and have dinner with me?" Jay opened his eyes and smiled and shook his head yes and then struggled to stand up, getting caught in his blankets. I reached in and took hold of him and pulled him out over the top of the crib.

"So do I get a hug for dinner?" I asked him, smiling. He leaned into me and put his head on my shoulder and stayed that way as I walked down the hall and towards the kitchen. I placed him in his high chair, pulled the tray in front of him, and put a small car on the tray for him to play with while I got his dinner on the plate.

After dinner I put him down, and he stayed in the kitchen playing with some of his toys as I washed the dishes and cleaned the counters. We went into the living room, and I turned on the television. Jay brought some of his toys to me, and we played several different games with his cars and trucks.

Around 8:30 P.M. Jay began to look pretty tired, so I asked him if he wanted a bath, and he giggled as he shook his head up and down. He loved his bath times as we would always make a game of it. I bent down and scooped Jay up from the floor and walked to the washroom with him, singing to him about the ABC's, and he sang along with me. When we got to the washroom I sat him down on the lid of the toilet and gave him one of his bath toys to play with while the water began to fill up the tub. I removed his clothes and put him gently into the tub and began washing him down while singing to him: "It's raining, it's pouring, the old man is snoring…" Jay laughed and finished the song for me.

After the bath I got him ready for bed. As he lay down in his crib I picked up a book and began to read him a story about a little train. I looked over at him as he was being really quiet and saw he was fast asleep again. I put two fingers to my lips and touched his cheek, giving him a kiss. I turned the night light on, and then I went back to the living room. Just as I was about to sit down, there was a knock at the door. I went to answer it, and Jim's sister Vera and brother-in-law Mario were standing there.

"Hi," I said surprised. "Come on in and have a seat. Do you two want a coffee?"

"Sure," they replied as they made their way to the sofa and sat down.

I went into the kitchen and prepared the coffee. While I waited for it to finish brewing, I went back into the living room and sat down with them "This is a nice surprise," I said, trying to sound casual but wondering why they were there. I was worried they would notice the red blotches on my face. If they did, they didn't say anything.

"We haven't seen you in a while and thought we would stop by and see how you and Jim and Jay are doing," Vera stated.

"We're all fine. Jay is in bed and hopefully asleep for the night," I replied, smiling.

Mario asked, "Where's Jim?"

"Jim just got back today from out of town again. When he left he said he was going out for dinner, but he hasn't come back yet so I assume he is now at his favorite spot, the pool hall," I replied, trying to smile.

Mario smiled and shook his head knowingly. "It must get lonely for you," Mario said.

"Lonely?" I asked "I don't have time to get lonely with Jay around." Vera smiled and said, "Yes, I'm sure he keeps you busy."

Just then the door opened and Jim walked in. "What's this, a party I wasn't invited too?" Jim asked, not looking amused.

Mario laughed and said, "Well, if you came home once in a while then you would know what is happening in your home," Mario teased Jim.

"Maybe that's why I don't want to come home. I don't want to know what's going on around here," Jim replied.

With that Mario and Vera began to pick up on the fact that Jim was not smiling and joking around.

Vera cleared her throat and said, "Well you have a nice home, a beautiful wife, and a handsome son. There are a lot of men out there who wish they could have half of what you've got."

At this point I got up and went into the kitchen and began to get the coffee. I felt really uncomfortable, as it seemed they were saying all the wrong words without realizing it. I knew Jim well enough to know he was going to get out of control again.

I could hear them talking in the living room, and I heard Jim say, "Well, then tell those men to come on over, and they can take my place. This isn't a home; it is a shell I come home to."

Mario said, "Jim, sometimes we don't appreciate what we have until it's gone."

"What are you trying to tell me?" Jim yelled. "Is my wife telling you she is leaving?"

"No, she hasn't said anything to us like that," Vera jumped in. "We were just joking and trying to have a conversation with you."

Jim got up and came into the kitchen at this point. "What have you been telling them?"

"I haven't said anything," I replied.

Mario walked in the kitchen at that point and said, "You're taking this the wrong way, Jim. We just came over to see how you are both doing, as we haven't seen you in a long time. I think we'll forget about the coffee and we'll just go now. I'm sorry, Jenny."

With that he turned and walked to the doorway, and I stood there watching Mario and Vera walk out. There was a small part of me that wanted to run after them and beg them to stay or take me with them.

I sat the tray of coffee on the counter and started to put the cups back into the cupboard. Jim grabbed me by the hair from behind and twisted me around. "If I find out you are talking to people about how things are around here, I'll have to make sure you never see anyone again." He let go of me and walked out of the kitchen and down the hallway into the bedroom.

I stood there taking a deep breath. I wondered why he was like this. It seemed that I never could find an explanation for his outbursts; they just seemed to happen for no real reason. One moment everything could be fine, and then the next he would be exploding and I would be left trying to figure out why. I often wished he was an alcoholic, because with an alcoholic you knew that when they took a drink they could become obnoxious or mean, but with Jim I had no warning. Sometimes I felt like I could see his eyes glass over when he was going to get out of control. I swear I could feel the air change like a barometer measures; I could sometimes measure an explosion coming, but then the other times there was no warning.

The next morning he got up and came into the kitchen. I handed him a coffee and asked him, "Do you want something to eat?"

"No, this is fine," he said, tipping his coffee in my direction. "You need to find a babysitter, as my company is throwing a Christmas party on Friday night."

"I don't really have anything to wear. It's been a long time since I've gone anywhere. Do you think you could leave me some money so I could buy a dress?"

He laughed as he took another sip of his coffee. "You don't need a dress; it won't change how you look." He finished his coffee and then grabbed his bags and left for the rest of the week to work out of town. He never mentioned the night before, and I didn't either. I was just glad that he seemed to be over his angry mood and that he was at least being civil.

I received the baby bonus, and because of Christmas I was determined I would spend most of it on gifts for Jay, hoping that Jim would continue to buy food and diapers, as he sometimes would stop buying food or things we needed to punish me for something. When he would withhold food from us, he always said it was my fault for making him angry about something. One time he didn't buy food for two weeks because he didn't like the way I cleaned the bathroom. I had forgotten to empty the garbage can for two days.

I called my mom and asked if she would babysit on Friday night,

"I'd love to," she said, "how about I come up and spend the week."

"Oh, I would love that, Mom." I got dressed and put some makeup on to cover the red marks on my face. I hoped they would fade and not turn into bruises. I cleaned the apartment while I waited for her to arrive.

Jay woke up, and as he ate his breakfast I said to him, "Guess what?"

He stopped eating and looked at me with wide eyes as he answered, "What?"

"Grandma is coming over to stay for a few days. She is going to be surprised by how big you've gotten."

His eyes glowed and he laughed and said, "Grandma is going to play with me. Love Grandma," he stated as he puckered up his mouth and then kissed the palm of his hand and then made it look like he tossed the kiss into the air and then laughed.

"She loves you too, and yes she is going to play with you."

My mom arrived later that day. Any time she came over to visit Jay, it was like celebrating Christmas. She always carried a navy blue cloth shopping bag. She would sit in a chair and Jay would climb up on her knee and they would go through the bag together and see what was in it. She always had a couple of books to read to him. He loved the coloring books and crayons she always brought. She often brought pencils and plain paper so they could sit and draw pictures together. He loved the gifts but more than that he loved the special attention he got from her.

A knock came on the door, and Jay went running to the door. He tried to open it by standing on his tip toes. With my help he got the door opened and grabbed my mother's hand and led her to the chair. She sat down laughing and picked him up on her knee. They gave each other a big hug and kiss and then he got down and said, "Grandma, I'm bigger now."

"Yes you are. You are quite a young man," she said as she looked at him and said, "I think you've grown a lot taller and more handsome."

"Yup I did," he agreed. "What have you got, Grandma?"

"Oh, well you'll have to help me look and see." She laughed as she opened the bag for him to peer inside.

I had been standing back and watching and feeling at ease finally. I smiled and interrupted and said, "How about a cup of tea, Mom?"

"Love one," she said as they both held the bag and peered inside.

While my mother was there I told her about a program I had heard about. "I can take art classes from home. It is a correspondence course that is sponsored through the Government of Ontario. I could start and then maybe someday do something with my art."

"Oh Jenny, that is such a great idea, you can study while Jay is sleeping. You have always been artistic, and I think it is an excellent idea for you to expand your talent."

With her encouragement I called the phone number I had and spoke to a person. They explained about the different courses available and that they could sign me up then. I gave them all my information and I was told that within two weeks I would receive my first course. I was so excited when I hung up. It was the first time in a long time I felt positive about something.

My mom bent down and said to Jay, "Your mom used to say when she was a little girl that she was going to be an artist someday, and guess what?"

"What?" Jay asked.

"Your mom is now going to be an artist."

Jay laughed as she hugged him, and he hugged her back.

The week went too fast. I enjoyed having her there. I was always able to relax and feel safe just like I did when I was a little girl. When I was a little girl, if she knew I was scared she would talk and tell me stories and all the world's monsters would disappear. She had a way of making me feel safe. She had no idea she was still doing that for me now. That there were times the monster would disappear, even if it was only for a little while, when she visited.

During the week I found an old black dress I had hanging in the back of the closet that I had worn for a funeral. I looked in my jewel box and found some small white beads. I carefully took the dress from the closet and surveyed it. I can probably do this, I thought, so I began to hand sew them onto the dress, trying to make it look more festive than something you would wear to a funeral.

Jim arrived home on Friday afternoon. My mom was sitting in the living room when he walked in. My mom spoke to him, saying, "Hello Jim, how are you?"

He just looked at her and nodded but never answered. He put his bags down and went into the kitchen. He grabbed an apple and then walked into the bedroom.

My mom said, "Go ahead and get ready for the party. I'll make dinner for Jay and me. We'll be fine, as we are going to have a picnic in front of the TV tonight."

"Thanks, Mom," I said as I went to get ready.

Jim took a shower and put on a shirt and tie with a grey suit and then sat tapping his foot while he waited for me to dress. I put my long blond hair up on my head and then I put on the black dress. I walked out of the washroom and he looked at me, grunted his approval, and off we went to the party.

Large, soft, fluffy flakes of snow were gently falling, covering the houses, trees, sidewalks, and roads, making it look like a Christmas card as we drove to the party. Christmas lights glistened in store windows and the spirit of the season was apparent on houses as the neighborhood streets shone with Christmas decorations on the lawns, and people walking down the sidewalk were leaving their footprints in the freshly fallen snow.

Jim seemed in a relaxed mood, and I thought maybe this was a good time to tell him what I wanted to. I had been working up the courage for a long time. I cleared my throat and said, "Jim, I have been thinking, and I want to go and get my driver's license so I can drive Jay to doctor's appointments and things. Since you are out of town most of the time, it makes it difficult to get to a doctor's appointment, especially if he is sick."

Jim kept looking forward and said, "No wife of mine needs to know how to drive."

"Jim, it would be good for both of us if I knew how to drive, then you wouldn't have to drive me around."

"The discussion is closed; you are NOT getting a driver's license." There was silence in the car after that. I thought to myself that learning to drive would be a form of independence, and that was something he tried so hard to make sure I didn't have. I couldn't understand why, if I was independent, it would be such a threat to him.

When we arrived, the party was in full swing. People were smiling and laughing as they sat at their tables listening to the DJ playing dance songs. A few people were on the floor dancing, while others were at the bar in a corner getting their drinks. The room was festively decorated with balls and lights hanging throughout the room, and there was a big tree fully decorated off in a corner with flashing lights.

As we took off our coats and checked them in, we heard our names being called over the music. I turned and saw one of Jim's co-workers beckoning for us to come and sit with them.

We made our way around the dance floor to the table, trying not to bump into people who were up and dancing.

"Hey you two, come and join us," Max said. He was one of Jim's co-workers. "This is my wife Hazel, and these people are Fred and Alice. Fred works with Jim and me," Max said as he made the introductions to me.

Jim already knew everyone at the table. I sat down beside Hazel. She was dressed in what looked like an expensive gown with sequins shining around the neck and arms of the dress. The other women at the table also looked very festive in their gowns and expensive jewelry. You could tell that the women had spent half their day at the salon having their hair done. Everyone seemed so happy and was having a good time. I tried not to let myself feel out of place with these well-dressed people. It had been a long time since I had been around people in a party atmosphere, so I felt like I didn't know how to act.

Everyone seemed to know everyone else and have something in common as they laughed and talked about the party the year before. I knew I couldn't match up to the way they looked, so I just hoped no one would really notice that my outfit was more homemade than anything. The men all looked like their designer suits were made for them. No matter how hard I tried, I really felt uncomfortable around these people. Everyone looked so self-confident and assured, and I felt completely the opposite. The men were handsome and charming, the women were beautiful and educated, and I felt I could not measure up no matter how hard I tried.

I found myself pushing the thoughts to the back of my head: that I wasn't good enough to be there, and that Jim would have been happier to have left me at home, which, at this moment, I was wishing he had because of the way I looked.

Hazel seemed to pick up on my discomfort and stopped talking to the person on the other side of her and began a conversation with me.

"My kids asked me to leave them money for pizza tonight so that way I didn't have to cook, so that gave me time to go out and buy this gown before coming here tonight." She laughed and said, "Max said I have enough dresses to open a dress shop of my own." She smiled.

I smiled and asked, "How old are your children?"

"Our son is thirteen, and our daughter is fifteen."

The DJ began to play some slow music, and everyone jumped up from the table and began dancing. Jim, sitting beside me, leaned over and asked, "Do you want something from the bar?"

I nodded my head and said, "Yes, I would like a glass of white wine if you don't mind." With that he got up and walked over to the bar.

I sat alone at the table and watched the couples dancing on the floor. They all seemed to be happy, and laughter was between all of them. I envied them, as I knew I could not have that kind of relationship with Jim. It must be so nice to have someone who really loves to be with you and enjoys your company, I mused to myself.

The music stopped and everyone came back to the table. The lights were turned up, and the DJ announced that there was a buffet set up in the adjoining room and that people could line up for their food. Once again everyone left the table.

Jim arrived back at the table a minute later, and we moved into line in the next room. Soft music continued to play, people talked back and forth in line, and laughter could be heard throughout the room as we all waited for our turn at the tables.

Hazel was in line just in front of me, and she turned around and starting talking to me again. "It's turning out to be a really nice evening. Everyone seems to be having a good time. I hope it's not still snowing when we have to leave. I hate slippery roads."

I just had time to agree with her when our turns arrived at the tables. We each grabbed a plate from a stack of dishes and picked up our cutlery out of a tray that had them all individually wrapped in a napkin. There was a large assortment of salads, a tray of lasagna, plates with assorted cold cuts and cheeses, and then there were many festive-looking dessert trays. Everyone filled their plates and went back to the table to enjoy their choosing.

Once again Hazel and I began to talk, while Jim talked with Fred and Max. Hazel explained to me how hard she was finding it to work and run a household at the same time.

"Really, some days I just don't want to go to work. I hate my job. I've been working at the same restaurant for fifteen years and I still make minimum wage; if it wasn't for the tips I would quit."

"I'm sure it's got to be hard, especially with teenagers," I said.

"You know Jenny, we should get together sometime and do lunch or something."

"I'd like that," I said, knowing deep down inside that it was never going to happen as Jim did not want me associating with anyone. I felt really sad at that moment, as I really liked her. She sounded so sure of herself when she spoke. I wished I could be that sure of myself, I thought.

"You and Jim could bring the kids over to the house one day," she said as she broke into my thoughts.

I smiled at her and nodded yes, and then I said, "With Jim out of town a lot we don't go out usually. He hates for me to get a babysitter."

All of a sudden I realized the discussion Jim was having with Fred and Max was turning into an argument. What it was about I was not sure, but Jim was being truly obnoxious and trying to get Max even angrier by egging him on, saying, "Do you want to step outside?"

Max looked at him for a moment and then said, "How would you like me to tell Jenny what you really do when you're out of town?"

With that Jim shut his mouth. Everyone at the table and the surrounding tables became very quiet. You could feel the tension in the room as all eyes were adverted towards us. About two minutes went by, and then Jim stood up, pushed back his chair, and looking at me, he said, "Let's go."

Hazel started to say something, but her husband Max put his hand on her arm and shook his head no. She lowered her eyes, and Max looked at me and said, "I'm sorry, Jenny."

With that Jim put his hand on my back and guided me to leave in front of him. We got our coats from the check out, and as I put my coat on I could still feel everyone's eyes on us.

We got outside, and Jim pushed me up against the side of the car and said, "You listen to me: it's none of your business what I do when I'm not home, do you hear me?" Shocked, I just looked at him, and he yelled, "Do you hear me?"

"Yes, I hear you," I replied. At the same time I thought to myself, I really don't care what you do when you're out of town.

With that he opened the car door and tossed me into the car. He never spoke on the drive home.

My mom was still up watching TV, and she turned the sound down as we entered the living room. I could see the way she looked at us that she knew there was something wrong.

Jim said to her, "Get your things, and I'll drive you home."

"It's late," I interrupted, "why don't you just get some rest, and we will take her home tomorrow."

He glared at me and repeated, "Get your things, and I'll drive you home."

She stood up and said she had everything ready to go. She put her jacket on and then stopped and gave me a hug. They left, and as I heard the ding of the elevator arriving I felt so totally alone and empty.

It was about a half an hour drive to my mother's place, so I figured that Jim would be back in an hour, making his arrival home around midnight.

I went to the bedroom and took my dress off and hung it up. I looked at it one last time before closing the closet door. I thought it looked old, and I felt older even though I was only twenty one.

I crawled into bed and awoke around three am to hear Jim coming in the front door. I rolled over, hoping he would just fall asleep on the sofa. A few minutes later I heard him snoring from the living room, and I gave a sigh of relief as I drifted of back to sleep.

It was early in the morning, and Jim was in the bathroom. I had been in the kitchen preparing breakfast. Jay was sitting in his high chair having scrambled eggs, and I looked at my wrist to see what time it was and realized I had left my watch on the night table beside the bed. I looked at Jay and said, "I'll be right back, I'm just going to get my watch."

Jay looked at me and smiled as he popped a piece of egg in his mouth with his chubby little fingers. I walked down the hallway, and as I entered through the door of the bedroom, Jim just happened to be stepping out of the in-suite washroom and into the bedroom, which was on the opposite side of the room. I looked over at him and maybe I had a startled look on my face, because I was not expecting him to come out of the bathroom at the same moment I entered the room. I'm not sure really what happened, but all of a sudden he jumped across the bed and grabbed me by the throat and pushed me into the wall.

"What are you looking at?" he screamed into my face. I felt my legs go weak with fear and shock. He banged my head several times on the wall and then let go of me. I started to fall to the floor, and he grabbed me by my arms and stood me up. With one hand he held me up against the wall again, while with the other he took a swing and punched me in the face.

I hit the floor hard, and I think I was unconscious for a few minutes, and when I started to come around he was standing over me, kicking me, and yelling, "What were you staring at? Answer me or I'll hit you again."

I tried to get up, but my legs wouldn't let me. I could taste blood. Then I began to become more aware of what was happening, and I could hear Jay crying in the kitchen.

Oh my God, I thought. Has he fallen out of his highchair? I could feel tears begin to run down my face. Jim was still standing over me, but he had stopped yelling and kicking me.

I took a deep breath and allowed another minute to go by, and then again I tried to get up. It took all my strength to finally stand up on very wobbly legs. There was extreme pain in my face, and I couldn't see from my right eye. Jim suddenly turned and walked away and back into the bathroom again.

I held onto the wall in the hallway and made it back to the kitchen, where I found Jay still sitting in his high chair. He was safe, but he had heard what was going on and was scared. I picked him up and hugged him close to me.

"It's alright, sweetie," I whispered into his ear. He stopped crying, and he seemed to relax. I walked over to the window in the living room with him, and we both looked outside. I was feeling dizzy and sick to my stomach.

I spotted a squirrel, and I pointed it out to Jay. I could feel him take in a few big shaky breaths and continue to relax as he watched the black squirrel running around the grass and then up and down a tree. He started smiling and pointed the squirrel out to me and said, "See, Mommy, he's playing."

"Yes he's playing," I whispered. Within another minute Jay struggled to be put down. I then put him down on the floor with a couple of his favorite toys. He began to play as if nothing had happened.

Jim walked into the living room at that point, grabbed his jacket, and walked out the front door, slamming it behind him.

I was so relieved he was gone. I went to the bathroom and looked in the mirror to find that I had a black, swollen eye and nose and marks on my cheek and forehead. I put my hand up to the back of my head where I had hit the wall, and I had two large bumps there. I pulled up my shirt and saw I had several large red marks on my back and ribs where he had been kicking me. I washed my face and took a couple of aspirins for the pain, and then I went back to where Jay was still playing.

The phone rang, and I went to pick it up. "Hi honey," I heard my mom's voice sounding cherry into the phone. "I just thought I'd phone and see what you are doing." My heart skipped a beat as I said, "I was just playing with Jay."

"Your voice sounds strange. Are you feeling alright?"

"I'll be fine. Just a little tired from being out last night," I lied.

"Well how about I come up and look after Jay for the day so you can get some rest," she suggested.

"I don't think so, Mom. I have a touch of a headache, and if I'm coming down with something I don't want you to catch it. In fact, when I put Jay down for his afternoon nap I will lay down at the same time and rest."

I could hear her sigh and she said, "Well, if you change your mind, let me know."

I could feel my breathing change and my voice quivering as I said, "Alright, I'll let you go now, and I'll talk to you later." I hung up the phone and sat down feeling mentally and physically exhausted. I couldn't face having her know what my life was really like. I was so embarrassed that this was happening and yet I didn't understand what was happening.

I had been hiding the verbal abuse for a long time, and if someone did happen to hear something then I would try to make light of it as much as possible, by either ignoring the remark Jim had just made, or by making a joke about it. Bruises were harder to hide, and the best thing to do was just stay away from everyone.

I just felt like such a loser. I brushed away a tear I felt running down my face and realized how much even that hurt.

I got some ice and put it on my eye and went to sit in the living room where Jay was still playing. Jay saw me sitting on the sofa and came over to me. I gave him a big kiss and smiled and told him I was just playing with the ice. He touched it and said, "Cold."

"Yes, it is cold," I said as I watched him turn around and start playing with a Sesame Street garage he had.

A few hours later Jim came home. "Have you got my clothes washed?" he asked. "I'm packing to leave to go out of town again for the week."

"Why are you leaving today; it's only Saturday?" I asked.

He just gave me a look that let me know he was not about to answer that question.

"Yes, your clothes are ready," I said as I walked down the hallway to the bedroom to get his suitcase ready. I put his usual things in the suitcase, clothes for work as well as street clothes. He always wanted nice dress clothes for when he and his fellow workers went out to dinner in the evenings. When I finished, I carried the case and went into the living room. He was on the phone and hung up as I entered the room.

He picked up his suitcase and started to leave. As he started to walk out the door, he stopped, turned around, and said, "If you were a better wife, this wouldn't have to happen. It's your fault. Don't try to blame me if your face hurts." With that, the door closed behind him.

I went back into the living room and watched Jay playing so innocently with his toys. He was oblivious of what was really happening. I sat there for a long time with no real thoughts, just a sick feeling in the pit of my stomach. Sometimes it was like my mind would shut off. I couldn't carry a thought. My brain became empty of emotions, feelings, and thoughts. At these times I would be more like a zombie than a person. I was awake, I could see things around me, I could respond if need be, but things just didn't really register, and I wondered if this was some form of survival that I had found where I needed the break from the fear and shame, and this was my form of an oasis. With a big sigh I went over to Jay and sat down with him on the floor for a few minutes, and we rolled a car around a garage that he had and had it go through the pretend carwash.

After about ten minutes of playing together, I said to Jay, "How about helping me make dinner?"

Jay and I prepared dinner together. I let him sit in his highchair and stir a bowl of cake batter while I peeled potatoes. We sang songs he had learned from Sesame Street, and then he helped me pour the cake batter into the baking pans. He sat in his high chair licking his fingers while I popped the cakes into the oven.

"Alright young man, let's go have a bath while we wait for dinner to cook." I picked him up and we continued to sing songs on our way to the bathroom. I ran the water into the tub while Jay tossed a few of his rubber toys in to get washed with him. When the water was ready, I put him in the tub and we made a game of getting the cake mix off him. He laughed and splashed around in the water. By the time we were done, I was just as wet as he was. Laughing, I wiped him down and got him into his pajamas, and then we went back into the kitchen to eat dinner.

After dinner we played a few more games, I read him a story, and by this time he was looking pretty sleepy. I picked him up and gave him a hug and a kiss as I gently placed him into his bed.

I had a shower and got ready for bed. I laid there most of the night, not sleeping. Close to daylight I fell asleep for a couple of hours until I heard Jay stirring in the next room. I crawled out of bed and went into get Jay. I washed him down, put a blue t-shirt and pants on him, and combed his hair.

"My, you are a handsome boy today," I said as I tickled his tummy, and he laughed and doubled over, expecting some more tickles. I carried him into the kitchen and put him in his high chair with a cup of juice and a bowl of cereal.

"I've got to go to the washroom," I told Jay as I turned and walked away. I looked in the mirror and found that my face and eye looked even worse this morning. There was more swelling and bruising. My vision was really blurry, and my head still hurt. I washed and combed my hair and went back to the kitchen to check on Jay.

"Are you finished?" I asked him, smiling.

Jay kicked his feet back and forth and gave me a big smile that would melt the arctic and said, "I go play now."

"Yes, you can go play now," I said as I lifted him out of the chair.

I put him on the floor with his garage set, and he began to play with his cars driving them down over the built in roadway in the set.

I went to the phone and called the doctor. I was worried I had a concussion and thought it best to get my eye checked as well. I was given an appointment for 12:30 pm that day.

I got dressed, cleaned the apartment, and then gave Jay some lunch. The morning seemed to go quickly, and before I knew it, it was time to leave for the appointment. I put Jay in his stroller and grabbed my purse. I took out my sunglasses and put them on even though it was a cloudy day. I wanted to try and hide the bruising as much as possible. I looked in the mirror as I started to walk out and realized that the bruising came down below my glasses. My swollen nose was very noticeable. I took a deep breath and talked myself into going out in public.

"You have a concussion," the doctor said as he looked into my eye with a flashlight. "How on earth did this happen to you?"

I cleared my throat and said, "Well, I walked into the bedroom and my husband thought I looked at him in the wrong way and the rest is kind of a blur."

The doctor continued to examine me and then said, "Well, some young European men have a lot to learn about how to treat a lady." With that he prescribed a pain killer and gave me some drops for my eye so that it wouldn't get infected and sent me home.

I'm not sure what I thought a doctor would do for me, but I left feeling like an idiot and that even though he did not say it, I felt like it was my fault, just like Jim had said.

When I got home I fixed some juice for Jay and read him a story as he lay in his crib for his afternoon nap. When his eyes started to close I allowed my voice to become softer and softer with each word I read from the book, and then I pulled his blanket up over him as he slept, and I walked out of the room.

Scared that Jim would do this again, I phoned his sister Ellen, thinking that maybe she could shed some light on why he was so moody and unpredictable. I waited, listening to the phone ring. I had a guilty feeling that I was breaking some sort of secret between Jim and me, that I should not tell anyone. I knew that Jim would be more than angry if he knew I was talking to his sister or anyone about his. She answered the phone on the fourth ring. "Hello?"

"Hi Ellen, it's me, Jenny."

"Hi Jenny, this is a surprise. You don't call too often."

"Well, being on my own with the baby keeps me pretty busy," I said, feeling really uncomfortable now.

"So what's up?" she asked.

"Well, you have to promise to keep this between us," I said

"Yes, alright," she agreed.

"Jim hit me really hard yesterday because he thought I looked at him the wrong way."

"Listen Jenny, my husband used to beat me all the time, and for no reason. My dad beat my mom for years, and he had no reason. This is what Italian men are like." She laughed and said, "You'll get used to it, I did, I don't get beaten anymore; he just grew out of it, or he got tired of doing it. I think he realized it took more energy to beat me than it did to just leave the house when he gets mad, and now everything is fine. Same for my mom, my dad quit beating her too because he just got too old to do it. You didn't grow up with a dad, so you don't know what is normal or what to expect." She laughed at this point and asked, "So how big is the bruise?"

I swallowed hard, trying not to let the tears rising up in my eyes begin to fall. "Don't worry about it," I said.

"Listen Jenny, it will heal up in a few days. Jim will be back on the weekend and all will be fine, you'll see."

"Alright," I replied weakly into the phone, trying to sound stronger than I felt. "I'll let you go now, I hear Jay waking up," I lied so that I could hang up quickly.

She was right; I had not grown up with violence of any sort, and I did not know how to handle this. Her attitude of this being normal and I should just accept it was no help. I just kept feeling I was sinking deeper and deeper into something I could not get out of.

Our second son, Al, was born on April 23, 1978. Things continued on the same course as before. Jim was out of town most of the time. I was still never left with any money, nor did I have access to the bank account because only his name was on the account, so if I ran out of something like diapers, I had to find an ingenious way of coping until he got back.

I would take the kids outside to get fresh air, but only after Jim had called, and then only for about half an hour just in case he decided to call back. If I wasn't home when he called, I had hell to pay when he came home on the weekend.

I had received my art course package in the mail months ago, and I hid the fact that I was taking the course. I knew he probably would not approve, and I just didn't want anything to spoil what I was enjoying doing. Within a couple of months I managed to finish two courses. The first course I only got eighty-three percent on. It was a study of different artists and the techniques they used. They gave a few assignments that you had to complete and send them in, but I felt I did not do as well as I should have.

I was nervous about getting caught doing it, so that may have had something to do with what I felt was a low mark. The next course was on city planning, and I felt I could be much more creative. At the end of the course I got to draft and design a city. I loved the challenge of the assignment, and I was shocked when I got my marks back with a letter from the teacher who had marked on my assignment that I had received the highest mark in his class during that session: ninety-seven percent.

I was so thrilled that I called my mother on the phone with the letter still in my hand and said, "I got the highest marks in the class for the city planning course."

"I am so proud of you," I heard her say over the phone as I continued to look at the letter. Wow, it felt really good to hear someone say that they were proud of me.

"Thanks Mom, that means a lot to me."

"How about I come up for a few days?"

"Yes, I would love that. See you soon," I said as I hung up the phone and then went to hide the letter and my marks in a dresser drawer.

It was Friday afternoon around three when Jim arrived home from being out of town. I was sitting in the living room talking to my mother, who had arrived that morning and was holding Al and giving him his bottle while Jay played quietly on the floor. Jim walked in, tossed his bags on the floor in the hallway, nodded to me, and walked into the kitchen and opened the fridge. "There's no food in here," he yelled from the kitchen.

"No, we didn't have too much food when you left on Sunday. You never went shopping last weekend, so if you go shopping now, I'll make you something when you get back," I replied, trying to sound cheerful but feeling embarrassed that my mother was hearing this.

"Forget it," he replied, "I'm hungry now so I'll go out and get something to eat." With that he walked out of the apartment and slammed the door behind him.

My mother raised her eyebrows at me and was silent for a few moments, and then she said, "Jenny, is he always like this?"

I really hated to hear that question, because the true answer was no, most of the time he was worse, but I couldn't tell her that.

"He's just tired, I guess," I said as I got up and walked into the kitchen to look into an almost empty fridge and wondered if he would go grocery shopping this week. He had to feel some kind of guilt not to shop for the kids, I thought.

While I was taking the art course, they had sent supplies, and in those supplies there was enough sketch paper and charcoal and paints that a few times I had sketched out charcoal pictures of some kids in the building.

I sat outside and the parents would see what I was doing, and they would want one done of their kids. I would charge them fifteen dollars for each one I did. I made enough money to keep the kids and me eating, but I always made sure there was no evidence of this food around when he came home on the weekend so that he wouldn't catch on to what I was doing. I just prayed he would not come home early or unexpectedly and find the food, as then I would have some explaining to do, and I was not sure what I would say as I really wanted to keep my art classes secret. I just could not bear anyone destroying the pleasure I was getting from them. Maybe even a bit of self-respect.

A couple of hours later he came home again and walked into the bedroom, and we could hear the dresser drawers opening and closing. "Hey," he yelled from the bedroom, "where's my favorite blue shirt and the rest of my socks?"

I felt my heart go into my throat, as I knew I would end up being blamed for him not having what he wanted to wear. Trying to keep my voice steady and not start breathing hard, I yelled back from the living room,

"Oh, they are still in the laundry, as I did not have any laundry soap this week while you were gone."

"Well, I see you and the kids wearing clean clothes. How's that possible if you didn't have any detergent?" he yelled back.

Rather than keep yelling back and forth and having my mom hear everything, I got up and walked down the hallway and into the bedroom. I stood in the doorway and said as calmly as possible, "I washed things out by hand and used hand soap."

"Well, if you have that much energy, then you could have at least washed my favorite shirt for me, knowing I'd be home today." With that he pushed me aside and walked out of the bedroom and back down the hallway into the living room.

He looked at my mother and said, "How long are you here for?"

"I'll be leaving in another hour or so," she responded. Jim turned and walked back down the hallway. A few minutes later we heard the shower turn on.

My mom looked at me and asked, "Are you alright?"

Avoiding her eyes, I bent down and picked Jay up of the floor and pretended to be busy playing with him. "Sure Mom, I'm fine."

"Well, maybe I'll go now so you can relax. Put Jay down for his nap, and you should lay down too for a while. You look really tired." With that she gave me a hug and kiss on the cheek and walked out of the apartment.

I laid Jay down for his nap with his favorite bear. Al was all curled up in his crib, fast asleep, and looked like a peaceful little angel. I stood there for a moment and watched him breathing. I wish I could feel that peaceful, I thought to myself. Then I kissed two fingers to my lips and touched his forehead. I turned and walked out of his room just as Jim was walking down the hallway towards the living room.

As he entered the room he said, "Good, she's gone." With that he sat down on the sofa and turned the TV on. I stood there for a moment, and then I sat down in a chair across from the sofa. I picked up a book I had started to read days before, and just as I was getting back into the story, Jim said, "I think I'll go out for the evening. I'll be back later." With that he stood up and walked towards the door.

"When are you coming back? Aren't you going to go shopping? The kids need diapers and food; even if you don't want to buy food for me you still need to buy for the kids."

"I'm busy tonight, maybe tomorrow," he said as he walked out.

I walked into the kitchen and opened the fridge once again. Why I bothered I don't know, as nothing had changed in there. It still contained a bottle of juice and several bottles of formula that was mixed up. On the second shelf there was a few pieces of cheese I had managed to make last all week. There was a bowl of pudding I mixed up the day before when I found a package of pudding in the cupboard. There were two apples in the crisper that had been there for about two weeks, but they were still in good shape. I went into my bedroom, where I had hidden in the back of a drawer some canned goods. I then had placed some t-shirts and sweaters over top of them so that if Jim ever opened the drawer for any reason he would never see the food. I took a can of soup, heated it up, and put some into a bowl. I sat at the kitchen table and tasted a spoonful while I watched Jay eating his bowl of soup. I decided I wasn't really hungry anyway and covered the rest and put it into the fridge and thought that might be my meal tomorrow.

Al woke up, and I prepared his formula and then went into his room and picked him up and changed him. I chopped up one of the apples from the crisper and gave it to Jay, and he munched happily on that for his dessert while I gave Al his bottle.

After dinner I turned the TV on, and Jay sat on the floor and watched the Muppet show while I held Al and patted his back.

After the Muppets were finished, Jay came and sat on the sofa beside me and said, "Can I hold Al?"

So I had Jay sit back against the sofa and showed him how to hold Al and support his head. Al looked pretty contented with his big brother holding him.

"You're a good brother," I said to Jay.

"Yup, I am," he said, smiling proudly at his brother.

We sat there and I said to Jay, "Why don't you sing one of your songs to him? It will help him fall asleep." Jay giggled and said, "Okay," and with that he started to sing a song he had just heard on the Muppet show. He made up his own words as he went along, but overall he did pretty good job. I was impressed with his enthusiasm, also how he stayed pretty much on key. I just sat, listened, and enjoyed.

"He's going to sleep," Jay whispered.

"Here, I'll take him now and you can come with me and help put him in his bed." With that I bent over and took Al from Jay, and we got up off the sofa and walked to Al's room. Jay got a chair from the corner and brought it over to the crib so he could stand on it and look into the crib.

"Be careful you don't fall," I said as I laid Al down. We both stood there for a few minutes and Jay was humming his song still to Al.

When he finished his song, I said, "You did a good job, he's sound asleep. Let's go now so we don't disturb him."

With that I lifted him off the chair and helped him put it back in the corner. Jay and I went to his room and he picked out a book he wanted me to read to him. We went back into the living room and sat on the sofa together, and I read to him while he pointed to the pictures and helped turn the pages. When we finished I took him and gave him a bath and put his pajamas on. I laid him in his bed and kissed him good night. I turned the light out and started to walk out of his room.

"Mommy, I love you."

Those words form Jay made my life worthwhile. "I love you too. Sleep good." I smiled and left the room.

I went back in the living room and turned the TV on. There was a movie playing, and I tried to concentrate on it but found I couldn't get interested in it. I turned it off and put the stereo on. I tried to find some soft music, and I picked up my book and began to read.

Around midnight I put my book down, turned the stereo off, and went to get ready for bed. When I came out of the bathroom from having a bath I found Jim sitting on the side of the bed. "Oh you're home," I said, surprised.

"What do you mean by that?" he asked.

"I mean, you're home. I didn't hear you coming in."

He grunted something and got up off the bed and left the room.

I crawled into bed, and surprisingly enough I feel asleep not long after. Around two am I woke up to hear the TV going. I got out of bed and walked out into the living room and found Jim sound asleep on the sofa. I stood there for a moment, wondering if I should wake him up, and thought I would rather let him sleep than take the chance of waking him up and finding he was in a bad mood. I walked over, turned the TV off, and went back to bed.

I woke up about six am, hearing Al crying. I got up and went into his room. I picked him up and snuggled into him for a moment while I tried to wake up. He stopped crying and snuggled into me as well. After a few minutes of standing and holding him close, I walked over to his change table, undid his sleepers, and took off his diaper. I cleaned him up and put on a new one. I put on a fresh sleeper and then picked him up and made our way into the kitchen to get his bottle ready.

Jim heard us and woke up. He got up off the sofa and came to the kitchen door and looked at us and then turned and walked into the bedroom. After I finished feeding Al he fell back to sleep instantly, so I put him down in his bed. I went to look in my bedroom and saw Jim lying on top of the bed, sound asleep.

I thought I heard sounds coming from Jay's room, so I went to the door to find him sitting up in his crib playing with his teddy bear. I walked in and whispered, "Good morning, Jay."

He smiled and whispered, "Good morning, Mommy."

I picked him up and gave him a big hug, and he gave me one back. I carried him to the kitchen, where I said, "How about some of my famous scrambled eggs this morning?"

He laughed and said, "Yup and Shreddies too."

I poured some Shreddies cereal in a bowl and put some milk and sugar on it and gave it to him and said, "Your eggs are coming up."

He bent his head down to the bowl and listened, placed some Shreddies on his spoon, and then he hummed the ABC song as he ate his cereal.

I looked to see if there was enough coffee to have one, and I thought there was, so I made a coffee and sat down at the table. Jim left his cigarette package on the table and I took one, thinking it would be great to have a smoke after being without cigarettes all week. I lit a cigarette and sipped my coffee while Jay ate his breakfast.

After breakfast Jay and I went to the bathroom where I washed him down and he brushed his teeth. I combed his hair with his help, and then we went into his bedroom where he decided what he wanted to wear that day. A few minutes later he was dressed in a red and white striped top and shorts to match, white socks, and a pair of his favorite running shoes.

It was a beautiful, sunny July day, and we went outside and sat on the balcony. Jay brought out a ball, and we tossed it back and forth for a while, and then he got bored and went and got his favorite truck.

Al woke up about an hour later, and I went to get him so he would not wake Jim up. The more he slept the better it was for all of us.

Around eleven am Jim woke up and came into the kitchen to see if he could get a coffee. I made him one, and he went into the living room and sat down. Al was getting hungry again, so I went into the living room and handed him to his father and went back into the kitchen to prepare his bottle. Surprisingly enough, Jim sat there holding Al and watching TV. I came back into the living room and took Al from Jim and sat down in a chair and proceeded to give Al his bottle.

"I think I'll go get dressed," Jim said as he got up and left the room.

About an hour later he came back into the living room and said, "I'm going to go visit my Mom, I'll be back later." I just sat there and watched him walk out again.

Around six pm he came home and actually brought some groceries with him for the kids and even me. I knew it was not a lot, but at least I could get the kids through another week.

I put the groceries away while he went to watch TV again. Around eight pm, after the kids had been fed, washed, and put to bed, I went into the living room and sat down across from Jim. "Can we talk?" I asked.

There was about three or four minutes while I waited for a response and was beginning to think he was not going to answer me at all, when suddenly he said, "Sure, about what?"

"Why do you seem so angry all the time?" I asked.

Another few minutes went by, and then he said, "This is not the life I wanted. I don't need a wife and a couple of kids to feed. I want my freedom to do what I want. I don't need to answer questions about where I'm going or what I'm doing." He stopped talking and looked straight at me and then said, "I don't need to feel guilty every time I leave here."

I sat quietly for a few minutes with a lot of thoughts going through my head, and then I said, "So do you want a divorce?"

Without hesitation he said, "It's too late for that, I don't believe in divorce. It's admitting to the rest of the world that you failed at something. I am never going to admit that to anyone. I'm not happy here with you. You're much too innocent for me. You look innocent, and you have an angelic kind of look. I like a woman who looks tough and hard.

"Women who look and act like sluts are a real turn on. Wives aren't supposed to act the way I like my women to act. Therefore, I have to put up with what I got married to." He just stared at me for a few more minutes, and then he said, "Really, what do you think a lot of European men do when they have wives like you? They have a few girls on the side to keep them busy. We can do things with them that you don't do with the mother of your children."

I sat there stunned for a few minutes. I tried to comprehend all he had just told me.

At last I said, "You're not the only one disappointed in this marriage." With that I got up and walked into the bedroom.

I heard him call after me as I walked down the hall. "Too bad bitch, you're stuck now. This marriage is the point of no return."

The next morning I woke up to an empty bed and found that he was nowhere in the apartment.

He finally came home later that day and said, "Have you got my things packed? I'll be gone for two weeks this time. While I'm gone I'd prefer you not have your mom around, as she was a single mother raising you, and she's a bad influence on you as far as I'm concerned."

I didn't answer him and just turned around and went to the bedroom where I had his bags ready to go. I walked back down the hallway and handed them to him.

"What about your sister?" he said. "I don't hear you mention her much."

I looked at him and said, "What's to say? I haven't seen her in almost a year and probably won't be seeing her any time soon."

As far as my sister was concerned, she had her own problems with raising her kids and trying to make ends meet. I never told her what was happening with me. It was just easier to keep my distance, and that way I didn't have to worry about her finding out what my life was really like. I could hide my bruises behind the phone calls we had. We talked often enough, but Jim didn't need to know about that.

"Good," he said as he took hold of his bags. A few minutes later he left.

Each time he went out the door I always felt like a weight was being lifted off my back, even if I knew it was only for a little while. It was like getting a breath of fresh air during a dust storm.

I had seen in a newspaper that there was an ad stating that if you needed to talk to someone there was a phone help line that you could call. In the article it had talked about abused women, people feeling suicidal, or someone just being depressed and needing to talk to someone. I had cut the phone number out and hidden it in a dresser drawer.

The kids were sleeping, and I went to the drawer and got the help phone number in my hand. I walked into the kitchen where the phone was. I sat at the table, trying to get up the courage to call. I realized that my heart was pounding really fast, the palms of my hands were sweaty, and my breathing had totally changed. I wasn't sure what I expected them to say. I knew they could not cure my problems, but just having someone to talk to might make it a bit easier.

I got up and made myself a coffee and tried talking myself into making the call. Finally I got up the courage to call.

I picked up the phone and dialed half the number and then I suddenly panicked and hung up. I thought to myself that if Jim ever found out he would kill me. The fact that I was actually going to tell a stranger that there was a problem in my marriage was really hard to do.

I took a couple of sips of coffee and started to dial the number again. This time I got to the sixth number and then I hung up again, feeling like I couldn't breathe. I actually felt dizzy.

I sat there thinking about how guilty I was feeling for doing this. This is ridiculous, I thought to myself, Jim will never know that I've made the call. These people can't see me and they will never know who I really am. Finally I talked myself into trying one more time.

I heard the phone ring, and on the second ring a man's voice answered. Just the fact it was a man's voice started to throw me off and I wanted to hang up, but I hesitated a moment while the voice on the other end of the line said, "Hello," again for the second time.

I took a deep breath, and I said, "I am having some problems in my marriage, and I don't know how to handle them."

The voice on the other end said, "Well, we're not marriage counselors."

I sat there for a few seconds and said, "Well, I thought you listen to people and guide them as to what they might be able to do."

"Look lady, we have people with real problems calling in all day long. If you've had a fight with your hubby you should talk to him."

At this point I was so embarrassed that I just said, "Thanks," and I hung up.

I went and sat on the sofa for a long time. I don't think I moved for a couple of hours. I just sat there feeling numb. This was where I thought people turned if they needed help or even just to talk. Now I knew there were no one who cared and no one I could tell about this.

Even though I often felt alone, I think this was the first time I had begun to realize I was alone, not just because Jim wanted to keep people away from me, but also because I didn't know how to face people any more. I had this sense of worthlessness and despair.

I still saw my mom so that she could see her grandchildren, but the stress of trying to keep a lot of the abuse away from her was taking its toll on me as well.

I found that I really did not want to be around people. I always felt like I wasn't as good as they were. Everyone seemed to have their lives going the way they wanted, and they all seemed so happy. I really couldn't relate to anyone. I felt I had nothing in common with anyone.

If I found myself in a room full of people, be it in a doctor's office or even just a grocery store, I would feel very inadequate. I felt I couldn't measure up. In my mind they all dressed better. They spoke better. They looked better and they were smarter and better educated. They had a right to be happy, but I didn't believe I had that right.

I was also really exhausted most of the time. The less I saw of people the less I had to try and act as if everything was alright. I stayed inside except for a few times a week when I would sneak out to take the kids outside for fresh air. I always felt like I was doing something wrong, even if we were just sitting in the playground out back.

I knew that Jim would be furious to find us out there. A woman's place is in the home, he would say. If the husband is a good husband then the wife never needs to leave the house. The man will bring everything to her. She needs no one but him. She should relinquish all ties with her past family, such as her mother, father, brothers, sisters, and friends. A good wife only needs her husband and kids.

I began to find that it was harder and harder for me to walk out of the apartment, even if it was only to take the kids to the playground. I would actually break out into a sweat. My heart would be pounding, and I would feel like I couldn't breathe the whole time I was outside.

I would look out the bedroom window, which over looked the playground, to see if anyone was there, and I would take the kids out only if there was no one else around. I hated to face people. I felt everyone could see through me. I often felt like people were staring at me.

One afternoon while Jim was out of town I took both kids outside because no one was around. Jay played on the swings and in the sand box with one of his toys while I sat on a bench watching with Al sleeping in the carriage.

There was a gentle breeze blowing and the birds were singing. Jay called me over to the sand box to show me a few roadways he had built. I sat down on the edge of the sand box and watched him for a couple of minutes.

"Mommy, can you hand me those cars to me?" I picked them up and handed them to him, and I heard Al begin to cry from his carriage. I got up quickly and went over to check on him. I picked him up and was about to turn around just when another mother and her son arrived at the playground.

"Oh, may I see you baby?" she asked as I started to put Al back in his carriage.

"Sure," I said as that same old anxiety started to come over me. She bent over the carriage as I quickly went to the sand box and gathered up the toys and Jay.

"Please Mommy, I want to stay and play."

"We have to go," I said as I put the toys in a bag and put the bag in the carriage.

"It would be nice if you could stay so your son and mine can play together."

"I'm sorry," I said as I started to push the carriage with one hand while holding Jay's hand with the other. The discomfort of feeling like I was not as good as her was overcoming me, and I quickly escaped, much to Jay's disappointment. I felt torn, as I believed it would have been so nice for the kids to play together, but I couldn't risk Jim finding out. I also didn't want the woman to notice how panicked I had suddenly felt.

Jim didn't stay out of town for two weeks; he arrived home in two days. The job had gotten cancelled, and everyone returned home. He sat on the sofa for the first day looking pretty miserable and then he did a turnabout and became sociable.

"Well, if I have to be here at home we may as well make the best of it," he said. "It's going to be a hot day, so let's take the kids to the beach."

Jim was all smiles that day and for the next couple of days. He played with the kids and seemed to really enjoy the time he spent with them. I began to think that maybe things could change. Maybe he didn't mean to be so miserable all the time. Then the weekend rolled around and his old personality came back full force.

We had the kids outside most of the day in a local park. Jay had fun running around the playground, going up and down on the slide and being pushed on the swings while his little brother Al slept in his stroller.

We had packed a lunch and had spent most of the day there. We sat on a blanket, ate sandwiches, and Jim played with Jay, kicking a ball back and forth. Al sat on my knee for a while and drank his bottle and also enjoyed the fresh air and sunshine. The day was really nice, not too hot or too cold. I began to feel that this was what a family is supposed to feel like. I wished that it could be like this all the time.

When we got back to the apartment building, we had just entered the elevator when the woman who had been in the playground the other day got onto the elevator at the same time.

"Hello," she said. I felt my heart go into my mouth as she continued, "Maybe the next time you and your son can stay in the park longer so the kids can play together."

Just then the elevator stopped at our floor. I smiled at the woman while I could feel my heart skip a beat, knowing I was in trouble again. Jim didn't say anything at that moment, but I could feel the air change and the tension arrived again.

We got to the apartment, Jim opened the door, and when he closed the door behind us he grabbed me by the hair and said, "See how I always find out what you're up to."

He pushed me into the door and said, "You're lucky I don't flatten you right here, but I'm too tired to bother. Just know the next time you do something wrong you'll pay double. Remember this one thing, if I want to, I can move to Italy and take the kids and you will never see them again." That was the one statement that scared me more than anything else he could do or say.

I took the kids and went down the hall to their rooms. I fought back the tears of frustration and fear as I left Jay sitting on the floor in his room beside his toy box as he played with a ball, rolling it back and forth. I went into Al's room and got him ready for bed. Jay came in a few minutes later and asked if he could help put Al in his bed. We got the chair and together we laid Al down and covered him up with his blanket. Jay handed him a stuffed toy, and then we left to go into Jay's room to get him undressed and ready for bed.

As Jay crawled into his bed he handed me a book and said, "Let's read."

"Alright," I smiled, and I read the book as he pointed at the pictures and sometimes commented on what he saw in the picture. He always enjoyed turning the pages. After we were finished I gave him a kiss, turned his night light on, and left the room.

I could hear Jim in the living room with the TV on, and I thought I just needed more time before facing him, so I went to the bathroom and ran the shower. I went into the bedroom and got out of my clothes and took my night gown into the bathroom with me.

I stepped in to the shower and stood there for a few minutes, just letting the warm water sooth away some of my tension. I could feel my muscles that had been so tight start to loosen up.

The water was running down over me when all of a sudden Jim pulled back the curtain and grabbed my arm. "The phone just rang and no one was on the line. Who's calling here and won't answer when I'm home."

I stood there, stunned. I had not heard the phone with the running of the water. I had no idea who would be calling.

"Answer me," he yelled as he squeezed my arm.

"I don't know who would call. Wrong number, I suppose," I said as I tried to wipe away water that was running down my face and into my eyes.

"That's bullshit, I know you have someone on the side when I'm not home. You'd better tell me who he is before I have to beat it out of you." With that, still holding tightly onto my arm, he pulled me out of the tub.

The water dripped all over the floor, and I started to slip on the tiled floor. He took advantage of that and pushed me up against the vanity. I felt the counter top cutting into my back as he pushed against me. He slapped me across the face and yelled again, "Who is it? I'll kill you both."

He slapped me again. I tried to struggle free of him, and he just pushed harder up against me. This just seemed to excite him, as I could feel him getting aroused. He stepped back from me at this point and said, "Men should only have sex with their wives if they want kids. The good stuff is for the girlfriends." With that he laughed and turned and walked out of the washroom. I wrapped myself into a towel and stood in front of the mirror and stared at myself, wondering if it would ever get better. A few minutes later I heard the front door close behind him.

I sank to the floor and sat there, curled up in a ball for a long time. There were no real thoughts going through my head, just empty spaces where feelings and thoughts should be. Finally I got up because I began to realize that I was freezing and shaking. I got ready for bed and then laid there most of the night, not sleeping and not thinking. It was as if something inside of me shut down that night. A switch got turned off, and I became cold inside.

CHAPTER TWO

There was a subdivision being built north of where we were living. The builders where advertising in the newspapers, and it looked enticing. Jim went to look at the blueprints and plans that were on display at their sales office. He came back and said he wanted to buy a house there. He took me to see the plans and put a deposit on a house.

I gave birth to our third son, Paul, on August 1, 1979, and on December fifth of the same year, the house was ready. We moved into a detached three bedroom, two story brick home. There was no snow on the ground, but it had rained the day before, and just like any subdivision under construction there was mud everywhere. The U-Haul moving van was fully packed up, as well as some of the relatives' cars and vans that had shown up to help. My mother-in-law sat in the front seat of our car, holding Paul on her knee, while I sat in the back with Jay sitting beside me. I held Al on my knee.

When we got to the house we had to park at the end of the driveway, as the moving van was up close to the house. I was undoing Jay's seatbelt as I heard my mother-in-law getting out of the car. Suddenly I heard her scream, and I looked just in time to see Paul almost head first in the mud. She had dropped him as she stepped out of the car. I opened my door and jumped out and grabbed Paul with one hand while I still had a hold of Al in the other.

Paul was covered with mud from head to foot. I looked at him and thought, I don't think I've ever seen a mud baby before.

Jay struggled out of the car and looked at Paul with wide eyes and said, "Wow, is he ever dirty. Is he going to be in trouble for playing in the mud?" I smiled at him and said, "No, he won't get in trouble."

Jim saw what had happened, and instead of treating it like an accident he began to yell at his mother in Italian. Even though I don't really speak Italian, I knew enough to know that he was telling her off. You could see she felt bad enough already and did not need him to act like this. So I spoke up and said, "The baby is fine, just a different color." I tried to smile at her but she was too embarrassed, and she apologized and rushed into the house to get to the kitchen where she felt more comfortable.

I got the kids inside and went to find some towels and clean clothes for Paul. About half an hour later, Paul was washed and falling asleep in clean clothes, a bottle of formula in his little tummy.

Since we didn't have time to put the kids' beds together yet, I decided to unpack a box and use it for a bed. The items in it turned out to be kitchen items the women were wanting. I found a couple of blankets and used them as a mattress in the box. I laid Paul down in the box and covered him with a baby blanket. He snuggled down and was fast asleep.

There were ceramic tiles in the hallway, first floor washroom, and kitchen. Mud got tracked through everywhere as Jim and several members of his family moved in the furniture and boxes of clothes, toys, and things that needed to get unpacked eventually. Jim's father helped as much as he could. He carried in the lighter boxes and sat them on the floor in the hallway, while the men carried the heavy things into the house. The women all made themselves at home in the kitchen, preparing food to feed everyone. I tried to look after the kids, and every few minutes I would be called into the kitchen so they could ask me if I knew where something was. By three o'clock in the afternoon most of the things were moved in. Boxes sat everywhere.

The amount of food being prepared looked more like a party rather than a simple moving day. Wine flowed freely, and many beers where consumed even before the food was ready.

All the men sat down in the kitchen and passed food around the table as the women waited on them. The men ate, drank, and carried on conversations in Italian with the occasional laugh mixed in.

I had learned a long time ago that it didn't matter if everyone in the room could speak English, they would always speak Italian. I felt this was rude since they knew I could not speak Italian. I had managed to pick up a few words, but to carry on a conversation I could not do that.

I fed Jay and Al and then went to get their cribs ready so they could take a nap for a while. I heard my name being called a few times, and I ignored them, thinking that my kids come first. Actually I was feeling a little peeved, as I didn't think I needed thirteen people to help move us in when six of those thirteen were women cooking for the men.

After I got the kids down for a nap, I went back downstairs again. I entered the kitchen to find everyone still sitting and eating. The women had stopped serving and had now joined the men in eating.

"Jenny, if you find the boxes with the kids clothes in them, then I will unpack some of them and put them in the dressers that you have for them," said my sister-in-law Suzanne as she sat across the table from me, biting into a cold cut sandwich.

"Thanks, but I think I'll do it as I come across them. There is a lot to do today, and first things first, I need to make sure I have all their food supplies, diapers, wipes, and other things the kids will need right away," I replied with a smile.

Jim spoke up and said, looking directly at me, "You should take all the help you can get while you can get it."

"Yes," I replied, "and I am very grateful, but moving takes time, and I see no need to get everything done today. I have three small kids that come first. As long as I know where their things are that will be needed, then I will make do with what I have for now." I sighed.

Jim started to say something, and his brother-in-law jumped in and said, "You're right Jenny, the rest can wait until tomorrow."

Most of them left shortly after they had finished eating. Jim's mother and father stayed the night. I went to prepare their beds while my mother-in-law started to clean the kitchen. After I had finished getting the beds ready, I went back downstairs to find Jim and his dad watching TV while his mother made coffee.

I went into the kitchen and prepared some pasta for dinner, as I had sauce made and had brought it with us from our old place. My mother-in-law came into the kitchen and helped to prepare the meal.

After dinner Jim and his parents went into the living room where Jim turned the TV on, and they sat watching the news.

Al had crawled into a cardboard box and was holding Paul on his knees while Jay pulled the box up and down the hallway.

33

I found the camera, and I went and stood in the hallway and took of a picture of the three smiling faces. Cardboard boxes can sometimes be more fun than toys, I thought to myself, as I remembered how I used to love to play in one when I was young.

I went back into the kitchen to clean up after dinner and unpack some more boxes. I managed to unpack and put away the contents of four or five more boxes when suddenly I heard Jim and his dad arguing about something. Jim was waving his arms as he yelled in Italian. His father looked really angry but said nothing.

Jim's mother stood up and yelled something back at Jim in Italian and then turned as I walked into the room. When she saw me, she turned and sat back down, but I could see that she was still very angry about something.

"What's wrong?" I asked as I walked in. No one answered. They just glared at each other for a few more minutes, and then his mom and dad got up off the sofa and went upstairs to bed.

Jim got up as well and pushed me out of his way as he left to go upstairs as well. I never did find out why they all were arguing. I was starting to get used to this, as they often had yelling matches and argued amongst themselves a lot.

Growing up with just my mother, I never heard people yelling and screaming all of the time. It was pretty quiet around our house. If she got upset she would usually cool off and then speak to me about it quietly. It was rare for my mother to raise her voice.

The next morning I was up first, feeding the baby, when everyone came downstairs.

I had coffee waiting, and I offered to make breakfast, but his parents just wanted to leave. Jim pulled the car out of the garage and his mom and dad left, saying good-bye, but I could see they were still upset.

Jim was gone most of the day. Jay helped as much as he could to unpack different boxes and help put things away.

When Jim came back I offered to make him some dinner, but he said he had already eaten. "I need my clothes packed, as I am leaving tonight to go work out of town," he said.

I stopped putting things away and went to look for the boxes that contained his clothes. I found them and began to pack up his suitcase.

He came to the bedroom door and said, "Don't leave this house while I'm gone, and no one needs to come here either." He started to walk away and then turned around again and said, "I own you, don't forget that. You gave up your freedom to me. If you don't listen, the kids and I will be living in Italy and you won't be able to get near them." Then he walked away. I hated hearing that threat.

The following day, the kids and I went outside and sat on the front steps for a while. It was a warm, sunny day and hard to believe that it was December. There were a lot of construction trucks going back and forth, and Jay was fascinated with watching them. Jay sat beside me while Al sat on my knees and watched the trucks as well. Paul sat in his little baby seat, and even at his age of only four-and-a-half months, he was entertained as well, watching the trucks come and go.

After about an hour I took them back inside. The phone rang, and it was Jim. "Where have you been?" he said in a whisper into the phone, as if he was trying to speak without someone close to him hearing.

"I took the kids outside on the front steps so we could watch the construction trucks go by," I said, not thinking anything could be wrong with that.

"You slut," he murmured into the phone. "You're just out there looking the construction workers over. You think I don't know how your mind works? You're just trying to pick up one of them to keep you busy while I'm away from home. You can't be trusted anywhere."

I got so angry at this point. I was so tired of being accused of things I hadn't even thought of. "You're right," I screamed into the phone. "If I'm going to be accused of it I might as well do it." With that I slammed down the phone.

Within a minute the phone rang. I stood there looking at it as my heart beat wildly against my chest. I knew I was going to pay for that outburst. The phone continued to ring on and off the rest of the afternoon. He finally stopped calling about six o'clock that night. Then he never called back after that day, which was truly unusual as he always phoned several times a day to keep track of where I was and what I was doing.

As the week neared Friday, my nerves got worse. I was throwing up throughout most of Thursday night. The anticipation of waiting for him to return was taking its toll on me. I went to make Jay a piece of toast on Friday morning, and I put the slice of bread in the freezer instead of the toaster. It took me a few minutes to realize what I had done, and then I put the bread into the toaster with tears in my eyes, thinking I was totally losing it.

He arrived home around three P.M. He left his suitcase in the hallway and came into the kitchen to find me. I was sitting at the table with Al in his high chair next to me. Jay and Paul where both upstairs having a nap.

Jim walked over to the kitchen drawer and opened it. He grabbed a knife, walked over to the table, and pointed it at me and said, "I've thought all week about what I was going to do to you. I could cut you up so no man will ever look at you. I could take the kids and move to Italy so you never see them again, but for now I think I will just let you sweat it out, wondering what I am going to do."

He tossed the knife on the table and then left the house. I heard the car drive off and gave a sigh of relief. He was right, I would worry about what he was intending to do next.

I got up from the table and took Al upstairs to have a nap, and then I walked back downstairs into the hallway and picked up the suitcases and took them upstairs. I unpacked them and took his laundry downstairs to do them and prepare them for the next time he would leave, which I assumed would be on Sunday night again.

I started wondering again what it was that he had planned to pay me back, and I thought he was probably not going to buy food again.

He had stopped buying food several times before, usually for about a week each time. There was one time when he didn't buy any food for about two weeks, and I finally asked him what I had done to make him so angry. He said, "I didn't like the way you looked in that outfit you wore when we went grocery shopping a couple of weeks ago."

I was so surprised to hear the reasoning for not providing food for at least the kids. "What outfit was I wearing?" I asked as I tried to remember.

"You had on a pair of tight dress pants and a top that I thought made you look attractive to other men. You manage to dress for other men, but not for me."

"I dress for myself. I don't really care what others think," I explained, still shocked that this was his reasoning for not providing food for at least the kids.

It was times like this I would usually paint pictures or do sketches of kids to make money for food, but now that we were in a new subdivision, there were not that many people around yet, as most of the houses were still not built yet, and I knew no one in the area.

I got up and looked in the fridge, the freezer, and cupboards, and tried to estimate how far I could make things stretch. Not for three weeks, that's for sure. I thought to myself.

Jim came back later that night. He made himself a sandwich and said, "I had dinner out, but I'm still hungry." He took a big bite and laughed as he said, "Just think how hungry you three are going to get." He polished off his sandwich, had a drink of pop, made a big burp, and rubbed his stomach as he laughed again and left the kitchen to go upstairs to bed.

I followed him up the stairs a few minutes later. By the time I had gotten ready for bed Jim was already sound asleep.

He got up and dressed the next morning and was gone again for the rest of the day.

I spent the day looking after the kids, doing laundry, and getting Jim's clothes ready for him to leave again. When he came back he smelled of beer.

"I miss the pool hall when I'm on the road. There are some pretty cute little girls hanging out there lately. One is a little older and a real hard-core hooker. I gave her a drive home tonight, and guess where she is living?"

I looked at him and said, "I have no idea."

"Well, she's not far from here," he replied with slurring words.

"How nice for you, I'm sure," I said sarcastically.

"Hey, do I detect a hint of jealously in my wife's voice?" he asked, laughing. I thought to myself sadly that I don't think I feel anything.

Then he sat down at the kitchen table and said, "Did I ever tell you about the time that I picked up this girl hitchhiking on Bloor Street? I drove her home, and I made a date with her for the next night. I told a few of the guys at the pool hall that I had this hot chick on the hook and that they could join me for a night of fun with her. I went to pick her up and took her to the park where I told the guys to meet us, but they never showed up. They chickened out, and I had her all to myself."

I felt my stomach turn as I listened to him. "Maybe the guys don't believe in gang rape," I said as I turned and walked out of the kitchen. I went to the wash room, and I fought the urge to throw up. He really is heartless, I thought to myself.

It was about an hour after that when he made his way upstairs and lay on the bed with his clothes still on and passed out. He slept like that all night. He awoke the next morning with a headache and moaned and groaned about his upset stomach. He took a shower and put fresh clothes on. With his suitcase in his hand, he made his way to the front door where he turned and said he was going to be gone all week.

I listened to him drive off and realized I was still feeling sick to my stomach.

I had enough diapers to last me most of the week. Once I ran out I would have to find an alternative. I had enough food in the house that I could make baby food of vegetables and fruits. I had a small roast in the freezer, so I took it out and cooked it up. I kept back a few slices for me and pureed the rest, turning it into baby food. I had enough cereal to keep us going for about two weeks. I spent a day just preparing us for the rest of the week. I could do without, but not my kids.

By Thursday morning I had run out of diapers. After giving the kids breakfast and putting them in their bedroom to play, I went to look through the dresser drawers and closets to try and find a substitute for diapers. I went into the bedroom and opened the door of our walk-in closet. I stood looking at my side, and then surveyed Jim's side of the closet. He had seven white shirts hanging there; five of them were Italian cotton shirts. I couldn't think of anything better to use them for except the babies' bottoms. So I took the shirts and prepared them to be transformed from dress shirts to designer diapers. I removed all the buttons, and I have to admit I had a smile on my face while I cut them up. I found that after cutting the sleeves and collar off, you only had enough material for one diaper. When I finished I gathered the kids up and took them outside to play.

I was outside with the kids enjoying the fresh air. I was standing at the end of the driveway watching the kids play in the garage when I felt a tap on my shoulder, and I turned around to see a young mother standing there with her two small children about the same age as Jay and Al.

"My name is Ann, and this is Mary and Crystal, my two daughters. We thought we would come over and introduce ourselves and see if the kids would like to play together," Ann said, smiling.

She was a bit taller than me, and she had long brown hair down to her shoulders, tied back in a tight ponytail. She would say a few words and then stop to yell at her daughters.

"Mary, stop hitting your sister," Ann said as she turned back to me. "We moved in a few months ago, but I have only met a few people so far. Crystal, stop throwing things." Ann turned back to me and started to say something and then suddenly yelled again, "Crystal, if you throw one more thing I am going to take you home."

Ann looked at me and laughed. "So what do you in your spare time? Do you read?"

"Well actually, I do sketches of children, and this helps me to make ends meet," I answered.

"Oh, how wonderful," exclaimed Ann. "My parents are having an anniversary next week. I know it is short notice, but could you do one of these two? I know my parents would love it. I've been wondering what I could give them, and this would be perfect."

"Yes I would love to do it for you. I charge twenty-five dollars. And I just need you to give me a clear photo of each of them, and I will do the rest," I smiled and felt a sense of relief.

She gave me the twenty-five dollars, and I put it in a hiding place for when I needed it. I had no way of getting to a grocery store, as it was more than a mile away and there was no transportation up in the area yet, as it was still relatively new. If worse came to worse, then I would ask my new friend Ann to take me or pick a few things up for me when she went shopping.

The next day was Friday, and Paul was wearing his designer diapers when his father came home. Jim took one look at the label on Paul's butt and said, "What on earth have you done?"

I smiled at him and said, "Why, I'm just showing you how much we needed you this week when we ran out of diapers."

Jim raised his hand to slap me, but for some reason he didn't. He turned and went upstairs, and I heard him throwing things around in the bedroom. A few minutes later he came back down and went out without another word. In about half an hour he came back to the house and dropped off three boxes of diapers and then left again. He didn't speak for the rest of the weekend while he was home, and on Sunday night he left to go back out of town again.

Spring finally arrived, and the construction work was still going strong. The kids loved going outside every day to get fresh air. The subdivision was made up of mostly young families with two or three kids each. Every time I took the kids outside, I would open the garage door where the kids had riding toys as well as other toys. It was like a magnet to all the kids on the street who were my kids' age.

The neighborhood kids outside with their parents would see my kids playing, and they would beg to come over. So within a few minutes of us being outside, I would have the neighborhood kids and their parents in my driveway.

Quickly we got to know just about everyone living on our street. We would stand and discuss parenting and all the issues associated with it. We would talk clothes, toys, recipes, schools, and anything else that our kids' lives revolved around. I began to make a few close friends. It was like opening a whole new world for me. I suddenly enjoyed my days and even looked forward to going outside with the kids so that I could see everyone.

Jim was beside himself, as I refused to keep the kids inside. "I don't want you and the kids outside. Why can't you understand that? Good mothers listen to their husband's desires and do what he wants them to do. Why do you have to defy me?"

Jim was angry, as he had been out of town all week and had called several times, but I was outside with the kids and not inside answering the phone. When he arrived home he had to wait at the end of the driveway for the kids and their new friends to move all of their toys out of the way so he could drive in the driveway. He parked on the driveway and got out and glared at me without saying hello as he walked into the house.

Ann noticed the angry look and said to me, "Wow, he's been away all week and he didn't say hello to you or the kids."

"He's probably tired and hungry," I said, turning to face the kids so that she could not see the embarrassment I was feeling. "Come on you guys, let's go in and see your dad."

"Aw Mom, do we have to, we're having fun," Jay said. "Can't we see Dad after we finish?"

"No, we can play again tomorrow," I responded. "Let's go inside now."

Ann said, "That's alright, we have to go now anyway as I need to go grocery shopping for something for dinner. We'll see you tomorrow." With that she walked towards the girls and took their hands and walked away, yelling "bye" over her shoulder.

I quickly put the toys away in the garage with the kids' help, and then we went inside. The kids quickly went upstairs and into their rooms where I could hear them talking and whispering as I walked into the kitchen.

Jim was sitting in the kitchen, looking really pissed. I walked past him, pretending not to notice.

"Are you hungry?" I asked as I walked over to the counter and grabbed a cup from the cupboard and poured myself a coffee from the coffee maker.

"I've been calling all week, and you are never here. Is this what you do all day? Stand outside and entertain the neighbors?"

"The kids and I enjoy being outside. The neighbors come over when they see us out so that the kids can play together. There is nothing wrong with that."

Jim got up from the table and walked over to me. He ran his had up my back and then grabbed my hair. "How would you like me to show you what is wrong with that? Most husbands would beat their wives for being belligerent and not listening. You're lucky I'm not like that."

"Jim, you can beat me all you want, but I am not going to stop taking the kids outside. I'm sorry if you don't understand that, but they need to be allowed to run and play and make friends," I told him and looked him in the eyes as I said, "You would have some explaining to do if the neighbors see bruises on me all the time. You can't keep us hidden forever. Whatever your problems are, you may as well get over it, as I am not going to hide my kids or me anymore."

Jim didn't know how to react with my taking this stand. I think he knew it was true that you couldn't keep the kids inside. Soon they would be going to school, so then what was he going to do? Begrudgingly, he finally conceded that the kids could go out to play.

"You can't trust people. You're too naïve, and they will take advantage of that. I've only been trying to protect you and the kids," Jim said and then continued. "You can't bring anyone into our home. No kids and no adults. You may think these neighbors are your friends, but they don't care about you. They can see you're not smart. They know you're useless, and they are only feeling sorry for you, and they feel sorry for the kids for having a mother like you. Come to think about it, even your own father didn't want you when you were young. What makes you think people are going to start liking you now? What's there to like?"

I stood there, feeling like ice water was being poured over me. I fought back the tears that were stinging my eyes.

"Why are you always degrading me?" I choked out in a whisper.

Little did I realize that all the abusive things he was saying were starting to take effect on me. I didn't realize what was happening, as it began slowly. He would allow me to go to a mall or grocery store with him only once in a while, and I would suddenly start feeling like I couldn't breathe, sometimes to the point I would think I was going to pass out.

If I thought someone looked at me I would have this impulse that I wanted to run and hide. I would see people in a store and start feeling like they were better than me and I had no right to be there.

Jim, realizing how uncomfortable I was feeling to be out in public, would make it worse by saying, "What kind of an idiot are you? Do you know how embarrassing it is to have a wife that can't handle being out in public? What am I supposed to think except that the only place you should be is in the house with the doors and windows closed so you can't see people and they can't see you?" He would laugh and say, "You're so lucky you have me, as no other man would put up with you and your eccentric problems."

I would go home from those outings with tears running down my face. I had no explanation of what was happening. I didn't understand any of it. I just knew that I felt so worthless. My kids deserved so much better.

For some reason I did not relate it to the fact of the abuse I was receiving. In fact, it had gotten to the point that I didn't realize or even think that I was being abused. All I knew was that I was uncomfortable all of the time, no matter where I was, always feeling inferior to everyone around me. It was getting to the point that I thought I was not good enough to raise the kids. I would watch them playing and think to myself that they would be happier if they had another mother. I believed they needed someone who was smarter and prettier than me.

I was determined for the kids' sake that they were going to live as normal a life as I could try and give them.

Some days I would stand at my front door and look out and see the other mothers and kids outside, and I would have to talk myself into going out because I knew that once we were outside they would come over. Some days I could handle it, and then other days I just wanted to run back inside and close the door.

I had never heard of panic attacks or about people that panicked when they left their homes. Even if I had, I don't think it would have made any difference, as I was living in this hell and I had no idea of what to do about it.

I didn't think anyone would ever be able to understand what I was going through. I had begun to feel like I had to hide who I really was, this terrified stupid person. I had to pretend for the kids' sake that I was normal. I tried so hard to be like the other mothers, but I never felt I measured up.

It had been hard enough to hide the verbal and physical abuse from everyone I knew, including family. Now I had this monster I had created of being terrified and inferior everywhere I went. I hated who I had become.

I also had a terrible time every morning as I would have to deal with the dreams that I had the night before. Jim had convinced me that he would take the kids away from me if I ever tried to leave. So I had a reoccurring dream that I was lost and looking for the kids and couldn't find them. I would be searching everywhere. I would wake up exhausted, as if I had actually been running all night. Many times I would wake up gasping for air, and I would feel sick to my stomach. I would be so nervous that I just wanted to cry. Instead I would get up early before anyone else was up, and I would sit and smoke one cigarette after another, trying to calm down. Trying to talk myself into believing that I could cope and carry on throughout the day and not let the kids or anyone else know just how scared I was. I felt like Jim was right. If I was a better person then everyone would be happier.

Most mornings I would put on some makeup before waking up the kids so that they would not notice I had been crying in my sleep.

When I was outside and talking to the other mothers, they would be laughing and talking about going shopping and buying things for their kids. They loved to get out of the house. Most of them had their husbands home each night, and the fathers would look after the kids while the mothers went grocery shopping and just got out of the house.

They all drove, and they teased me that I didn't need to drive because I was living a pampered life style because Jim would do all the shopping when he came home for the weekends.

I would watch my kids laughing and having a good time, and I thought they also can never know what a basket case their mother is. They had to deal with so much when it came to their father they didn't need to know what an idiot they had for a mother.

So every day I would force myself to take them outside to play with their friends.

It was like fighting this war going on inside me, not to allow myself to become that house hermit that Jim wanted me to be and that I now discovered that I wanted to become.

I dreaded having someone come to my door unexpectedly. If the doorbell rang, my heart would start beating fast and my hands would get sweaty, and by the time I got to the door my legs would feel weak and shaky. I guess I was scared that someone would want to come in, and I knew that I had to face a beating or verbal abuse if I let them in and Jim found out about it.

THE WEB

One day I was outside with the kids, and like always the neighborhood kids and parents came over. We were watching the kids playing on the riding toys in the driveway, but we were having a hard time keeping them from going into the area that was roped off in front of my house where the construction workers were about to start pouring the sidewalk. Since it was a new subdivision there was only dirt roads, and the sidewalks were not built yet.

The construction workers arrived and starting getting their tools out and preparing for the cement to be poured. One of the workers came over and said, "The cement truck will be arriving shortly. You might want to take the kids inside so that they don't get hurt."

"I think that's a good idea," I said. "It's almost time for Paul to take his nap. How about I take the kids inside with me and they can all watch TV together, you guys can come over later and pick up your kids when they are finished pouring the cement."

The mothers asked their kids if they wanted to stay or go home with them and they all opted for staying. So I took seven kids into my living room, turned the TV on, and made sure they had cartoons to watch.

I went into the kitchen to prepare a bottle for Paul so I could put him down in his crib. With the bottle ready I picked Paul up out of his high chair and checked on the kids in the living room on my way upstairs to put Paul down for his nap.

I closed his bedroom window as the noise from the cement truck outside was fairly loud and I thought it would just wake him up.

You could hear the construction crew yelling back and forth to each other over the sounds of the truck. I turned to look at Paul, who was lying down in his crib, and was surprised to see that his eyes where closed and he seemed to be asleep. I walked over and kissed him and whispered, "Wow you can sleep through anything." Then I quietly walked out of his room and made my way back downstairs again.

Once again I checked on the kids in the living room and they were all engrossed in a kids TV program. I asked them, "Does anybody want a snack?"

Several of them shook their heads yes and a couple of them said, "Yes please."

"Alright, I'll be back in a few minutes with some snacks."

I went into the kitchen and got out a small bowl and poured some raisins in the bowl. Then I went to the fridge and got an orange and an apple, and I cut them both into wedges and put them onto a plate.

I was standing in the kitchen at the sink getting some water when I looked out a window above the sink that over looked the side of the house as well as where they were putting some of the sidewalk down in front of the house.

When I looked out I saw a few of the construction workers leaning on their shovels and laughing as they pointed to what looked like a hard hat about twenty-eight inches tall going down the sidewalk they had just poured.

Oh no, I thought to myself. I went to the living room and looked, and sure enough my son Al was missing. I looked at Jay and said, "Do you know where Al is?"

He looked at me and replied, "No, I'm watching TV."

"All of you stay here," I said as I turned and ran outside and saw Al running down the sidewalk, completely nude except for the hard hat he had gotten from somewhere. The construction workers were laughing as they watched him go.

"Please catch him," I called to one of the workers who were closest to Al. With that he stepped into the cement and scooped Al out of the cement. By this time I had caught up to him, the worker turned and handed him to me, laughing. "I guess he wants to join our crew."

"I'll let him do that when he gets some work clothes," I said as I took of a hold of Al.

With that, the guy laughed even harder.

"All joking aside, I am really sorry about your sidewalk," I said as I started back towards the house. Several of the workers waved to Al as I carried my cement-covered baby back home. Al waved and smiled back.

A few weeks later there was a knock at the door one evening. I went to answer it, and there was a tall black man standing there. His smile instantly drew me into him. "Hi, my name is Bart Clerk. I and a few of the other parents in the community are trying to put together a Soccer Association. We are hoping that we could talk parents into coming out and letting the kids get together. If we can get enough kids interested then we can start having teams. We believe that it is good exercise for the kids, and also they will be making friends and learning to get along with each other. The youngest team we would be having is four year olds. Would you be interested in coming to our meeting on Saturday night? I am holding it at my house at seven P.M."

"It sounds like a great idea," I said. "I'll tell my husband, and hopefully he will come to your meeting."

Bart smiled a warm smile and handed me a piece of paper with his address and phone number on it.

When Jim came home, I told him about the meeting and that I thought it would be great for the kids be involved in sports. "I believe that if you keep kids busy with sports and school then they won't have time to get into trouble," I said

Surprisingly enough, Jim agreed. "I'll go on Saturday night," he said.

Jim went to the meeting and came back and told me he thought it was a good idea. He said they had a bit more organizing to do, but there seemed to be enough kids to make a few teams. There was going to be a team for Jay's age group.

The following night Jim had a stag to go to for one of his friends from the pool hall who was getting married. Dressed in his finest and smelling of strong cologne, he set off to the party with a big smile on his face.

Since the kids and I had the night to ourselves, we rented a movie, I made a pizza, and we settled down to have a nice evening together.

Around ten P.M., the kids went to bed and I had a bath and was sitting up in bed reading a book when the phone rang around eleven P.M. I answered the phone, and it was Jim on the line.

"I got beat up," he said into the phone.

"Why, what happened?" I asked.

"They sold tickets to get into the stag, and I won first prize, but another guy said he won first prize."

"Well, what is first prize" I asked innocently.

"What do you think would be first prize at a stag party?" Jim asked me sarcastically. "Really, sometimes you do amaze me with your stupidity. The reason I'm calling is I want you to have Tylenol ready for when I get home, as I am pretty banged up."

"Hold on, and I will look to see if we have any," I said as I put the phone down to go and look.

I went and checked the cupboard, and sure enough we had Tylenol. I went back to the phone and said, "Yes, we have Tylenol. So what time are you going to be home?"

"I don't know, I have to wait until the other guys are finished first. Once I get my turn I'll be home."

"Your turn at what?" I asked.

He laughed and said, "The hooker." Then he hung up.

I stood there holding the phone and feeling numb. I think wives are supposed to get upset at times like this but I never do. I just don't feel anything.

A few days later Jim came home from work early. I was in the kitchen preparing dinner and had my back to him as he came in. The kids were sitting at the table playing a game of cards.

Jim walked over to the counter and grabbed a bowl of pudding I had just made for dessert. He took a spoon out of the silverware drawer and took a bite of the pudding. I turned to him to say something to him, but just as I opened my mouth, he put the spoon of pudding in my mouth. I could feel something hard in my mouth, and I spit it out onto a napkin and was shocked to see a diamond cluster ring. I stood there looking at it, and then I looked up to see Jim standing with a smile on his face, and he said, "See, I'm not so bad. I bring you gifts home." With that he left the kitchen, laughing. The kids gathered around to see the ring; they were as surprised as I was that Jim gave me this for no reason.

Strangely enough, a couple of weeks later he brought another diamond ring home and put it on a ring holder I had on the kitchen counter. "I bought it off a guy at work. He is into selling diamonds rings."

I was really shocked, as this was not like him at all. "Thanks," I said as I admired the ring.

"Well try it on and see if it fits."

I slipped it on my finger and said, "Yes, it fits."

"Good," he said, and then he left.

Shocked I watched him walk away. It was not often that I saw a nice side of him.

A soccer organization was formed, and parents all volunteered their time coaching and getting things set up. Local business people and stores were talked into sponsoring the teams so the kids could have equipment and uniforms. The kids were all so excited.

For the next few years, the soccer organization grew, and the kids looked forward to playing. After the first two years the teams started going to tournaments and holding tournaments. The uniforms got nicer and the kids now carried soccer bags with their team names and sponsors.

I volunteered on the association, and I was voted in to be their secretary treasurer. I went to the meetings being held. No one realized that each time I walked in the door and sat down at the table my heart would be racing and that I was fighting my fears to be there. I would have a strong impulse to want to run and hide. The other volunteers got to know me and seemed to give me respect.

They decided that we should organize a tournament and send out letters to as many clubs as we could all across Ontario. It was going to be held on a long weekend. After I mailed out letters to all the teams, I began to get their responses back, which was turning out to be very positive. I decided I would get in touch with the Toronto Sun and see if I could talk them into sending a reporter out to cover the tournament. I called the Sun and spoke to a gentleman in charge of the sports section coverage and told him what we were doing and asked if he would support us.

On the day of the tournament I was on the field with the kids, and as they prepared to play I went around and checked with everyone to make sure things were going well. There was an ambulance on site just in case of an accident. I had talked a couple of food vendors to come out and set up, and I was standing talking to a police officer about the amount of traffic when I got tapped on the shoulder, and I turned around to find two men standing there.

"Are you Jenny?" one of them asked.

"Yes, I am."

"We were told to report in to you. We are from the Toronto Sun. We will be following you around today from field to field and taking photos and covering the events."

"Well, that's wonderful," I replied. Once again I fought the urge to just run and hide. I pushed back all of my insecurities and just tried to make it through the day.

Throughout the day we traveled from field to field, where they took pictures and talked to several of the parents. At the end of the day they packed up, and I thought that would be it, but much to my surprise they said they would meet me back at the same location the next morning.

The kids and I went home that night. They were thrilled. Their teams were doing well. Everyone attending seemed to be having a good time. There had been a few scraped knees but no serious injuries.

Jim was very quiet, and after the kids retired for the night he walked into the living room where I was sitting going through papers for the next day's tournament. He sat down on the sofa across from the chair where I was sitting.

"I don't appreciate you hanging around these guys on the soccer fields. Everyone is going to think you have something going with one of them," Jim said as he stared at me.

"Well, I guess that it is their prerogative to think what they want. I am going to continue to do what I have to do for the kids' teams. I promised to do a good job, and that is exactly what I'm going to do. If you have a problem with that, then that's too bad. It's too late to pull out now, and so far things look like they are going well. Hopefully everyone is having a good time and all the visiting teams will want to come back next year. If we get good coverage from the Toronto Sun, then it is going to help our cause of trying to get soccer recognized in Canada."

He sat there for another moment and then got up and walked out.

Wow, I thought to myself, that went too easy.

The next morning the kids were up bright and early. As soon as they ate breakfast they were ready to go back to the fields.

The kids all went in different directions to link up with their teams. A few minutes after we arrived, I was standing and talking to a child who recognized me from our street.

"Hi Jenny," he had called as he came running up to me. He gave me a hug and then asked, "When are the games going to start?"

"Real soon," I said as I looked up and saw the two men from the Toronto Sun standing back and watching and smiling.

"Good morning," I said as I walked towards them.

"It looks like we are going to have another nice day for this tournament," one of them said.

"Yes," I replied as we started to walk the length of the field. "I have the soccer schedules here, and I thought we would start with this field as we have some of the older children playing the first game."

"Sounds great," the photographer said as he began to set up his tripod to hold one of his cameras. The reporter went to search for some parents to interview.

I went to check on things with some of the other volunteers. They all seemed happy with the way things had gone the day before and were looking forward to today's events.

"Jenny, the teams that are from out of town are saying this is one of the best organized tournaments they have been to," said Margaret, who was one of the volunteers.

"The coaches and referees are also saying they are very impressed with the hospitality they have been shown," another mother said.

I felt a hand on my shoulder, and I turned around and saw Jay's coach standing and smiling at me.

"Hi Bart," I said smiling.

"This is turning out to be a great event for the kids," Bart said as he patted my back and then walked away.

We all dispersed at this point, and I walked back over to the photographer. The reporter had a few parents lined up to talk to, while the camera clicked.

The game began and the crowd became involved with cheering the teams on. The day went quickly, and by the time that the last game was being played the kids all looked exhausted.

At the finals Bart took the microphone and announced the winning team in each age group. He handed out trophies to each of the players, and the crowd cheered the players on as they were handed their trophies. I proudly stood on the sidelines and watched and clapped.

I went and found the photographer and the reporter from the Toronto Sun and thanked them very much for their time. "I really appreciate you two coming out for two days to give us some coverage."

Our tournament took place the same weekend that the World Cup had played, so I said to them both, "Maybe someday you'll see one of these kids playing the World Cup." They laughed and packed up their equipment to leave.

"We had a lot of fun watching the kids. We don't often get assigned to the younger teams, usually just the professionals. So this was refreshing." With that we shook hands, and they got in their jeep and drove away.

I walked back to the activities that were still going on. I stood and watched the kids' faces as they looked at their trophies and patted each other on the backs, and I heard many of them saying to each other, "good job."

It was worth fighting my fears to see the smiling faces of all the kids, including my kids.

My kids came running over at the end of the evening, and we all walked home happy and exhausted.

The next morning I went downstairs early and walked to the end of the street where there was a Toronto Sun box sitting, full of newspapers. I put my money inside, pulled open the door, and took out a paper.

I walked back to the house and poured myself a coffee. I sat down at the kitchen table and opened the paper. I turned the pages until I got to the centre section, and there it was: beautiful photos of the weekend's events, plus a long write-up. They had interviewed me when they first got to the field, and they had put that in the paper with the photo coverage they had done.

I sat there, shocked. I never expected to see the tournament receive centre section of the Toronto Sun, especially during the World Cup. I really thought we would get a small picture on the corner of a page.

The kids came downstairs and looked at the paper, and they were also surprised to see the amount of coverage we had received. Jim came down and took a look at the paper. "That is a lot of coverage," he admitted.

For the next few days my phone rang of the hook, people thanking me and congratulating me.

I picked up the phone and called the Toronto Sun. I spoke to the gentleman that I had originally spoken to, trying to get the coverage.

"Thank you so much for the coverage," I said.

"You're very welcome," he replied.

"I wasn't expecting so much coverage. How come you gave us the centre section?"

"Well, I thought that it would be refreshing for people to read about the grassroots soccer trying to get started in Canada, and it is only going to happen if people like you push it."

"Thanks you again," I said as we hung up.

It felt good, but more importantly it began to show me that I could do things if I put my mind to it. I was slowly learning to have some self-confidence.

It made it a little easier for me after that to go the soccer meetings or even walk from one soccer field to another. I was still managing to hide from the kids and everyone else that I came in contact with that I was terrified every time I stepped outside my front door.

The shame and embarrassment I lived with daily suddenly was starting to subside a bit, or at least I was learning to live with it a bit better.

The following year Paul was old enough to play soccer as well. I asked him if he wanted to join, and he seemed really enthusiastic.

"Will I have a uniform like Jay and Al?" he asked.

"Yes, of course you will."

"Yaw, I want to play." So I took him to sign him up as well.

He was so excited the night of his first game. He couldn't wait to get his uniform on. We packed his soccer shoes in his bag along with a juice to drink. Al was not playing that night so he came with us to cheer his brother on while Jim and Jay went off to a game in another field.

When we got to the field there were a lot of children he already knew. The other team was there that he had never seen before. When the referee came onto the field and called the players to the field, all the children walked out onto the field. You could see the pride on their faces and in the way they walked. Some of them pat each other on their backs and nodded.

The whistle blew, the ball got tossed up in the air, and when it came down, Paul got a hold of the ball and with a lot of control he managed to work his way up the field past all the other players on both teams and scored the first goal. The crowd roared from the sidelines. Paul jumped up and down and clapped his hands, and his teammates all ran up and patted him on the back. His face shone with a lot of pride.

I thought to myself that he had learned a lot by watching his brother's games. Al, on the side of the field, was clapping and yelling, "Way to go Paul."

Paul came running over and slapped hands with his brother. I heard the referee blowing his whistle and trying to get the kids to pay attention to him so he could carry on with the game.

"Okay Mom, let's go home," Paul said.

"Why?" I asked.

Al looked at him amazed and said, "The games not finished, you can't go home yet."

"I don't want to play anymore. I scored a goal and I want to go home." With that he sat down on the sidelines, and no matter how much I or his coach tried to talk him in to going back onto the field, he really did not want to go.

THE WEB

For the rest of the year I had to argue with Paul or coax him into going to his soccer games. I finally promised him that I would not sign him up again next year, but we had made a promise to play and his team was counting on him, so he finally agreed to play.

Not much changed during the next few years, but as the kids got older the less Jim would hit me in front of them. The verbal abuse continued towards me and the kids.

It fact, the less he physically abused me the worse the verbal abuse got.

It seemed that daily I was told how stupid I was. How I wasn't good enough. He had to tell me constantly how he was disappointed in me.

I was standing in the kitchen one day, and I was wearing a blue dress my mom had bought for me. Jim came home from work and walked into the kitchen. He looked at me and said, "There is a girl at work that wears that same dress. She looks a lot better in it that you do. She weighs about twenty pounds more than you, and she just seems to fill it out so much better."

I took a deep breath and thought about not saying anything, but I couldn't resist so I said, "Well Jim, I appreciate the info. Does this mean I should tell you every time I see a better-looking man?" He just turned and stormed out of the kitchen.

That weekend there was a big tournament going on out of town, and Jay's and Al's teams were going to be playing. The kids were both excited and looking forward to the weekend events.

All of the parents and kids travelled and checked into a motel for the weekend.

The teams were all going to be playing on the same fields, so that meant we just had to pack a picnic, and we would probably be there all day.

Jay's team played first, and they won their first game. About an hour later, Al's team was playing on the same field. I was standing back from the field so that I could watch, but at the same time I could see Paul playing with some of the younger children.

The teams seemed to be close in skills and ability, and the score was three for the other team and two for Al's team. Al had the ball and shot on the net but missed. Suddenly, I saw Jim jumping over a chain link fence to get onto the playing field. He grabbed hold of Al. He slapped him twice while yelling at him. "You are such a loser. You embarrass me and your team members," Jim yelled at Al as he slapped at him.

The referees and coaches from both teams ran towards Jim and tried to stop him from attacking Al.

There was a chain link fence that ran around the field. I heard the commotion and ran towards the fence yelling at Jim to stop.

Al ran from the field and got in the car. His team mates just stood there, shocked. Al was one of the better players on the team, and this was such a shock for the kids to have to witness.

My heart was in my throat. I told Paul to come with me, and we went to the car. Jim had broken away from the coaches and the referee and was on his way to the car.

I got to the car first, and I opened the door and asked Al if he was alright. He didn't answer me. Red faced, he kept his head down.

Jim got in the car, and all the way home he ranted and raved about how embarrassed he was that his kid wasn't even trying to play the game right.

I felt sick to my stomach. I just wanted to fix the damage I felt was being done. How do you fix pain? How do you take away hurt? How do you, as a parent, help your kid when you don't know what to do or where to turn?

All three of the kids strived so hard to be the best at everything that they did. They tried so hard to put a smile on their dad's face, which didn't happen too often. They actually were turning out to be the best players on their teams, as well as good students in school. They did whatever it took to try and get their father to give them credit for working hard. They all wanted his approval so much. Jim, on the other hand, just refused to give any credit to anyone. It was almost like he went out of his way to hurt them with his words all of the time.

I had stopped going to Al's hockey games as I could not stand to watch and listen to Jim yelling at Al in front of the team. Al would endure all of Jim's insults and still go out and play the game with his heart on his sleeve. My nerves couldn't take it. I would fight tears and feel so embarrassed for the way Jim would act.

Al was one of the best players on his hockey team. Every week you could pick up the local newspaper and read about the team's success and read about Al's hat trick or goals.

It got to the point that Jim was obsessed with Al playing hockey and soccer. It was almost like he was trying to relive his own childhood and make Al into something he had not been himself. The pressure he would put on the kids when it came to sports was terrible. Nothing meant anything if there was not a few goals scored every game.

I was sitting in the living room with Jay and Paul when Al and Jim came in from one of Al's weekly hockey games. Jim was angry, and you could see on Al's face that he was stressed out. It looked like he had been crying, as his eyes were red and swollen.

THE WEB

"Get in the kitchen and give me the wooden spoon," Jim ordered Al.

Al, with a pained expression on his face, dropped his hockey bag on the floor in the hallway and went immediately to the kitchen. I jumped up and went to the kitchen door and asked, "What's going on?"

Al walked over to Jim and handed him the spoon, and Jim grabbed it, turned Al around, and slapped him hard on the backside, then hit again, and the third time he went to strike Al. I grabbed at the spoon, and Jim pushed me away and hit Al again. This time Al screamed and began to cry.

I could feel my stomach rise up in my throat and again I grabbed the spoon. I felt the impact of the spoon across my hand as it hit Al again as I struggled to get it from Jim.

Jim just pushed me against the wall and again he struck Al.

"That's enough," I screamed.

Jim threw the spoon on the floor and walked upstairs.

Al ran upstairs to his room.

I felt so sick at this point. How was I going to protect them? How could I stop this from happening? As a parent there is nothing in this world that is worse than hearing your child being beaten, and you can't stop it. The sounds of Al's cries will live with me forever.

The next few hockey games that Al played all ended up the same way. I even taped it one night, Jim hitting Al with the wooden spoon because he didn't like the way Al played.

The next day I took the tape and went to my family doctor. "I need you to help me," I said to the doctor. "This can't be normal, and I believe Jim needs help. I can't stand to have this happen."

I turned the tape on, and the doctor listened to the recording of the beating.

The doctor looked straight at me and said, "If it wasn't the fact that I know you so well I would turn you into the Children's Aid right now. Legally that is what I should be doing, but I know you are a good parent and that you do love and try to protect your kids. My advice to you is to get rid of that tape now before someone else hears it. If Children's Aid heard that you would lose the kids."

I left his office shocked and dismayed. I was hoping I could get some help, but instead I learned that not only could Jim maybe take my kids from me if I didn't do what he wanted, but now I had to fear that Children's Aid would take them too.

I stood outside the doctor's office and wondered, what do I do now? I can't have the kids live like this. I won't have my kids beaten, I whispered into thin air. "I have to do something, but what?"

Paul wanted to take karate instead of playing soccer or hockey. His father tried to put him down every time he mentioned it. "You won't learn anything, and you're too fat, so why bother?" Jim would say.

Paul stood his ground and continued to ask to be allowed to take lessons. Even though Jim was against it, I took Paul and signed him up.

The karate school was not that far from home, and he could walk there after school and on the weekends. What a nice smile Paul had as we stood there listening to the man who would be his instructor. It was like giving Paul a million dollars. It meant so much to him that he was going to learn self-defense. He was going to do something that his brothers didn't do.

Paul excelled at karate, and within the first year his instructor had Paul going in to help with the younger children. He was learning self-confidence and respect for others as well as himself. He loved the lessons and the environment. He was always bubbling about what he was learning.

Then it got to the point where he had learned enough that there was going to be a display of skills. The parents were invited to attend and give moral support and also see what the kids had learned. Jim did not want to go, but I finally talked him into it. We all sat in the gym while the kids sparred with each other, and then it was Paul's turn. He sparred with his instructor and did very well. At the end of the evening there were refreshments served.

I spoke to Paul's instructor, and he said how proud he was of how much Paul had achieved in such a short time. I thought the evening had gone really well.

Jim did not seemed pleased and was not encouraging Paul at all. In fact he told him he would like him to quit.

The next day when the kids had left for school, Jim said to me, "Now I know why you wanted Paul to take karate, you're having an affair with his instructor."

I was shocked to hear that. "Where do you get these ideas from?" I asked.

"I saw how he looked at you when you were talking to him." Jim said.

"You always have to destroy anything that means a lot to these kids. Why is that?" I asked. "Why do you get such pleasure in making everyone else miserable? It seems that the only time you are happy is when you see everyone else is upset."

It got to the point where I believed that Jim hated to hear laughter or see people happy. During a birthday party, Christmas celebration, or any other get-together, he would always find a reason to lose his temper and make everyone around miserable. It was as if he had to be the centre of attention, even if it was negative attention.

CHAPTER THREE

In June 1983 my mother called me one Saturday morning, as she was having a hard time speaking or breathing.

"Hang up Mom, and I am going to call an ambulance, and I will call you back." Jim was sitting at the kitchen table having breakfast and looked up and listened while I hung up and called the ambulance and then called my mother back. She picked up the phone. "Mom, can you get to the door to let the ambulance attendance in?" I already knew the answer.

"Don't worry Mom, the superintendent will let them in. You just stay on the line with me. They will be there in a few minutes."

I knew she was having trouble talking, so I just wanted to keep her calm until they arrived. A few minutes later they arrived and started to work on her. One of the attendants came onto the phone and told me they suspected that she was having a heart attack and they were taking her to the Wellesley Hospital, which was just around the corner from where she was living.

"Thank you, I will meet you there. Please let her know I am on my way. It will take me about forty minutes to get there, but please assure her I will be there." With that I hung up the phone and said to Jim, "We need to go, my mom is having a heart attack."

Jim was actually accommodating at this point and told me that we could take the kids and drop them off at his mother's, as it was on the way to the hospital. After we left the kids at his parent's house we drove the rest of the way to the hospital in silence.

We went upstairs at the hospital, and I was met by the doctor who said my mother was in very bad shape but hopefully they would know more in a few hours. She was so weak at this point that I was allowed to see her for only five minutes every hour. I went in and spoke to her, but there was not much response. Within a few minutes the nurse was asking me to leave, and I went to sit in the waiting room.

Jim was there waiting to tell me he was ready to leave.

"I'm not leaving here," I stated as I sat down.

Jim stood up and said, "I think you had better come with me, as my mother doesn't need the kids all day. There is nothing you can do here, and they will call you when there is any change."

"I'm not leaving," I repeated. He stood there a moment and then turned and left. For the next five hours I was allowed in to see her for five minutes and then would be ushered out again.

She looked pale and weak and most of the time she did not know I was even there.

Jim came back around four P.M. and asked, "Do you want a coffee?"

"Yes please," I answered as I sat in the waiting room, waiting for the next time they would allow me back into her room.

Jim took off and a few minutes later returned with a coffee. As I sipped on the coffee, Jim said, "I think you better come home now as the kids are crying and wanting to know what is happening."

I went to my mother's room and spoke to her. "Mom, you can't leave me. You have to get better. I need you and I love you. I'll be back tomorrow." I turned and left her room.

We drove back to his parents' house in silence.

Jim's mother was there and said to me in broken English, "No cry Jenny, you just upset kids."

I resented her telling me that. My mother was the only person I really had all of my growing up years, and I did not want to lose her now. I wanted my kids to get to know their grandmother and see how special she could be.

We drove home basically in silence. The kids looked tired. They asked a few questions about their grandmother, and I tried to answer them as best I could, but there was a steady lump in my throat I couldn't get rid of and tears were just a drop away. My strength was totally gone. I felt drained and just wanted to sit in a hot bathtub and cry.

The next day Jim said he would take me to the hospital to see my mother. The kids and I got in the van and we drove down to the hospital, which was about a forty-minute drive from our house.

Jim pulled up at the door and said, "You go in, and we'll wait here. I expect you back in fifteen minutes."

I looked at him, shocked. "What do you mean I have fifteen minutes?"

He said, "If you want to come and see your mother again you will be back in fifteen minutes. Don't waste my time, I have things to do. You'd better hurry up; the clock is ticking."

I got out of the van and walked into the hospital, still shocked.

I got in to see her as soon as I got there. She looked the same as the day before, and she still did not realize I was there. The machines hooked up to her were all beeping, and the oxygen seemed to breathing for her.

I went to the nurse's desk and asked, "Is my mother's doctor around?

"No, I'm sorry, but he has left for the day," one of the nurses replied.

"What does her chart say?" I asked the nurse.

"Well the nurse said she is stable, and we are hopeful."

I held my mother's hand and watched her sleep. She was hooked up to different machines, and she was receiving hydrogen, as it is lighter than oxygen. She looked very pale as she lay there unaware that I was beside her.

"Mom, you have to get better. I need you and the kids need you." With that I kissed her and let go of her hand. I walked out and got into the elevator to go back downstairs to the van, but I was leaving a piece of my heart with her.

Jim took me back to the hospital every day, and he would say the same thing every day: that I had fifteen minutes to visit, and I had better be back on time so I could continue to see her.

Within five days she was beginning to show a marked improvement, and she was moved into a private room. She was breathing on her own, and she was starting to eat small portions of food.

She was sitting up when I walked into her room. "Wow, you're up and active," I said, smiling as I walked in to see her.

"Yes, I feel really good. The doctor was in and said I was improving and that tomorrow I can start walking around the hospital."

"That's great," I replied.

She looked really serious and said, "I want you to bring your Aunt Gina in with you to see me."

I was surprised to hear this, as Aunt Gina was Jim's aunt. I was very close to her. She was the one person in the family that treated me like I was her family. She always had a big hug and kiss for me and the kids when we walked in. She had met my mother a few times at baptisms and different family events. They seemed to like each other, but hearing my mother asking to see her surprised me.

"I just want to talk to her," my mom continued.

"Alright, I'll call her when I get home and see when she will be able to come." My mom was happy with that answer.

I left the hospital that day feeling good. I got in the van and gave Jim and the kids the good news that she seemed so much better. When I got home I called Aunt Gina and told her that my mother wanted to see her. She said she would love to go to the hospital to talk to her.

The next afternoon I received a call from the hospital that she had just had another heart attack.

"Oh God," I said into the phone when I heard the news.

"I think you had better come to the hospital," my mother's doctor said.

Jim dropped me off, and again he said, "Remember, you have fifteen minutes."

"Take your fifteen minutes and shove it up your ass," I said as I got out of the van and quickly walked into the hospital. I had no idea if he would be there when I came back out or not, and at that moment I didn't really care.

The doctor was waiting for me, and we went into a small office and sat down.

"Jenny, your mom is in very serious condition. I don't know if she will pull through again. I need you to make a decision on what you want us to do."

"I'm not making that decision, you're the doctor, and it will be up to you and her, not me."

"Well, let's wait to see what happens," her doctor replied.

I went into her room in the ICU, and she was hooked up to everything again. "Mom, I'm here with you. Don't you give up."

She opened her eyes and squeezed my hand. A nurse came in to check her vital signs and said that someone would be staying with her throughout the night. I held her hand and just stood beside her for a long time. Finally the nurse said that I would have to go.

I kissed her, and once again she opened her eyes, and I said, "I'll be back tomorrow." With that I left her room. I glanced at the clock over the nurse's station as I walked by on my way to the elevator and saw I had been there for about an hour.

I went outside and was surprised to find that Jim was sitting on a bench with the kids. They were watching people coming and going from the hospital. As I approached, the kids came over to me, asking how she was.

"We will have to wait and see," I replied.

Jim got up from the bench and started walking towards the van. I expected to hear him yell and scream on our drive home, but instead he was silent the whole way. I was relieved, and it gave me time to just look out the window. The kids chatted amongst themselves in the back.

After the kids had gone to bed, Jim came into the kitchen where I was preparing lunches for the next day. "I thought about it, and I've decided to drive you to the hospital again tomorrow. She is your mother, and I guess you have the right to see her." He then turned and walked out of the kitchen.

I wondered to myself how he would feel if someone was trying to hold that kind of power over his head, as I watched him walk away.

For the next two days she seemed to get better and stronger and was even sitting up in the ICU having breakfast on the second day. She asked the nurse to give her a phone so she could call me and talk to the kids if they were around. The kids spoke to her for just a couple of minutes, and then she asked them to put me on the phone.

"Wow, Mom, it's great to hear your voice. I'll be in later today; do you want me to bring anything?"

"No, just you, will be enough," she replied.

Then she said something that really surprised me. "If I have another heart attack and they don't think I will make it, I don't want you to come to the hospital."

Shocked, I asked her, "Why?"

"I think this is too hard on you, and I want you to be home with your family."

"You're my family, and I will be with you. I don't want you to talk like that; you are going to get better. I'll be in later." With that we hung up. I was excited that she sounded like she was getting stronger but worried that she sounded like she was ready to give up.

Later that day, Jim pulled up at the hospital, and again he said to me, "Fifteen minutes."

I got out of the van as if I didn't hear him and went up to her room. Once again they had moved her out of ICU and were in another private room. She was lying down resting when I arrived. A few minutes later Aunt Gina arrived to visit her.

My mother was thrilled to see her, and she took a hold of Aunt Gina's hand and said, "My daughter thinks the world of you, and I have watched you with her, and I know you love her just like I do. From one mother to another, I want you to look after her for me."

Aunt Gina, with tears in her eyes, said, "She is like my daughter, and yes I will watch over her."

We all chatted for a few minutes, but my mother seemed to get really tired, so I said I would leave so she could get some sleep. Aunt Gina said she was going to stay for a little while longer.

Before I left, my mother caught my hand and said, "I want to ask you to do something for me."

"Sure, what is it?" I asked her.

"I want you to go to my apartment and move my piano to your house. I want you and the kids to have it."

"Mom, let's wait until you feel better, and then you can be there when we do that. You will have to live with us anyway, as you are not going to be on your own anymore, so let's just wait."

"No, it's really important to me that you do this now, in the next few days. Promise me that you will."

I could see that she was starting to get agitated, so I finally said, "Yes, I'll have it moved to my place."

With that she seemed to relax, and we said good night to each other. I gave her a kiss and kissed Aunt Gina good bye, and then I left the two of them talking. Aunt Gina had pulled up a chair and sat beside the bed, and as I walked down the hallway I heard laughter float from the room. The sound made me smile as I neared the elevator.

On our drive home I told Jim and the kids what she wanted. Jim was not in favor of having the piano, but I think he knew there was no way he was going to win this argument.

The next morning I phoned a friend of mine and asked if her husband would help me to move it, as he had a truck. She assured me he would love to help. A couple of hours later the phone rang, and it was the hospital again.

"Jenny, your mother has had another heart attack."

"I'll be there as soon as I can get there." I knew it was going to take me about an hour and a half to go by bus and then subway. So I called my friend back and asked if she could drive me.

I spent the rest of the day at the hospital. There was a machine breathing for her. She was once again back in ICU. I sat in the waiting room and was allowed to see her once every hour for five minutes.

Each time I went in to see her she did not respond. I felt like I was being worn down as well at this point. There was no one else in the waiting room. A few times when I left her room I would go back to the waiting room and sink into a chair. I felt so drained. I wished she would open her eyes and tell me she was alright and that she would get better.

Once when I came back into the room I stood looking out a window and remembered my growing-up years. She always seemed to be so strong. She would make my fears disappear and just make my world seem like a better place to live. "Don't leave me," I whispered. The motion of my words made a teardrop fall onto the window sill, and that was when I realized I was standing there with tears running down my face.

I turned around and walked away from the window and went to sit on a chair they had pushed up to a table. There were several small tables and chairs as well as more chairs to choose from. Magazines were spread out over an end table. This is a pretty lonely place to sit when no one else was around, I thought to myself.

Jim arrived around six P.M. and did not look happy about the fact that I had been at the hospital all day and that the kids had stayed with my friend.

"How can you just leave them all day? You need to be home with the kids and not hanging out here all day. There's nothing that you can do here," Jim stated.

"They're fine," I said. "They were going to spend the day with Sally's kids and have a great time. The hospital is no place for them to be for a full day."

I went in to see my mother one more time and told the nurse I was leaving for the night, but I would be back tomorrow. "Please call me if there is any change," I said.

The next day she had another heart attack. I was called to the hospital, and I sat with her again all day. There was no change when I left for the night.

I found I was having trouble sleeping and eating. Every time I tried to get food down I would feel like I was going to choke. I stood on the bathroom scale that night and was shocked to see that I had gone from one hundred pounds to eighty-three pounds.

Within a few days she seemed to perk up, and on the fourth day they took her off the machines and she sat up and ate an egg and some toast. She called me from the hospital, and we talked for a few minutes and I told her that I would be in later to see her.

For the next few days she seemed to get stronger and her color came back.

"Will you bring a fingernail file tomorrow with you and do my nails?" she asked. "Of course I will."

The next day I had the file in my purse and some pictures of the kids that I thought she would like to see and even keep if she wanted. I had dinner cooked and the kids were sitting watching TV.

It was around four o'clock when the phone rang. I answered the phone, and once again it was the hospital. "Your mom has had another heart attack. This time she has requested that we do not resuscitate her. We think she has probably got about an hour. You need to come to the hospital now."

"I won't make it there in an hour, it's going to be rush hour traffic out there now," I cried into the phone. "Please don't let her die without me being there," I begged.

Tears streaming down my face, I called my friend and asked her to look after the kids. Just then, Jim walked into the house. I told him what was happening and he said, "I'll take you in a few minutes. I want to change my clothes."

"What?" I cried. "You must be joking, my mother is dying and you want to change your clothes?"

"Don't get mouthy or we won't go at all."

"You can stay if you want but nothing is keeping me from being with my mother." Within two minutes we were on the road to the hospital. It was rush hour and traffic was barely moving.

We finally made it to the hospital. I went into her ICU room and spoke to her. She opened her eyes. She couldn't talk and made signs that she wanted a paper and pen. The nurse got her a pen and paper and handed it to her. She put a clipboard under the paper, and my mother tried to write what she wanted to say. I couldn't make it out. I saw how much energy it drained from her to try and write, and I didn't want her to use up her energy so I pretended that I knew what she wanted to say.

"Just rest Mom. Know I am here with you. I love you, and I will keep you alive in my heart and in my thoughts."

My mother had spent the last couple years of her life writing poetry. It was a past hobby that she really enjoyed. Some were funny, some were sentimental, some were religious, but most of all it was a pastime that gave her great pleasure.

"Mom, I promise that I will publish some of you poems someday so that people will be able to read them." My mom tried one more time to write down what she wanted to say, but again I could not read what she was writing.

"It's alright Mom, everything will be fine. Don't worry about anything." With that she looked at me and she managed to get up the strength to say my name, and then she slipped into a coma.

I stood there for a long time wanting her to open her eyes, but she didn't. Tears streamed down my face as I held her hand and said, "Mom, I still need you, please don't leave me." But I knew she wasn't able to come back.

A nurse came over and put her arm around me, and I turned into her and sobbed. "Please don't let her suffer," I cried.

"She won't," the nurse assured me. The nurse looked at me and said, "You look exhausted. Why don't you go home, and we will call you if there is any change. I think she's going to hang on until morning."

"I don't want to go," I said, but Jim came into the room at that point and said, "The kids need you home. I'll bring you back in the morning." With that he led me out of the hospital.

I don't remember the drive home. I just remember lying on my bed and reading a book because there was no way I would ever fall asleep. Jim was in the living room watching TV.

Around midnight there was a loud knock at the front door. I jumped up from the bed and ran downstairs.

Jim had fallen asleep and did not hear the knock at the door. I opened the door to find a policeman standing there.

"Are you Jenny?" he asked.

"Yes," I replied, surprised to see him standing there.

"May I come in?" he asked.

"Of course," I replied as I stepped back from the door and beckoned him to enter.

"The reason I'm here is because Wellesley Hospital has tried to call you on several occasions this evening, and they have not been able to reach you. Your phone does not seem to be working."

"It was working earlier today," I said.

"Well, how about you trying to call the hospital and see what is happening," he replied.

With that I walked down the hallway and into the kitchen. I picked up the phone and got a dial tone. "I have a dial tone," I said to the police officer as I dialed the hospital. I asked for the ICU and was put through immediately. When the nurse answered the phone I spoke and said, "Hello this is Jenny Guccio," I said.

"Jenny, we have not been able to reach you. Did the police get in touch with you?"

"Yes," I answered, "the officer is here with me now."

"That's fine," said the nurse. "I'm sorry to tell you that your mother passed away about half an hour ago."

I could feel tears welling up as I hung up the phone. The officer asked me if I needed anything.

"No, I should be fine," I stated, feeling like I would never be fine again.

"Well, if you are sure, then I will leave you alone," the officer said as he walked down the hallway towards the front door.

He opened the door and turned.

"Thank you for coming," I said as he smiled and then walked away.

I closed the door and stood at the end of the staircase.

Jim had woken up while I was calling the hospital. He heard the news and stayed up until the officer left.

"I'm sorry about your mom," he said as he went back to lie down on the sofa. I went back upstairs. I lay on the bed and cried for a long time.

She had five heart attacks from the time she entered the hospital. She fought it and held on as long as she could. She passed at the away at the age of sixty on June 23, 1983, and took a part of my heart with her.

I realized then that I would always tell anyone that I loved how much I loved them, and as often as I could, because it might be too late in another moment.

She had been my best friend, and she could make me laugh with her silly stories or jokes. She was full of talent, writing poetry, and painting beautiful pictures, making music, and more. She should have done something with her talent, but instead she spent her life raising and worrying about me.

A few days after her funeral I moved her piano into my home, her gift to us all.

I will sign the kids up for piano lessons, I thought to myself, as a form of respect to her for her gift. I hope the kids will enjoy learning to play it.

I suddenly had no one to talk to anymore. We would talk on the phone almost every morning. She would call me or I would call her. Even though I would not tell her what was happening between Jim and me, the sound of her voice would still make me feel better.

I found that I was having a hard time getting through eight am to nine am every morning. I would sit at the kitchen table during this time and remember our phone calls and conversations. I loved to remember the times we had together and the stories she would tell. She could put a smile on my face no matter what was happening around me.

One morning, she phoned me about a month before she had her first heart attack, to tell me about the night before.

"Hi Jenny, if you have a few minutes I have something to tell you," she said into the phone when I picked up the receiver.

"Sure, I have a few minutes," I said as I looked around the kitchen and grabbed my coffee off a counter and sat down at the table to listen.

"Well, last night I was going to church with my friend Eva. We had previously agreed that we would meet in the lobby of my apartment building around six P.M. and then we would go to church together.

"I sat down on a bench in the lobby and waited for Eva to show up as I got there first. As I waited in the lobby for Eva I noticed that there were several shopping bags sitting in a corner. Everyone coming and going paid no attention to the bag. The longer I sat there the more my curiosity got peeked about what could be in the bag, so when my friend Eva arrived we went over to inspect the bags. We found lots of beer bottles in the bags. We decided they should not be left there because some kids might break them. So after a short discussion between us we decided we should carry them down to the janitor's apartment and give them to him. We tucked our bibles under our arms and picked up the shopping bags with the bottles. Giggling like school kids, we proceeded to walk down the long hallway that led to the janitor's apartment."

My mother began to giggle at this point as she told me the story.

My mom carried on telling the story. "I was just a few steps behind Eva, and suddenly one of the shopping bags broke and bottles went tumbling to the floor, most of them rolling in all different directions. A couple of them shattered and worse than that, beer splashed onto me and Eva. I could feel the wet beer marks on my legs. Eva looked horrified."

My Mom stopped talking and laughed again.

Smiling, I continued to listen.

"We were so embarrassed at this point, as if we had just been caught in some wicked act," my mom continued. "Think about it, here we are with broken beer bottles and the smell of beer all over the place as well as us, and we want to tell the superintendent that they belonged to someone else."

My mom started to laugh even harder now. Catching her breath, she carried on. "I said to my friend Eva, 'Look at us now, here we are two church-going old women, and here we are looking and smelling like two boozers.'"

Eva laughed also when she saw the humor at what they had gotten themselves into. It turned out that the superintendent was not home, so they left the bags at his door. They went back to the elevator to go back up to their apartments, as they felt they could not go to church smelling the way they were. They pushed the elevator button, and as they waited for the elevator to arrive, a young couple came into the building and stood beside them to wait for the elevator as well. My mother noticed that they were nudging each other and making faces, as they could smell the beer.

My mother laughed and said, "Just imagine what that young couple must have thought to see these two old women with bibles under their arms and smelling like beer."

Needless to say, they did not go to church that night, but they did get a good laugh, and so did I the next morning as she told the story.

I got myself a cup of coffee and sat down to remember another story about my mom that always brought a smile to my face.

My mom was at my apartment before Jim and I had purchased the house, and some of the apartments were getting broken into. Jim was out of town, and my mom had come over to spend a few days with me.

I was still recovering from giving birth to Al, and she was a big help with Jay, keeping him entertained while I looked after Al. It was just nice having her around.

She was asleep in Jay's room while I was up at two am giving Al a feeding. All of a sudden I heard a noise in the hallway just outside the apartment door. I listened for a moment, and then I went and laid Al down in his crib. Just as I was coming out of Al's room, my Mom got up and came into the hallway and asked what the noise was.

"I'm not sure, but I think someone might be trying to get into the apartment." I crept down the hallway quietly, making my way back to the living room. I stood in the alcove leading to the apartment door with the lights out.

A few seconds later my Mom bumped into me. We both stood there a few minutes listening to the sound getting louder, as if someone was trying to loosen the lock on the door.

My mom started to step in front of me, and I noticed she had a can of hair spray in her hand.

"What are you doing?" I asked.

She whispered her response. "I'm going to spray whoever comes through the door in the eyes and blind them."

"Mom, give me the hair spray before you end up spraying yourself." With that I tried to take the can away from her. "Mom, give me the can," I said, a little louder.

Neither one of us could see the hold in the nozzle where the spray was going to be coming out of, and for all I knew she would end up blinding us and not the person coming into the apartment.

My mother, getting frustrated by me trying to stop her, said even louder, "Leave me alone and I will stop this fool from coming in here with just one shot."

Suddenly the noise on the other side of the door stopped, and we heard footsteps going out the exit door and down the stairs. I stood there looking at my mother and started to laugh.

Here we were, two small women standing there with our dangerous weapon of hair spray, while the culprit was running away from the building thinking he was running for his life.

My Mom stood there looking at me, and then I said to her, "Thank goodness he didn't get in here because, I know you would have given him one hell of a hairdo."

With that she bent over with laugher. Tears streamed down her face as she said to me, "We always have fun no matter what is happening."

She was right about that.

When she finally stopped laughing, she turned and went to put the can of hair spray back in the washroom.

We never did hear of any more break-and-enters in the building after that.

"Way to go, Mom," I whispered into an empty kitchen. "I miss you, Mom."

After my mother's passing, it became harder for me to accept what Jim was putting us all through. His insults and innuendos just seemed to become more frequent. It was now a daily thing that I lived with.

Jim rarely worked out of town now, and most jobs had him home every night, which meant that the abuse was now daily instead of weekly.

Since the outburst on the soccer field and the embarrassment that Al had to go through, I felt that things were out of control and that I had to do something to protect the kids and myself.

I was tired of the threats of violence being made towards me. The biggest threat was him saying he was moving to Italy with the kids, and I would never get them back. That was the one thing he could hold over my head, and it would stop my heart.

I had heard about a woman's shelter that was about twenty miles north of where we were living, and I thought we might be safe there. I might be able to get some help and make a clean break from this situation.

I called them, and I was told they were completely full and that I had to keep checking back with them until they were enough spaces available to accept me and three children.

I would phone daily, and it began to feel like they would never have the space for us. Then finally, after about two weeks, I dialed their number again, thinking I would still hear the same thing, and instead they surprised me and said they had space for us and that I could bring the children and come.

I told them I was going to speak to the kids' school and let them know where the children would be. I worked it out with each teacher that the kids would receive school work for a few weeks, and then I got the children packed up to go.

The next morning when Jim left for work I called a girlfriend, Ann, and asked her to drive the kids and myself to the shelter, which she did.

During the first couple of days I tried to keep up with the children's school work as well as trying to see what was available for work and an apartment for us live while we started over again.

The shelter set up an appointment with me to meet with a counselor the following week, where maybe some of my questions might get answered.

The kids cried almost every day. They missed their friends, and they just wanted to go home. They didn't understand I was trying to give them a better life without abuse and that it was going to take time and some sacrifices on their part and mine. "I know you all miss your friends, but hopefully we will have a better life."

They did not want to hear that. They wanted to go to their sports games, see their friends, and just continue on with the only life they had ever known.

The third day that we were there I got called into the main office of the shelter, and I was told that Jim had found out where I was and that he was continually calling and making threats.

"We no sooner hang up the phone from one of his calls and he phones right back again. We have tried to reason with him, but he is not listening to anything we say. He seems to be obsessed with you and the kids. Maybe you can talk to him and explain that he cannot continue to call here."

Then they handed me the phone and asked me to call him and see if I could make him see reason.

I already knew there was no reasoning with Jim, but I felt I owed it to the shelter to try.

I dialed the phone, and on the second ring Jim picked up the phone.

"Jim, I hear that you are continually calling," I said into the phone.

"I'm going to do more than just make phone calls. You had better get my kids back here now. My patience is running thin, and I want my kids home now," he screamed into the phone.

"Jim, you have to realize the kids and I can't live with the abuse, and it needs to stop."

"You haven't seen abuse yet," he threatened into the phone. "Now get my kids back here at this house before I show you what abuse is."

He slammed the phone down.

I sat there with the phone in my hand. The workers looked at me and asked, "Do you think it did any good?"

"No," I answered, "I don't think so."

Within a few minutes the phone rang, and it was Jim again.

"Tell my wife that if she is not back in two days she will be sorry."

I looked at the supervisor and asked, "Why aren't the police doing anything?"

"We did speak to the police, but unless he actually does something there is not much they can do.

"At this point, we are feeling that maybe this is putting the other mothers and children in the shelter in danger, and we want to know if you and the children have some place else that you can go?"

"No, I don't. My mother has passed away. I have no father. My sister doesn't know how bad it is for me, and she has a family with her own problems. This place is it for me."

"Well, let's see if he cools off," they told me.

The next morning they called me back into the office again and said, "We're sorry, but your husband is not letting up. In fact he is getting worse. We have talked to the police but they still are insisting that until he actually does something, there is not much they can do."

The worker cleared her throat and then continued, "We are asking you and your children leave this facility by Saturday. This is only Thursday, so that gives you some time to maybe think of some other place that you can go."

"I understand," I said as I got up and left the office, knowing there was no other place for me to go but backwards.

As I walked down the hallway, I thought to myself, I never seem to belong anywhere. There is no hope for us, and I have no choice but to go back.

I went back to sit with the kids, who were in the TV room watching TV. I told the kids that we were going to go home and see if we could make things better. The kids were excited and happy to hear this and started making plans to go home.

I looked at their smiling faces and relieved expressions.

"We can see our friends again," said Jay while the other two nodded.

I wished I could feel as good about it as they did, but I knew it was probably only going to get worse now.

The next day was Al's birthday, and the shelter was planning a little party for him that the other kids in the shelter knew about and were all looking forward to.

The next day I went into the office and asked if I could use the phone. I picked up the phone and held the receiver in my hand for a few minutes. This was a call I just did not want to make but knew I had no choice. With a big sigh, I slowly dialed the phone number and prayed he would not answer, but Jim did pick up on the first ring.

"Hello," he said into the phone.

"Jim, the kids and I are ready to come home."

There was a slight hesitation on the other end of the line, and then he said, "I'll be there in about an hour to get you."

I didn't tell him we had been asked to leave the shelter. I thought it might go better for us if he thought it was our decision to come back. I also thought I was better off if he thought we had someplace to go if we ever left again.

"No, we're not ready. There is going to be a birthday party for Al, and we are staying for that. You can come later this afternoon, say around thee P.M."

With that I hung up with a heavy heart and thought that I would probably pay a big price for leaving.

There was a festive air in the living room where several presents sat wrapped up on a table. The room was decorated and there were balloons tied to several chairs. The kids were playing a few games, and there were smiles on all the kids' faces.

Al received a few games, and he was thrilled with each of them. The cake was cut and served after the children sang "Happy Birthday," and then Al made a wish and blew out the candles.

A few hours later we said good-bye to everyone and were in the car and driving home. The kids where very quiet, and Jim and I never spoke.

As soon as we got home the kids ran upstairs to their room and began calling all their friends to tell them they were back.

I cooked dinner, and we all ate in silence. I had not felt comfortable since we had gotten in the car to return home. I felt like the air was heavy with tension. Jim sat in the living room and watched TV. After dinner the kids went back to their rooms. Later that night, after the kids had gone to bed, Jim came into the kitchen where I was trying to keep busy so that I could avoid him.

"Well, don't you feel like an idiot?" were his first words spoken to me since coming home.

I didn't answer him, and I continued to wipe down the kitchen counter.

"You really are a piece of work," he said angrily. "You are just trying to embarrass me. I am so ashamed that my wife would do this. What do you think my family would say if they knew?"

Still I kept quiet and didn't answer.

I never looked at him, and I continued to clean. Suddenly he grabbed me by the arm and squeezed really hard and started to twist it and said, "I could break you in half if I wanted to. Don't ever try that again, because the next time you try to take my kids, I'll kill you."

Things were going to be tough from here on in. I now knew I had no other alternatives, and I was now here in this situation until the kids became older. I had to try to do whatever I could to make sure the kids and I stayed safe.

The next day I phoned Ann. I heard the phone ring, and I was actually looking forward to hearing her voice and telling her what had happened.

"Hello," I heard her say into the phone on the fourth ring.

"Ann, it's me, Jenny. The kids and I are home."

She was silent for a moment and then said, "Well then, you're on your own. You had me take a chance, driving you and the kids to that shelter. If Jim had found out I was the one who helped you get there I would have to deal with him. Who knows what he would do if he knew I was involved. Now you phone me less than a week later and tell me you're home."

I tried to interrupt her at this point and said, "Ann, he'll never know it was you. The kids and I will never tell him."

"I don't care," she said. "I don't want anything to do with you or your family any more. Your husband is crazy. Almost everyone in this neighborhood has witnessed it at some time or other. I don't need the trouble I know he could cause."

I heard the click of the phone as she hung up. I stood there for a few minutes, shocked.

I never realized she was scared of Jim. In fact, I had never thought of anyone else being scared of him except me. I felt so sorry that I had made her fearful. I knew there was nothing I could say to make her feel any better and that it was best to just let it go.

I felt terrible that I was losing a good friend because of Jim but knew that it was best.

I had one more friend who had been close to me since we had moved in. Her name was Eileen, and I wondered if she was going to take the same stand and tell me to get lost.

She was always stopping in to see the kids and me on her way home from work every day. Her kids came down and spent time with the kids and me as well, even though they were a bit older than my kids. Her husband Will was also always in touch and joked around with the kids.

I felt like I might as well find now out if she was still going to at least speak to me. I picked up the phone one more time, and when I heard her voice I fought back the tears as I told her that the shelter had asked us to leave and that we were back home again.

"I'm glad you're back," she said, much to my surprise. "I hated walking by your house knowing you were not there. We missed seeing the kids around, and hopefully you can work things out with Jim."

She had known we had problems, but I never told her to what extent they were. Some things you just can't say. I hated anyone to know about the physical abuse. They heard the verbal abuse towards the kids and me, but I would try and make it not sound so bad or laugh it off. I was relieved to hear I still had her as a friend.

Since the kids were in school full time, I decided I had to do something so that I would not sit around thinking about my problems all day long. So I made some flyers stating that I would paint wall murals and then I went throughout the subdivision and handed them out.

The next day I got a call, and I went to see the person. I ended up being hired to paint a doctor's office. While I was doing that mural, I got some more calls to do wall murals in private homes.

Kids' rooms where a big thing, I learned. I had no idea that it would take off like this when I made up the flyers. People would tell me what they wanted, and I would go to their home and sketch out what I thought they would like, and once they approved it I was painting their walls.

I was working on several homes at the same time when I got a phone call to come into a Burger King store in the north end of Toronto. I discussed with the owner what he wanted for a kid's party room. I did sketches that he looked at and liked, and I was hired to do the party room.

The day I went to paint the party room I took Al with me. Al worked just as hard as I did, and I was impressed with his skills and ability. I was wishing he was a bit older so I could talk him into working with me full time, but he was too young for that. He had school and sports, and that was enough on his plate.

We made six hundred dollars. That day and the next day I took Al, Jay, and Paul to a local pet store, and we purchased a little dog they had been looking at every time we went into the mall.

I knew Jim was going to be angry, but I didn't care. We had seen him angry for less than that. I felt the kids needed something that was positive, and I felt that the love of an animal could be a very positive thing. Like they say, a dog will love you without making any demands on you. Their love is unconditional, and I thought it was about time that the kids experienced that.

The dog was a little black and white Shih Tzu puppy, and as he was handed to the kids in the store, I asked them, "So what are you going to call him?"

They all agreed that his name should be Pepper.

Pepper became the centre of attention for everyone and, surprisingly enough, including Jim. Pepper was smart and loveable. He was full of life and had a real love for stuffed toys. He claimed almost all of the stuffed toys in the house as his. If we took him to someone else's house he claimed their toys as well.

He was so easy to house train. As soon as he ate, the kids or I would take him outside and within a few days he was fully trained.

The kids spoiled him whenever they were home. They played with him, and he knew he could get just about anything he wanted. The kids' friends loved him as well.

Pepper and I spent a lot of time together, and I thought it would be fun to teach him a few tricks. I was surprised how quickly he picked up a new trick. I could show him something a few times and he would catch on and start doing the trick. So one day, when the kids came home from school, I told them to stand quietly and watch.

"Pepper," I said, and when I knew I had his undivided attention, I said, "Pepper, say your prayers."

With that he laid his down and put his two paws together and bowed his head. He stayed that way, and within a minute I said, "Amen." He raised his head, and I gave him a treat.

The kids loved it, and they all tried it. After that Pepper learned a lot of tricks, closing the door, closing the fridge, dancing, giving a high five, and playing dead. Even people that did not like dogs seemed to like Pepper. He just had that certain puppy personality that everyone warmed up to instantly.

He loved going to soccer games and sometimes would try to get the ball away from the kids. He also loved to wear sweaters and t-shirts. It got to the point he didn't want to go outside without a shirt on. He became the mascot of Jay's soccer team one year.

Pepper brought some much-needed happiness into our home. He was something that we could all relate to.

One day my sister Isabell called and said she was throwing a birthday party for her daughter on Saturday and asked if I would come over and spend the day with her and help her decorate and get things ready for the party. I couldn't see why not, and I asked her if she would mind coming to pick me up.

My sister and her family loved my cooking, as most things I prepared were Italian foods made from scratch. So she wanted me to make lasagna and some appetizers. She said she would make the cakes and salads if I would do the rest.

I was looking forward to it but did not mention it to Jim until the day my sister was coming, as I did not want to listen to him rant and rave. I knew he would not be in favor of it because I wouldn't be where he could watch over me.

My sister called to say they were leaving and would be over in about half an hour. I hung up and went into the living room where Jim was lying on the sofa watching TV.

"My sister just called and is on her way over to pick me up. They are having a birthday party for my niece Lynn and they want my help to cook and get ready."

Jim never took his eyes off the TV and just said, "Well, call them back and tell them not to bother coming because you can't go anywhere."

I stood there for a moment and felt my anger rising, and I said, "Gee, I don't remember asking permission, I was telling you that I'm going to help them out."

He sat up and said, "We'll see about that."

I turned and walked into the kitchen. My heart was in my throat, as I knew he was going to cause trouble when they got there. I picked up the phone and called their house, but they had left already. There was nothing more I could do but wait.

Half an hour later I saw my sister Isabell and her husband Rob drive up the street and park in the driveway. I grabbed my purse and jacket and went outside.

Jim jumped up from the sofa and ran out behind me. I got to the van and opened the door and got in.

Rob rolled down the window and tried to speak to Jim. "Hi Jim, are you coming to the party for Lynn?"

Jim shook his head no and said, "My wife can get out of your van now as she is not going, either."

Rob, trying to be diplomatic, said, "Well it's not going to hurt for her to come over and help her sister."

Jim just ignored Rob and said, "Get out of the van now before I drag you out."

"No," I replied, "it's the principle of the thing. I am not doing anything wrong, and there is no reason for you to stop me."

"You're my wife, and you'll do what I tell you." He started to turn towards the house and said to Rob, "Just wait here, I'll be right back."

While he was gone my sister said, "Maybe you should stay, I don't want to cause trouble for you."

I could feel tears coming near the surface. "No, I should be there helping you. I am not doing anything wrong."

Suddenly Jim walked out of the house holding the dog. He held Pepper up by the scruff of his neck and said, "Get out of the van right now or I will kill this dog."

I heard my sister take in a deep breath. Rob sat quietly. I opened the van door and stepped out. Jim walked over and tossed the dog at me and grabbed my arm as I caught the dog.

He turned to Isabell and Rob and said, "Don't ever try to get my wife away from here again." With that he pushed me towards the house. I heard the van start, and I glimpsed the van pulling away from the house as I walked into the hallway.

Jim walked back towards the living room and said, "You are such a stupid bitch. You just can't learn that I will always have the upper hand. I will always control you. I will never let you go. I will kill you first before you leave me. You can try all the tricks you want but you will never have your freedom. I own you. Don't forget that." With that he lay back down on the sofa and started watching TV again as if nothing had happened.

I went upstairs to my bedroom and sat on my bed with the dog in my arms. The phone rang, and I realized I had been sitting there for almost an hour holding the dog and not really thinking of anything. I always found that something inside me would shut down at times like this. My mind would go blank and time could pass without me realizing it.

I got up and went around the bed to get the phone. As I picked it up I could hear Jim pick up the extension downstairs.

It was my sister Isabell. "Are you alright?" she asked.

I swallowed hard and said, "Sure," trying to sound alright.

"What happened, why did Jim act like that?"

"I don't know," I said.

My sister and I stopped talking for a moment. I could hear Jim breathing into the phone.

"Well, I just wanted to call and see if you and the dog are alright. I'm sorry if I caused trouble for you, I just thought it would be a nice surprise for Lynn to have you at her party, and you know how much she loves your cooking."

I hated the fact that my sister thought she should apologize for something that was clearly not her fault. "Thanks for calling," I said, fighting back tears, and then I quickly hung up. I heard Jim hang up the phone downstairs and go back into the living room.

For the next few months, every time the phone rang, if Jim was home he would wait until I picked up the phone and then he would pick up the extension.

Just another form of control, I thought. He was putting me through hell. It was hard to live with someone who suspected that every minute of the day was another minute that I was planning an escape. I couldn't understand why someone would want to hold onto someone that didn't want to be there.

I began to feel like I was an insect caught in a spider's web; the more I struggled to get free the more excited the spider became. There is no escape. There is no way out of that web. The panic, fear, and anxiety of being captured are overcoming.

A few weeks later Isabell called and said she wanted to come over with Rob and the kids and asked if it would be alright.

"Yes, please come over. I would love to see all of you." I hung up and walked to the kitchen to prepare some snacks for when they would arrive. About an hour later I saw their van drive up the street and park in front of the house.

I stood smiling in the doorway of the house while I waited for them to descend from their vehicle and make their way into the house. Jim had gone out hours before, and I was actually looking forward to spending time with them alone without him being around.

We made our way into the kitchen and we all sat around the table talking, laughing, and munching on snacks.

Eventually my sister cleared her throat and said, "So is everything alright?"

"Sure," I responded, trying to sound convincing.

"Well we were shopping at a dollar store in Scarborough and I saw this and thought you would like it," my sister said as she put her hand into her purse and brought out a small picture frame and handed it to me.

"Thank you," I said, smiling as I took the picture frame in my hand. "Thanks for thinking of me."

We sat around for a little while longer just having small talk, and I got the impression that they were there checking on me.

We were talking of nothing in particular when all of a sudden my niece piped up and said, "Aunt Jenny, I want to be like you when I grow up."

She caught me truly off guard, and I swallowed hard trying to hide the fear that she had just run through me. I cleared my throat and said, trying to sound casual, "No Lynn, you don't want to be like me." I smiled and then diverted my head so she could not see my eyes.

The last thing I ever wanted was for anyone to end up like me, especially someone I loved so much. This little girl was like a daughter to me. I had three strong, handsome boys, but she was the beautiful daughter I never had.

When I went to bed that night I kept hearing my nieces voice in my head. "Please God, don't let anyone ever go through what I am going through," I whispered into the darkness.

CHAPTER FOUR

The sun glistened through the kitchen window, spreading warmth throughout the room. I poured myself a coffee and joined my youngest son Paul at the kitchen table. Paul was now fourteen years old with curly hair like me, but dark coloring and dark eyes like his father. Jay, who was the oldest at seventeen years of age, looked a lot like Paul with the same dark hair and eyes, and Al, now aged fifteen, had the lighter hair and eyes like me. I could hear Al and Jay joking around upstairs as they got ready for school.

Paul sat with his head bend over a plate of scrambled eggs and toast. "Mom," Paul said, "Dad was doing it again last night."

I watched Paul as he pushed eggs from one side of his plate to the other. I thought for a moment before saying anything, as I already knew what he was talking about. What does a mother say to her son when she has no answers?

There are times during motherhood that you really just want to run and hide and say, hey I can't deal with this, but you can't do that. There were no magical manuals given to me when I became a mother that told me how to handle difficult situations. I took a sip of coffee as I looked at Paul sitting there, needing an explanation. I noticed that his curly hair was looking unruly, as if he hadn't combed it but I knew he had just tried so hard to straighten it with water a few minutes ago. It had begun to dry and was becoming curly again. His youthful brown eyes looked as big as saucers at this moment as he looked to me for an answer.

With my heart in my throat I softly said, "Was he in your room again last night?"

"Yup, I woke up and he was just standing there staring at me. I pretended to be asleep, and he stayed for a couple of hours, just standing there over me. I finally fell back to sleep and the next time I woke up he was gone. Why is he doing this, Mom?"

"I don't know," I sighed, "I wish I did. I wish I knew what goes through his head."

Jim had been going to one of our rooms almost every night and would stand there over one of us for hours and just stare at us while we either slept or pretended to sleep. Night after night he would be in someone's room. Sometimes he would sit in one of the bedrooms on a chair and just watch for hours. It was an eerie feeling to know he was there. None of us felt comfortable enough to sit up and confront him.

"Mom, he really makes me nervous."

"I know," I replied, "but I'm not sure what to do about it yet."

He pushed his plate of eggs away and said, "I'm not hungry."

I looked at him for a moment and then said, "I know how disturbing this is, and I wish I knew what to say to make it better, but at this moment I don't."

At that moment Jay and Al entered the kitchen and were in the middle of a conversation. Jay looked at Paul and said, "What's up, bro?"

"Nothing," Paul replied.

I rose to get their breakfast on the table. They all began talking about the hockey game that Al had played last night and the next game that was coming up.

Thank God for sports, I thought to myself. It gives these kids something to concentrate on other than what was happening here at home. It made life for them a bit more normal.

After breakfast was finished they all grabbed their books and off they went to school. I cleaned up the kitchen, and then I went upstairs and finished getting ready for work. We owned a decorating store not far from home. We had five people working for us, and each one of them was excellent with the store, the customers, and the knowledge of decorating. I was really fortunate as they could all be trusted and were hard workers.

The store was in the centre of a plaza, and then the rest of the plaza was built around it in a U shape. It felt like we were the hub of the plaza as people going other places in the plaza always stopped in. The store itself was filled with designer sheets and bedroom accessories, as well as kitchen and bathroom supplies. We were supposed to have the largest selection of shower curtains in Toronto. We custom-made just about anything anyone wanted for their home.

We also dealt with a lot of movie and commercial productions. We would custom-make anything they needed for a set or backdrop. We did most of the Tide commercials at that time, renting the merchandise out to them. We also rented merchandise out to movie productions that needed to create a bedroom or washroom scene in their movies, sometimes working closely with the production crew in charge of designing. We made everything from the designer sheets that we carried, unless someone brought in fabric to have something made. Our days were always filled with working with many of Toronto's top designers, and we would work closely with them, making sure their customers were happy. We made anything from comforters or duvet covers and bed accessories to upholstered headboards and so much more. It was always busy and we were fortunate that way.

I loved the work, as it was creative and I particularly enjoyed helping to design rooms for people. Customers often came in with just an idea and didn't know how to make it become a reality. Being creative was something I came by naturally, as my mother and grandmother had both been artists and loved painting.

I got to the top of the stairs and I could hear the TV going in my husband's bedroom. I walked down the carpeted hallway towards his room and stopped at the door and asked, "Are you coming to work today?"

He had become obsessed with X-rated movies, and he managed to get the ones that were too raunchy for selling in stores. He had connections to the underground X-rated videos and he just wanted to watch them, seven days a week, twenty-four hours a day. He rarely left the house now. He seemed to get out of bed to only go to the washroom and go downstairs to get food.

Once we had purchased the store and I was working, looking after the store, he quit work and life took on a different context for him. He would leave once in a while, but most days he just laid there on the bed. The big decision of the day was which video he would watch first. He lived in his own little world. Sometimes he would come into the store during the day. He would walk up to me and hold his hand out and I would hand him some money, and he would walk out again. Where he went and what he did I didn't ask. I just always felt grateful that he didn't stay long and cause trouble.

There had been a few months in the beginning when we first had the store that he would spend part of the day there. He worked behind the cash register, ringing in the purchases or unpacking orders coming in and putting merchandise on the shelves, but it was not what he liked doing. He was not a people person and did not enjoy working with the customers.

There was no answer to my question about did he want to come to work, but I thought I knew the answer already anyway. I turned and started to walk away, and then I heard him yell out, "I don't want anything to do with that place."

It was my turn now not to answer, even though I had a few thoughts fly through my head.

Once at work I got to concentrate on other things. Deal with the customers, place orders for new stock, direct the staff on several things, and basically just keep busy so that I didn't have to think.

The day seemed to go fast as usual and after locking the doors at nine P.M., I went home to see what was happening there. I had been feeling like I was several different people for a long time now. To the staff, sales people, and customers, I was this young businesswoman in charge of a rather large store, and by all outsiders' eyes I looked like I was doing very well.

To the kids I was Mom, looking after three strong boys who all were very popular and often brought their friends over to the house. Jay excelled at soccer, he was now on a Canadian team that traveled and competed in tournaments everywhere. They were currently preparing to go to a tournament that would take them to Brazil. He was considered the best left footer in Canada. It was really neat because soccer was becoming more and more popular in Canada and there was a Toronto Radio station that just did sports. Sometimes on the weekend I could turn the station on and hear them talking about Jay and the many goals he had scored that week. I would feel such pride to hear about my son on the radio. The announcer said one Sunday morning, "He is considered the Best Left Footer in Canada."

"Wow, this is my son they are talking about," I said into thin air as I listened intently to the radio show.

"This is a young man who is going to go far," the announcer continued on.

The coaches and team members loved him, and he thrived in sports. The previous year he had been become a gold-carded athlete, and they only handed out three gold cards in soccer that year in Canada. He worked so hard at being the best. He would go jogging at four or five am and concentrate on conditioning himself. Not only did he thrive in sports, but he also excelled at school as well. He could read a book and basically remember everything he read.

Al was fantastic in hockey, and the local newspapers had given him the nickname Go Go. He was popular with his teammates, a good student, and excelled at anything he put his mind too.

Paul excelled in karate in a very short time. He was amazing at playing the piano and showed promise in writing music as well. Very artistic, he showed an amazing talent in just about any type of art that he tried, and his imagination was astounding.

It amazed me how their father did not seem to notice the talents that each of kids had. Each one of them was a strong individual, and it amazed me to watch them excel at their own interests.

I took Jay aside one day when he was in my store helping out and I said to him, "Jay I can only tell you one thing that I hope you will remember, and that is to choose something you love doing for a career, so you will enjoy going to work each day. Don't be like more than half of the world's population who hates their jobs and is miserable most of their lives."

Jay had played hockey as well as soccer for a few years, but it was too much on his schedule trying to keep his grades up and play two very competitive sports at the same time.

One night Jay and I were home together while Al and Jim were off at a hockey game. I could tell that something was bothering Jay. So while we were alone together in the kitchen I thought I would ask him.

"Jay, is there something wrong?"

He was quiet for a few minutes and then answered, "Mom, I have been thinking that I want to give up hockey, as I have so much schoolwork and I can't keep doing hockey and soccer. With the soccer team I'm on, we play soccer all year round, and I would rather concentrate on soccer and give up hockey."

"I can understand that," I said as I sat down across the table from him.

"Dad is going to be really mad."

"Well, I think it is more important that you do what you can handle, and if you know that playing two sports is too much, then yes, you should let hockey go. Your dad will have to understand."

"I know he is going to be upset. I hate listening to him when he gets mad," Jay said with tears in his eyes.

"We'll tell him together tonight when he gets home."

About an hour later we heard the garage door open and the van being parked. A few minutes later Al and Jim walked into the kitchen. They were both smiling, as Al's team had won the game, and I guess Al had played a good game in Jim's eyes.

Perfect timing, I thought to myself.

Jay cleared his throat and then said, "Dad, I have to tell you something."

Jim turned around from the kitchen cupboard, stuffing a piece of bread in his mouth as he looked at Jay and said, "What?"

"I want to quit hockey, as it is too much on my schedule for school and playing two sports."

"You can handle it. You just need to try harder," Jim said as he stuffed another piece of bread in his mouth with a slice of cheese this time.

I could see that Jay was weakening, and his eyes looked like he was nearing tears again.

"I think Jay is right. It is better for him to concentrate on one sport and excel at that sport rather than spread himself too thin with too many sports. He leaves this house early in the morning and some nights he is not home until after ten P.M. He is old enough to choose what he wants to play, and he has chosen soccer."

Jim started to leave the kitchen, and I could see he was angry. He stopped in the doorway and said, "I knew you had put him up to this. Then it's your fault if he never succeeds at anything."

That went better than I thought it would. I felt surprised that it was done and over with so fast. I looked over at Jay and smiled at him.

Jay got up from the table and left the kitchen.

Al was superb in hockey and loved and lived for the game. Even though he played soccer well, hockey was his true love. If he wasn't in school then he was either playing or practicing hockey. He was good in school as well but preferred sports to school. He had made the junior hockey team, and there were scouts coming out and looking at him all the time. He had received a lot of concussions, and the doctors where leery of him still playing on such a competitive level for fear that he would continue to receive concussions.

Al also enjoyed playing soccer and was a good soccer player as well. He was popular with his teammates but hockey was his sports preference.

Paul, on the other hand, was into karate and excelled at this. His trainer was impressed at his dedication at such a young age. Jim was so against Paul taking karate, and I finally figured out that the last thing an abuser wants a family member to learn is self-defense. Therefore, he was always putting Paul down and making it hard for Paul to continue.

Jim would make snide remarks and try hard to make Paul feel too inadequate to do anything.

"You're too fat and you can't do anything," Jim would say, trying to get Paul to quit. Paul would have tears in his eyes, and I would find him sitting in his room just trying to stay away from Jim and his hateful words.

"Listen Paul, your Dad has a problem, not you. I'm proud of you and who you are. You're doing great with your karate classes. There is no reason you should quit."

I hated these moments of trying to find the right words. It was hard to repair the holes that someone else had put into my son's heart.

I knew that Paul only heard some of what I said and the rest was drowned out by the remarks and words of Jim.

It was moments like this that I felt like such a failure. How, as a mother, could I stop the hurt?

When the kids were around I would try to be as cheerful as possible, making jokes and always welcoming their friends into our house. It was important to me to try and portray as normal a life as possible. Little did the kids know what my life was like when they were not around. Of course I could not hide everything. They witnessed enough I felt they had to deal with, they did not need to deal with more. They saw how their father was, when one moment everything was fine and then the next he just exploded for no apparent reason. It was moments like that I would wish he was a drinker. There was never any advance warning about the storm that was coming. We could just be sitting and eating dinner and all of a sudden he did not like something, maybe the way someone was chewing, or the look on someone's face, or the fact that someone was not eating fast enough, or slow enough, or whatever else he could find to start screaming and throwing insults at one of us. He seemed to really thrive on putting us down. One by one we all got it somehow. The more I would try to stop him from calling the kids' names or giving insults to them, the more he would do it.

He verbally beat them over their heads. "You're an idiot. You're stupid. I'm ashamed and embarrassed of you," were just some of the remarks he would yell at them. Each time I heard Jim say something derogative it felt like a piece of me inside would die. It hurt me maybe more than it did the kids, because I felt responsible to protect them as I felt that if I was doing my job this wouldn't be happening.

Nothing was ever good enough. Nothing ever made Jim happy. It didn't mean anything to him to see his children being the best on the team or in school. He just pushed harder to make them feel inadequate.

I had grown to hate Jim. I hated the sound of his voice. I hated the way he looked. I hated to be in the same room with him, and I hated to think what he was saying to the kids when I was not around, as I knew what kind of things he would say to them when I was in his presence.

It was as if he thrived on the misery of others. He was only happy when he could make everyone else miserable. I often witnessed that when everyone felt at their lowest because of something he had said or did, then he was suddenly happy and almost cheerful. It was almost like a sick kind of way that he had to make people notice him when their attention was on one of the kids. He would go out of his way to make a disturbance and become noticeable.

We've all heard the saying, kicking the dog while it's down. Well I would think that he lived by that. He often would see the kids upset about something. He would yell at them, wanting to know why they were upset, and then he would verbally be abusive to them instead of being sympathetic and trying to give encouragement or advice.

It was nothing for him to fly into a fit of rage and slap whoever he was angry at, at that moment, and then ten minutes later act as if we were all idiots as he couldn't understand why we would be upset by his verbal or physical abuse.

One day I came home from work and found Jim sitting in the living room with a driver's instruction booklet that I had borrowed from a neighbor when she had gone and written the exam and received her license.

"What the hell is this?" Jim tossed the book at me as I walked into the room.

I bent down and picked it up and then said, "I am going to get my license."

"You're too stupid to learn how to drive. I'm not taking you to write the test. We've discussed it before, and I told you no wife of mine is going to drive. You think you are going to leave me someday when you learn how to drive."

I had turned and walked into the kitchen as he talked. I could hear him from the living room saying, "I told you I'll kill you first before you leave me." I walked over to the radio and turned it on so that it drowned out his voice.

When Paul was thirteen years old, he commented that he hated hearing the garage door open and then hearing his father drive in, because he knew it meant his father was going to be coming through the door, and who knew what he was going to explode about.

I knew exactly how he felt because I felt the same way. I'd feel my heart sink, and I would start feeling uncomfortable and depressed. We would all become quiet, waiting to hear what he is going to be like. If he's in a good mood then how long is it going to last? The air in the house changes as soon as he walks in. Even the dog becomes quiet and lies still, waiting to see what would happen.

One New Year's Eve we were all asked to go to a party that Al's girlfriend Sue's parents were throwing at a local restaurant. So we all went. The kids were having a good time at a pool table that was set up in a room off the dining room, and most of the adults sat around long tables that were decorated for the occasion, talking, laughing, and enjoying the music that played in the background.

We sat at a table with Sue's parents and several other couples that we had just met that night. I thought everything was going smoothly as we all took parts in different conversations. Even Jim seemed to be enjoying himself, as he was being sociable with anyone who spoke to him.

At midnight everyone cheered, raised their glasses, and took a drink. Then just like it has been customary for many years, everyone at the table exchanged kisses and good will, wishing each other a "Happy New Year." After the festive moment, Jim said he wanted to leave, and we gathered up the kids, said our good-byes, and left.

The next day, I cooked a lunch and the kids stated that they were looking forward to going to their friends' houses to spend the rest of New Year's Day.

Jim and I were left home alone. I was upstairs dusting the kid's rooms and straightening up when suddenly Jim came into the room and shoved me up against a wall. He held me there with his arm across my throat and screamed, "Who is he?"

"Who is who?" I asked, shocked.

"Who was the guy that kissed you last night at the table?"

"What are you talking about? There were three or four men at the table. Everyone exchanged kisses, including you, so how do I know who you mean?"

He pushed harder on my throat. "You're having an affair or want to have an affair with that guy," he screamed.

"News to me," I said, but at the same time I felt my airways closing, and I started to cough.

He put his arm down but grabbed me by my hair and held me still against the wall. "I'll make you tell me everything." He let go of me and went downstairs. I heard him in the kitchen. I didn't know for sure what he was doing, but frightened, I ran to grab a cordless phone and went and locked myself in the washroom.

I called Jay at his friends and asked for him to come home, and then I sat in the washroom and listened to Jim still in the kitchen. In another moment I heard him coming back upstairs again. He rapped on the washroom door with something that sounded metal.

"Open it up," he screamed. I didn't answer, and I didn't move. He kicked the door and said, "I have a knife here, do you want me to open the door for you?" With that I could hear him trying the door handle, and then he tried pushing against the door.

I dialed 911.

I heard someone on the other end of the line.

"Please help me," I whispered into the phone.

"Do you need fire, police, or ambulance?"

"Police," I answered, fighting back tears.

Jim continued to bang on the door and scream for me to let him in.

The woman on the line could hear the commotion and asked, "What is happening? Are you in danger?"

"Yes," I responded.

Jim now was kicking the door and swearing, "You bitch, I'll teach you a lesson when I get ahold of you."

"Please get someone here. I fear he is going to kill me," I begged into the phone.

"Alright, stay on the line with me while the police are on their way. They say it will be four minutes before they get there."

Jim continued to bang on the washroom door and yell for me to open the door.

"You bitch, you are going to be so sorry for this."

The woman on the line could hear what was happening. "Please try to remain calm. The police are on their way. Does he have a gun?" she asked.

"No, but he said he has a knife. He is going to break this door down if the police don't hurry," I said.

I could hear the woman's breathing change on the phone. "Hang on, stay on the line with me," she stated.

In another moment the dispatcher announced "The police are now in your driveway. Can you get to the door and let them in?"

"You must be joking," I said. "I am not opening this door and walking past him. I weigh about one hundred pounds. Jim weighs about one hundred eighty pounds. I am assuming that the police are stronger and bigger than I am. They are supposed to be coming to protect me from him. It's not my place to protect them from him," I said into the phone.

"Alright, stay where you are, they are going to ring the doorbell and see if he answers." I heard the bell ring about a moment later and then Jim going downstairs to get the door.

The police came in, and I left the bathroom. I told them what was happening and that I was shocked, as I had no idea that Jim was even upset. One officer spoke to Jim in the kitchen while another officer kept me in the living room. Jay arrived home about ten minutes after the police arrived. About twenty minutes after the police had arrived they felt that things were under control, and they warned Jim that if they had to come back he would be arrested. With that they left.

Jay stayed home for the rest of the night. I went to my bedroom and just sat on my bed fully dressed for the rest of the night. I could not understand what had happened. I had no idea that Jim had been upset in any way. Life was so unpredictable with him. You just never knew what was going to happen or where.

THE WEB

I heard Al and Paul come home around ten P.M. They all went straight to their rooms. I didn't move until about five A.M. when I finally got up and went to the washroom and then got washed and changed for work.

Not much changed for the next few months. The kids went to school and sports and spent time with their friends. I went to work every day and tried to make sure that things ran smoothly. I was grateful for the hours I got to spend there, as I could at least for a little while each day put behind me how miserable my private life was.

Sometimes after the kids would leave for school and I would be alone in the house with Jim, he would come downstairs and try to intimidate me.

"Do you know how easy it would be for me to kill you?" he would ask. "In some countries men don't even need an excuse to kill their wives. They just have to say she was no good, and that is enough for the country to accept her murder."

Other times he would stand over me if I was sitting at the table and run his hand down my back or over my hair and say, "It's a shame really that someone like you has to be killed." He would often laugh and walk away. I would try not to show fear. I wouldn't allow my voice to waver if I spoke, and it would make him angry to see that I was not intimidated.

I think he realized that now that the kids were older, and he couldn't take them away from me any more than it was harder to keep me under his thumb. His control tactics didn't work, and he was losing control and he didn't know how to handle it.

It was early May and the weather was just starting to get warmer. I woke up to hear my husband Jim screaming at someone. I jumped up and looked around. The room was dark with the drapes closed, and the only thing I could see clearly was the time on the digital clock showing that it was 5:30 am. What on earth could be going on? I thought as I ran from the bedroom and in the direction of the screaming. I found Jim standing over Paul as he lay on his bed. He raised his hand to strike Paul, and I pushed him away.

"What are you doing?" I asked as I pushed him away from the bed.

He stood there glaring angrily at Paul and then he finally spoke in a loud gruff voice. "He used my toothpaste."

I was shocked, and I stood there for a few seconds staring at him, trying to make sense of what he had just said. "What are you saying?" I finally asked.

"You heard me, he used my toothpaste."

I tried to push Jim towards the bedroom door, but he just stood over Paul and ranted, "You little bastard, you had no right to use my toothpaste."

At this point Paul jumped up from his bed and ran from the room. Jim started to go towards the door as if he was going to go after him, and I used all my strength and pushed him back.

"You are mad," I yelled, and with that I turned and left the room. I heard the front door slam shut, and I cried out, "Paul wait," but it was too late; he was gone already.

I ran to my bedroom and threw on some dress pants I had worn the day before and a sweater and slipped shoes on and ran down the stairs and out the front door. The day was just starting to get light. I had no idea where Paul had gone, and all I could do was walk around and call his name.

There was a park close by, and I went into the park calling out his name. About an hour had gone by, and I was getting cold. The sun was rising, and it glistened and sparkled on the dew on the ground. I felt a chill go down my spine, and I was not sure if it was the dampness of the early morning or just the fact of why I was out walking through the park for the third or fourth time. I wondered if Paul was cold, as I knew he did not have anything but his pajamas on. I started to walk by a jungle gym set in the park and I looked up, and there he was lying down on the top of it as if trying to hide from the world.

My heart broke for him. What do you say to try and make it better? I didn't understand what was happening, so how could I make him understand. All I knew was that it was not his fault, and it was important to me to try and make Paul understand that.

"Paul, I know you are up there. Please come down so we can talk."

There was no sound for a few minutes, and then I heard Paul start to slowly move. He came down and we sat for a few minutes not speaking.

"Paul, your dad is mentally ill, and it's not your fault that he is the way he is," I tried to explain. "It doesn't make it any easier for you or anyone else. I know it's not fair, but right now we have to stick together, and we will get through this. I hope you'll come home with me. I'll make us some breakfast, and I'd really like it if you will come to the store with me today."

I looked over at Paul and saw the stress written all over his face.

"I don't think that your dad is home, as he was going to be taking Al to a hockey tournament, and I'm sure they have left already."

We both stood up at the same time, and we walked home in silence.

This was when I had a hard time being a mom. I always thought that moms were supposed to have all of the answers, but I had none. I had to wing my way through everything. Most of all I had to try and hide how scared I was most of the time. I was always questioning if I was doing and saying the right things. I wanted to protect my kids, and I felt that I had really failed them in this area.

I wanted to support my kids in everything they did, be it school, sports, or whatever they chose to do, but I had gotten to the point where I had a hard time going to a soccer or a hockey game because I knew there was more than a seventy-five percent chance there was going to be a scene of some sort, and at those moments, I had a hard time to fight back the tears in front of people.

There were times when we would be at a soccer game or hockey game and Jim felt they had not played the way they should have. He would take it as a personal insult if they did not score a goal. Or if he perceived them as not playing up to his expected standards, then they had to listen to him on and off the soccer fields, hockey arenas, or anywhere else that their father would decide to explode. Jim had gotten to the point that he did not care if people witnessed him screaming and swearing at the kids. It was as if he felt no one could touch him. He was right, and everyone else was wrong.

Parents and the other children would be horrified at the way the kids were being treated, but they did not know what to do any more than I did. I spoke to one of his sisters and asked her what she thought. I told her of several of the incidents and said there had to be something mentally wrong with him. I explained that he had become obsessed with X-rated videos and that his life revolved around them. I told her he had no interest in anything except sports and X-rated videos. I also explained that he was verbally abusive to me and the kids. Her explanation was just so simple

"Oh, that's just Jim," she replied, ending any discussion we might have.

Oh well gee, why didn't I think of that, I thought sarcastically as I hung up.

Really, there was nowhere to turn, and there was nothing that I could think of to do to protect the kids and myself.

Jim was lying in bed watching his videos. Jay was out at a soccer practice, and Al was at a friend's house.

I walked up to Paul's bedroom door and tapped on the door.

"Come in," I heard Paul call out.

I opened the door and walked in to find Paul reading a book.

"Hi," I said. "I was wondering if you would like to come with me to the store and help me out, as I gave the staff the day off."

"Sure," Paul answered as he got up off his bed.

"Great," I said as I turned and walked out of his room.

Later as we arrived at the store, I turned the alarm system off as Paul went to the back to turn on all of the lights.

Since it was Sunday I knew it was not going to be too busy, so I told Paul that he could go and get us something to eat at a nearby restaurant.

The store was a little over four thousand square feet, and it was too big for just one person to run it alone. So when Paul came back with his food, we stayed at the front of the store so we could watch what was going on.

About an hour after opening, Paul and I were at the front of the store, waiting on customers, when Jim arrived. He looked at us and continued on his way to the back of the store where my office was. Paul and I looked at each other and continued to work with the customers.

Jim stayed at the back of the store for about ten minutes and then came to the front of the store and put several files from my filing cabinet on the counter and said, "That's for you," and then turned and walked back to the office again.

There were still a couple of customers in the store, and Paul was with one of them while I was with another one. Paul had become a great little salesperson, and the customers always enjoyed being waited on by him. He would tell them what they could use to decorate and how it would look and even explain how it could be custom-made for them if they needed or wished. He had that special touch that the customers really liked.

A few minutes later Jim came back to the front of the store again and left a few more files on the counter. As he turned to walk away, he again stated, "That's for you."

Paul came over to me and whispered, "What is he doing, Mom?"

I shrugged and said, "I don't know."

Jim had a strange look in his eyes, and something told me not to even attempt speaking to him.

On Sundays we closed early, and by the time we were locking the door at five P.M. I had all my files on the counter at the front of the store. Paul and I got into the car with Jim and no one spoke on the drive home. When we arrived home Al and Jay were both home. They seemed to sense that something was wrong, and they stuck around at home, which was unusual for them as they normally were out with friends playing sports.

I walked upstairs to my bedroom and closed the door. I changed out of my suit and put on a pair of jeans and a blouse and combed back my long hair and just sat down on the bed when the kids came into the room.

They all had a questioning look on their faces, but I did not know what to tell them, so I said, "Who wants to play cards?" trying really hard to make it sound like there was nothing wrong.

They all agreed and we all sat down cross-legged on the floor and began to play cards. We talked in general and joked around, and I started to feel the tension start to slip away from all of us.

All of a sudden the bedroom door opened and Jim was standing there staring at each one of us and said, "What are you laughing at?"

"We're playing cards," I responded. He turned and left, closing the door behind him. We continued to play cards, but I could feel the tension come back again, but maybe even worse this time. I tried to sound cheery as we continued on with the game, but I started to get a sick feeling in the pit of my stomach.

We played cards for a little while longer, but it seemed like none of us could enjoy ourselves now. We all agreed that we had played enough and each of them retired to their rooms and they seemed quiet.

I went downstairs and made dinner. When I had finished preparing the meal, I called Jim and the kids.

The kids came downstairs and sat at the table.

Jim did not move from the sofa in the living room.

The kids and I ate in silence, each one of us in our own thoughts.

After dinner the kids and I all went back upstairs, each one of us in our own rooms. I could hear Jim every once in a while walk around downstairs, and sometimes he came up and looked into the rooms and then would go back downstairs again. He was acting as if he was uneasy about something and not sure what he should do next. This in itself was making me extra nervous. I kept trying to figure out what was on his mind and why was he acting so strange.

Around nine P.M. he came into the bedroom and said, "You wait, you'll see."

I looked up from a book I was reading and asked, "See what?"

He just stood there with a strange look in his eyes, and then he turned and just stood in the hallway between all of the bedrooms. He acted like he was listening to something, but no one was talking. He stood there for about ten minutes and then slowly walked downstairs again.

The kids went to bed early and the house was unusually quiet. I sat upstairs reading a book but having a hard time concentrating. I could hear Jim every once in a while get up off the sofa and go into the kitchen. He seemed so unusually restless. I had never seen him like this before, and it was unnerving.

Finally around eleven P.M., I closed my book and got up and went to the washroom where I ran a bath. I sunk into the tub and felt some of the tension slip away.

I heard someone outside the washroom door, and I sat up in the tub and listened. I thought I could hear Jim breathing, but I also thought it might be my imagination. I got up out of the tub and quickly dried off with a towel and then put my nightgown on. I rinsed out the tub and stood in the washroom and listened again before opening the door. I was just about to open the door when all of a sudden I heard footsteps descending on the stairs. I waited another minute, trying to hear anything else. Then I slowly opened the door. I walked to the kids' rooms and peeked in on each one of the kids, and they were all lying down and it looked like they were asleep. Therefore I now knew it had been Jim that was standing out in the hallway almost the entire time I was bathing.

The next morning I woke up at my usual time of 6:30. No alarm clock, just years of training that I needed to get up every day at that time to make sure I was ready for work and get the kids ready for school.

Even though, it was June 13, there was a bit of a chill in the air, and when I threw back the bed covers I felt the cold air touch my skin. I sat on the side of the bed for a few minutes looking at the sun trying to shine through the drapes. I got up, stretched, and walked over to the window and drew back the curtains. I turned and walked to the bathroom. I washed and combed my hair. I walked out of the bathroom and saw on the clock that it was now almost seven am. I wrapped my robe around me and walked down the carpeted hallway and stairs.

In the downstairs hallway the walls were mirrored, and I looked at my reflection and thought I still look tired even though I slept. I entered the kitchen. The sun was streaming through the windows and the white cupboards and counter gave off a glow that hurt my still-tired eyes.

I walked over to the coffee maker and grabbed the pot. I walked towards the sink, and then I noticed there were pill bottles all over the counter. Some sitting straight up, while others where turned on their sides. I picked up each one with a frown on my face, and I noticed they were all empty. I stood there for a moment, and then I got this weird feeling in the pit of my stomach, and I walked out of the kitchen door and into the living room.

There, lying on the sofa, was Jim. I walked to the sofa and stood over him and watched him for a few minutes. He just looked like he was sleeping. I spoke to him but there was no reaction. So I shook him and again no reaction. I stood there for another couple of minutes and just stared at him. I had a thousand thoughts going through my head at this point, none of them making any sense. Again I spoke to him and shook even harder, but still nothing. Nothing was really registering with me. I thought he was just ignoring me. I turned and walked up the stairs.

For a couple of minutes I stood in my bedroom. The vision of the empty bottles on the kitchen counter kept coming back to me. I began to wonder if that was what he was doing last night when he was acting so weird.

I ran back downstairs again and into the living room. I stood over him, examining his color, which looked normal. Again I shook him and called his name. No response.

"Oh shit," I whispered.

I stood there for a moment and thought, this could be my escape. I could just wake the kids up and go to work and pretend that I didn't notice anything wrong. As quickly as that thought came, I also thought: I can't be like him. He would let me die. I can't do that, because I have to live with that knowledge. I have to look at myself in the mirror every day.

I tried again to wake him up again, but still nothing.

I ran to the phone and called an ambulance. Then I ran upstairs and woke the kids up.

"Get dressed, hurry," I said urgently. "Your dad has tried to commit suicide and the ambulance is on the way."

I could hear the disbelief in the kids as they tried to grasp what I had just said.

I quickly threw on some clothes, and I went back down the stairs. As I quickly walked into the living room again I felt so very angry. I could hear the kids upstairs and thought to myself, why would you do this to them?

I opened the front door and stood looking out the screen door. I heard Al hit the wall upstairs in anger. Then there was complete silence, except off in the distance I could hear the siren of the ambulance getting closer.

The sun shone through the glass door and warmed the hallway, reflecting off the mirrored walls and casting shadows that danced across the ceramic floor. People were walking past the house on their way to work or school. Birds were singing in the trees, and there was a slight breeze blowing. Everything seemed so normal except where I was standing.

Just as the ambulance pulled up to the front of the house, so did a couple of police cars. They all entered at the same time. One police officer took me into the kitchen while the rest all congregated in the living room. The officer who was in the kitchen with me had just asked, "Have you noticed anything unusual lately?"

I thought to myself, how do you answer that one? It would be easier to answer the question, is there anything normal lately? It was always unusual or unexplainable around here with Jim.

Before I could answer, an officer from the living room walked into the kitchen and said, "We have managed to bring your husband around enough that he is talking a bit. He seems very concerned about a piece of wood, and he is asking for it. Do you know what he is talking about?"

"I have no idea what he is talking about," I said, surprised.

The officer went back into the living room only to come back in another few minutes and said, "Your husband is refusing to go to the hospital until we find his piece of wood. He said that there are nails in the piece of wood. I think we should humor him and all of us look around to see if we can find it."

I was stunned but moved towards the living room. We all started a search for the piece of wood, and finally an officer did find it behind a wall unit we had in the dining room.

"What is it for?" I asked a police officer as he handed it to Jim.

"We are hoping he'll tell us. It seems to be very important to him. Is this what you where wanting?"

"Yes," Jim replied.

"What do you need that for?" asked the officer, and Jim just smiled and said, "I was going to use it on her."

The officer who was holding the piece of wood looked over at me and said, "We'll take this with us."

I stood there watching them roll the stretcher down the hallway, and then one of the ambulance attendants turned to me and asked, "Do you want to come with us in the ambulance?"

"No, I have to get ahold of my staff and tell them to open up the store. The children and I will meet you at the hospital."

I quickly contacted the staff and asked them to open up the store and that I would contact them later.

About half an hour later we arrived at the hospital only to be told we needed to wait around as the doctors where working on him. They were pumping out his stomach, and they would let us see him when they were finished.

We all went and stood outside the hospital, and after a few minutes I thought I should call his sister and let her know what was happening. She could call and tell his parents, as they did not speak good enough English to understand if I tried to tell them, and I did not speak Italian.

I walked back into the hospital and found a phone booth. I found change in my purse and I proceeded to call Jim's sister Eve. She answered on the third ring. When I told her what had happened, there was silence on the other end of the line, and then she said, "I'll call my parents and then I'll come over to the hospital." I told her to wait as no one could see him right then, but I would call her as soon as there was any change.

I walked back outside to find the kids standing around talking. About an hour later we were finally allowed to see him. We entered the room to find him all hooked up to machines, and we were told he was in a deep sleep at that point. I asked how he was doing and was told that it would be a few hours before they knew for sure, but at this point they thought he would be alright. They had pumped out his stomach and now it was time to wait and see what happened next.

The kids and I left the hospital and went back home. I called the store and spoke to my staff to find out how things were going. I just told them that Jim was in the hospital but did not tell them why.

The kids were acting angry and frustrated. I didn't blame them, as I felt the same way, but yet I did not know what to say to them to make it any better.

Al kicked things around his room, and Jay seemed to be extra quiet. Paul just looked shocked.

I was so angry at this point. Why does he keep hurting us? Doesn't he care what he puts the kids through?

Each one of us went to our own rooms and spent time in our own thoughts at this point. A couple of hours later the phone rang, and it was the hospital saying that he seemed to be coming around and that it would be good for us to come in and see him. I felt like yelling into the phone: what about what is good for us? I sighed and said we would be there soon. I called his sister back and told her that if his parents wanted to see him they could.

We went back to the hospital and into his room where he still remained hooked up to the machines.

"Jim," I said as I stood beside the bed.

He looked at us for a few moments and then he said, "I saw Heaven, and it is beautiful, with gorgeous flowers, and I want you all to come with me and see it."

Oh great, I thought, I needed to hear that.

A few minutes later his sister and parents arrived, and they all began talking in Italian and that gave me time for my mind to try and comprehend what was happening. The kids went off to get drinks and I stood there in the room wishing I was anywhere but there. Wishing I was anyone but me.

A week passed, and we went to the hospital every day to see him. He was always talking about heaven and what he had seen. He often spoke about how he was going to take us all to see it. I dreaded going there and hated listening to him. This is absurd, I would think to myself. He has now created this imaginary place that he is convinced was going to save us all and take us there to live happily ever after.

When we weren't at the hospital Jim was on the phone telling me how much he liked heaven and couldn't wait to get back there.

"All our problems will be solved, and everything is going to be beautiful, you wait and see. You will love it there. The kids will love it too."

"You're crazy," I said to him. "Do you realize what you are saying? You are going to kill us all?"

"Yes that's right. I'm doing us all a favor," he replied.

I would receive calls like that from him six or seven times a day. At the hospital when we went to see him each day he talked about the same thing.

I was at work when the phone rang and it was one of the doctors on the phone saying that I could bring his clothes to the hospital as he was being released.

The kids and I walked into the hospital and I went to his room.

"Where are my clothes?"

"At home," I responded.

"You bitch, you go get them now as I am coming home."

"Not if I have anything to do about it," I responded as I walked out of his room and down the corridor to the nurse's station. I walked over to the desk and asked, "Is Doctor Francis around, I need to speak to him about my husband?"

The nurse looked up from reading a chart and said, "No I'm sorry, but he has left for the day. You can take your husband home now and then can call the doctor tomorrow with any questions you may have."

I shook my head and said, "No, I'm refusing to take him home. He has been telling the kids and I that he has seen Heaven and that he intends to take the kids and me to see Heaven with him, therefore if I am made to take him out of here and something should happen to the kids or me, then I will sue you and this hospital."

The nurse looked shocked and said, "Well, he has been released."

I continued, "I am not bringing his clothes to the hospital so he can come home. I think the doctor needs to realize that my husband keeps calling my house and threatening all of us. You have a choice: to keep him or send him somewhere else, but it won't be at my house."

I stood there looking at her. She sat for a few minutes trying to decide what to do and then said, "Alright, I will get in touch with the doctor. Please wait in the waiting room while I try to get him on the phone."

The kids and I went into the waiting area, and a few minutes later a nurse came over and told us that they were going to keep Jim for three weeks, but they could not legally hold him after that time. While the nurse was telling us this, there were several male nurses and attendants going into Jim's room telling him he would not be going home. He didn't like what he was hearing. He especially didn't like the point that they were going to hold him against his will. I could hear him becoming agitated and yelling.

They walked him down the hallway holding onto him, to a room they were going to lock him in until he calmed down. As they tried to get him into the room he screamed, "You bitch, you'll be sorry. I'll get you back for this."

It was hard to stand there and face the person that had always threatened. I knew he meant every word he had just said. With a sick feeling in the pit of my stomach, I spoke to the kids, "Come on guys, it's time to go home."

The next day after the doctor went to see him, he managed to convince the doctor that he was fine and they should let him out of the locked room and back into a private room, which meant that he had access to a phone again.

The first thing he did was telephone me and said, "You are going to be so very sorry for what you've done to me. You think I don't know you are making them keep me here so that you can spend time with all your boyfriends."

I hung up on him. For the next couple of hours he called every few minutes and tried to threaten and intimidate me into bringing him home. The last call he made he told me to bring him some money because he needed it for the phone.

Needless to say, I never took him any money, and each time he would ask I would say that I would bring some the next day.

His calls became less frequent but he still managed to get money off other people going to visit him, and then the calls would resume again.

The next couple of weeks went by really fast. It was all happening at the same time that OJ Simpson had just been charged for murdering his wife. It seemed like every time you turned on the TV or radio they were talking about it. Everywhere you went someone was discussing OJ Simpson. It just seemed to drive deeper into me just how uncertain I was becoming on the safety of the kids and myself.

It proved to me that it didn't matter who you were or what you had, if your husband wanted to kill you, there was not much help out there.

On the twentieth day of Jim being in the hospital, I received a call from one of the doctors asking for me to meet with him so that we could discuss Jim and the situation. We arranged an appointment for that afternoon at two P.M. I hung up and looked at the time and saw that I had about an hour to go before leaving for the appointment. I talked to the staff on duty and told them I would be back in a couple of hours.

I arrived at the scheduled time and sat in a luxurious waiting room that was furnished with thick leather sofas and chairs, complemented with cherry wood coffee tables and end tables. A few original paintings hung on the walls, displaying lovely country scenes. I thought to myself that they were trying hard to create a nice calming effect while soft music played off in the distance somewhere. A few minutes of sitting there and the doctor, a tall man with grey hair and a mustache, dressed casually in jeans and a striped dress shirt, opened a door and beckoned me to come inside.

"Hello Jenny, please take a seat and relax." He went around the desk as I sat down in a high-backed leather chair. Positioning himself into a very luxurious office chair, he started flipping through some files on his desk. While he looked for Jim's folder, I glanced around the room and noticed that it was almost a carbon copy of the room outside, as there was another leather sofa and chair in here as well. The doctor found the file and opened it up.

"Well Jenny, we are getting close to the time when I am going to have to release Jim. There is a law that states I can only hold him for twenty-eight days and then he has the right to leave. I have spoken to Jim almost every day, and truthfully I can see where he is playing games with us and tries to turn things around to suit himself. He does not want to tell the truth about anything. In fact, I know that he does not see that he has a problem and that he thinks everyone else has a problem."

The doctor looked up from the chart and said, "Do you have any place that you and the kids can go?"

I looked at him and said, "No, there is no place we can go to get away from him. He would hunt us down anyway."

The doctor got up from his chair, came around the front of the desk, and sitting on the edge of the desk, he said, "Well I wish there was more that I could do, but I legally can't. My hands are tied. The only real advice I can give you is when you go home today get rid of all the sharp objects in the house."

"What do you mean, sharp object?"

"Yes, things like scissors, knives, anything that he can use to harm himself or someone else."

I looked up at the doctor and said, "In other words you are sending me home with someone not to be trusted."

The doctor shook his head yes and said, "That's a fair way of putting it."

He got up off the edge of the desk and went to stand at a window and looked outside as he continued. "Were you aware of the fact that your husband Jim tried to kill himself on two other occasions?"

Shocked, I said, "No, when?"

"Well, he says that he tried to hang himself in your basement from the ceiling rafters but something went wrong and it didn't work. Then I guess he was about to stab himself but one of the kids came into the house with a friend and he dropped the idea at that moment. Then he finally he took all of the pills you had in the house. Even that was calculating, as he went to the dentist and complained of pain and was given Tylenol with codeine, and he used those mixed with everything else."

I sighed and said, "I didn't know anything about it. I thought the pills had been the first time."

The doctor turned back to his desk and sat down again. He picked up Jim's file again and said, "I have tried to talk him into coming in for counseling, but he has refused that as well." He looked up at me and said, "You are going to have your hands full. At this moment he is full of a lot of anger and hatred towards you. He blames you for all of his problems."

I smiled and said, "Doctor, he's been blaming me for a lot of things for years."

"Well, be careful," the doctor said as he rose from his desk. "I think you should take him seriously."

I stood up and shook hands with him and then turned and walked out.

I went home and looked around the house. How do you safe-proof a house when someone wants to kill you and everyone in it? I went upstairs and looked around up there. Then I went into the basement, remembering what the doctor had said about Jim trying to hang himself down there.

I felt sick to my stomach. No one really knew how devastated I felt about all of this. How do I protect my kids from this lunatic? How do you continue to go on with your life of work when you don't know what is happening in your home and if everyone is alright?

The phone rang, and I went up the stairs thinking, I bet it's him. I picked up the phone and said: "Hello." Sure enough, I won first prize.

"What are you doing?" he asked.

"Just cleaning up," I answered,

"Well, you won't have to worry about that very soon. You will just have to enjoy heaven with the rest of us."

"I'm busy," I said, and I hung up. Within a minute the phone rang again and then again and then again. I went outside and sat on the front steps. The dog ran around my feet, and I just sat there smoking a cigarette and wishing I could run away.

Since Jim had been in the hospital, I realized I had begun smoking almost two packs of cigarettes a day. Not healthy, I thought to myself, but then again neither is a heart attack from stress. I had begun calling my cigarettes my stress releasers a long time ago. They still were that to me. It's not healthy getting murdered by your husband, I thought as I lit another cigarette.

That night we went to the hospital to see Jim, and he sent the kids to get a drink from the snack bar, and while they were gone he grabbed my arm and said, "Don't think you're going to escape me. You will never get away. I'm going to do you the favor of taking you with us to heaven, so just get used to the idea."

I looked him straight in the eye and said, "You can get used to the idea that I have no intention of going anywhere with you."

He laughed at that point and let go of my arm.

The next few days I could feel myself becoming more and more nervous. I hated the thoughts of him coming home. I wished I could find a way to prevent it from happening, but there was nothing I could do.

The day came too quickly, and before I knew it he was once again sitting in the living room and observing everything around him as if he was taking inventory.

The kids went out, and I went into the living room and said, "The day you were taken to the hospital you came around enough to want a piece of wood. It had a few nails in it. What was that for?" I asked.

"None of your business," he replied.

CHAPTER FIVE

Things did not seem to get any better. He was now playing games, and he had a captive audience: his parents, his sisters, the kids, and the police.

Almost every day after the kids would leave for school he would come downstairs and sometimes become really explicit on how he could kill me and end all of his miseries. "I can do anything I want to you, and I will never get locked up. Everyone now believes I'm crazy. I can smother you while you're sleeping, stab you, cut you into tiny pieces, and choke you or anything else I choose to do." He would follow me throughout the house. This eerie feeling of hatred and anger was always right there with me everywhere I turned.

I would try really hard to show no emotions. I would continue on with whatever I was doing and pretend I didn't hear him. When he couldn't get any reactions out of me, then he would become quiet but still continue to follow me around. Little did he know that inside I was terrified of being in the house without the kids being around.

,Day after day after day this continued. I got away from him only by going to the store but I got to the point that I couldn't concentrate on work anymore. His words were always going through my head.

Then, after he was home about two weeks, he began to come into my room every night and would keep me awake all night long. If I started to fall asleep, he would wake me up or shake me or slap me to wake me up. This went on for several weeks. Night after night, he would not let me sleep. "I'll kill you when you fall asleep," he would whisper in my ear. "I can't stand the fact I have no control over your dreams. You are probably dreaming about some man. Do you think I don't know you? You're a slut, and you can't wait to have sex with other men."

I think that somewhere during this time I started to learn how to rest without sleeping. I would start singing a song in my mind, and I would sing it over and over again. Doing this would relieve some of the tension, and I was able to make my mind rest even if my body couldn't. Counting numbers was another form of concentration, or I would make up games in my mind with numbers.

Jim would sit quietly on the side of the bed until he thought that I was falling asleep and then he would start up again. "Wake up bitch, if I can't sleep you can't either."

Then one morning after the kids went to school and I was getting ready for work, the doorbell rang and I went to answer the door. I was surprised to see that there were two police officers standing there. One of them spoke, "Are you Jenny?"

"Yes," I answered

"Well, your husband has called and reported that he is thinking of killing you. May we come in?"

I stood back from the doorway and beckoned for them to both come into the house. They stepped inside, and as I began to close the door Jim came to the top of the stairs and said, "Good, I'm glad you came. I was really fighting the impulse to kill her."

"Have you been arguing?' one of the officers asked.

"No," I answered as I watched my husband walk down the stairs. "I have been getting ready for work and didn't know he called you."

"Let's go into the kitchen," Jim said as he led the way down the hall and into the kitchen. The officers sat at the table and listened to Jim tell them I had him locked up in the hospital for weeks while he was sure I was out screwing around and probably not even home at nighttime for the kids. He believed I had convinced the kids not to tell him about me having different men in the house while he was gone.

The officers listened to him rant and rave for more than an hour, and then they tried to convince him to go back to the hospital with them.

He smiled and said, "You know what? I feel so much better now that I have all of this off my chest. I don't need to go talk to the doctor. I'll be just fine now. Thanks for coming and listening to me." With that he stood up and dismissed the officers.

"Well we can't force you Jim, but I think you'd be better off if you let the doctor talk to you," one of the officers said.

"Thanks for your concern, but I'll be just fine now."

I followed the officers down the hall and to the front door. They turned and said good-bye and then left. I closed the door behind them, and when I turned around there was Jim standing just a couple of feet behind me. Smiling, he said, "See how easy that was? Now the cops think I'm crazy too. It's on record at the hospital that I'm crazy. If I kill you I won't spend any time in jail at all." With that he laughed and went back upstairs.

I just stood there for a few minutes letting it sink in what had just happened and how calculating he had become.

I left for work and tried to get it out of my head, but I couldn't shake what he had just done and maybe what he was planning on doing.

Every day I would come home after work, and the kids would tell me that they found Daddy crying when they got home from school.

"He is just sitting in a chair and crying." I now knew that everything was an act. He had the kids feeling sorry for him. He had his family feeling sorry for him, and I was becoming the cold bitch in everyone's eyes as I was having a hard time showing sympathy. No one was seeing the vicious side of him that he was showing me when no one else was around.

After about two months of this truthfully I was beginning to feel like I was losing it. My nerves were shot. I began to sleep on the dining room floor because I could see in the hallway mirrors and see what was happening upstairs, and if he was going into the kids' rooms I would go upstairs to see why. Needless to say, lack of sleep and nervous tension was beginning to take its toll on me. I decided I could not live like this anymore. Not sure what to do, or what the outcome would be, I decided I was going to let the store go.

I felt that the store was just another tie I had to Jim. He had always felt that money was more important than anything else in the world. In the back of my mind I had decided that I was ending the marriage, but I was going to take it one step at a time. I had no plans of where I would eventually go or how I would do it, but at this point I was only ready for baby steps, and therefore concentrating on getting rid of the store was the first step.

When I got to the store I waited until the store was empty of customers, and then I called all the staff up to the front of the store. They all looked at me with questioning expressions on their faces. I smiled at them and said, "For right now, please don't take any orders from customers for stock that we don't have. I have decided that for now we are going to just work with the inventory that we have. I am going to set up with Chin Radio to have them come out and broadcast from here for a couple of days."

I had Chin Radio come out on a few occasions and broadcast from the store for a couple of sales we held, and it always brought in the crowds.

I went back into my office and within a few minutes I had a date set up for Chin Radio to come back and broadcast from the store, which would be in two weeks from that day. I went back to the front and wrote it on the calendar for the staff to see.

For the next two weeks I prepared the store for the sale and the day finally arrived.

The radio station was there and sales were being broadcasted. The store was packed full of people. The staff were run off their feet for the two days that Chin Radio was there.

The store was over four thousand square feet, and so when I stopped ordering stock, and with the sale that had just taken place, the shelves were looking pretty bare. With the money that I made on the sale, I made out checks to pay off as many of my suppliers that I could. I did not want to close the store still owing my suppliers.

The rents in this area where very high, and I was paying twelve thousand dollars per month in just rent because of the store being just over four thousand square feet, so I decided to move the store to a smaller location in the same plaza to sell off the rest of the inventory.

Within two months most of the stock was sold, and I was ready to claim bankruptcy. The bank manager called me into the bank and told me to sign over all my RRSP which was valued at over sixty thousand dollars, because they could not touch my husband's as he was considered mentally incompetent. So I did. This was to cover a personal loan we had taken on the store when we first bought the store to purchase supplies.

I went home that day and told Jim what I had done, and he said, "Good, they won't touch mine then."

The store closed down a few weeks later. I told my staff not to come on that day, but they came anyway saying that we were like family and that they would see it to the end.

Even though it was my decision to close down the store, it was an emotional time for me. It had been the one positive thing I had in my life. It was my escape from the insanity, but I had to let it go as I had to somehow find a way to get free from all of the abuse.

One step at a time, I thought, but I had no idea where my steps would take me. My sister Isabel came that day with her husband Dan and watched as papers got signed and the keys to the store got handed in. It was an emotional time, and I was glad she was there.

Some of my suppliers came in that day as they had heard what was happening and they came to say good-bye and wish me luck. The man who had looked after my security came in and took down the security system and then came to my office and handed it to me and said, "You'll need this someday as I believe you will be back in business." With that he turned and went outside.

Several of my other suppliers made excuses to come into the store. They would be there for only a few minutes and then say good-bye and leave. I was so stressed out at this point that I didn't really think about what they were doing.

When I finally handed over the keys and walked outside, there standing beside their cars where several of my suppliers and the security man, all just standing there watching as if they were giving me a send-off. I broke down then and started to cry. I never knew that these people cared so much.

I asked my sister if I could stay there for a few days. I went there and slept that night, and then I went back home the next day as I could not leave the children in such an unstable situation.

When I got back home the first thing I did was call one of the guys that Jim used to work with and asked him to come over. I met him at the door and asked him to come into the house. I took him into the kitchen and told him a bit about what had happened. I explained about Jim trying to commit suicide and that I closed the store. I asked him if he would go upstairs and talk to Jim and see if he could convince him to go back to work.

He did, and when he came back downstairs he said that Jim was thinking about coming back to work. I thanked him and he left.

Within a few minutes Jim came downstairs. "I should kill you for calling him and telling him my business." I walked out of the kitchen and into the living room and he followed me. "I'm going to kill myself and take you with me, that way no one will ever have you. If I can't have you no one is going to."

I got really angry and thought he can't destroy me much more than what he has already. "Come with me Jim," and I walked back into the kitchen and opened the cupboard door and pointed to the pill bottles that he had sitting there. "See those pills? You are welcome to take them any time you want." Then I walked him over to the phone and grabbed the phone book. I looked up the closest motel to us and said, "Here, call it and make a reservation for a room and then you can go there, take the pills or anything else you want to use to get rid of yourself. Go ahead and kill yourself, I really don't care. Just get it over with, will you? I'm sick of listening to this, and if you try to kill yourself here, then I have to stop you. If you check yourself into a motel and do it there, I can pretend that I don't know anything about it. As far as me standing still and letting you kill me? Well, let me tell you something, I don't want to spend time here on earth with you, what makes you think I'm going to go to Heaven with you? As far as going to hell with you, I live there already."

I left him standing there with a shocked look on his face. Wow, that felt good, I thought to myself as I went to the washroom and locked the door, waiting for him to explode, but instead he just disappeared up stairs without another word.

A few days later I spoke to my bankruptcy trustee, and he told me that I did not have to get rid of the house. I told Jim and said I thought it would be a good idea to keep the house for the kids' sake, as they had been going through enough lately.

"No, I don't want the house," he replied. "It's nothing but bad memories here. I want to get an apartment somewhere, and we can all start over again."

I looked at him for a moment and then said, "I'll talk to your parents to see if they would like us to move in there with them."

His parents were in their mid-seventies, and I felt maybe they could use some help. I also thought that if they were around it might help keep Jim under control. They had a large three-story house, and I knew the kids would not mind it there as they had a close relationship with their grandparents. When I spoke to them they thought it would be a good idea.

The house got listed with a real estate agent, and within a few days I got a call from our agent. I answered the phone. "Hi Jenny, I have an agent that wants to come by in half an hour to show the house to a couple that might be interested. Is it alright with you?"

"Yes, sure, that will be fine." I hung up the phone and went into the kitchen to make sure that it was clean.

The kids had a small exercise equipment set-up in the basement and would often go down with their friends or just alone and spent time working out. I forgot that the kids were downstairs. The doorbell rang, and I answered it and told them to feel free to walk through and see the house. The couple, in their fifties, and the agent walked down the hallway and through the kitchen. They stepped up into the raised dining room that led from the kitchen and as they stood in the dining room looking around and down into the sunken living room, suddenly one of the kids downstairs turned on the theme song for the Movie Rocky really loud, and then suddenly you could feel them starting to work out on the punching bag. The bag just happened to be attached to the rafters under the dining room where these people were standing.

I stood in the kitchen in horror as I watched the real estate agent and the couple all grab onto the dining room to try and steady themselves on the now bouncing floor. The real estate lady had a pair of glasses on that was now bouncing down her nose to the beat of the music. She dropped the papers that she had been carrying when she grabbed the table for support.

The music and whoever was working on the punching bag suddenly stopped. The couple jumped off the floor and the agent left her papers lying there as she quickly followed them out of the room.

Needless to say they did not want to see the rest of the house. They scurried down the hallway and out the front door with me in pursuit, trying to apologize and explain what was happening, but it turned out they did not really speak English.

As the door closed behind them I turned and started to walk back up the hallway and then stopped and started to laugh at the picture of the three people in the dining room moments before looking like they were jumping up and down in an exercise class.

The day came finally that we moved out. As the last box was being put onto the van, I turned and looked at the house for the last time. Memories came flooding back to me about all the years that we had been there.

"Jenny, when you are ready? The van is packed, and we're all ready to go." I heard my brother-in-law call from the front steps.

"I'll be there in a moment," I called out as I walked into the kitchen for the last time. I stood there in the doorway and looked over at where the table had once been. There was the vision of three small children sitting there talking and laughing. I turned and went to look in the living room. I touched the spot on the wall where the piano had touched and thought I could hear the sounds of the keys being played. I turned and quickly ran upstairs. I went to the door of each of the children's rooms and stood, remembering the many times I stood in their doorways and had a conversation with them.

I remembered my mother being there, all smiles as she would say good night to the kids and tell them stories and jokes as they would lay there giggling before falling asleep.

I remembered the many times I sat in the kids' rooms while we would talk about things on their minds. So many memories came flooding back, many of them happy, but sadness was the biggest memory of all. I turned and went back downstairs, took one last look around at the bottom of the stairs, and then I walked out for the last time.

Jay wanted to stay at a friend's house for the next few days. I consented and told him to call me each day.

It was a couple of weeks after that, that someone told me that Jay was actually going through the dining room window of the house and sleeping there. That broke my heart.

Jim's parents were wonderful, sweet people. They couldn't do enough for us, but they also could not see anything wrong with their son. They would witness him flying off in fits of temper, and they would say the same as his sister once did, "That's okay, that's just Jim," and they would say shaking their heads.

Jim seemed to pull himself together and actually started working again full time doing flooring. The threats continued, but he had a harder time trying to say that I was having an affair as he knew I was home all day with his parents.

Now he had everyone's attention on him as they all felt sorry for him for having tried to commit suicide. A lot of times he used it to his advantage. Anytime he would argue or be rude with someone, they would just back down and let it go, not wanting to get him upset. One of his sisters actually was afraid of him, saying that he was unpredictable, and she didn't need him coming to her house to cause trouble.

The kids continued to go to their old school with their life-long friends. They would take the TTC and arrive at school about forty-five minutes later. It made for a long day for them but they preferred that to changing schools. I could understand how they felt. It was hard enough to lose the only home they had ever known; they didn't need to lose their friends too.

To help pass the time away and to keep myself occupied, I started taking a correspondence course to become a paralegal. There were a lot of courses to take, and I didn't know if I would ever pass them or not, or even how far I would go with it, but for the time being it was something that I thought was positive. I was allowed to pick the course that I wanted to take first, so I choose Wills and Testaments. I found it not to be too hard and enjoyed the reading and just learning something new.

Jim did not give any encouragement, nor did his parents, but I felt that I needed to do something for myself.

When I wasn't studying or cooking, then I helped my mother-in-law to clean this big three-story house. It was a large older home in the heart of Toronto, and it was a lot for someone her age to look after. I helped to vacuum the stairs, which were particularly hard for my mother-in-law. I would do laundry and wash the ceramic floors in the hallway, kitchen, and bathroom. I would help her with any outside chores as well as inside. I went with my mother-in-law and father-in-law to any doctor's appointments that they had. They found this to be a big help, as they did not understand what the doctor would try to tell them, and I could try and portray what was happening even if I did not speak Italian.

We managed to converse somehow without much trouble. If there was something that they did not understand, then I would tell Jim when he came home and he would convey it to them.

I loved to go downstairs and sit with them while they watched Jeopardy on TV.

They could not speak English but had learned that you had to guess the alphabet. If you guess the right one then it went up on the board; the wrong one and the audience would moan. They would sit there and yell out different letters of the alphabet. Sometimes they disagreed with each other as to the right alphabet, and they would begin to argue. When they got it right they would laugh and clap their hands.

They lived near Honest Ed's, which is a large discount department store in the city of Toronto. It was started by a man who had believed that sometimes if you gave to the community you would go farther. He was right, everybody loved Honest Ed's, and Ed Mervish had started this store many years before dollar stores were ever thought of.

My in-laws, even though they didn't have a mortgage or struggled to pay bills, they still liked to save money where they could, just like a lot of other people. So if they heard that there was going to be a bag of sugar on sale for five cents, they would go and stand in line for hours waiting for their turn to get it. They would usually go together because the store would maybe sell only one per customer so that everyone would get a chance at getting some. It really did not matter what the sale was, if it was good they were there.

One morning I was downstairs vacuuming when they came up behind me and unplugged the vacuum cleaner so that I could hear what they wanted to say.

"Jenny, you come with us to Honest Ed's, we go get a bird."

I smiled and asked, "A bird?"

"Big bird, what you call it?" My father-in-law said as he struggled to find the right word.

"You mean turkey?" I asked. "Yes, yes, turkey," he replied, smiling.

"Alright, I'll come with you." I unplugged the vacuum and grabbed my jacket and off we went.

The line-up was almost a block-and-a-half long. So we settled into our place in line and began our long wait. A couple with orange hair stood in line a few people ahead of us. My father-in-law kept looking at them, and then he turned to my mother-in-law and said something in Italian. She asked him in Italian what he had just said, so he repeated it and again a little louder. She still did not understand what he was trying to tell her. Finally, out of exasperation, he yelled at her: orange hair.

Everyone looked at them, and my mother-in-law said, "Young people crazy."

The young man turned around to stare at my father-in-law. He looked back at the young man and said, "Wife crazy, you look good," and with that the young man turned around and my father-in-law had a big smile on his face as everyone in the crowd began to snicker.

When we got up to the front of the line where they could get their turkey, they had just about run out and had only one more to sell. They got the last one. They acted like they had just won a prize. The rest of the crowd started to disperse with some of them moaning and groaning. My father-in-law held the turkey high over his head as if it was trophy and bowed to a few people who looked angry at this point. Laughing, he carried his turkey home.

I loved these two people. Why couldn't their son be like them? They knew how to laugh and enjoy simple things.

We now lived just a few blocks away from Jim's Aunt Gina that my mother had asked to come to the hospital to see her. I would see her every week, and she would drop by the house every time she was out shopping. She had kept her word to my mother; she was always watching over me.

I never told her what my life had been like with Jim, but I still felt close to her. She had told me once that when she married into the family there was a lot of people who didn't accept her. They looked down on her. I guess that was our first bond, as I felt that way from some of my in-laws.

We just became good friends from the moment we met, and the friendship grew over the years. I never told her about the abuse, but she knew I was not really happy.

"It will all work out some day, you'll see," she would tell me.

I never met anyone who could find four leaf clovers like this lady could. I would go for walks with her sometimes. We would walk down some of the side streets, and she was always bending down and picking up four leaf clovers off people's lawns.

"How do you do that?" I would ask her. "I could go for twenty years or more and never find one, and you find twenty of them in a year."

She would laugh and say, "I'm just lucky."

One afternoon I was walking with Aunt Gina and I said, "It's not getting any easier with Jim. I don't understand what he has done or what is wrong with him, but I have to try and figure it out somehow. I have to learn to accept it or change it. I have heard there is a group that meets every week, and they give support to each other."

Aunt Gina asked, "What type of support group are they?"

"Well they all suffer from a mental illness of some sort, and they give each other support. Do you think I should call them and see if they will let me go to try and understand about mental illness?"

"I think it is an excellent idea," she replied.

When I got back to the house I looked up the phone number and called it.

I heard the phone ring several times and then finally on the fourth ring a man answered, "Hello."

I cleared my throat and then spoke, "I have a husband who has tried to commit suicide on several occasions. He was locked up in the hospital for several weeks, but he is far from cured. He has mentioned on several occasions that he would like to take my kids and myself to heaven with him. I really need help to understand depression and everything associated with it. Will you please give me permission to come to your classes and try to understand?" I stopped talking and waited a few minutes with my heart pounding from nervousness.

There was a long pause on the phone, and then the voice said, "We are having a meeting on Thursday night, and we will have to discuss it and let you know. Everyone must be comfortable having you there, as normally we don't allow anyone to come who is not suffering from some sort of mental illness."

Friday morning I received a call. When I picked up the phone I recognized the same voice.

"Is this Jenny?"

"Yes, it is," I replied nervously.

"We had our meeting last night, and we took a vote, and it was unanimous that you could come to our next meeting to learn more about mental illness, but we want your husband to come with you."

"I will try and convince him to go. Thank you for calling and letting me know."

I hung up the phone and wondered how I would convince Jim to attend these meetings.

For the next few days I did not say anything about the meetings. I just needed time to think about how I would approach him about it.

The weekend came and went, and then on Monday night when he came home I sat down on the sofa beside him as he watched the news and I said, "Jim, there is a support group north of here that holds meetings every Thursday night. I spoke to them, and we are welcome to come and listen to what they have to say. There are no doctors or lawyers allowed there, only people suffering from a form of mental illness. I hope you will consider going. I've already told a few people, such as your Aunt Gina, about the support group, and they thought it was a good idea."

I sat there waiting for a response. A few minutes lapsed and then he finally turned to me and said, "Why would you tell people about the meeting?"

"I wanted to see if anyone other than me thought it was a good idea."

"I think you are just trying to coerce me into going," he stated as he looked at me angrily.

"Truthfully, whatever it takes to get you there. I need to understand what happened and what is happening, and they won't let me come to their meetings without you."

"Oh, so you need me to go," he leered.

"Yes, I need you to go. So will you?"

"I'll think about it," he said, and with that he got up and walked out.

When Thursday arrived I pretended I thought we were going, and I was ready. When he came home from work I served him his dinner. When he finished eating, I removed his plate from the table as I said to him, "Time to go to the meeting."

Surprisingly, he got up from the table and said, "Alright, let's go."

When we arrived they asked me to take a seat and for Jim to wait outside while I explained to them why I wanted to be there. As I spoke my heart was beating rapidly.

"My husband has been very abusive verbally and physically over the years. I have three sons, and they have been abused as well. Jim tried to commit suicide on several different occasions, and now he says that he has every intention of killing himself, the kids, and me and taking us to heaven. I have tried to get help from doctors and police, but it seems everywhere I turn, there is a reason why I can't get help. So I can only help myself, and I can't do that if I don't understand what I am dealing with. I hope you can help me to learn about his illness. I have no other place to turn."

A man stood up and said, "We voted last week that you are to be allowed to be here. We just wanted to hear it from you why you feel you need to be here."

I looked around the room at the people sitting watching me and listening. "Am I still accepted to be here?"

"Yes you are still welcome here. Hopefully we can help somehow," a woman from the left side of the room said as she stood up.

"Alright let's call your husband Jim back in here, and then we will introduce ourselves to each of you," said the man who had first spoken.

Jim entered the room as the man held the door open for him and beckoned him back inside.

We all sat around a long table and each person began by saying their name and what they suffered from.

There were six people there, all fighting their own battles and each one giving support to the other one. They talked about medications and side effects, and what worked for one person did not work for another.

They asked Jim that night if he would like to talk. "Yes, I would," he said as he looked around the table at everyone. "I don't have any problems like the rest of you do. I'm only here because the wife wants to be here."

"Well that's fine, Jim. You are both welcome, and we hope you will come back every week."

So every Thursday we would go to the meetings. Jim seemed to be enjoying it. I could see he was using it to his advantage. On our trips home he would laugh at some of the people who had been there that night. It was as if he was collecting information to help him prove his point that he was crazy. Even though I suspected this was happening, I also was using it to my advantage to try and understand how the human mind works. If I could get an idea of how to cope, it would be a big help.

In the meeting room there were chairs and a table. People would sit around the table and talk about what had happened to them that week and if they were having problems with anything. Some struggled just to get through each day. Some had compulsive disorders. Some had anxiety attacks while others suffered depression, but no matter what the problem was, they were there to help give information, ideas, and support to each other. Some just needed someone else to listen and understand what they were going through.

I did learn a lot from these people, and I admired all of them for what they had to face and go through each day. There is such a stigma attached to mental illness that a lot of these people were being shunned from society. Their friends, neighbors, and even family did not know how to cope with the problems that they were living with, so the easiest solution to the problem is just don't get involved. Therefore, someone suffering a mental illness feels alienated from everyone. Loneliness can be a very real problem for many suffering with a mental illness. Support groups are great, but these people still need the support of family and friends.

I had always believed that Jim had a need to be the centre of attention, and he was beginning to show that here at these meetings. While people would be talking he would interrupt and give a comment or make a wise crack. People where becoming more and more agitated with him each week.

The meetings were two hours long starting at seven P.M. and finishing at nine P.M. Around eight P.M. they would break for fifteen minutes and have coffee and go outside for a cigarette for those that smoked. Outside the meeting usually continued. Whatever the discussion was going on inside, we would go outside and it was still being discussed over a coffee and smoke.

Sometimes emotions where pretty high at this point in the evening, depending on the discussions, and it was not unusual to see someone off in a corner wiping tears away as they tried to regain composure. These people were real people, with real problems, and sometimes two hours per week just were not enough time to try and deal with everyone's issues.

Inside around the table you would hear heartbreaking stories of what someone had to go through in their life. I was really hoping these stories would help Jim to understand that his life was a breeze compared to some people.

One night we started off the meeting with a young man in his late twenties talking about how he had lived in a rural area north of Toronto, and he traveled by bus to school. There were no other children in the area to play with, and he was made to work hard on a family farm.

He would be tied up in the barn for days at a time if his father got drunk and decided that he didn't want the kid around. He would be left with no food or water. His mother was also an alcoholic and never wanted him around either, except to do chores around the house or barn. He spoke of beatings and threats that the parents made to him if they thought he was too slow with his chores. He spoke of how they would laugh at him if he cried.

One year for Christmas his mom and dad went away for three days and left him tied up in the barn, but because it was Christmas they left a sandwich and a glass of juice for him to eat on Christmas Day.

He spoke of how he tried to make the sandwich and juice last until Christmas Day, but he got too hungry and thirsty so he finally broke down and ate it the day after they left, leaving him with nothing to eat and drink for the next two days. He cried as he spoke of how cold he remembered it to be in that barn that Christmas. He said he sang Christmas songs that he remembered hearing at school, and that helped to get him through the days of being tied up.

They had a dog who would come into the barn and lay with him and keep him company. His parents fed the dog like they fed their child, once in a while when they were feeling generous. The dog was the only friend he ever had.

He did not learn how to read or write, as he had a hard time concentrating at school.

He began stuttering when he was about four years old, and it only got worse the older he got. The kids would make fun of him for the way he talked or the way he dressed, as most of the time his clothes were too small and always dirty from working on the farm. He was an outcast from any school activities, and when he was allowed to go to town the people would just stare and point fingers and whisper.

Everyone who came to these meetings had become his friend. He had a hard time speaking of these times, as it brought forward a lot of emotions. Tears rolled down his cheeks as he carried on.

"When my parents arrived home from their Christmas vacation they went into the house and came out a few minutes later walking towards the barn with my father carrying his shotgun. They entered the barn and said to me that they could not afford to feed me and the dog. With that my father raised the shotgun and shot my dog. They then untied me and left me there kneeling over the dog, crying."

Tears rolled down my face and almost everyone else's in the room.

While he and everyone else in the room tried to regain some composure, a lady began to talk. She was in her mid-sixties, and she spoke about how she had suffered with a compulsive disorder for more than thirty years. She spoke about how she had to count all the doors in her apartment several times before she could leave. She had to turn a light on and off ten times before turning a light on. She said that she would count all the bottles on a shelf in a store if she was going to buy something off that shelf. She could not cross at a light at an intersection if she had not counted it going on and off and least four times first. Then she said that she would find herself pulling her hair out one strand at a time without even realizing she was doing it. Hence she wore a wig most of the time, trying to get her hair to grow back in again.

She spoke about being sexually abused when she was younger by her father. Her mother had died when she was about five years old, and by the time she was seven her father was sexually abusing her. When she was around twelve or thirteen, her father would have friends over for a drink, and if they brought him a bottle or a case of beer then they could have sex with her too.

She cried as she spoke about leaving home when she was fourteen years old. Her father threatened to kill her because she had her first boyfriend.

"You're mine and always will be," he had yelled at her as she walked out of the house with her suitcase in her hand.

She never looked back. She ended up living on the streets of Toronto. She survived by giving sexual favors. Sometime she would do it just to get a case of beer or a bottle of whisky. When she turned thirty no man really wanted to pay for her favors anymore. Too old, they would tell her. Too used up.

She kept her eyes down and twisted a napkin through her fingers as she talked.

Now in her mid-sixties, she lived alone in a small one bedroom apartment where she spoke of the walls peeling and the floors rotting. She was basically totally alone with no family and no friends to speak of.

She laughed as she said the word. "Friends, that is someone who comes over, uses you for the night, and you never see them again, and if you're lucky they don't steal from you while they are there."

She turned and put a comforting hand out to the young man who had previously spoken. "We're two of a kind, you and me," she said with a sad smile on her face. "Nobody's child." He looked over at her and gave a weak smile and then he too looked down.

Then another woman spoke about the loneliness she was living with. A tear rolled down her cheek as she said her family had not spoken to her in six years, since she had tried to commit suicide. She had suffered depression for years. "When I'm going through what I call a bad spell, I am unable to get out of bed, get washed or dressed, and basically cannot cope with everyday life.

"My family never did understand what I'm going through and just made it worse by getting angry at me and telling me to pull myself together and get a job."

My family would look at me and say, "Do what everyone else in the world is doing and start working. Just get a job and make it last for more than a few weeks. You'll be surprised how much you feel better."

"I tried it, but the depression just got worse because it was like I had just proved to myself that I was not normal like everyone else. I would arrive late for work because it took me forever to get ready. I could not concentrate."

Finally she had tried to commit suicide, and that was the last her family had anything to do with her. Since then she had tried to face the illness on her own with the help of her family doctor.

Everyone in the room had a lot in common when they spoke of their experiences with their illness.

The stigma of mental illness was a common bond between them all. They had all experienced what it was like to be misunderstood to some degree.

They all agreed that medication was a big factor with how they felt. Some felt that they were being experimented on. Some drugs were better for some than others, and it can be a hit and miss situation until the right medication is found. Some medication made them sleep constantly. Some meds made them feel like they were stoned and could not make a decision for themselves. Others felt like their medication was not working at all, as they were having panic attacks and other disorders that kept them from living a normal life. They all agreed that medication was a factor to feeling better, but only if they could find the right one, but that it was like living in hell until they did.

Jim disagreed with them, as he did not take medication. He didn't believe it was a good thing for anyone to do. "It's better to depend on yourself rather than depend on medication," he stated, "you can live without it."

"Is that so," said one of the men sitting at the table. "You are telling me that you are not on medication, and that you are not depressed and everything is fine in your life?"

"That's what I'm telling you," Jim replied.

"Well then, why did you try to commit suicide?"

Jim glared back at the man for a moment and then said, "None of your business."

Suddenly you could cut the tension in the room with a knife as Jim and the man glared back and forth at each other. A few people began to shift around nervously in their seats, expecting that something was going to start.

Another man sitting at the table cleared his throat and then said, "I think that is enough for tonight. We will all meet back here next Thursday night. Everybody try to have a good week."

With that chairs began to scrape across the tiled floor and people began to raise and leave the room. Jim got up and walked quickly out of the room, leaving me behind. I picked up my jacket and purse and started towards the door, saying good night to people as I passed them by.

One woman took a hold of my arm as I neared the door and said, "You need to leave that man, he will never change," and with that she smiled and walked away.

When I got to the car Jim was already seat, belted in and waiting impatiently. "What took you so long?" he demanded.

I didn't answer and just put my seat belt on. He grabbed my belt and said in a deep, ugly voice, "You have everyone in there feeling sorry for you, having to live with someone like me. Well, let me tell you that if they really knew you they would feel sorry for me instead."

I sighed and thought I did not have the energy to say anything back. He started the car, and as we drove home he grabbed my hand and squeezed it really tight. "You try to portray yourself as such an innocent, don't you?" he said. "Face of an angel, acts of a devil."

I suddenly realized how very tired I really felt. Tired physically and emotionally. I felt like the years of trying to understand what was really going on was taking its toll on me. I could educate myself on mental illness all I wanted, but it was not going to help someone who did not want any help.

The one thing that I had learned during this education venture was that if I did not show any emotions, such as fear or anger, then it seemed to calm Jim down. He did not have the same amount of power without those emotions. It was hard to do, but each time he showed an outburst, I would try to show no emotion, and I was getting better at it. Each time he would try to intimidate me, it was as if he got a bit weaker while I got a bit stronger. I did not have to yell or scream. I did not have to threaten him, as any of those emotions are what he was trying to create. I just had to be silent and look him straight in the eye and not blink. If I spoke, my voice had to be strong and clear, never waver, and my words could not be hesitant. I had to make him believe that I had confidence in whatever I said and did.

This was hard to do, as I had no self-confidence, but I was getting better at it. If I could make him believe that I had self-confidence, then maybe someday I could make myself believe it.

Also during these weeks of sitting through these meetings, I had learned about myself, even if I wasn't learning about Jim. I found out what I had been suffering all those years of being afraid of going outside. Afraid of being in malls and panic attacks. I finally could put a name to what I was going through.

I had fought it for so long, and it actually had gotten a lot better with me forcing myself to face the fears and go out with the kids and try to live as much a normal life as possible. I refused to allow to be locked inside like Jim wanted me to be. Knowing now what I had suffered made it easier. Knowing that others suffered the same thing made me feel like I was not alone.

I did not talk at these meetings about the things I had experienced, as I did not want Jim to know how bad it had gotten for me. I didn't need to give him any ammunition that he could use against me. I had managed to hide it from everyone who knew me up to this point, and I wasn't about to let that change.

One thing that was happening that was new to me was that I would wake up in the middle of the nights or in the mornings and I would have my fists clinched so tight that my fingernails were digging into the flesh of the palm of my hands, and I had cuts and bruising most of the time now. I knew the stress was taking its toll on me. I was able to hide this from everyone.

The following week was filled with Jim trying hard to intimidate me. He was beginning to see that I was getting stronger, and the threats were not having the same effect on me that they used to have. This just made him even angrier and obsessed with the thought that he had to gain control somehow.

He came in from work, and the kids were not back from school yet. I was in the kitchen preparing dinner. I was standing at the kitchen counter cutting vegetables and had my back to the kitchen door when he came through. He never spoke but just walked up behind me and grabbed the knife out of my hand. He pointed the knife at me and then ran it down the front of me, then laughed and dropped the knife on the counter and walked out of the kitchen and into the living room, where I heard him turn the TV on and sit down on the sofa as if nothing had just happened.

I stood there, frozen to the spot, and when I heard sounds coming from the television, I finally took a breath, closed my eyes for a moment, and then picked up the knife and with shaking hands continued to cut vegetables.

It was moments like this that I had to fight this strong urge to run. Where would I run to? What could I do? Who would believe me that he was doing these things, and even if someone did there was nothing they could do about it. Police and doctors couldn't help, so what was left for help?

The next Thursday night they all voted that Jim should have the floor and talk about what was bothering him.

"I don't need to talk about anything."

"Well, we all disagree and think it is time for you to accept that you have some problems," the person who was chairing the meeting said.

"Alright," he said, "if you want to really know what's bothering me, she's bothering me," he stated loudly as he pointed to me.

"Alright then, tell us how and maybe we can help," said one of the group members.

"You can't help me with her. She's a bitch, and I have to live with that."

"So is that why you tried to kill yourself?" another one asked.

"She refuses to do what I want her to do. She refuses to make me happy. If she was a good wife I wouldn't have any problems."

"What is it you want her to do?" another person asked.

"Everything I say, with no questions asked," he responded as he started to get irritated. "You guys don't understand what it is like to be embarrassed when your wife doesn't do what she is supposed to do."

"You are still not telling us anything. You're talking too general. What is it you want her to do that she refuses to do?"

"None of you God damn business," Jim yelled.

"Well, let me tell you something," another one jumped in at this point. "If it wasn't for your wife, you would have been thrown out of these meetings a long time ago. We don't condone rudeness, and we believe you are treating these meetings like a joke."

"These meetings are a joke, and so are all of you. I'm out of here," he yelled, and with that he grabbed my arm and pulled me up from my chair.

"She does not need to leave. We have nothing against her, and if she still wishes to remain then she's welcome, but you can only stay if you are going to be civil," one of the men said.

Jim didn't acknowledge him and continued on towards the door, pulling me with him.

One of them began to rise and come towards us.

I looked at him and said, "It's alright." The man stopped, and everyone in the room watched as Jim and I walked out.

That was the last time we were at one of those support meetings. I had learned enough that I didn't think it really mattered, and I knew it was not helping Jim.

My father-in-law began to feel ill, as he was having a difficult time breathing. I spoke to Jim and told him he had better convince his father to go to the hospital. After a couple of days he consented to go. We went with him and checked him in. The doctor who examined him did not like the way his chest sounded and said he would like to keep him for observation overnight. So we said our good-byes and left for the night. I promised him that even though Jim would go to work, I would come back the next day with Maria, his wife.

The next morning I woke up to a beautiful, sunny day. I stretched and lay there for a moment looking out the bedroom window. I got up and got washed and brushed my hair and then threw on a light-colored cotton blouse and jeans, as it looked like it was going to be another hot June day. Then I descended the stairs to the kitchen and made breakfast.

Al rushed in and grabbed a piece of toast and said, "I'm in a rush. I have to be at school early." With that he grabbed his school bag and ran out the door. As I heard the door closing behind Al, Jay and Paul entered the kitchen and sat down at the table. I sat their breakfast down in front of them.

"Are you going to the hospital to see Nonno?" asked Paul.

"I'm going to go there later this morning," I answered as I poured a glass of juice and sat down with them.

Jay took a bite of toast and said, "Tell him we want him to hurry up and get better."

I smiled and said, "I'll try to relay that message."

Jim ran into the kitchen at that point and took a couple of sips of coffee and then ran toward the front door. I hear him speak to his mother on his way out.

After the kids went to school, I called the hospital to see how my father-in-law was doing. They said he had a good night, and he was doing fine. I went downstairs and told my mother-in-law the good news and said I was going to clean up the kitchen and then we could go to the hospital.

I went back upstairs and cleaned the dishes off the table and put them in the sink. I stood over the sink, allowing the water to run over the dishes. I listened to the radio with the morning news and road and weather reports. A few minutes later I had finished washing the dishes, and I wiped the table and counter down. I looked around the kitchen and was satisfied that it looked clean enough and was just about to pick up my purse and go back downstairs when I heard the phone ring. As I walked down the hallway, I heard my mother-in-law answering the phone.

"Hello," she said into the receiver.

A few seconds later I heard her calling me. "Jenny come, I no understand what they say."

I ran down the stairs and took the phone. "Hello?" I said into the receiver.

"This is the hospital calling. I regret to inform you that Allen has just passed away."

I stood there looking at my mother-law, stunned. "What do you mean? I just called there about half an hour ago, and I was told he was fine."

"It was very sudden, a heart attack."

"Oh, my God," I said as I looked at my mother-in-law, who was standing anxiously beside me waiting for me to explain what this call was about.

I hung up and took my mother-in-law by the hand and led her to the sofa. I sat her down wondering to myself, how do you tell someone their lifelong partner of more than fifty years has just passed away?

She studied my face as I struggled to find the words she would understand as well as tell her gently. I started to speak and suddenly she threw herself into my arms and cried, "No, no, no," and then continued on speaking in Italian. At this moment we did not need to speak the same language. We understood each other perfectly. We shared the same pain of losing someone we loved. We could read each other's body language, which just spoke of shock. I kept remembering his smiling face as I had said good bye the night before.

I tried to keep her calm while I thought about what I should do next. I called the school to tell the kids to come home. Then I called Jim's work and asked them to give him the news. Then I called my sister-in-law and told her and asked her to contact everyone else she thought should know.

I stayed near my mother-in-law. She went and got a picture of her husband and then the bible and sat down in the living room. With her prayer beads in hand, she sat whispering prayers on each bead as they passed through her fingers.

Knowing that people would soon be arriving, I went to the kitchen and made coffee. The shock was still there, and I had this sense of disbelief. I cut some bread and placed it on a tray as I laid out assorted cold cuts. Then I made another tray of cakes and cookies. I kept going back to the living room to check on her. Finally I made up a small fruit tray and then went back to sit with my mother-in-law. She was still softly praying and every once in a while she would stop long enough to wipe away a tear.

The next few days are pretty much a blur. Many people coming and going, giving their condolences to the family. Telegrams arrived from Italy as well as from some relatives in California and on the West Coast of Canada. There seemed to be a constant vigil going on in the house. Food was plentiful, as people brought food with them as well as the food that was already prepared and waiting for more people to arrive.

On the day of the funeral the sun shone warmly down upon us all. Jim and the kids dressed in black suits, I wore a black dress, and my mother-in-law dressed in the typical black dress and head scarf. It was a hot morning, and beads of sweat appeared on most people as they entered the funeral home.

The family went to the funeral home first, where we sat in a room with the coffin, and the family members got to say their last good-byes before going to the church. My mother-in-law cried and wailed as people walked up to the coffin. One of my sisters-in-law, Betty, tried to climb into the coffin as they were closing the lid. There was screams, and several people had to grab her and pull her back. This just upset my mother-in-law more and made the rest of the ceremony harder on her. We left the funeral home and made our way to the church.

As people entered into the church I stood outside on the steps for a few moments. I watched people as they arrived. Most of them nodded at me as they entered the church. I continued to stand there breathing in the fresh, warm air. Cars lined the street because the parking lot of the church was full. As I walked into the church I realized just how many had turned out. The church was packed full.

The rest of the morning, the service, the grave yard, is pretty much a blur. After the funeral was finished, we all went back to the house where people gathered. More food was served, and people continued to come and go all day.

We were all exhausted mentally and physically when the last person left that day. I was having a hard time with the passing of my father-in-law, as he was the only real father I had known, and I was going to miss him a lot. Even though he could not speak English, we always managed to understand each other. He has a sense of humor that I enjoyed. Instead of calling me Jenny like everyone else did, he would refer to me as Jenasee, and then he would laugh.

After his passing Jim was around even less. For the next month he would come home, change, and leave, going to a local restaurant for coffee. He would walk the streets as if he was looking for something.

One night he came home, had dinner, and then went for his usual coffee. He came back within an hour and said, "I want you to move out."

I had been sitting on the sofa and looked up him to see if he was joking. He had a serious look on his face.

"Alright." I got up and made my way upstairs to the bedroom to begin packing.

This was not planned, and I had no idea where I was going. This was my opportunity to leave, and I was going to take it. I would figure out the rest later. The kids were home, and I went to their rooms and told them that their dad had asked me to leave. Then I went back to the bedroom to finish packing. The kids seemed shocked and came and asked me why. I didn't have a specific answer to give them. I just gave them a look and continued to pack.

Jim came to the bedroom door and said, "You don't get any money to take you."

"Well, that is a surprise," I said sarcastically as I continued to pack.

When I was ready to leave I went downstairs and found the kids waiting; they had all packed and were coming with me.

"Are you sure you want to come?" I asked as I looked from one to the other.

"We're sure. We want to come," Al answered.

"I have no place to go. I don't know what we will do," I responded.

"We'll figure it out," Jay responded.

We got into the kids' car and drove away. I never looked back. We decided between us that we would go back to our neighborhood, where the kids would visit their friends.

As we drove north to our old neighborhood, I had this sense of being in a dream. Since I didn't have time to plan anything, I had no idea at this point what we were all going to do.

We went to drop off Jay at his friend's house, then we drove Paul to his friend's house, and I went with Al to his friend's house, where we spent the next few days. I hated intruding on people.

Everyone in the family were great, welcoming us into their home, but I felt so out of place. I wouldn't eat their food. I accepted the occasional coffee, but mostly I did without because I knew at this point I could not pay them for anything. When I left I had seven dollars in my pocket and nothing else to my name except a few clothes in one suitcase, the family dog, and the kids. I needed to find a home for all of us.

I went looking for work every day, but it was hard. I went looking for an apartment, but it was hard as well, as I had no money and there were very few places in the area to rent. I understood how the kids wanted to be in the area where they had grown up, but it was going to be a hard place to be as it was an expensive area to live in.

I eventually bought a bag of bagels and fed the dog and myself a bagel a day.

The kids ate at their friends' houses, which I was so grateful they could do. I felt that I had spent too much time with Al's friends; they were very kind but I really felt like I was imposing.

So at the invitation of Jay's friends I went there for two days. I would leave during the day and look for work and a place for us to live, but I was having a hard time finding anything. On the third day I came back to the house about four o'clock in the afternoon, feeling really depressed and scared, as I still was not finding any place to live or any jobs. I sat on the front steps when I arrived back and watched the kids playing and joking around on the front lawn. The husband noticed me sitting there and came to the door and said, "Jenny, will you come in for a moment?"

"Sure," I responded as I rose from the steps and entered the door.

He had walked to the back of the house where the kitchen was, and I could see him standing, leaning up against a cupboard and motioned me to come in.

As I walked into the kitchen he cleared his throat and said, "Jenny, my wife Rebecca asked me to talk to you. She is not comfortable knowing that you could be here all day with me while she is at work. She doesn't mind if the kids stay, but you know what women are like. She's jealous and just wants you to leave. I feel bad, but it's her house too."

I looked at him for a moment and then said, "That's alright, George."

"I'd like to give you a few more days to get things arranged, but she is the boss around here," he said, looking uncomfortable.

"That's fine," I responded. "I think I might have a place and a job," I lied as I tried to give him a reassuring smile. "So please don't feel bad. I'll go put my things together and leave now."

"You are welcome to stay for dinner."

"No thanks, I ate already," I lied as I walked away.

I had been sleeping in their basement. I went downstairs and started putting my things into my suitcase.

Jay came into the house and went downstairs. "Where are you going?"

"I am going to go and stay with a friend for a few days."

"Why?" Jay asked.

"I need time to think."

I smiled weakly at Jay as he looked confused. I was too embarrassed to tell him what had just happened and that I was asked to leave.

I said to Jay, "All of us will get together every day, and we will try and work out something. We'll find a place to live, and a job or something."

A few minutes later I took the dog Pepper and we left.

I did not want the kids to worry about me and the dog. I went and sat in the car every night after the kids were safely in their friends' houses. The kids believed at that point that I was at a friend's house. Every night I would sit in the car, too nervous to sleep. Pepper would curl up beside me and put his head on my lap. I would count the hours until I would see daylight again.

THE WEB

Throughout the night I would relive all the years of abuse. All the threats Jim had ever made. All the times he promised to kill me. I would hear his words, "You're no good. You're not worth anything. You are so lucky that you have me to look after you, because you would never make it on your own."

The dog became ill after a couple of weeks of living like this, and I took him to the vet's. They ended up putting him on intravenous. After two days the dog came out of the hospital with the vet saying that the dog was suffering from bad nerves.

I continued to look for work. One problem I had while trying to find work was I did not have an address or a phone number to put on the application forms. Finally I went to the welfare office and asked for help explaining the situation. I felt like such a loser.

I sat that first day in the office of a social worker with tears in my eyes as he explained what I could get, which was not enough to keep the kids and myself in food and a place to live. "You need to get approved," the worker stated at the end of the interview.

It took a week, and then they finally approved us for welfare. They said it would take about two weeks before we would receive a cheque.

This meant I still had to live in the car without the kids knowing and try to make sure that they could continue to eat at their friends' houses.

One of Al's friends was trying to rent out a basement apartment, and the kids and I went to see it and talk to them about maybe moving in. It was one long room that contained a kitchen sink and a few cupboards at one end. The rest of the room was to be used for a living room and bedroom. There was a small washroom off the other end of the big room. It was the end of July, and it was already cold down there with ceramic tile throughout the room. We decided to take the apartment as soon as we received the cheque.

The kids went to their friends' houses each day and continued on with their sports. I looked for work each day but was not having much success.

Isabell, my sister, and Rob, her husband, had a trailer just east of Peterborough, so I called and asked if I could go with them on the weekend. This way the kids could have the car to themselves, and it also gave me someone to talk to. So they came and picked me up on Friday afternoon. We arrived at their trailer and prepared dinner. After we ate we sat around the campfire and talked about different things, but even then I could still not tell her everything that I was going through. I was so ashamed that I was living the way I was, trying to get my life started over again after an abusive marriage. I felt like Isabell and Rob would not understand.

I would sit on a picnic table most nights I was there. I had gotten to the point that I never slept. I think only fear kept me going. I would sit there watching cars that passed by, and I would wonder if one of them was going to be Jim driving up to kill me. After all the years of hearing the threats, it was hard not to think about it now.

It was like I had been brainwashed. I now did not know how to cope or how to survive or what to do. I couldn't eat, couldn't sleep, and had a hard time concentrating and making decisions.

Pride is a funny thing. It can make you strive for the moon, and at the same time it can make you hide the truth from everyone. There was no way I could tell my sister that I was living in the car. I had always wanted to appear like I was in control of what was happening, but I had no control over anything. The only thing I knew for sure: I was not going back to Jim.

The next day people came to the trailer who I had never met before. They were supposed to be neighbors living near the trailer park. They sat around and talked for a long time to my sister and brother-in-law. Everyone around seemed happy and joking around, and it felt good to be around people who were having a good time.

I sat at a picnic table nearby and would take part in conversations when directed at me, but for the most part I just let my mind wander, trying to figure out what I'd do on Monday. God, I felt lost. I felt like I did not belong anywhere. Not good enough for anything. No confidence and no idea of what to do next. I felt like I was ugly, damaged goods that were not worth anything.

As the day progressed, one of the people, a young man named Sam, asked me where I was working in Toronto. I told him I was currently looking for work. I explained that I had just broken up with my husband and that I was taking the first few steps towards putting my life back in order. With that, he said he worked in Toronto and he had contacts and would ask around to see if he could help me find a job. I told him I would really appreciate it. He gave me his number and told me to call him during the week, and he would let me know if he found anything.

The next day we all packed up and went back to Toronto. My sister dropped me off at Al's friend Cathy's house and said she would pick me up the following weekend.

Cathy's father Mike was selling kitchen cookware at the time and said that I could go to the classes and learn how to do this, and there was a chance I could make good money selling on commission, if I worked hard at it. So the next morning I started going to classes. Al also went and was taking classes as well.

It was not something that I had a lot of faith in. When working on commission you really need to sell a lot to pay all your bills, and I could not see me doing this to support myself and three kids. I did not have a car, and at this point in my life I did not even have a driver's license. I thought it might just be a bit hard to take a set of pots and pans on the local TTC and give demonstrations.

First thing you need if you are going to be a salesperson and work with the public is a lot of self-confidence, which I did not have. Therefore I already had one strike against me before I even started.

When a woman is coming out of an abusive relationship, the first thing she needs is a lot of support. She needs someone around her who understands what she has been through and a lot of encouragement for her to take the necessary steps of getting her life together.

At this point it was as if I was jumping from the frying pan right into the fire, as I did not know how to cope with what laid ahead of me.

They talk about men coming back from fighting in a war, and they suffer from Post-Traumatic Stress Disorder, which is a clinical term used to describe the acute psychological and emotional injuries caused by an extremely traumatic event. This usually results from a life-threatening situation or witnessing extreme violence. They say that people suffering this disorder have a hard time sleeping, and they suffer from nightmares. They also have a hard time coping with everyday life.

I was suffering the same as anyone who had witnessed violence during a war. I did not have to travel to another country to witness the violence. I lived it for more than twenty years right in my own home. The war was daily, struggling to survive.

Mike was a photographer as well as selling pots and pans. "Hey Jenny, how about staying and helping me out? There is a desk, chair, and phone in the basement. I could really use someone phoning people in the area by going through the phone book and seeing if you can get me some bookings for photo work. Let them know I will do weddings, anniversaries, or anything they need."

"Yes, I would be willing to try and help you. You and your family have been great helping me and the kids. I really appreciate it, so I would be willing to do anything that I can do to help you out."

"That's great. I'll show you where everything is, and you can go there anytime you want and work." He walked to the basement door and then led me down the stairs.

"I can only pay you a percentage of everything that you book."

Even though I was now taking these classes, I still could not sleep. I would sit up night after night outside the house waiting for morning to arrive. Early in the evening there would still be people moving around, and there would be lights on in the houses, and then as the night wore on, the people would disappear and the lights would go off one by one until finally the neighborhood was in darkness except for the street lights casting a soft glow. All night long I would sit there, frozen to the spot with the dog by my side. He usually lay down and would put his head on my lap. I would listen to the sounds of the night. Sometimes you would hear a car off in the distance and maybe the barking of a dog somewhere, but overall the subdivision was quiet. I watched and waited for Jim to show up and carry out all the threats he had made over the years. I couldn't sleep, so there was no use even trying. I would tell myself that if Jim arrived I could make sure he did not get near the kids. This was the time of day that I felt the loneliest. The silence was deafening, as my thoughts would turn to memories and then turn to fears.

There may not have been much logic in what I was thinking, but I wasn't thinking logically about anything anyway.

I phoned the guy Sam on Thursday, and he said he had some information for me and could he meet with me to talk. We met at a coffee shop in the area.

I entered the coffee shop and placed an order for a coffee and then went and found a table to sit at and look out the window while I waited. About ten minutes later I saw Sam drive up and come into the coffee shop. He waved as he came in, acknowledging the fact that he knew where I was. He went up to the counter and got a coffee and came over to the table and sat down.

"How's your week going?" he asked as he took his first sip of coffee.

"Rough," I sighed, "I have been going to classes all week to learn about selling cookware, but I don't believe that it is the answer to my problems. I need a job nine to five that I can count on a certain amount of income each week to pay rent and bills."

"Well, I have several of my friends putting out feelers for you, and hopefully they can come up with something. My sister up in Peterborough has someone who wants a wall mural painted, if you are interested. I remembered you saying that you know how to do that."

"Yes I am more than just interested. When do they want it done?" I asked.

"I'll find out the details, and I will let you know." He finished his coffee and we talked small talk after that. Just as he was leaving, he said, "Call me tomorrow, and I will let you know what I find out about the wall mural." He left then, saying that he had to meet someone.

I finished my coffee and went back to Al's friend's house. I felt like I might just have a chance to make things come together.

The next day I phoned Sam again, and again he told me to meet him at the coffee shop.

THE WEB

This time he was there before I got there, and as I entered he beckoned me over to the table.

"I took the liberty of getting you a coffee, I hope you don't mind."

"No, that's fine," I said as I sat down. "Do you have any information for me?"

"Well, my sister tried to get a hold of them, but they weren't home. She'll try again tonight."

"Tell her I do appreciate what she is trying to do."

"Yes, I will tell her."

He put his hand on mind, and I jumped back as if I had been burned. "Sorry, I was just trying to comfort you. You look so tired and distraught. I didn't mean anything by it."

"I'm sorry," I said. "I guess I am just a little jumpy. I haven't been getting much sleep, and it is clouding my mind as to clear thinking."

Sam smiled, finished his coffee, and said, "Well I have to go. I will probably see you this weekend when you go to your sister's trailer. Maybe I'll have some information for you then."

I sat and watched him leave. I had a long walk back to the house where Al's friends where living, and I just needed to get some energy before leaving. I sat for a long time and my mind drifted. It has to get easier, I thought to myself.

The next day at the selling classes for the cookware we were told there was going to be a booth set up at the Toronto Exhibition Centre in two weeks, and that we would all be required to be there to sell the cookware.

The first thing I felt when I heard this was that it was so public. Jim could be in the crowd, and I wouldn't see him. I got really scared. What if he tries to do something in front of all these people? Stop it, I told myself. I need to try anything, and fear is not going to stop me.

That Friday my sister came and picked me up, and we went back to their trailer.

Sam arrived about an hour after we arrived and helped to make a campfire and just hung around as my sister and I unpacked what she had brought up for the weekend. I helped her prepare dinner, and then after dinner we all sat around the campfire and other campers came over.

Sam said to me, "My sister Sue is still trying to get in touch with these people, but as soon as she does I will let you know. So how was the rest of your week?"

"Truthfully, I am finding it really hard. Not having our own place and depending on everyone to get me from place to place. I really hate this. I wish I could find a decent job. I don't suppose your friends have come up with anything yet?"

"No, not yet, but I'm sure someone will. They all have good contacts."

I sat watching the flames and felt the warmth of the fire start to feel like it was burning my face, while at the same time I could feel the cool air on my back.

Someone around the fire piped up and said, "Look at all the stars. You don't see anything like that in Toronto."

Before we knew it, it was two am and people began to go back to their trailers and cottages. Sam got up, stretched, and said, "Well I'll go, and I'll see you tomorrow."

My sister and her husband got up and went into the trailer. "Aren't you coming to bed?" my sister asked.

"Yes, in a little while." I sat on top of the picnic table and watched the fire. The flames got smaller and smaller until they finally burnt themselves out. No one was moving in the park anymore. There were no street lights, and off in the distance I thought I could hear wolves howling. I got up and quietly went inside and grabbed a sweater and put it on. I put a little jacket on that Pepper had, and I picked him up and sat him beside me on top of the table. "It's just you and me again," I whispered to Pepper as he snuggled into me and closed his eyes. This is hard on him as well, I thought as I patted his head.

The next morning my sister got up and came out. "Did you sleep?"

"Yes, I slept a bit," I lied.

"Do you want a coffee?"

"I'd love one," I said as I got up stiffly off the table and walked into the trailer behind her. I felt my legs shaking as if I was weak. I pushed the idea to the back of my head.

After lunch Sam was back again. "Do you want to go for a drive and see the area?"

"Sure," I said as I looked at my sister, and she just smiled.

We drove towards Peterborough. He stopped at a chip truck on the way and bought some fries that we shared. He pointed out some tourist spots along the way that led us back to the trailer park.

He just hung around the rest of the day. I went into the trailer and helped my sister get things ready for dinner.

I was standing washing and peeling potatoes, and my sister all of a sudden said, "I think Sam likes you. How do you feel about him?"

"I feel confused about everything. I don't know how I feel. I just need a job, and hopefully his friends can help me."

She just smiled and continued on with making salads.

After dinner, the campfire was started and again people from around the park came over and sat and talked. Someone played a guitar, and several people sang songs as the evening went on.

As people dispersed for the night, Sam said, "I'll come over before you leave tomorrow just to say good bye."

"Alright," I answered

Once again I sat on the picnic table and watched the sky all night with Pepper. I hummed a few songs to try and make the night go faster. This is the loneliest time of the day. There is no other soul around, and you feel like you are the only one left on earth.

The fire crackled and sparked as it burned itself out. The dog and I sat and shivered. Even through it was now August, it was still cold really late at night. I could feel the dampness in the air as dew settled itself over the blades of grass and wildflowers in and around the park. "I wish I could sleep," I whispered to Pepper.

The next day Sam was back again as we were packing up. "How about I come by tomorrow and pick you up and take you for a coffee? I might have some news for you."

"Yes, that will be fine," I said as we walked towards the van.

When we got back to my sister's apartment, I called the kids and told them I was back and to see if they could come and pick me up at her apartment.

"Hi Mom." There was a hesitation, and then I heard Al say, "Do you want the good news or the bad news first?"

My heart jumped into my throat and I said, "Give me the good news first."

"Okay, no one got seriously hurt."

"Oh my God," I gasped, "What happened?"

"Well we were in the car, and we were stopped at the lights at Finch Avenue and Dufferin Street, and when the light turned green we started to go through, but we got broadsided really hard by a woman who couldn't stop her car."

"Are you sure that you guys are not hurt?" I asked

"Well, we all got hurt to some degree, and the doctors are recommending therapy for all of us," Al explained, "but the car has been totaled."

"Well, if you guys are alright, that is the main thing. We can replace a car, but I can't replace you guys. I'll get a ride home from here. I'll see you soon."

I hung up and sat and cried. This was like the final straw. My sister came into the room and said, "Jenny, what's wrong?"

I looked at my sister and answered. "The kids were in a car accident, and they all got hurt to some degree, but not seriously. The car, on the other hand, is totaled."

My sister tried to make me feel better by saying, "Well thank God they aren't seriously hurt."

"Yes, you're right. There is only one problem that no one realized up until now. I've been living in the car most of the time. Al would think I was at Jay's friend's house, and Jay would think I was at Al's friend's house, and I would just hang around them until they all went to sleep, and then the dog and I would spend the night sitting up in the car or on the front steps of someone's house. So I guess in some ways they not only wrecked the car, but they wrecked my house on wheels."

When I got back to Al's friend's house the kids were there waiting. I was so relieved to see them. They all looked banged up but reassured me that they were alright.

That night, when they all went to their friends' houses to sleep, I sat on the front steps of Al's friend's house and cried. I think I spent probably four hours crying. "What are we going to do?" I whispered in Pepper's ear as he snuggled into me for warmth, as the evening was cool. There was a slight sprinkling of rain, and the dampness of the night was hard to take.

The next morning I contacted the insurance company and told them what had happened. They gave us a loaner car to use for about a week. They said they would make out a cheque and send it to Jim, as he was the one who paid the insurance on the car.

I told the kids to contact him and tell him what had happened, and that they would need the cheque when it came, as they were the ones injured in the accident and they had therapy that they needed to get to, so they would need to get a cheap car just to get them around and back and forth to the doctor's and therapy.

Sam arrived the next afternoon and took me out for coffee. As we sat in the coffee shop, he surprised me by saying, "Jenny, I was talking to some people who say they know your ex. They warned me that Jim is looking for you, and that you need to be careful."

It became a daily thing that Sam would arrive to take me out for a coffee and tell about his friends who supposedly knew Jim. "You hear all the time about husbands killing their wives when the wives try to leave. You have to watch your back."

Then on Wednesday he said that his sister had word from the people who were wanting the wall mural, and that I needed to go and price it out. "I'll drive you up and have you back by five P.M. so that you can still go to your classes."

"Alright, let's do it," I replied. "I'll tell the kids where I am going."

He drove me to the address that he had been given in Peterborough. He sat in the car as I got out and rang the doorbell. A few seconds later a man came to the door, and I told him who I was and why I was there.

"Yes, please come in," he said as he stepped back, and I entered the house. He took me into the kitchen where his wife was sitting, and then she took me upstairs and had me look at a wall in their son's room.

"Our son is ten, and he wants airplanes and jets on the wall. Could you draft up something and let us see it, and then we can let you know if we will do it or not? We have just been thinking about it, but our son Jamie really wants it done, so we thought maybe it could be a birthday gift for him."

As I looked at the wall I thought about telling her that it was difficult for me to go back and forth because I was in Toronto, but I needed the work so bad that I didn't want to risk them getting someone else. "Sure, I can draft up something for you," I said.

I went back to the car and told Sam what had transpired.

"Well you draft up something, and I will bring you back so you can show them and hopefully get the work."

"That's so nice of you," I said, amazed that someone would go out of their way to help me out.

"My sister has dinner ready," Sam said as we pulled away and drove down the street.

I looked at the dash clock and said, "Dinner this late?"

Sam just smiled and said, "Ten o'clock is when I finally get to eat dinner most weekdays."

We got to Sam's sister's house, and as he ate I went to use the phone. I called my sister and asked her if I could stay at her trailer for the night, as I was in the area.

"What are you doing up there?" she asked, surprised.

I explained what was happening, and she said, "Sure, go over to the trailer, as my son Dale is there. He wanted to spend the week up there so we let him."

"Great," I said.

I went back into the kitchen where Sam and his sister where sitting.

"I'm going to go over to my sister's trailer and spend the night. Her son is there, so I can get in. If you don't mind just pick me up in the morning, and I will go back to Toronto with you."

Sam stood up from the table and said, "I'll walk you over to the camp-ground."

"No, don't be silly, it is less than five minutes for me to walk there. I'll be fine."

I walked down the side of the highway that led to the trailer park. Since it was a weekday, it seemed pretty quiet. In fact it seemed eerie with no one around and no lights or campfires going. It was nothing like the weekends, when you could hear music playing and see people walking around with a beer in their hands.

I walked up to the trailer and knocked on the door. The trailer was dark and there were no sounds inside. I was beginning to think that Dale wasn't there, and I had turned to go and sit on the picnic table, but finally Dale came to the door. Surprised to see me, he said, "Aunt Jenny, are you alright?"

"Yes, I'm fine. I am just going to hang out here tonight, but I will be gone early in the morning to go back to Toronto."

"Alright," Dale said as he walked back to his room. I guess I had woken him up.

I sat down in the outer room, which was a closed-in sun porch they had added on, and it had a sofa sitting up against one wall. I sat there for a long time. I finally lay down but within an hour I was back up again. I looked at the time in the kitchen and then went back to sit on the sofa again. This is better than sitting outside, I guess. Most nights now it was beginning to get really damp, and sometimes by morning my clothes would be damp from sitting outside all night.

The next morning Sam drove in about four am and off we went back to Toronto.

"You know Jenny, you are not safe in Toronto. You should consider moving out of there and try getting a job maybe up in this area."

"Well, I never thought about it before, but you may be right," I said

When he dropped me off, it was just around 5:45. I sat on the front steps of Al's friend's house. They would be waking up in about another hour.

Later that day I received a call that I could go pick up the welfare cheque that day, and that meant we could now move into the basement apartment we had found.

Later that day we started to move our things in. We set up with Bell to get a phone installed, and they gave us the number right away.

Jay arrived late that day from his friend's house, and I asked him where he had been.

"I was over at Vanna's house because her mother wanted us to do some stuff for her."

"Jay, I needed you to help us out today as well."

I felt really hurt that he thought her mother was more important than his. I told myself that due to lack of sleep I was becoming too sensitive.

The kids all went off to their friends or sports or whatever they had scheduled, and I sat in the apartment wondering how I was going to do this. I looked around me and felt lost and began to panic.

The kids came back late that night. They all got ready for bed, talking and laughing and acting as if everything was alright. I wondered how they could feel that way. I was so scared about what was ahead of us. I tried to push all the negative feelings away and concentrate on something positive. I decided I was going to take another paralegal course as soon as I could.

We had a few dollars left after paying the rent, and the next day I went to get a few groceries. This was not going to last us long, but it was at least it was a start.

The weekend came, and my sister picked me up again to go to her trailer. Sam arrived the next day and said he thought one of his friends had a lead on a job. I got so excited. Maybe things will work out, I thought to myself.

Sam hung around and then asked me out to dinner that night. "I know this really good fish place in Peterborough. I think you would like it."

"Alright," I said as I turned to go and tell my sister where I was going.

"Enjoy the fish," she said as she waved good bye.

We ordered our dinner, and while we were waiting for the food to arrive, Sam said, "You are so pretty. Your ex is crazy to have treated you so badly."

I sat there a moment and thought, I feel really uncomfortable, I can't remember the last time someone gave me a compliment.

I looked down at the table, not knowing how to respond.

Sam seemed to pick up on my discomfort and said, "Sorry, I didn't mean to make you uncomfortable."

The waiter arrived then, and it gave us something to concentrate on other than the awkward moment.

When Sam took me back to my sister's trailer, he got out of the car when I did. I walked over to the picnic table and put my purse down. My sister and her husband were sitting around the campfire with a few of the other campers.

"How was dinner?" my sister asked.

"The fish was really good," I answered as I sat down at the picnic table. Sam sat down across from me, and we both were quiet as we watched the flames of the campfire as they danced and flickered in the soft breeze.

Later people started going back to their trailers, and my sister and brother-in-law went into their trailer for the night. Sam continued to sit, not saying anything for a long time and then finally he said, "Well, I think I'll go." With that he stood up and came around to where I was sitting. He bent over and kissed me lightly and then walked away. I watched as he drove off. I had no real thoughts or emotions at this moment.

The next morning, we were just about to leave when Sam arrived and said, "I'll be in touch with you to let you know what is happening."

"Oh here, I forgot I have a phone now." I handed him a piece of paper saying, "Here is the number, and you can call and let me know. The kids and I also moved into our apartment." I then gave him the address as well.

Isabell and her husband Rob dropped me off at the apartment. This coming week was when we were going to be down at the exhibition. I washed a few clothes by hand and hung them up to dry. I figured I was going to need them to wear for the week.

The next morning Al and I went to his friend's house, and we got a ride down to the exhibition. We helped to get the displays set up and talked to people as they arrived at the booth. On the first day I made a sale with the help of Al's friend's father. I could not have done it alone, but it did feel good about at least having made a sale.

All day long people came and went to the booth. I took a break a couple of times and walked around to see the other displays that were there in the same building. It was a long day, and I felt completely exhausted when we left for the day. We took the transit back up to our apartment.

The apartment seemed empty, as Jay and Paul where at their friend's houses. Al went to see some of his friends, and once again I was left alone with my thoughts and fears. I washed out a few more clothes and tried to clean up as best I could. All of us were living out of our suitcases, as we didn't have any closets or dressers to put our clothes in.

It was about six o'clock when the phone rang. I picked it up, and it was Sam on the other end.

"Jenny, I need your help. I got hurt at work today. I fell and broke my ankle. I'm in so much pain that I won't be able to drive home tonight. Could I stay at your apartment with you and the kids?"

I didn't feel good about it, but I felt like he had done so much for me by trying to find me a job that I felt I had no choice but to say yes.

"Yes, come on over and we will put you up for the night."

"Great, I really appreciate it. I'll be there soon." With that he hung up.

Paul came in, and I told him what had happened, and he said it was fine with him.

About half an hour later Sam arrived. I let him in and he sat at the table and showed me his ankle. He was walking with crutches, and he took a couple of painkillers when he sat down. I made a coffee for him.

"As you can see, it is not much of an apartment, and we don't have much furniture. You are going to have to sleep on the floor on a blanket," I said.

"That's fine," he said. "I would never make it home tonight."

Within an hour Sam was feeling drowsy from the painkillers, and I handed him a blanket and he went and lay down up against a wall. Around ten P.M. I decided to lie down on a mattress that was there on the floor. I left a light on in the kitchen so that when the kids came home they would see that Sam was there asleep on the floor, and they wouldn't trip on him.

I woke up the next morning and the kids were all still asleep. Sam was just coming out of the washroom and said he had to leave. I told him I was going to be down at the exhibition, and he said that if he finished at the doctor's early enough he would come down and give us all a ride home.

After he left I went into the washroom and got washed and dressed, and then I woke Al up so that we wouldn't be late.

Down at the display booth people were coming and going, and I talked to a few people and handed out brochures to others who looked interested as they passed by. Around lunch time I went outside and sat on the steps and lit a cigarette. Within a few minutes Al came out and sat down beside me.

"I didn't appreciate coming home last night and finding some guy asleep on the floor."

"I didn't think you guys would mind," I started to say.

"You must be kidding," Al said angrily. "I come home late at night, and there is my mother's new boyfriend asleep on the floor. Mom, I don't want you living there with us anymore. I want you out of there today."

"Al, he got hurt at work," I tried to explain.

"I don't want to hear your excuses. I just want you out of there," he said as he got up and walked back into the building.

I sat there, shocked. I didn't know what to do. I had not expected this, and I felt like someone had just knocked the wind out of me. My heart felt like someone had taken my heart and twisted it and then threw it up against a wall. I continued to sit there and fought the tears that kept welling up in my eyes. It took about half an hour to gain some composure. I thought I had myself pulled together, and I went inside and tried to find Al so I could try to explain everything that had happened, but I didn't see him. I hung around the booth, but he had gone off somewhere, probably so that he could avoid me.

Sam did arrive later in the afternoon. We went for a coffee, and I told him what had happened and said, "I don't know what to do."

Sam listened and then said, "Well, you should move out for a while and give him a chance to cool down. In the meantime maybe you can find a decent job not trying to rely on one sale to pay the bills."

"Where I am going to go now?" I said, close to tears. "I have no money and no place to go. I think I will try to work it out with the kids, after all I really have done nothing wrong."

"No, you did nothing wrong, but the kids are upset about you and their dad breaking up. Everything is uncertain for them. They need time to adjust. You just need to give them some time to accept what is happening."

"I guess what you are saying makes sense. I can't think straight. I feel like I am in a bad dream and I can't wake up, no matter how hard I try. I feel so exhausted. I really have not had much sleep in weeks, and I don't trust making decisions right now." I put my forehead in my hands and said, "I've had a headache for weeks."

"Then let me make the decision for you. You need to go someplace and just rest. Your kids need time to work things out for themselves, and so do you."

"Where am I going to go?" I asked.

"I have been thinking about moving out of my sister's house and getting my own place. I will find a place, and you can move in with me until you work things out."

"I don't know if that's such a good idea." I said

"Well do you have a better idea? Where do you want to go?"

"I'll think about it and let you know tomorrow," I responded as I looked away at people walking around laughing and talking.

I went back to the apartment at the end of the day. As I walked up the street and neared the house, I noticed that a vehicle was parked in front of the house. As I neared the car Jim opened the door and got out. I stopped in my tracks and watched as he walked towards me. I slowly looked around, but I didn't see anyone walking on the street.

"I've been waiting for you," Jim said as he got closer.

"What do you want?" I asked, trying to keep my voice from quivering.

"I want you and the kids to come home now. This is ridiculous. You can't survive without me. You've had time to learn a lesson, and now it's time to come home. My mom misses you and told me to tell you she wants you back."

"Tell your mother I miss her too, but I'm not coming back."

"Are you crazy?" Jim asked. "You know you won't make it on your own. So let's stop playing games and just come back now. I'll help you get your things together and drive you back."

I just gave him a look and then tried to walk past him toward the house.

Jim caught my arm as I tried to pass and squeezed it. "Don't make a scene. I'm here to take you home. The kids can come when they are ready. They are all at their friends' houses right now."

I pulled my arm away from him. "I'm not going anywhere with you."

Again I tried to walk away, and again he grabbed my arm. This time he squeezed even harder. "You'll be sorry. I'll make your life hell. You are never getting a divorce, and if I can't have you then no one else is going to have you either."

This time I was determined that he was not going to stop me again. I just wanted to get away from him.

"Let go of me now. I will never come back. You really can't make my life any more hell than what you've already done. I have nothing more to fear. You wish to kill me, then do it now."

Just then a neighbor walked out of their house and looked at us. Jim dropped my arm and stepped back as I walked away and into the house. My heart was pounding. My head hurt, and I felt like it was hard to breathe. I sank into a kitchen chair and folded my arms in front of me and rocked back and forth. I could feel tears begin to run down my face. Maybe about ten minutes had passed, and the phone rang. I picked up the phone and Jim was on the other end of the line and said, "I'll be back."

I slammed the phone down. A few minutes passed and then the phone rang again. I sat looking at it and on the fifth ring I picked it up. I didn't say hello this time, but just listened. For a moment there was no one talking, but I could hear breathing and then Jim said, "Listen bitch, I'll make you pay for this."

Again I slammed the phone down. Almost instantly it rang again. I picked it up and laid the receiver on the table and walked away. About half an hour later I went back and listened for a moment and then hung it up.

Al never arrived home, and I knew he was avoiding me and probably waiting for me to leave.

Sam called about two hours later and asked, "So how is everything going?"

"Alright, I guess I'll do it. I'll move in for a few days, and we will see what happens in a few days."

It broke my heart to leave the kids, especially under these circumstances. I didn't tell Paul or Jay that Al had asked me to leave. I felt that Al would tell them himself. I really didn't know how to handle what was happening. I felt so mentally and physically drained, I couldn't think straight. Was I hurting them to stay?

I was really devastated that Al was acting like this. If he had allowed me to speak to him I was sure we could work things out.

Sam had found an apartment in Peterborough. I had an appointment to see the couple to paint the wall mural to give them a draft of what their wall would look like. They said they would hire me, but it would not be for a few weeks.

I tried to relax and feel comfortable around Sam, but there was something that made me uneasy, but I didn't know what. He was always so nice, kind, and considerate. I told myself that it was just me. I wasn't ready for a relationship, and I had told Sam this and he said he understood.

When Sam would fall asleep at night I would sit in the living room and just stare at the walls. I missed the kids, and this was not what I wanted. I was so torn apart, as I knew Al still did not want me around, and it broke my heart. I didn't want to be here. I tried to accept the way things were but I couldn't.

I tried to get ahold of the kids at the apartment, but no one was ever there. I tried to call their friends, and I was told that they had seen them and they seemed to be doing fine.

I worked on the wall mural and finished it. When they handed me the money I put it in my purse with the thought that I would now buy the second paralegal course and hopefully pass.

Sam drove me back a couple of times, but I never really saw the kids. I would go from their friend's house to friend's house, but I would never find them. I'd leave messages but still I was unable to make contact.

School started and the kids all went back to school, and at this point I was doing another wall mural in Peterborough and that just gave me enough money to help buy some food and pay some bills.

I finally got the next part of the course and started reading and studying every time I got a chance. It helped to keep my mind occupied, and I was hoping that if I ever finished the course the kids would finally have a reason to be proud of me.

The first few times I talked to the kids, I tried to convince them to go back with their dad; at least they would have a roof over their heads and food in their bellies. They did eventually go back, and I was relieved. I knew Al did not want me around, and Jay was not speaking to me any more either.

Eventually Al moved out of the house and got his own apartment. He needed his space. He never said, but I can just imagine that things did not get any easier after I was gone.

I felt like I had totally lost everything. Nothing meant anything to me anymore. I didn't have my kids. They all seemed not to want anything to do with me. Paul would speak to me once in a while but not very often.

After about two months, I had made enough on several wall murals that we were able to find a better place to live. We rented a bungalow on a highway just outside the small town of Norwood.

Winter set in and it was bitter cold, especially for me because I didn't have a winter coat. I wore a cloth trench coat all winter. I didn't have winter boots and walked around in just a pair of dress shoes I had worn when I left Jim in July, and by January I was very ill with pneumonia.

Sam was acting weird. Every time I spoke to the kids he would question me as to what we were discussing. Then one day with no warning, he just exploded and began yelling, "You're planning on leaving me, aren't you?"

"No, where did you get that from?" I asked, surprised. I had been sitting on the sofa reading a book when he started.

He rushed over to the sofa and grabbed me. "I see why your husband beat you. You're secretive and you can't be trusted."

I was totally shocked, as I had not expected this to be happening at all. He stood up and pulled me to my feet and screamed into my face, "Admit it, you're planning on leaving."

"I don't know why you are acting like this, but you had better stop now or yes I will leave," I said. "I left my family because I was being abused. Trust me, I'll never stay in another abusive relationship again."

He seemed to change as soon as I said that. His face changed, and he let go of me. He stepped back and said, "I'm really sorry. I don't know what got into me."

I walked away from him and tried to get my thoughts clear. I looked at him as if it was the first time I was really seeing him. I thought to myself that I had read somewhere that women, when they leave an abusive relationship, will a lot of the times get into another abusive relationship right away.

I realized I had to be truthful to myself, and I did not want to be in this relationship. I was not comfortable. I always had a feeling of distrust and deep down inside that I really did not like this person very much. He had just been someone who was there when I needed someone, and I was grateful for that, but really I was not happy and I just wanted out.

Sam never mentioned it again and I didn't either, but it was always at the back of my mind now, and I didn't trust him after that.

My landlord Frank lived next door, and he stopped in daily to talk. He lived alone, and he would knock on the door and then come in and sit down. We would discuss politics, what was happening in the area, and he would try to give advice on where to try and find a job. He had a girlfriend who he was having problems with and sometimes would tell us what was happening, saying he needed a female's point of view. I enjoyed his visits, and while he was around I found that I felt relaxed.

Frank would often ask how I was doing with the paralegal courses and encourage me to keep up with my studies. "You are really smart, and you can do it if you want to."

It was refreshing to have someone encourage me. I really appreciated that.

One day as he stood in my living room, he said, "I want you to come with me to meet the lady living next door. I know you two will like each other."

"Alright, "I said as I grabbed my jacket. I looked at Sam and said, "I'll be back in a few minutes."

As Frank and I walked over to my neighbor's house, Frank said, "Do you want to tell me what on earth you are doing with that guy? He looks like an idiot, and you deserve a lot better than that."

I was shocked and looked up at Frank and was about to say something when he jumped in and said, "I'm sorry, I didn't have the right to say that." Just then we arrived at my neighbor's door. Frank knocked loudly on the door, saying, "She's deaf, and you have to knock loudly." He was just about to knock again when suddenly she opened the door. She smiled and opened the door.

"Eva, this is Jenny, the girl I told you about who has moved in next door to you." Frank said, giving the introduction.

Eva grabbed me and pulled me into the house where she gave me a big hug and said, "I am so happy to finally meet you. Frank has told me all about you, and I've been wanting to meet you. Please come in and have a seat."

We followed her into the living room and sat on chairs opposite the armchair she sat in.

She picked up some knitting and said, "I've been knitting mittens for the kids at the local school. I do it every year." She held up a pair of mittens, and I could see that she was doing a beautiful job on them.

"They are beautiful," I said as I picked up one and admired her work. "Not one stitch missing. If I did this, there would be big holes everywhere."

We sat and talked with Eva for about an hour, and then I could see she was getting tired and I said to Frank that I thought we should go. As we stood up to leave, she came over to me and gave me another hug and said, "You and I are going to be great friends."

"Please come over any time you want," I said as I walked to the door.

"She really liked you," Frank said as we walked back to the house.

"I like her too. She is a lovely person." I said, smiling.

"I'll say goodnight to you then," Frank said.

"Good night," I replied and started to walk away.

"I'm sorry for what I said before," Frank said. "I have no right to say anything about anybody when I have my own problems." With that he walked away and left me standing there wondering what he meant.

When I went into the house, Sam was on the phone talking to someone. There was an old girlfriend that would call him or he would call her, so I assumed this was probably who he was talking to. I went into the kitchen and made myself a coffee. I looked over at Sam and beckoned to him if he wanted a coffee. He shook his head no and continued talking. I took my coffee and went into the bedroom and got changed and ready to go take a shower.

When I came out of the washroom Sam was off the phone and had left the house. I went to look out the window and saw that the car was gone. I sat down and turned the TV on. I watched TV for about an hour and then turned if off. I got up off the sofa and walked round the house, wondering if there was something to give me a clue as to where Sam had gone. I found nothing, and I decided to go stand outside to get some fresh air. As I went around the front of the house I found Frank sitting at a picnic bench that he had in front of his place. I walked over and said, "Is this a private party or can anyone join in?"

Frank smiled and said, "Please sit down; I would enjoy the company. Where did Sam rush off too?"

"I have no idea. I was in the bath when he left, and he never left me a note, so I don't know what is happening."

"Well I was sitting here when he came out, and he seemed in a big hurry." Frank said as he looked at me with a questioning look.

I shrugged my shoulders and said, "I guess he'll tell me when he gets back."

Frank and I sat at the picnic table for several hours. He told me all about his life and some of his dreams. I was surprised to hear that he had helped to build the very first Batman car with one other man. He got up and went inside and came back out with a photo album and showed me several photos of the car being built in different stages.

"Wow," I said as I looked at the photos. "You just never know who you are going to meet and where you will meet them."

"That's true," he said. "I would never have thought that I would sit in my office, and I would have the woman I would fall in love with just walk in off the street and ask me to rent my house out to her."

I sat there, stunned. I didn't know what to say. I didn't know how to act. I looked at him trying to figure out if he was joking, but he had a very serious look on his face. He tipped his beer bottle towards me and said, "You have no idea how I feel about you. Do you remember the day you came here, my friend Steve was here as well. We had been to the legion and he came back with me to have a sandwich and just talk. After you had come and gone, I turned to Steve and said that is the woman of my dreams. I am going to make her mine. Steve laughed at me and said it would never happen."

My heart was beating really fast as I watched Frank telling me this. I didn't know what to say or do.

"I believe in love at first sight," Frank continued on. "Sometimes there is a reason for everything, and I believe there is a reason you walked into my life."

Just then I heard a car pull into the driveway, and I turned to look and saw that it was Sam coming back. I sat there a moment and wondered what I was supposed to say.

"It's alright Jenny, I know you think you are with that guy, but I think you also know he is a big mistake."

I stood up, still feeling shocked. "I'll see you tomorrow," I stammered as I started to walk away. I walked over to the house, and Sam was already inside.

"I went out for a while," Sam said as I walked through the door.

"Yes, I noticed," I said as I went over to the sofa and sat down. "What happened that you had to leave in such a hurry and couldn't leave me a message?"

"That phone call had been my ex-girlfriend, and she wanted to meet with me to talk." Sam said as he walked up the hallway to the washroom. He went inside and closed the door.

I sat on the sofa and thought to myself, this just feels like I am back living with Jim again. Sam came out of the washroom a few minutes later and walked into the living room and turned the TV on.

"Well I'm tired," I said and I got up and went to bed. I laid there thinking about what Frank had said. I really liked him, but I was not going to keep moving from one mistake to another. I rolled over and tried to sleep but I couldn't. I couldn't get Frank's face out of my mind, and the look he had when he said, "You have no idea how I feel about you."

The next evening the phone rang, and I answered it, and Paul was on the other end of the line. "Mom, is there any way I can come and stay with you for a few days? I just need to get away."

"Why, what is happening?"

"Well you know we all moved home with Dad. He doesn't buy any food, and he won't give us a key to get into the house, so if we come home when he's not here then we have to sit outside and wait for him."

"Well, tomorrow is Friday, and you can come and stay for the weekend if you want."

"Yes, I would like that."

I looked over at Sam, who was sitting reading a magazine and listening to the TV.

"Sam, would you mind driving me down to pick up Paul tomorrow after school?"

"Yes, that's fine."

"Alright I'll meet you in front of your school tomorrow afternoon."

"Thanks Mom, I'll see you then. Love you, bye."

We hung up and I went down the hallway to go to the bedroom.

We left around lunchtime the next day and arrived at the high school just as the kids were getting out of class and making their way to the parking lot in front of the school.

Paul finally came out of the school and made his way over to the car and climbed in the back seat. We stopped and picked up a hamburger and drink for Paul to eat, knowing that he probably did not eat that day.

When we arrived back at the house a couple of hours later, Paul sank onto the sofa and began telling me what his father was acting like and putting him through. "Sometimes, I find that he is standing over me when I'm sleeping like he used to do. Then there are other times that he is screaming about something, and I don't even know what he is talking about. Yesterday he accused me of taking his socks."

"How are your brothers handling it?" I asked.

"They just don't come home very much. They stay at their friends' houses, and they play sports or they are working. Jay is working at a bank, and Al is working at a restaurant up near where we used to live. Mom I don't want to go back."

I looked at Paul and wondered what the right thing to do was.

"Paul, what about your school work?"

"I'll get the teachers to give me work and let me finish it here."

"Alright, let's see what we can do," I answered. I felt a sense of relief knowing that he would not have to put up with what Jim was doing.

On Sunday we drove Paul back down to Toronto and told him to get his clothes ready and anything he felt he would want or need and take it to the school with him and work out with his teachers the work that he would need. Then I would pick him up at the school on Tuesday, giving the teachers time to get Paul's work together.

On Tuesday we picked up Paul at the school and brought him back to the house again.

I introduced Paul to Sam's sister's son, Darryl. He was about the same age, and it would be good for both of them to have someone to talk to. They seemed to hit it off right away and started hanging out together.

They would go to Peterborough and meet up with some other kids that Darryl knew.

About two weeks of Paul living there, he brought a girl home to meet me. "This is Sally. She lives in Peterborough with her mom," Paul stated as he introduced us.

"Hi Sally. It's nice to meet you," I said.

"Thanks, it's nice to meet you too."

Sally seemed like a nice girl. She told me that her mother suffered from a split personality and that life up to this point was pretty rough for her and her younger siblings. She spoke about how her mother had tried to commit suicide. I could see where Sally and Paul would feel like they had a lot in common.

Paul began spending more and more time at Sally's house. "I'm helping out around the house because her mom is just having such a hard time coping."

One morning I saw the mail being delivered, and I called out to Sam, who was in the washroom, "The mail is here. I'm going out to the box to get it, and I'll be right back." With that I walked out of the house and opened the mail box. "Bills," I said as I took the envelopes out of the box. Then I noticed there was a letter from the paralegal school. Excitedly, I tore open the envelope as I walked towards the house. I read the print and saw that I had passed another course. I got eighty-three percent, which was alright. I would have preferred more, but I was happy just to have passed. One of the other envelopes was advertising, addressed to the home owner. Then another one was an envelope full of coupons, and the last one was the phone bill. Standing in the living room, I pulled the bill out and took a look at it, expecting to see about thirty-five dollar at the most that I would owe. I almost fell over when I saw the total owed was six hundred fifty-six dollars.

I stood there, shocked, looking at the page showing a lot of long distance calls. I read them all and saw there were three I had made to my kids, totaling, $10.35, and the rest I had been unaware that they had even been made. Some were to Newfoundland, where Sam was originally from, and the rest were just everywhere.

I looked up as I heard Sam coming down the hallway, and I said, "I just got the phone bill. There must be a mistake, as it says that I owe over six hundred dollars for a lot of long distance calls. I know I made three of them, but there are places mentioned that I have never even heard of."

Sam walked over and took the bill from my hand and read it over and then laid it down on the counter and said, "Yes, I think it's right."

"You think that's right?" I asked, astonished. "Where are these places, and why would you be calling them?"

"That's where my ex is," he said as we walked into the kitchen and opened the fridge.

"How can your ex be in all of these different places?" I asked

"Oh, she's a truck driver and she travels around from province to province, and then sometimes she drives into the States as well to take orders," he stated without any emotion.

"So why is it that you have to call her in all of these places?" I asked, still trying to figure out what was going on.

"Well, she gets lonely when she is on the road, and I just want to make sure she is alright."

"So do you have six hundred dollars to pay for this bill for being a good Samaritan to your ex?"

Sam came over to me and picked up the bill off the counter, crumpled it up in his hand, and shoved it in my face as he yelled, "I do what I want, remember that."

I started to walk away, and he grabbed me and pushed me into the counter and said, "Where do you think you're going?"

I struggled with him, and he slapped my face.

I pushed him away from me and said, "I do what I want also." With that I rushed into the bedroom and grabbed a jacket and started to go out the front door.

Sam grabbed me from behind and stood screaming in my face, "No one leaves me!"

He pushed me up against the door.

Frank had been outside and heard the yelling and came rushing over to the house. He pushed open the door and said, "What the hell is going on in here?"

Sam stepped back from me and said, "Nothing."

Frank rushed over to me and said, "You're bleeding." He turned and looked at Sam and said, "I want you out of here now." Then he took ahold of my arm and walked me over to the kitchen sink and put some water on a paper towel and handed it to me. "Your lip is bleeding."

Sam walked out of the house and slammed the door behind him.

"What brought this on?" Frank asked as he stood there watching me.

"I guess we had a fight over a six hundred dollar phone bill. He made a lot of calls to his ex-girlfriend to make sure is alright. I don't think I should have to pay that."

"Did you eat yet?" Frank asked.

"No, I'm not sure I'm even hungry."

"Well, come over to my place. I have a pot of soup on, and it's pretty good if I say so myself. I'd enjoy the company."

With that he guided me towards the front door. As we walked across the yard to his place, I thought to myself that this was probably a good idea just in case Sam came back and tried to start trouble again.

Inside Frank's place I looked around and was surprised to see how neat and tidy the place was. "The soup smells lovely," I said as I took a chair at the table.

"Don't sit down so quickly. You can help set the table and cut some bread that we can eat with the soup."

I smiled and walked over to the cupboard where he handed me some dishes and silverware. While we ate, Frank told me all about his mother and what it had been like for him growing up in Toronto.

I watched him as he spoke of her very fondly. I finally said to him, "You show the world that you are this big tough guy, and you are really a pussy cat deep down inside."

He looked over at me and smiled. "Don't tell anyone. It would ruin my reputation in this town if they knew that."

I helped him clear off the table, and he continued to talk about himself as if it was really important that I get to know him right away. "I'll help you wash the dishes."

"I can't refuse an offer like that," he said, laughing.

After the kitchen was clean and everything put away, I said, "Well, I think I should go."

"I wish you wouldn't. I've enjoyed the evening, and I could put on some old records and we could listen to music."

"You have a record player and records?" I asked.

"Follow me," he said as he led the way into his office and turned a light on. "Here it is," he said as he grabbed a few records and then opened a record player that was sitting on a stand. He put a few records on and then sat in his office chair. He pointed to a stool that was in front of a counter that was in the office and said, "Sit and relax. Where do you want to go?"

I took a seat on the stool and listened to the first record. "Frank Sinatra," I said as I listened.

"Yes, he was my mother's favorite," Frank said as he closed his eyes and just listened to the music.

"You miss her, don't you?"

"She was my best friend. I think of her every day. That's why I get upset if someone hits a woman. That woman is someone's child, someone's sister, or someone's mother. No man should ever raise his hand to a woman. Not if he's a real man."

I sat there watching him. Here was a man in his early sixties who missed his mother. Here was this man who displayed to the rest of the world that he was a big tough guy with a gruff exterior. He owned and often rode his white police special motorcycle, which was his baby. It was in mint condition, and he looked after it the way someone would look after a treasured possession.

He opened his eyes and caught me staring at him. He sat up straight and said, "You probably think I'm crazy."

"Actually, I was thinking how refreshing it is to see someone who honors his mother the way you do. She was a lucky lady to have a son who loved her so much. I hope that my kids will love me half as much as you seem to love your mom. I think it says a lot about your character for you to care so much about her."

He just sat and watched me for a few moments, and then he said to me, "I'm glad you feel that way."

"I have a confession to make," I said. "This was the first time in a very long time that I actually felt relaxed, and I thank you for that. I've enjoyed this evening." I got up off the stool and said, "I think I'd better go."

I walked towards the door, and just as I was about to push the door open, Frank said quietly, "I'm falling in love with you."

I stopped in my tracks and turned and looked back at him. Thank goodness he couldn't see all the butterflies that had just suddenly appeared in my stomach. "Good night, Frank," I said as I walked out.

I really didn't know how to deal with this. I liked him but I wasn't ready for any more relationships.

The next day Sam came home and said he was moving out. He packed up his things and left.

Frank came over to the house, and I said to him, "I can't afford to stay as I only get an occasional wall mural to do, and I have no other income."

"Just move in with me," he said.

"No, I can't do that. I went from my mother's arms into Jim's, and then from him to Sam, and now I am finally on my own. I have to work things out in my mind as well as try to find a way to support myself. I feel like I have lost everything. My kids really don't want anything to do with me at this moment, and I don't know where my life is taking me. I just know I am never going back to someone who abuses me. I can't live that way anymore."

I called my sister and her husband, and they came to pick me up. I stayed with them for a few days, and then I left to find my own way. I felt like I was imposing on her and her family, and I needed to get my life together and not depend on people.

I ended up on a native reserve called Curve Lake and spent most of the next couple of months there trying to get my head together and find out what I could do. There was a Native Artist, Norman Knotts, who had an art gallery on the reserve. I worked for Norman running a small restaurant that he had there for visitors. He would put his art work out every day, and sometimes he would leave for a few days at a time to visit a girlfriend—they had a baby together. He would go to spend time with her and the baby, and while he was gone I was left in charge of looking after his gallery and trying to make sales for him while he was away.

This place was something I had never experienced before. There was no hydro or heat. There were no washrooms, just outhouses, and there were no showers. You prayed for rain so that you could take a shower.

I slept in a teepee that had a dirt floor, and the dust was thick. The roof of the teepee was open, and you could actually lie on a mattress on the floor and look at the stars. There was a circle of rocks and stones that were in the middle of the floor, and you could build a fire there, but I never did.

Outside there was a fire pit, and every morning when I woke up I would sit by the fire and drink my coffee and watch the sun rise. I loved this time of day, as it was so peaceful and quiet. You could hear animals walking in the woods that surrounded the property.

Sometimes if Norman got up early enough he would come out of his art studio where he slept at the back of the building and he would join me. We would talk. He would tell me about his past and his future dreams for his art work and gallery. He had a good sense of humor, and his deep laugh would carry on the wind and echo off in the distance.

"It's so peaceful here," I said to Norman as we sat there one morning. "I think this is the first time in many years that I feel truly at peace. I needed to come here and experience all of this nature and tranquility."

Norman looked over at me and said, "That's what this place is all about. I have been an elder for years. People from many walks of life have come here searching for something that they need in their life. If I had electricity and modernized this place. then it would lose that peaceful, back-to-nature feeling. It's a good place for people who have lost their way."

"Yes, I can see that," I replied. "I feel like I have been lost my whole adult life."

"Well, maybe you will find yourself here."

I was there about two weeks, and Sam found out where I was. He arrived one afternoon and asked if he could stay in one of the teepees. Norman gave him permission on the basis that he not cause any trouble.

The next day Sam said to me, "I have to go to Toronto, and if you want to come along then I will take you to see your kids."

I jumped at the chance to go and see how they were doing. The couple of hours' drive going to Toronto was rather quiet, with neither one of us really speaking. When we arrived, Sam dropped me off in the old neighborhood where I thought the kids were still living. Sam went to a doctor's appointment and I walked around from house to house trying to reach one of the kids.

Finally I met up with one of their friends, who told me they had all moved back with their dad.

I knew there was no way I would be allowed to see them. I left a message for them that I would phone them the next day.

Sam picked me about in about two hours, and I told him I would find a phone the next day and call them.

We arrived back at the reserve, and he went to his teepee and I went to mine. Norman came over about an hour later and asked me how it went. I explained what had happened and asked where there was a phone.

"It's about a mile down the road inside a park; there are two phone booths there."

"Alright, I will go there tomorrow when I think the kids will be home and try to contact them."

"Good night, Jenny," Norman said as he walked away.

The next day I was running the cafeteria for Norman on the reserve and watching over some of his paintings he had outside.

Sam hung around, and it seemed he was just trying to be nice and even helpful when people would show up at the gallery while I was busy waiting on people at the cafeteria. Later that night, after I had closed the cafeteria and the paintings were all safely placed back inside the gallery, I started my long walk to the park. I looked at all the trees and how silent this area was compared to the city.

When I arrived at the park I walked in, and it felt a little eerie as there was no one else around. There was a pole with a light on shining down on the phone booth, but other than that there were no lights around at all, and as the night progressed the darker everything seemed to get, to the point that it was beginning to get hard for me to see a few feet in front of me.

I entered the phone booth and deposited the coins into the phone to make the call. I dialed the number of Paul's girlfriend's house and listened to the phone ringing, and then finally someone picked up the receiver and it was Paul saying, "Hello."

As soon as I heard his voice, I had to fight back tears as I missed him so much.

"Hi Paul, it's me."

"Mom, where are you?"

"I'm on a reserve at this moment trying to work things out."

"Mom, I can't stand it here. Sally's mom is giving us a hard time, and we just need to get out of here."

"I'll come tomorrow around lunchtime to pick you up."

"Thanks Mom. I love you."

"I love you, too."

When I hung up, I dialed my ex's house, hoping he would not answer. On the fourth ring he did answer.

I took in a deep breath and then I said, "May I speak to the kids, please."

I heard the bang of the phone as he quickly hung up. I stood there holding the receiver, and then finally I hung up the phone and walked out of the phone booth. Tears slid down my cheek as I walked away from the light on phone booth.

I became nervous as I started my journey back again. I could barely see in front of me because it was now so dark. With tears in my eyes, it obstructed my vision even more. I fumbled in my pockets trying to find a Kleenex as I walked out of the park. A car came down the street and then turned around and seemed to come after me. I felt my heart start to beat wildly, and my legs suddenly felt weak, like they wanted to give out from under me.

The car pulled up alongside me, and I heard Sam calling from the driver's side. "Do you want a ride?"

With a sigh of relief, I accepted the ride and got into the car. I told Sam about talking to Paul, and he said that he would take me the next day to get Paul.

"I feel terrible that I have nothing to offer Paul at this time. The best I can do is have him stay in the next teepee."

"I'm sure he will survive. and he will probably see it as an adventure. Think of all the kids that go to camp. This isn't much different, but he may need the peace and quiet just like you do, at least for a while."

"I guess," I said as I nodded. "I feel like such a loser to be in this situation at my age. It is not easy to start over again."

"You'll get through it," Sam said.

I looked over at Sam and thought to myself that maybe he wasn't such a bad person. Maybe it was my fault that he and Jim had acted the way they did. Maybe I make them act that way without realizing it.

Sam parked the car, and I walked over to my teepee. I went inside and sat for a while with my thoughts rambling over the past and wondering about the future.

The next morning I was up early again. The sun was just coming up and there was a dampness still in the air. I sat down beside the campfire and listened to the flames as they slowly burned themselves out. The birds were just beginning to sing. There were animals noises off in the distance, but there were no other stirrings from humans anywhere around that I could hear.

Norman came out of his gallery and walked towards the campfire and sat down on a rock next to mine.

"I like coming out and finding you here every morning. It almost is like something is telling me that I am going to have a good day when I see you sitting there."

I looked over at Norman and smiled. "That's a nice compliment," I said.

"Well, it's true. A lot of times the people who come here are fighting demons and they can't cope with life. You are here, but the demon is your past not your present, and you will survive. You have a good head on your shoulders. You're smart enough that you will make the right choices. I have no doubt that you are going to be alright."

"That's encouraging," I said as I smiled. "I wish I felt that confident about my future."

"Give it time, and you will feel the same way."

"Norman, I need to let you know that my son Paul wants me to pick him up and bring him here with me for a while."

"I think that is a great idea," he said as he got up and walked away.

Later that day, Paul crawled into the back seat of the car with Sally and we drove back towards the reserve.

Though Paul and Sally did not seem to mind that I had nothing to offer them. They acted happy to just get away from everything and chill out for a while.

CHAPTER SIX

One morning I was sitting around the fire sipping my coffee, and Norman came out of his gallery and came over and sat down.

"I've noticed that you seem far away lately," he said after a few moments of silence.

"I guess I have been," I said. "I've been thinking that it is coming time for me to make a decision on what I want to do with the rest of my life. I feel so at peace here, but this is not where my life should be."

"Where do you think you should be?" Norman asked as he looked at me thoughtfully.

"That's where I am struggling. I don't feel like I belong anywhere."

"Everyone belongs somewhere. Only when we are lost do we feel that everyone else has a purpose. You have a purpose. Your art work is beautiful. You have taught me things I didn't know."

"Wow, that is such a compliment, to think I taught the great Norman Knotts something in art." I laughed then, and he smiled back at me.

"You are welcome to stay here, and I will help you get a career in art, and I have the contacts that I can help you become well known."

I looked over at him, and I thought for a moment that this was such an honor. Here is this man who people travel from all over the world to see his art, and here he sits with me drinking coffee and watching sunrises each morning and telling me he thinks I have artistic talent, and he is willing to help further my career.

"I don't know what to say to you, Norman. I am so honored by your offer to help me."

Norman stood up and stretched. "It looks like the day is going to be a bit cool. The leaves are changing color, and the feeling of frost is in the air. Fall is almost here, another changing season." He stood still for a moment and then said, "Your life is changing, too."

"Yes, you're right, it is. I guess I just want to feel that I have control over the changes and make them be the right changes."

"What bothers you the most?" he asked. "Is there someone you are thinking about?"

"I'm not sure," I answered, "but I guess I should find out."

Within the week I found a small two-bedroom house for Paul, Sally, and me to move into. It was even farther from town, and it was a great distance to get to anywhere. We got settled in and tried to decide what to do next.

I spoke to Paul about Frank and that I did miss him.

"Mom, you should call him and see how you feel after talking to him. It doesn't matter that he is a bit older and not well. You just need to make the most of every day that you both would have together if that is what you both decide to do. You have my blessing."

I listened to the ringing of the phone, and I felt like I was having a hard time breathing.

I had no idea what the reception was going to be. For all I knew Frank was just going to hang up the phone when he heard my voice. I wouldn't blame him. I had been gone for five months with no contact to him, and he had no idea where I was.

On the fifth ring he picked up, and I closed my eyes as I heard his voice saying, "Hello."

I swallowed hard and said, "Hi, it's me Jenny."

There was a slight pause and then he spoke. "God, where are you? I have been looking for you everywhere. I've had friends looking for you as well. I've been worried sick about you."

I was shocked and touched that he had been looking for me. "I'm in a phone booth on my way to Peterborough. I was hoping you would meet me at a restaurant so that we can talk."

"Just tell me where."

"I don't know, there must be a Swiss Chalet in Peterborough."

"Yes there is, I'll meet you there. Just tell me when?"

"I'm on my way now."

"Wow woman, you don't give a guy much time."

I smiled as I hung up. He sounded like the old Frank. I realized how much I had missed him telling me stories about his past and all the other things we'd shared.

Paul and Sally drove me to the restaurant. We had loaded up a suit-case in the back of the car just in case it sounded like things were going to work out.

Paul, Sally, and I had rented a house on the reserve, and we had been living there for a while now. Sam was living in an apartment somewhere off the re-serve. I felt that I was a fifth wheel hanging around Paul and Sally.

I had talked to Paul about Frank, and he looked at me and said, "Mom, I understand your apprehensions, but you need to take a step forward and let the past go."

I looked at Paul and wondered why I was so lucky to have a son like him.

When we arrived at the restaurant we stood outside waiting for Frank to show up. As we stood in the parking lot, we saw Frank drive by. Paul and I jumped up and down, trying to flag him down, and then a few minutes later we saw him drive by again going the other way.

"What is he doing?" I questioned as I watched him drive by the second time.

We waited a few more minutes and still he did not arrive. We decided to get in the car and see if he went somewhere else. About half a mile down the road we saw him sitting in the parking lot of a donut shop.

Paul drove into the parking lot as I got out of the car and went over to Frank's truck. "What are you doing here?" I asked as I opened the door.

"You told me that you were at a donut shop," he replied, "but I have been to every donut shop in Peterborough and still could not find you."

I smiled and said, "Oh boy, I can see this is going to work," I laughed.

Frank smiled, "Well, where do you want to go?"

"Let's just go to the Swiss Chalet down the street. I'll meet you there and go with Paul and Sally."

When we arrived at the restaurant, Paul and Sally went to sit at another table.

"You two need time to talk," Paul said, "and we just want to eat."

We sat at a booth and ordered dinner. Frank looked at me and said, "I have looked everywhere for you. Where have you been?"

"I have been on a reserve working in a restaurant and in an art gallery. I have gotten to the point that I have to make a decision about what I want to do with the rest of my life."

"What do you want to do?" he asked, looking down at his plate that the waitress had brought, but neither one of us had touched. Then he said, "Before you answer that, I want to give you something." With that he took a ring out of his pocket and grabbed my hand and put the ring on my finger. "This ring was my sister's before she died, and she gave it to me. It is an eternity ring, and I want you to have it. My love for you is for eternity, not just for the moment."

I had tears in my eyes as I looked at the ring. "I don't know what to say."

"Just say you will give us a chance. Let me be the decision that you make. I will make you happy. I will never hurt you, and I will do everything I can to make your life with me the best you have ever had."

I sat there with tears still in my eyes. I never expected this much. "Frank, I…"

Frank cut in and said, "I have to be honest with you, and that may make you change your mind." He looked uncomfortable, as if he was trying to find the right words.

"What is it?" I was almost scared to ask.

"I have had major heart surgery, and I have certain problems that are associated with the operation and the medication that I am on. We will never be able to have a normal sex life."

I was so relieved to hear that was what he was worried about. "I thought you were going to tell me that you were married or that you had a sex change or something," I said, smiling at him.

He looked relieved as he laughed and said, "I'll love you in every other way more than any other woman has ever been loved. If you can accept that, then we will have a great life."

"I'd be a fool to accept any other offers."

"Oh?" he said. "How many other offers have you had lately?"

I laughed and said, "None, but I thought it sounded good."

"Let's go home," he said, laughing.

With that we got up from the table, our dinners still untouched. We walked over to where Paul and Sally were sitting.

"I have to thank you for bringing her back to me," Frank said as he shook hands with Paul.

"My pleasure, as long as she is happy," Paul said.

"I'll be in touch with you in a couple of days," I said as Paul stood up and gave me a hug.

Frank and I left the restaurant and drove back to his place. The house I had rented from him before he now had rented to someone else, and we began our life together in a one bedroom apartment he had built in the back of his office.

Tiny was not the word for it, but for the first time in my life I started to feel like I was wanted. That just seemed to make everything else so much easier to deal with.

Not having a sex life really didn't seem to matter. He was so attentive in every other way.

He would get up extra early just to make me coffee, as he knew I would be awake about six am, to have a smoke and coffee. He would sit beside me as I drank my coffee, and he would pick up the lighter and light my cigarette for me.

About a week after I moved in, Frank said to me, "I think we need to talk. I have to tell you something I probably should have told you before, but I didn't want you to think I was a big loser."

"I would never think that. What do you want to tell me?"

"I have not been able to keep up with the payments of this place. I haven't made enough to pay the taxes and all the bills. Therefore, I am behind in the taxes, and I run the risk of losing this place this year unless I can turn things around."

"How many years has it been since you've paid them?"

"This will be the third year, and I also have had to put some of my stock and items I needed for the truck on my visa card," he said, looking really embarrassed.

"Well I guess we are going to have to find a way to change things," I said.

He looked over at me and said, "I don't know how we can."

"Give it a few days, and we will come up with something," I said.

A couple of days later Frank came to me and said he heard about a chip truck that was for sale, and he knew someone once who had made a living off a chip truck during the summer and went to Florida for the winter.

We went to look at the truck, and we purchased it on the spot. We towed it back to our location on Highway 7. We took all the equipment out of the truck and had it thoroughly cleaned, and then we painted the outside and put shutters on the serving windows, and when we were finished we had one of the nicest chip trucks I had ever seen.

We fought hard and finally convinced the town to give us permits to run the chip truck.

Everything fell into place and we were ready to open for the long weekend in May.

"Here is the deal," I said the night before we opened. "We take enough out from each day to buy supplies, and the rest goes every Monday morning on the taxes and the visa bill until we have paid them off."

"Alright, I think that is a great plan," Frank said.

That first long weekend we made just over one thousand dollars, and I took out four hundred for stock to get us through the next week, and then just like I told him I went to the town hall and put three hundred on the taxes and then I went to the bank and I put three hundred on the visa.

Frank had run a sign shop from his office since he had moved in. He was actually very good at what he did. So when we weren't too busy on the chip truck, he would go back over to the office and make signs if he had any orders.

The first time I had watched him make a sign I said to him, "I had no idea how signs were made."

Frank laughed and said, "What is really amazing is that I had no idea either. After my heart operation I decided I needed something to do and be able to make a living at. I bought this computer used from a guy who was getting a new one. I purchased material from several suppliers, and I taught myself what I needed to know. Since I've moved here I have been able to build the business up a bit, but I have never been able to make enough to pay all the bills. I always thought it would be easier if I had a son to help me out."

After I had put the money down on the taxes and the visa, Frank said, "Let's go to the legion and celebrate with a beer."

"I don't really drink," I said.

"That's alright, you can have a pop."

As we entered the room everyone turned around and looked as if they were shocked to see us.

Frank went around the room, table to table, and introduced me. "This is the love of my life, Jenny. She has accepted my proposal and has moved in with me. Needless to say, I am the luckiest man in the world."

One woman looked at me and said, "You're a lot younger than Frank."

Frank jumped in and said, "No not really, she just holds her age well. She's actually older."

"Oh thanks," I said, smiling. Inside I was really smiling. I never thought I would ever experience someone that would be so proud to be with me.

Frank introduced me to a woman whose name was Helen, but they nicknamed her Fluffy. "That is an unusual nickname. How did you get it?"

"Well when I met Bob, I told him I was not fat, just Fluffy, and that is what he has called me ever since."

I liked her instantly. She was from Scotland and had a thick accent. Sometimes if she got excited it was hard to figure out what she was saying.

"We're going to be good friends," she said as we said our good byes that afternoon.

When we got back to the apartment, Frank cooked dinner. "I want you to do some of your art work, and we will take it into Norwood and Havelock and see if we can sell them. Even if it doesn't sell you are still getting some exposure." While I worked on the glass etchings, Frank looked after the cooking and the clean ups. He wouldn't let me do anything. "It is more important that you show off your work. I can handle the rest," he said.

Every time I worked on one of the glass etchings, I would cough and choke. I tried different types of masks, but they all allowed in some sort of glass dust.

I sold a few pieces in town. At the same time Frank got this idea in his head that I should paint a wall mural in the office, and that way any one coming in would see it. I agreed, and I painted a waterfall on a small wall.

Paul and Sally moved from the reserve and into Peterborough. They got a small apartment, and Paul got a job at a local factory. He worked long, hard hours. Sally stayed home most of the time, except when she visited her family who also lived in Peterborough.

Things where tough for the both of them, and within a short time they broke up, with Sally going back to her live with her mother. Paul stayed at the apartment and continued to work. The stress of living alone and working long, mostly nighttime hours was taking its toll on him.

I got a phone call from Paul the day before Christmas saying he was going to commit suicide.

My heart went into my throat, and I fought back the tears as I talked to Paul. Frank knew instantly that something was wrong when he looked at my face. As I talked to Paul, Frank caught on what was going on, and he dialed Al's cell phone. While I talked to Paul, Al was on the cell phone and was driving to Peterborough to get to Paul's house before he did something.

The long drive from Toronto to Peterborough is about two hours. Al drove as fast as he could and continued to stay in contact with us to let us know how much farther he had to go. We gave him directions to get to Paul's house, as he had never been there before. At the same time I continued to talk to Paul and made him stay on the phone with me and kept him talking.

Eventually Al arrived at Paul's house and talked him into coming to Frank's and my place for dinner so we could talk.

After the meal was finished, Al talked Paul into going back to Toronto with him. This made me feel much better, knowing that Paul would be with

Al and that Al would watch over him. I also knew that Al would try and make Paul talk about things.

Paul eventually moved back to Toronto and was working in a Swiss Chalet restaurant where he met the girl who would change his life.

When he brought her to meet me, I knew instantly that this beautiful young lady was going to be the love of his life. I also knew we would be the best of friends.

Frank had a good sense of humor, and he loved playing practical jokes on people. That made us a good pair, as I love to see people laugh and be happy. One day he was sitting at his desk, and he had just opened the mail and there were a lot of flyers and coupons in the mail. As he looked everything over he said, "I have a collection of envelopes in my desk drawer that have the prepaid postage on them already, as they came in the mail by different companies advertising. I have kept them thinking I could use them someday." He looked at me and said, "I also have a letter here that is a joke that I got from somewhere that I think we should do something with." He got up and went over to his filing cabinet and took out a letter that was supposed to be written from a Reverend James. In this letter the reverend was looking to hire someone who would travel with him to take the place of his last assistant who had died. The last person had traveled with the reverend and would sit on the stage and would make rude remarks at the audience, while doing even more rude finger and arm gestures. The reverend liked to use him as an example as to what drinking alcohol could do to someone. I laughed as I read it and said, "Yes you're right, it would be so much fun to send this out to a few people."

"I knew you were my kind of girl," he snickered as he got all the stamped envelopes down and put them on his desk. "Who do you think we could send them to?"

I thought for a moment and then said, "Let's send them to some of the people who go to the Havelock legion."

"Great idea," he said, laughing.

We spent the rest of the evening copying the letter and putting people's names at the top and then putting the letters in the envelopes, and then we were able to get most of the addresses out of the phone book.

Frank suggested the next morning that we should travel to several of the local towns and mail the letters so that way they would not all come from the same place. After breakfast we gathered all the envelopes up and off we went. We had about twenty letters going out, and we had three towns that we were traveling to in order to mail them. We dropped six in the post office box in

THE WEB

Campbellford. We dropped another six off at the Norwood post office, leaving us with eight to mail in Havelock. We were like two giggling kids as we mailed off the final letters. Then we waited with gleeful anticipation for the mail to arrive to our friends.

Two days later I met Frank at the Havelock legion in the afternoon. As I walked in I saw him sitting at a table facing the door, watching for me to arrive. As I crossed the room I could see a slight smirk on his face, and as I got to the table he stood up and pulled out my chair. He bent over and whispered in my ear, "You have to keep a straight face."

I sat down, and he sat down beside me. "Here, I got you a ginger ale," he said as he pushed a glass and a can of pop towards me.

I looked at him, and he leaned over close and said, "Just listen, as some of them have received their letters already. Some are sooo mad," he said as he tried hard not to smile.

Within a few minutes another person walked into the legion waving his hand above his head, gripping a white envelope in his hand. "I just got a notice in my mail box to pick up this letter. I had to pay postage on it only to find out some jerk mailed me out a stupid letter to work with him as his alcoholic assistant."

Others in the room began nodding their heads and confirming that they too had to pay postage to get their letters.

"Oh no," I whispered.

"Don't say anything." Frank said smiling.

The room became a buzz as they all compared their letters. It turned out that the letters mailed in Norwood and Campbellford went through fine, but for any letters mailed in Havelock, the people were then charged postage. I have no idea as to why that happened. Sitting there it was like listening to an angry mob, and they would lynch the first person they could get ahold off.

I had such a hard time keeping a straight face.

Frank pulled out a card from the post office and said, "Well I'm glad I didn't pick mine up. Now that I hear what you poor suckers have been through, I don't think I'll bother."

A man sitting at the next table turned around and looked at Frank and said, "So you got one too?"

"No actually I didn't, this is addressed to Jenny."

I burst out laughing at this point and said, "Oh, thanks."

The man turned around and said to several people sitting at his table, "This reverend character must be really desperate if he is sending Jenny out a letter. She doesn't even drink."

Frank and I laughed so hard at this point. When I finally could catch my breath I whispered to Frank, "I think we should tell them it was us."

161

He shook his head and whispered back, "no way, they're having way too much fun trying to figure out who did it. Why spoil it for them?"

I smiled and said, "You mean they will hang us both."

"Well that too," he laughed.

A few days later it was Halloween. I had never dressed up for Halloween before, but I felt like a little kid as Frank took me from store to store trying to find the best Halloween costume for me. "The legion is having a dance, and it will be a lot of fun, and you have to look great," he said. He finally decided on a long black dress with a long black wig and, of course, a witch's hat. "You will look fabulous."

He decorated the house and outside on the grounds. "We don't get any kids because we are on the highway, but kids do drive by with their parents, and they will appreciate the way it looks."

I just stood back and watched. "You really enjoy Halloween, don't you?"

He stopped tying a witch to a post and looked at me and said, "You have to enjoy life."

"So what are you dressing up as?"

"You'll see," he smiled and then went back to work decorating.

Around five P.M. Frank asked me if I needed the washroom for a while, and I said no.

He went into the bedroom and got a bag and then went into the washroom. I prepared dinner and set the table, and then I heard him coming out of the washroom. I turned around and gasped as he walked into the kitchen looking like a female. He had a long dress on, a wig, and a mask and a pair of female dress shoes. He twirled around and asked, "What do you think?"

"Wow, you look so different that I wouldn't know it was you, except that I recognize your voice."

"Well I am going to put a name tag on, but instead of a name I am going to put the name of a drink. Everyone knows I drink beer, so that will throw them off. I will point to the tag each time I want a drink," Frank said. "I will sit on one side of the room, and you sit on the other side and say you are waiting for me to show up later."

"Sounds like a good idea," I said.

Eva said she wanted to come with us to enjoy the evening, so she came and had dinner with us.

After dinner I helped him put his mask back on. Then I drove him into town, but I drove onto a side street and let him out, and then he walked back to the legion so that he would not arrive with me.

When Eva and I arrived at the legion, I went to get my usual ginger ale, and Eva just wanted a coffee, so then we went to sit down at a table where there were a few couples sitting already.

"Where's Frank?" one of the men at the table asked.

"He was helping a friend of his, but he'll be here later."

I looked around the room and was surprised to see that just about everyone there was in a costume. Music was playing, and everyone looked like they were having a good time. There were a few couples up on the floor dancing as I noticed Frank coming into the room. People watched him, all trying to guess who he was. I listened, but no one was guessing him.

As the evening progressed, people would stop by the table and asked me about where Frank was, and I always gave the same answer.

There is a man named Tim who goes to the legion all the time who thinks he is God's gift to women, and I saw him approaching me and I thought to myself, no please go away. When he got to the table he came over to where I was sitting and asked, "Where is Frank?"

"He was busy, he should be here any minute."

"Well, I came with a date," he said as he pointed to an older lady sitting and watching him. He waved at her, and she waved back. "I hate to see you sitting her by yourself. Would you like to dance?"

"That is nice of you, but I think I'll pass for now. I'll just sit here with Eva and wait for Frank to show up."

He looked a little perturbed but said, "As you wish," and he walked away.

A few minutes later I saw Frank stand up and walk over to Tim and tap him on the shoulder. Tim looked up and smiled. Frank made it plain with his hand in a circular motion that he was asking Tim to dance.

Tim stood up so fast that he nearly knocked his chair over. A big smile was on his face, and he looked around and pointed out to several people nearby that this tall creature of a woman had just asked him to dance.

A few people looked shocked, and I heard one whisper, "I wonder who that woman is? She doesn't know Tim."

I sat straight up and smiled at Frank as he looked my way as they proceeded to the dance floor. When they arrived on the floor, Frank grabbed Tim and pulled him close. Frank towered over Tim by about three inches. I watched as Tim's face shone with glee as he danced with this newfound woman who he thought was real hot. Tim slid his hand down Frank's back and grabbed his butt. The music came to an end, and Frank let go of Tim. Frank walked Tim back to his table with Tim in front of him, and just as they reached the table Frank grabbed Tim's butt. He then pulled out the chair for Tim and then walked away and went back to his own table. Within another minute Tim was over at Frank's table, trying to have a conversation with Frank.

Frank continued to not speak and just tried to act shy as Tim became more aggressive.

Then the DJ of the evening said, "Alright folks, we are now going to decide who wins best costume for the evening. Anyone who wants to take part please come stand up here, and everyone else will vote by applause who you think should win."

People from all over the room got up and went to stand at the front of the room.

Frank was one of the last to stand and walk up and stand in the row of about fifteen people.

The DJ went down the line and held his hand over the person's head and the audience clapped. When the DJ got to Frank, he held his hand over Frank's head, and Frank suddenly removed his mask.

Laughter erupted in the room as people realized Frank had been the hot woman that Tim had been hitting on.

Frank won first prize.

We left a short time after that and drove Eva home.

"I had such a good time with you two ladies," Eva said, smiling.

Frank nodded and said, "I'm glad you had a good time."

As she got out of the car, she turned and said, "I'll be over tomorrow to see how the first-prize winner is feeling."

"Good-night," I said, "we'll look forward to seeing you."

Eva stopped by almost every day, and she was quickly becoming my biggest art critic and also my best friend. She would stand back and look at whatever I would be working on and would say, "I like this, or I don't like that."

I appreciated her honesty, and I also loved listening to her stories of what the area had been like fifty years ago when she first moved here from the Ottawa area. Sometimes she would sit for hours as she had nowhere else to go, and she would watch me work and tell me story after story about the area and the people. I loved listening to her, and I looked forward to seeing her each day.

"So how come you leave your house every morning around seven? Where do you go and what do you do?" I asked her one day as we sat around having a tea and looking at a painting I was doing.

"Well my dear, I go for breakfast every morning to a local restaurant and have breakfast with a group of people I have known for years. We talk about what happened yesterday, what will happen tomorrow, and what we hope will happen," then with a big laugh, "but most of all we just talk gossip and enjoy each other's company."

I admired this lady, so full of life. She never complained, and she was always so very positive about everything.

Sometimes Frank would join in our conversations, and she would start something and lose a word and I would fill it in for her, or vice versa, and Frank would look at us and say laughing, "How do you two finish what the other one is thinking?"

Eva would laugh and say, "We're connected."

"That you are," he would say, getting up and leaving the room, leaving us smiling at his back.

I would call the kids at least once a week, and sometimes I was lucky enough to get ahold of them, but a lot of times I just got a click on the other end if their father answered. It was really frustrating, and I would usually end up in tears.

I could only hope and pray that they would phone me. I always accepted the charges every time they could call, but as a mother I could never hear from them enough. I missed them so much. I wished that the happiness I was experiencing they would someday have the same experience with someone that they loved. I prayed for that. I didn't want them to ever experience the stress of a bad relationship.

Their grandmother, Jim's mom, passed away. The kids called to tell me, and I felt really bad. I knew the kids would miss her. I also knew I couldn't go to the funeral, and I felt bad that I could not pay my last respects.

Within a few months of her passing, Jim put her house up for sale. The contents he auctioned off as well as any possessions we had. I told Paul to tell his father that the piano was mine, and I preferred him to keep it for Paul, but if he wouldn't then at least give the cash from the sale to Paul. Needless to say he never saw any of the cash from the sale of the piano.

The house sold soon afterwards, and Jim purchased another house and a store that his aunt had owned. So Jim and the kids moved just a few blocks from where they had been living.

He didn't run the store but rented it out to people, and then he also rented part of the house he purchased. He was doing well, but Jim was one of these people that no matter how much you have it is never enough. He measured his life and everyone else's life by how much they had, monetary and financially.

Paul and Sally had broken up, and he had moved back to his father's house.

One day Paul called me and was telling me a story of him and his brother Al sitting outside their home in downtown Toronto, and it was late at night. "We were sitting outside as it was a really hot summer night, too hot to be inside. Al just had a shower and was sitting beside me with a pair of tear-away pants on. (Those are the pants that have snaps up the side of the leg.) We were just sitting there and talking when these two guys went walking by. I think they were high on drugs or alcohol," Paul continued.

Oh no, I thought to myself as I listened to the story. I felt the palm of my hands getting wet with perspiration as I anticipated that something happened.

"One of the guys started yelling at us, 'What are you looking at?' Then the other guy started yelling obscenities. Al told them to mind their own business and just carry on down the street.

"The guy who had yelled the obscenities didn't like that, so he came up on the steps and grabbed Al and pulled him down on the sidewalk. I knew that Al could take him, so I wasn't worried," Paul continued. "I held the other guy back so that he couldn't get involved. Al and this guy are fighting back and forth. Al is wearing those track pants that snap up on the side of the legs. The guy fighting with Al, and all of a sudden pulls Al's pants, and the snaps let go and his pants go flying across the sidewalk, and all the cars are honking their horns and whistling at Al as he tried to get his pants off the sidewalk. The guy keeps trying to fight Al. Poor Al had just had a bath a few minutes before and had just slipped these pants on with no underwear on underneath, as he just wanted to have a cigarette and then he was going to go to bed."

Paul laughed, and I interrupted at this point and asked, "Was he hurt?"

"No he wasn't hurt," Paul giggled. "But it looked really funny, Mom."

I laughed as I could picture all of this happening, and I was also relieved that nothing serious happened.

"No one got hurt or charged," Paul said.

"I miss you guys," I said.

"I miss you too, Mom."

When we hung up I told Frank about it, and he got a big laugh out of it as well.

About a month later Al moved out and into his own apartment. He told me all about his apartment, and he took a lot of pride in making it look good.

A few months later I got another call from Paul, but this time I didn't laugh. "Mom, Al has been arrested."

I felt my heart go into my throat as I asked, "What for?"

"He had a fight with Dad, and Dad charged him, and he is in jail awaiting trial."

"Oh my God," I said. "Please tell me what you know."

"Well, Al came to the house to say hello when he finished work early on Friday afternoon and was having a pop and relaxing. He had another job to go to and was just relaxing until it was time to go to the next job. The guy who works with Al was with him, and they were sitting in the living room, and Al had a can of pop in his hand. Dad came in and told him to move his car, as the tenant he rents to is allowed to park there. Al said he was only visiting for a few minutes and then he would be leaving to go back to work. Dad called him an asshole and told him to do what he was told. Al stood up and Dad grabbed him, so Al threw his pop in Dad's face. Dad took ahold of Al and tried to throw him down a flight of stairs. Al managed to stop himself from falling all the way down the stairs by grabbing the railing part way down. Then Al left the house, but Dad called the police and had him charged and thrown in jail until the hearing."

"What jail is he in? Will they let me see him?"

"No one can see him until Tuesday, the day of his trial. They are requesting that you be there around eight in the morning at the Old City Hall of Toronto."

"Yes, of course I will be there."

Frank went with me and we sat for hours waiting for Al's case to be brought up to the docket. Finally they brought him in and they addressed his case.

"Is his mother here?" the judge asked, looking around the court room.

"Yes your honor, I am here."

"This case is going to be remanded for a day next month. I am putting your son in your custody. I understand he does not live with you, but he does work here in Toronto."

"Yes, that's right your honor," I said, looking at Al.

"Well, then you have to agree that you will call your son every day at eight P.M. He is going to be under house arrest. He will be allowed to go to work, but he cannot go anywhere else. Strictly work and home."

"Yes, I agree to call him, every day."

I had to put up bail for Al, but it turned out I couldn't afford to do it. So his friend who was there put up bail, and then Al was released.

Frank was not feeling well, and I needed to get him back home so that he could get his medication. We were looking at a two hour drive. It was now getting close to rush hour traffic, and I knew the ride could be even longer. Frank looked drained, and I just wanted to get him home.

"All right Al, we have to go, but I will call you later this evening." I gave him a big hug and kiss and left to travel back home.

At eight P.M. that night and every night after that, I called Al without fail. He was good about the whole thing. He didn't complain when his friends were out partying on the weekends. He stayed at home and did work around his apartment. He took pride in his place. His friends who he had since he was a toddler came to visit him and keep him company.

I requested if we could meet with the court and ask permission for Al to come up to our place for Christmas. The Christmas season was upon us, and I couldn't bear it if he had to be locked up in his apartment during the holiday and not with family.

Frank said to me, "If we have to take a mortgage on this place so that we can put up some sort of bond so that he can be here for Christmas, then we will do that. In fact if he needs me to take a mortgage to pay off his lawyer, then we will do that too."

The day came for us to be back in court. The case got remanded for another date, but I did get a chance to request that Al be allowed to spend Christmas with us. The judge looked over the paperwork in front of him and then said, "Alright, he can go as long as he stays with you the entire time."

"Yes, your honor, that is not a problem. Thank you."

It was arranged that Al would stay at his apartment and continue to work until a couple of days before Christmas, and then he would be allowed to take the bus up to our place.

I enjoyed having Al around for Christmas. It meant so much to me. After feeling like I had lost my family, it was so great to have him there. I enjoyed getting up and making breakfast and then spending the entire day with him around. I felt like I was on cloud nine the whole time he was there.

Frank wanted to take Al to the legion so that he could play pool or shuffleboard. "He has to have some sort of fun. Let's have a small party and invite a few people over. We can serve food and just hang out for a day. I know they are not his age, but it's better than just sitting here."

After the Christmas season was over and Al went back to Toronto, Frank said to me, "Your kids are like my kids now. They are my family, as far as I'm concerned. I'll do whatever I need to let them know that.

"I think we should get a dog, so that if anything happens to me you have something around that will protect you. What do you think?"

"I think it sounds like a good idea, but not because it will look after me if something happens to you, because nothing is going to happen to you. I think it would be good company for us both."

It was almost a year later, just before Christmas, that we finally got a beautiful little puppy. A sheltie who is a herding sheep dog. The breeder said he would be an excellent dog for us. "They are intelligent and are great family dogs."

"What do you want to call him?" I asked as we both stood looking at this little ball of fur running around the living room chasing the two cats we had.

"If you don't mind, I think Chimo is a nice name, as it means friend in Eskimo, and it is also supposed to be the national cheer for Canada."

"That sounds like a great name." I bent down and picked up our new addition to the family and said, "Chimo, you look like you will be a good friend. You suit your name."

That Christmas the kids came and spent the day. It was great. There was laughter and everyone seemed happy. They all loved Chimo, and the pup loved them and the attention that he received.

I finally found a job as a manager of a local resort. I was to work in the office as well as look after the staff and order supplies and do any trouble-shooting that may arise. I considered myself so lucky, as jobs were hard to come by in this area. It is basically a tourist area and also a lot of retired people.

The first couple of weeks I was introduced to the setup of the park. We needed staff for the coming season. We had another three weeks to pull it all together. The park needed to be prepared and paperwork galore needed to be done. My biggest problem was that the owner of the park lived in the park. The main office and store were in the house that he lived in and that created a bit of a problem, since he was never sober.

I would go to work every morning at nine am, and I would probably not see the boss until about lunch time or later, and when he did get up, he was still drunk from the night before.

He often would stagger into the office and stand over me reading the computer or whatever else I might be working on. The smell of booze would be enough to knock you over.

For the first couple of months I tried to work around the fact that he was just not a working part of this park. I tried to hide the fact that he was drunk from the other staff members and anyone staying in the park, but they all knew and were just being polite to me, allowing me to pretend that the boss was a little under the weather today.

I found that there were a lot of problems in the park and that someone had been taking advantage of the fact of him being so drunk, and things, including money, had gone missing.

Finally one afternoon as he sat at his kitchen table reading a newspaper and sipping on another drink, I confronted him and told him he had to sober up.

He took a long drink and said, "Well that's why you're here, to run things for me. I don't need to worry about anything if you're around."

"That's not true. You have to pull yourself together and take an interest in this park. There are a lot of things going on that you are not even aware of because you are having a liquid lunch all day."

"Now listen here, I don't need you tell me what to do."

"I beg to differ with you. Yes, you do need someone to tell you what to do. You are drinking yourself to death. If I'm supposed to pick up the pieces every time I come to work, then I deserve to know why you are trying to kill yourself."

"My wife died years ago, and since then nothing matters. My sons have their own lives and they don't have much time for me."

"Well, stop feeling for yourself. There are a lot of people who have lost the ones they love, and they don't have anything going for them. You are a rich man with this park to look after. You have staff and customers and you need to pull yourself together."

He stood up and said, "Alright, I'll give it a try."

I was really amazed and wondered how long it would last.

For the next few days when I got to work he was sitting up having a coffee, and he looked sober.

Then the weekend rolled around, and I never worked on the weekends. As I left on Friday, I looked at him and said, "Alright Harry, I'm on my way. Staff will be in the store until eight P.M. The maintenance crew will work all weekend. All the cottages are booked. Boats are rented out for the weekend, and it looks like it should be good weather, which means there will probably be a few parties throughout the park."

"Alright, I'll see you Monday," he said nodding towards me and then looking down at some paperwork I had put in front of him a few hours before.

On Monday morning when I arrived the house was full of smoke. I opened the windows and doors and tried to air it out. I called one of the maintenance men in and asked him what had happened.

"I have no idea, but Harry was drunk again this weekend."

I checked around the house and found that he had tried cooking something that now looked like charcoal in the oven. He must have fallen asleep, and it burnt to a crisp so that now it was undistinguishable as to what it was. He must have come around with the fire alarm going off and turned the oven off.

I went into the office and did some work. Around one P.M. I heard Harry up, moving around in the kitchen. He was trying really hard to look as if he was alright, but you could see he was hurting. His legs where shaky and his hand shook as he tried to pour himself a cup of coffee.

"What happened to you?" I asked. "You were doing so well. What made you slip up?"

"How do you know I slipped up?" he asked, not looking at me.

"Call it a woman's intuition," I said, smiling.

"I knew I should have hired a man for the job of working in the office," he smiled and then said, "Alright, I slipped up, but it won't happen again."

"Alright, we'll see." I got up from the table and walked into the office.

For the rest of the week I caught Harry trying really hard to make it look like he was sober, but he would grab a glass and walk into the bathroom. He suddenly spent a lot of time in the washroom. So much so that I and anyone else had to go out in the park and go to one of the public washrooms.

I gave him the week to try and work it out, but I could see he was getting worse again.

So the following Monday morning I went to work thinking that I would talk to him about counseling.

As I walked into the house I noticed there was blood everywhere, on the floors, on the walls, and even on the furniture.

I picked up the walkie talkie and called the maintenance crew in. "Does anybody know what caused this?" I asked, pointing to the blood.

They both stood there with blank looks on their faces. "Well, I want you to go in his bedroom and check on him. Wake him up and make him talk to you to see if he is alright. Tell him I want him to get up now."

I stood in the kitchen and waited as the two men went into the bedroom. A few minutes later they came back out and said he was getting up.

"Thank you," I said, "could you please get a couple of the cleaning staff to come in and start to get this cleaned up. We can't let anyone staying in the park see this."

Within about five minutes Harry walked into the kitchen.

"Good Lord, look at you. What on earth has happened to you?" I asked as I saw that he had cuts on his face, arms, and hands. He had dried blood on his skin as well as on the shirt and shorts he was wearing.

He stood holding onto the back of a chair and said, "I don't remember what happened."

"Well, go get washed up and changed. The cleaning staff is coming in to clean up, and they don't need to see you like that."

He turned slowly and walked into the washroom.

I gave the cleaners instructions to clean quickly and then just let themselves out. I went into the office and prepared to do paperwork and wondered how I was going to handle this.

When he got himself pulled together he came into the office. He was walking on shaky legs and needed to hold onto the wall as he made his way. I pushed a chair in his direction and pointed to it for him to sit down.

"You need to get some help. You're in bad shape, and if you like it or not you are not coping with anything. You can fire me if you want for being so blunt, but you expect me to come here each day and look after this place while you are on a mental vacation. I need you to straighten up so that I can explain to you what is happening around here."

He sat there for a few minutes not saying anything, and then he said, "I guess you're right. I do need to get some help."

"Well, I will call the hospital and see if we can you into some sort of counseling, and maybe you can try in the meantime to cut back a bit on the booze. I know you are trying to hide the fact that you are drinking, but you're not fooling anyone."

"Alright, you make the call. I'll do what they say."

I turned and looked up the hospital phone number. Within ten minutes I had an appointment made and he agreed to go, which really surprised me.

Harry went to several of the meetings scheduled for his alcoholism. He seemed to be getting better. They had him on some type of pills that helped him to stay dry. He was not supposed to drink and take the pills at the same time.

Friday rolled around and the park was alive with excitement, as it was a long weekend and the park was full with campers, cottagers, and trailers who had pulled in for the three days.

The staff was all scheduled and in place and looking forward to working the weekend. We had security working to make sure that the weekend was going to be peaceful.

"All right Harry, I have paid everyone for the week, and the staff have all been given their instructions for the weekend," I said as I prepared to leave to go home.

Harry looked up from reading a book at the kitchen table, which was his favorite spot to sit as he could watch who was coming and going on security monitors that were in the kitchen. "Okay, have a great weekend."

"I will," I said as I walked out the side door of the house.

When I got home Frank had dinner ready, a bottle of wine on the table, and music playing, there were even wild flowers in a small vase in the centre of the table.

"Wow," I said as I looked around. "What's the occasion?"

"No occasion, just the fact that I missed you and thought this would be a nice treat."

"Well you're right, this is a wonderful treat. Thank you."

He pulled out my chair as if he was the waiter serving in a luxurious restaurant.

Once he had me seated, he then pulled the napkin off the table with a flair and laid it down on my knees and smiled and said, "Madam, your dinner will be served in a moment. Please allow me to pour your wine." With that he threw a white dish cloth over his arm and picked up my glass and poured the wine. "Enjoy," he said, bowing to me and then turning and walking into the kitchen.

We talked small talk over dinner, and I told him I had set up appointments for Harry. "Well don't expect too much from him. It might work, but there's a bigger chance it won't."

After dinner we both cleaned the kitchen and then went and sat outside and just sat quietly, taking in all the wonders of the area. You could hear the cry of some baby wolves that where in their den in a mixture a trees just off to our right. The sky was clear, and you could see thousands of stars twinkling as the moon shone down on the surrounding area. "Do you want to have a campfire?" Frank asked.

"Yes, that sounds great," I said, nodding. I heard the phone ringing, and I ran to pick it up. "Hello," I said.

"How are you doing?" a familiar voice asked.

"Hi Fluffy, we haven't seen much of you lately, what have you been up to?"

"Not a lot. I haven't been feeling that great. I guess I have a cold or something."

"I'm sorry to hear that. We are just about to light a campfire out back. Why don't you and Bob come over for a little while, I would love to see you."

"I'll pass for now, maybe in a few days when I am feeling better." We talked a little longer and then we hung up.

Frank got up and walked to the back of the property. He picked up some kindling and went to work making us a fire. Before long the flames sparked and shone against the night sky.

Eva from next door saw the fire and made her way over. "I'm not intruding, am I?"

"Not at all," I said. "Please have a seat and enjoy the night with us."

As we all sat around the fire Eva asked how my day had gone. I told her and then we were all quiet again, each one of us enjoying the warmth of the fire.

"You know, I wish my kids could have experienced these types of moments when they were growing up. The pure peace and relaxation, with friends around a fire."

Eva said, "Well, it is never too late for them to experience what this world can offer. These types of moments are just as important for the soul as food and water is for the body."

"That's very true," I said.

The next morning I got up around 6:30 am. Frank was still sleeping, and I was sitting in the office having a coffee and watching the traffic passing by on the highway when the phone started ringing.

I jumped up and went to the desk and picked up the receiver. "Hello."

"Jenny, we need you down at the park right now. Harry has gotten hurt, and there are a few very upset campers that we can't calm down."

I was surprised to hear one of the maintenance staff sounding frazzled on the phone.

"What happened? I asked.

"Please just come down, and I'll explain everything when you get here. The police are on their way, and I think you should be here when they arrive."

I could hear Frank stirring in the bedroom, and before I hung up he was standing beside me in the office.

"Alright, I'll be there shortly." I said as I hung up.

"What is happening?" Frank asked.

"I'm not sure, but that was Nick from the park, and he sounds pretty upset and said that Harry has gotten hurt and the police are on their way. He thinks I should be there when they get there."

"Get dressed while I make your coffee and a piece of toast. I'll drive you so you can at least eat and drink something on your way."

"Thanks, I appreciate it."

I ran off to the washroom, and when I came out Frank was dressed and coffee and toast were made.

Frank dropped me off in the park where there was four or five staff members standing waiting for me. They all descended on the car as we came to a stop. As I stepped out of the car they all started talking at once.

"Wait," I said, "I have no idea what you guys are trying to tell me. You are all talking at once. Let's go into my office and get away from all the people who are now staring at us."

They followed me into the office, and then I turned around and said, "Okay, one at a time, tell me what happened."

"Harry had a few too many drinks again last night, and he was walking around the park and he fell into someone's campfire. He got burned on his right side, his arm and hand. They got him out and brought him back to the house. He went out again later and got into an argument with someone else, and he threatened them that he was going to kill them. Another camper heard what was happening and talked Harry into coming back to the house again. Then Harry went out again, but this time he took his van and went driving throughout the park and hit a couple of parked cars and did some damage."

"Well I guess he is probably sleeping now, as it sounds like he had a busy night."

"People are pretty upset, as he almost hit a little kid."

"Give me the people's names who are upset about all of these incidents. Also I want one of you to go in to his bedroom and wake him up. Tell him he needs to get in to this office now before the police get here."

With that one of them wrote down the information I was requesting and then the other one went to wake Harry up.

Jack, the maintenance man who went in to wake Harry up, came back in about five minutes leading Harry by the arm.

"Make some coffee," I told Jack as he helped put Harry in a chair.

Harry winced with pain as he sat down.

"You look like hell," I said. "What have you been doing?"

"I don't know what you're talking about," Harry answered as he looked down at his burnt side arm and hand.

"Stand up and take your shirt off. Do you have any medication for burns in the house?"

"Maybe in the medicine cabinet," he replied as he tried to stand.

Jack came back into the office with a coffee and handed it to Harry. Harry made a face and put the coffee down on the desk.

"Please Jack, can you help Harry stand up and take his shirt off. I am going to go look in the medicine cabinet for something for burns."

I was back in a few minutes with a spray I had found, and I told Harry to sit back down so I could spray the medication on him.

"Jack, go into his room and find him a clean shirt."

Within about ten minutes we had him cleaned up. The burns looked fairly sore, but maybe with the spray they might start to heal.

Just then another staff member came running into the office and said the police were on their way into the park now.

"What do the police want?" Harry asked.

"They are probably going to want to talk to you, as someone has laid a complaint that you were driving intoxicated last night and you hit a few parked cars and almost hit a child."

"That wasn't me. Someone must have borrowed my vehicle."

"No one borrowed your vehicle, and yes it was you causing trouble in the park last night. Tell me, do we need security to watch the owner of the park to make sure he doesn't cause trouble?"

The police arrived, and I said to him to go back to his room and let me see if I can deal with them for now until he had sobered up a bit more.

With that Jack helped him back to his room, and I went to the front of the house where the Police were waiting.

"Good morning officers," I said as I got closer to them. "May I help you?"

"Yes, we have several complaints that there were a few incidents here in the park last night."

"Could you please tell me about them, as I was not in the park last night? In fact, I just arrived a few minutes ago."

"We were told that the owner of the park has been seen driving, and that he hit several vehicles and created some damage. May we speak to him please?"

"He is asleep, as he is up most nights making sure that things are running smoothly. Would you be able to come back in a few hours, and I will make sure that he is here for you to talk to?"

"I think that we should…" He broke off what he was saying due to the fact that his radio went off. He walked a few feet away and talked into his two-way radio, and then he turned and came back over to me and said, "Yes, I'll be back later."

With that they both turned and walked back to their cruiser and got in and drove away.

I went into the house and Harry came out of his bedroom and asked, "So what is happening?"

"You are a very lucky man, and you have been given a few hours to get your story straight."

"Maybe I can talk to the people whose vehicles you wrecked and see if they are willing to accept a cash settlement. Are you willing to do that?" I asked as he stood there watching me.

"Yes, that is a great idea. Please talk to them and tell them I am sorry and that I will pay to have their vehicles fixed."

"I'll be back," I said as I walked out and found one of the people right away.

Within an hour I had talked to all involved, and everyone was willing to let it go as long as Harry paid for their damages. Then I went and spoke to the parents of the child that he had almost hit. "Harry is very sorry for what happened last night."

They looked at me and said, "Well maybe he didn't see her, as she is so small and it was dark. She really should have not been on the road at all, but you know what kids are like. They are unpredictable, and you just don't know what they are going to do next."

"Well that is kind of you to say," I started to feel like this was going way too easy.

"We would be willing to forget about the whole thing if he is willing to let us have our lot fees for free for this season."

"Well, I can tell you now that he will agree to that," I said as I got up and walked towards the door. I felt like that was a deal that these people should not be asking for. How do you put a price on your child for maybe getting hurt? "Well, I'm glad your daughter is alright and that nothing happened."

With that I walked back to the house and informed Harry about all that had happened.

"I'm out of here," I said as I walked over to the phone and called Frank and told him to come and get me.

Harry asked, "What about the police?"

"They will be back, and you stay sober until they come and talk to you. If not then you will probably get locked up anyway."

"I knew there was a reason I hired you. You're good at what you do. You are an asset to this place. Thanks."

"You're welcome," I smiled. "Do I get a raise?"

I stayed working as manager of this resort for five years until Frank got too ill to be home alone anymore.

I didn't mind giving up working there. I had promised Frank he would never end up in a home, and I was determined that I was keeping that promise. It had been fifteen years since he had his quadruple heart bypass, and the heart specialist had told him that due to other health factors he was not able to have another one.

I admired him so much, his strength and courage. He knew he was dying, and he still managed to joke around, laugh, and try to make every day we had together a wonderful experience.

"You need to get you driver's license. You need to prepare for when I am not here anymore. You need to remember that you can do anything you put your mind to. You're a smart woman, and you will survive without me."

I hated to hear him talk like that. "Please, let's just take one day at a time," I said, fighting back tears.

I had been trying hard to save money while I was working, and I said to Frank, "Do you mind if I get the outside of the house painted? It needs a new deck as well."

Frank thought for a few minutes and then said, "No, I don't, if that is what you want to do."

I purchased the paint and started preparing the house for painting. It was good therapy for me, as it gave me something to do and at the same time I was just a few feet away from Frank if he needed me. When it got to doing the top part of the house, I hired a guy from town who said he needed work. Within a couple of days he was gone, saying he had other things to do. I hired another person and finally got the outside of the house done. Then I hired a friend of Frank's to build the deck. Within two weeks that project was done.

Frank was sitting in the living room, and he had said all day that he was not feeling well. "Just a touch of the flu," he said.

He was sitting in a chair watching TV, and I was sitting on the sofa when he got up to go to the washroom. He seemed to stagger a bit, and I watched him walking down the hallway. He was in the washroom a few minutes and then he came out, and as he tried to make his way back to the living room, he acted like his legs were giving out. I jumped up and grabbed ahold of him. I tried to lead him back to the chair that he had been sitting in, but I weigh one hundred pounds, and I had a hard time trying to control him as he weighed about seventy pounds more than me. I got him as far as the chair, and I seemed to lose him. He slipped through my arms and went face first into the chair and then continued down onto the floor.

I tried to get him up, but he was of no help. "Frank, listen to me, you hold on. You stay with me. Don't you let go."

I heard a sound outside in the driveway, and I went out and flagged down a guy on a motorcycle who had come into the yard to make a U-turn. "Please, you have to help me. Frank has fallen, and I can't lift him up." He got off his bike and I was already in the house and on the phone with 911 when he entered. I told the dispatcher what was happening and that Frank was a heart patient. She assured me that the ambulance was already on its way.

I hung up and ran over to where Frank was still on the floor. The man I had flagged down was kneeling beside him.

"I'm glad you came out and flagged me down, Jenny."

I looked at him again as I didn't recognize him before, but now that he had said my name I realized we knew him from the legion in town.

"Strange that you were there when we needed you," I said.

"Yes, it is strange, as I should have not been here but I forgot something and had to turn around and go back, and that is when you saw me."

"There's a reason for everything," I said.

The ambulance arrived, and Frank was rushed to the local Campbellford Hospital.

Within a few minutes I was told that Frank had a heart attack. I was standing beside him, and he was hooked up to machines and heart monitors. Sud-

THE WEB

denly he took a turn for the worse. The nurse pushed me out of the room. There were doctors and nurses running from everywhere. I stood there shocked and then another nurse took ahold of my arm and led me out of the hallway and into a quiet room. I sat in the room for a few minutes, but I felt like I had to be as near to the room as possible. I got up from a chair and made my way back to the room that Frank was in. I stood quietly on the outside of the door. I could hear the doctors and nurses working hard trying to save him.

"Please God, let him be alright."

About twenty minutes later a nurse came out and got me, and I was allowed back in to see Frank. He looked so pale at this point. Our family doctor was standing next to the bed as I entered, and he said, "Jenny, we have to transport him to Bellville, as we don't have the equipment to look after him here. We need a machine that can breathe for him, and we just don't have it here. I have called the ambulance and I will go with him and make sure he gets there safely."

I stayed and waited until the ambulance arrived, and Frank was lifted into the ambulance. Our family doctor and a nurse both got in the back of the ambulance with Frank. The doctor held onto the machine that he had to manually pump by hand so that Frank could breathe until they got him to the Bellville Hospital.

I called Paul and told him what had happened. I asked him if he was working. "I was wondering if you and Mary could come up and stay with me for a few days until we see what is going to happen with Frank."

"Yes, we will be there tomorrow."

I went to the hospital that night and Frank had no idea I was there. When I got home I called Fluffy and told her and Bob what was happening. Then I sat in the bedroom and cried all night long.

The next day Paul and Mary arrived, and I felt a bit better having them around. Paul seemed to take charge right away and started cooking dinners and making sure I ate at least once a day. They both drove back and forth to the hospital with me and worried over Frank as much as I did.

Paul looked after chores around the house and property as well. There were a lot of things I had not been able to do and Frank had been too ill to do.

Days passed and finally Frank started to come around, and they eventually shipped him back to the Campbellford Hospital. He spent another week in there, but the day came that we went to the hospital to pick him up.

Paul knew that Frank had a sense of humor and that Frank had always joked around that when my kids came to visit we were left with an empty fridge. "They eat us out of house and home," he would jokingly say.

So Paul took a chain that he found in Frank's garage and wrapped it around the fridge and put a lock on it, and when Frank walked into the house that was the first thing that he saw. As weak as he was he sat down and laughed. "Well it's about time we stopped being left foodless."

Harry was in touch often, and when he heard that Frank was coming home he said that Paul and Mary could go stay there in the park. "I will enjoy the company. In fact I will give Paul a job, and if they want to stay when the park closes in the fall they are welcome to stay, and they can go back to school and finish their education."

Paul and Mary accepted the offer. They went to stay in Harry's house, and they called each day to see how Frank was doing and let me know how they were doing.

Paul worked hard during that summer, and when the park closed Mary and Paul decided to stay.

Frank was continually getting worse, and in January he had another heart attack. The doctor told him at that time that he had only about three weeks to live.

"I don't think so, Doctor. I will be staying around until my birthday."

"When is you birthday?" the doctor asked.

"It's in June."

"Well I hope you make it," the doctor said as he walked away, shaking his head.

Over the next few months I watched Frank deteriorate. It was very frustrating, as there was nothing I could do to stop it. It got to the point where the doctor wanted to see him every week, but he was not strong enough to travel the twenty minutes to see him, so the nurses started coming to the house and doing checks on him.

My girlfriend Fluffy had tests done to see why she was always feeling sick. She called me up and said, "Well you meet me for a coffee?"

"Yes, Frank is feeling alright today, so I can meet with you." A few minutes later I seated myself across from her in a local restaurant.

I smiled at her and asked, "How have you been feeling?"

"That's why I wanted to see you. I got the results from my tests done, and they confirmed that I have throat cancer. It is pretty severe, and they are going to be putting me in the hospital and giving me treatments."

I turned and looked out the window. It was late November, and snow was starting to fall and the ground was getting white. I felt like I was in a bad dream. Frank was sick, and now here was my best friend sick as well.

"I'm sure you can fight this," I heard myself saying.

"You don't have to worry about me. You have your hands full with Frank. I just wanted to tell you in person, not over the phone. I'm going to be fine. I feel very positive about the whole thing."

"I'm glad you feel positive. That is half the battle, they say. Your attitude is very important," I said.

We finished our coffee, and then I walked her to her car and I stood and watched her drive away.

I drove home with tears in my eyes. "Please let her get better," I whispered.

Within two weeks Fluffy was told that her cancer was in remission. I was so excited when she told me that. She came to tell me in person, which meant so much to me.

Then three weeks after that the cancer was back in full force. She was immediately put into the hospital and treatments were started again. She was receiving double doses of everything they could give her to try and fight it.

Frank had another heart attack, but they kept him in the Campbellford hospital this time. Fluffy and Frank both ended up in the same hospital and on the same floor at the same time.

I walked into Fluffy's room and laughed at her as she lay there in her bed and said, "You and Frank are at least making it easier for me this way. I can visit you both at the same time."

"You do have your hands full. Here you are worrying about me when you have so much happening with Frank."

"It's up to me if I think I want to worry about you both." I handed her some books I had brought her. I also had taken her in a small radio with batteries that she could listen to when she wanted.

Frank was sent home in about a week, but Fluffy continued to stay in the hospital. She was still receiving treatments, and she was feeling pretty ill from the side effects.

Frank was having his problems, too. He had lost a lot of weight, and he was feeling very weak most of the time. I would have to help him in and out of the bath. Help him get dressed and just watch over him if he needed anything. We were always checking his blood sugar, and he had to be weighed each morning before he ate and then again after he ate and then again at bed time. We needed to do this so we could keep track on any fluid that might build up in his lungs.

We now had a nurse come in once a week, and she would stay for about two hours so that I could just rest or go shopping or whatever I wanted to do. I would just go next door and vegetate mentally for the two hours. I was exhausted.

Paul and Mary came in for a visit and said, "Mom, you look terrible. This is taking a toll on you."

"I'll be fine," I said.

The nurse left, and I went back over to the house. Frank was watching a cooking show. "Look at this, she is cooking a pot of pasta, and when it was boiled she drained the water off and then she beat up a couple of eggs and threw it on top and put the lid of the pot back on. It looks really good. Would you make that for dinner tonight?"

"Sure I will," I said. It had been a long time since he had an appetite, and just the fact that he got a bit excited about some sort of food was enough for me to want to make it.

As I boiled the water and threw the pasta into the pot, I kept asking Frank if I was doing it right, making him feel that he was a big part of making the dinner.

While it was cooking I checked on Frank's sugar levels, which seemed fine, and then he felt that he needed to go to the washroom. By the time we got back and I had him seated in the living room, the pasta was cooked.

Frank was telling me a story about when he was young and his mom was cooking a special dish. At the end of this long story she had burned dinner and everyone went out to a restaurant.

While I listened to Frank I served the pasta onto the plate, and I got a tray ready for him.

"Don't forget to put the butter with grated garlic and cheese on top."

"I promise I won't forget," I said as I prepared his dish and then put it on the tray and took it over to him.

"This is terrific," he said as he ate almost everything on his plate. "I am really enjoying this. The egg makes a big difference. It's very tasty. I'm glad I watched the show and had you cook this up."

"I'm glad too," I said with a smile on my face as I watched him eat every bite on his plate. "You have done really well. That is the most you have eaten in a long time."

"Yes, you're right. I'm full," he said as he wiped his mouth with a napkin.

"So you really like that?"

"Yes that was great."

"And you think that the egg on top made a big difference?"

"Yes it really does. It gives the dish a really great flavor."

"Well I don't know how to tell you this, but I forgot the egg," I said, giggling.

"You little brat," he said, then he laughed out loud as well.

The phone rang and I answered it. "Jenny, it's Bob. There is no nice way to tell you, but Fluffy just passed away a few minutes ago."

"Oh, my God," I said as I looked over at Frank. "Is there anything I can do?"

"Not right now, I'll call you with the arrangements tomorrow." He sounded drained as he hung up.

I hung up and went over and sat down beside Frank. He sat looking at me with a questioning look. "Fluffy just passed away," I said, but my mind was not accepting the information yet.

The next day Frank had another heart attack and was put back into Camp-bellford Hospital. Doctor Williams walked in and checked him over. "You are a fighter, and you are doing better than I thought you would. By all rights you should not even be here now."

"I need to get out of here in two days for a funeral for a friend. I am not missing it."

"I don't think you are going to be in any shape to do that," the doctor said.

"We'll see who's right."

In two days Frank was checking himself out of the hospital, but we convinced him that he should take some oxygen with him and go to the funeral and then back to the hospital again. He was so weak, but he managed to get through the day and argued like a school kid when it was time to go back to the hospital.

The funeral was nice but very emotional for me. I had just lost my best friend, and I knew I was losing Frank also.

When Frank came home again he said to me, "I want you to sing at my funeral. You have such a wonderful voice. It is like the voice of an angel, and I want you to sing for me on that final day."

"Oh Frank, I know that is going to be the hardest day of my life. I won't be able to sing that day, as I will have tears falling all day long."

"Think about it please, as it means so much to me," he said.

I came up with a plan that I would borrow Paul's keyboard, and I would write a song for Frank and tape it so that it could be played the day of the funeral. So for the next week I worked on the song. Every day the nurse came and sat with him for about an hour so that I could take a break, so I would go next door and work on the song. When I finally finished it I taped it, and then I played the tape for Frank.

"Frank, this is the only way I could come up with a way that I would sing for you that final day. I wrote the song for you, and it is called, 'Heaven Needs An Angel.'"

Frank sat and listened to the tape with tears running down his face. When it finished, he said, "That is probably the most beautiful song I have ever heard. Thank you."

He sat for a few minutes and then he said, "I hope you do something with that song some day, as it is a song that should be played at funerals. It is so full of emotion."

"I'm glad you like it," I said, wiping a tear away from my face.

A couple of weeks later the nurse was sitting with Frank, and I was once again next door when Eva walked in and sat down. "You look awful," she said, then she stood up and came around to where I was sitting and touched my forehead and said, "You have a fever."

"I have been sitting here and thinking that I don't feel very well. I don't know what is wrong with me. I have been itchy around where my bra goes across me, and if I scratch then it hurts so much that I could just cry."

"Lift up your shirt and let me see," she said.

I stood up and lifted up my shirt and heard her exclaim, "You have shingles. I'm not surprised, since you are under so much stress."

"What is shingles?"

"Well, anyone who has had chicken pocks when they were young will have the germ of the chicken pocks still in their spine. When you grow up and you are under stress for a long period of time, then this virus comes out in the form of shingles. This is very dangerous, and people can die from this. I want you to come with me to the hospital to get checked."

A few hours later I got the official diagnosis from the doctor that yes, I had shingles.

"This can be very painful, and you will fell exhausted and sick to your stomach. You can also experience headaches."

"Listen doctor, I am looking after someone at home who is dying. I can't be sick right now. Can you give me something to help?"

"I can try, but you have had them for more than three days. The chances of stopping this are very slim."

Paul and Mary came over the next day, and I told them what was happening. I explained what it was and tried to explain what it felt like, but I could see the concern on their faces and decided they didn't need to worry about me as well as Frank.

As the weeks passed Frank continually got worse. He was on oxygen full time now. We had the machines in the house, and we also had the portable ones in case he had to go out. I also set up with the doctor that I had a hospital bed and other supplies that we needed to make him comfortable.

It broke my heart to watch him. He had gone from this robust man to someone now walking with a walker. One afternoon Paul and Mary were at the house, and Paul was cooking dinner to help give me a break, and Frank was sitting on the side of his hospital bed I had set up in the living room, and he was checking out his walker as he kept trying to figure out how the breaks work.

I got up and went to the washroom, where I sat with tears coming down my face.

This isn't fair, I said to myself. Here is the man who helped to build the very first Batman car, and he can't figure out how the brakes work on his walker.

I tried to pull myself together, but inside I was falling apart bit by bit each day. I felt that I should and needed to be strong, but I felt so weak.

As I walked back into the living room, Paul was just putting dinner onto plates. I went and got Frank's plate and tried to help him eat it. He really didn't want to eat, but I tried to coax him. He ate just a few bites and then his attention was back on the walker again.

I sat with my plate and listened to Paul and Mary talking.

They had been such a big help to me at this point. I don't know how to say thank you. I couldn't do this on my own right now. Just having them around made me feel stronger.

As we neared Frank's birthday I started to invite some of his friends that I knew he wanted there. I kept telling him that his birthday will be in another seven days, then six days, then five days and then the day finally arrived.

Paul and Mary were out shopping and getting things to set up for the party when my sister Isabell and Rob arrived.

"Isabell, will you help me get Frank dressed for the party?"

"Sure I will," she said.

I went into the bedroom and picked out some clothes I thought he would like, and my sister and I proceeded to get Frank dressed.

People arrived, and Frank seemed to start to come around. He realized that everyone was there and that we were celebrating his birthday. Some people went outside and sat in the fresh air waiting for the food to be served. Others played a lawn bowling game while others just sat around Frank and talked. Everyone seemed to enjoy themselves, including Frank. During the day one of our friends, Emily, took photos.

Early the next morning Emily came back to the house and handed me a photo album with the photos she had taken the day before of the party. That was probably one of the nicest things anyone could have done.

Frank was exhausted after the party, and when everyone had gone home, I got him ready for bed and he slept soundly all night long. When he woke up I asked him if he had enjoyed his party, and he didn't remember it. So I took the album Emily had brought and together we looked at the pictures.

A week later to the day, I woke up and got washed and dressed just like every other day, and then I went to wake Frank up to give him breakfast and his medication. I called Paul and Mary and they came over. The nurse arrived, and I had her check him. She put a call in to the doctor, and he said we should call an ambulance. Within half an hour I was standing in the hospital beside Frank's bed. He still had not come around. The nurse came in and said, "We are going to move him to a private room. If there is anyone you think should be here, then you should call them." I went to the phone and made a few calls to a few of his friends.

Once they had Frank in his private room, I sat down beside him. This all seemed so unreal. I kept looking at him and wishing he would wake up and smile at me one more time. I just wanted to hear his voice again.

Paul and Mary, Emily, and her husband George came, and another friend of Frank whose name was Bert all arrived about the same time. I spoke to them and let them know that the doctor had not arrived yet. When the doctor arrived, he checked Frank over and said that he would probably hang on until the next day.

I informed the doctor that I intended to stay with Frank overnight.

"That's fine, Jenny. We can bring a cot in, and you can sleep on the cot. If you want you can go home now and bring a bag back with things that you might want and need."

I spoke to Paul and Mary and said, "I'll go and get a few things and I'll be right back."

Bert offered to drive me home, and I accepted.

Once I got to the house I started putting things into an overnight bag. "I just wanted to take a quick shower," I said.

I took a shower and washed my hair. I quickly got dressed and walked out of the washroom and into the living room. I picked up the overnight bag and said, "I'm ready to go."

I opened the door and started to walk out when the phone rang. I stopped for a moment and then rushed to the phone. "Hello."

"Mom, you need to get back here fast."

"I'm on my way."

We ran to the car and sped down the highway. We took a side road so that we could speed even faster. The ride seemed to take forever. As soon as we neared the hospital I saw Paul and Mary standing on the road, waiting. I jumped out of the car and ran towards them. I saw the look on Paul's face and I screamed, "No, no, I have to be with him. I promised him I would be there."

Paul grabbed me and held me close while I sobbed like a child. Finally he pulled away from me and said, "Let's go in so you can see him."

I felt like nothing was real. I'm in a bad dream, and I'm going to wake up, and I will be home in my own bed and everything will be fine, I told myself as we walked into the hospital.

I entered the hospital room and saw Frank lying on the bed. A nurse had walked in the room with me. She walked over to the bed and pulled the sheet down from his face. "I'll leave you alone with him." Then she turned and walked out.

I walked over to the bed and stood there looking at him. He looked peaceful except that around his mouth he was getting dark. I felt so scared at that very moment and so totally alone. I took his hand; it felt cold and lifeless. "You were supposed to wait for me. I'm so sorry I left. I thought you would wait for me. Please open your eyes one more time and tell me you love me. I need to tell you I love you. Please don't leave me. I can't do this without you." I realized that tears were streaming down my face, and I could barely see him. I brushed away the tears and prayed, "Please God, tell him I'm so sorry I was not here."

I stood there quietly for a few more minutes, and then I whispered to Frank, "I take you with me in my heart and in my mind for the rest of my life. As long as I am alive, there is a part of you that is alive too." I let go of his hand and I left his room.

Paul and Mary were in the hallway waiting for me, and together we walked out of the hospital. I met Doctor Williams coming back into the hospital. He saw me and walked up and put his arms around me and just stood there holding me for a few minutes while I sobbed into his shoulder. "Let me know if you need anything," he said, finally letting go of me.

There were many things that had to be taken care in the next couple of days. I dreaded the day of the funeral, as I knew it would be hard.

Jay, Al, and Paul were all present, and I handed them things that Frank had wanted each one of them to have, and then we went to the funeral.

It was so emotional for all of us. The reverend said that it was one of the biggest ceremonies he had seen. There was standing room only. Paul read the eulogy, and then the song I had written was played. The kids had tears in their eyes, and I realized they would miss him as well.

CHAPTER SEVEN

After Frank's passing, I had a hard time focusing on the future. Nothing had any meaning anymore. I had no idea what I was going to do without him.

Isabell and Rob had put a small trailer that they owned in my backyard, and they came up on the weekends and would camp out in the backyard. My sister was always trying to convince me that I still had a life to life. "You can't give up," she would say.

There were times that I would only see them for a few minutes each day, as they would go off shopping and they would bring the grandkids with them and take them to a local park or swimming in a nearby stream. They would try to get me to go with them, but I just didn't feel like I could handle being around people. There were many times that Isabell would come into the house to say goodbye to me on the Sundays, and she would find me just sitting and crying. "I don't want to leave you. Come back with us," she would say.

"I have to get used to what my life is supposed to be like now."

I tried to pull myself together enough to take an interest in fixing up the rest of the property, telling myself that it was the right thing to do.

I spoke to a few people and finally found someone who said he was a contractor.

I discussed that I wanted a new counter made for the kitchen, and that when he was finished with that job then I would have work in the office building to be done.

For the next few days he came over almost every day. He said he had ideas for the place and that he wanted to discuss them with me. We sat in the office and he talked about changing the place totally.

"Sorry, I don't have the kind of money you are talking about," I said. "This will be fixed up to look good, and the repairs that need to be done, but that is all."

A few days later I had a friend call and ask if I could help them start up a new business in Toronto. So I planned to go and spend a couple of days and help them with the advertising and paperwork that needed to be completed. When I left on Friday I said to Paul, "Please keep an eye on things around here, as the contractor is supposed to be here to build the counter."

When I got back on the Sunday I walked into the house to find that all the carpeting in the house. There had been a small counter in the kitchen, and it was now gone, and Paul was standing with a sledge hammer in his hand, and he was about to knock down a wall between the living room and kitchen.

I stood in the doorway of the house and looked around and said, "My God, what happened?"

Paul looked over at me and said, "The contractor wants me to knock the wall down."

I looked at him and asked, "Why?"

"Well, he said that the counter he is building will have to fit right here without the wall."

"Well Paul, he can cut the counter to fit into the wall. He doesn't have to knock the wall down."

"He also wants to take the big front window out of the house, as he said the counter won't fit in the doorway."

"Why doesn't he put the counter together in the house?"

"I think because he has built it already, and it is there under the car port," Paul explained.

I stepped back outside and gasped as I looked at a mess of wood that looked like I had put it together. I asked, "This is the kitchen counter?"

"Yes, that's it," Paul answered.

"Let me tell you now that he is not taking the front window out of the house to get that mess into the kitchen. There must be something wrong with him, but he is not working for me anymore."

I told Paul to put the sledge hammer down and that I would take care of the contractor. I called him up and told him that his services where no longer required.

He argued with me and said he had over two hundred dollars of material into the counter.

"Well come by and show me your receipts and I will reimburse you, but your services are no longer required."

The next day he arrived and said he couldn't find all his receipts. I handed him two hundred and told him to leave the property. "It's worth the two hundred to get rid of you," I said as I handed him the money.

That day he called several times wanting to talk, and each time I said I was busy and we had nothing to discuss, and then he came to my office that night and said he needed to speak to me. I was sitting behind the desk so I pointed to a chair opposite me and said, "Alright, go ahead."

"Listen, I know this is going to sound crazy, but I know all about you. I know where you come from in Nova Scotia, and I know you have a sister and brother. I know about your son's girlfriend Mary and what she has gone through growing up. I know all about all of you."

I sat there shocked as to what I was hearing. I tried not to show how nervous he was making me. Paul and Mary had gone for a drive somewhere, and I had no one around so I didn't want to get him upset.

As causal as possible I said, "Well that is interesting. How do you know so much about everyone?"

"You're not going to believe me, but I can read people's minds. I've been doing it for a long time, and I have been able to read all of your minds since I started working here."

"Well, what do you want to do with this information?"

"Nothing, I just want to help you out. If you give me a chance you will see that I can be a big help to you."

"So what else do you know about us?"

He began telling me things that I didn't know how he ever got ahold of the information. My stomach turned while I sat there listening to him tell me about my sister, our lives as children. What our home town looked like, and then more information about Paul and his girlfriend Mary. He knew a lot about her life, and that really concerned me.

Why had this man gone out of his way to find out all this information? What was he up to? How dangerous was he?

We sat there, and I tried so hard to remain calm and show no emotions as he tried to convince me he was a great guy and that I couldn't get along in life without him.

Around eleven P.M. I said I was getting tired and that I was going next door to the house. I thanked him for coming by and that I was really impressed that he could read people's minds.

We both walked out of the office at the same time and he got in his car as I locked the door. I was relieved to see that Paul and Mary had come back and were in the house.

I turned and smiled and said, "Have a great night."

I went into the house and told Paul and Mary what had just happened. None of us could figure out how he managed to get all the information he had on all of us.

My sister arrived that weekend, and I told her about the contractor and asked if she would come with me to meet him and see if she could figure out how he had so much information on us all. She agreed and we met him for a coffee in town.

We sat around and made small talk, and then I asked him if he could read my sister's mind and tell us what she was thinking.

"No I can't," he said, "it doesn't happen that way. I can't make it just happen."

You could see on his face that he was getting really uncomfortable, and he just wanted to get away from us.

"I gave up going fishing to come here and have coffee with you two," he said.

"Well let me tell you, you had better find another place to fish because if you bother my sister again you will have to deal with me."

I stood there smiling as my big sister threatened this guy.

I never heard from him again.

The summer was coming to an end. Paul and Mary moved back to Toronto, and that's when I really fell apart. I would sit on the sofa all night long and watch traffic fly by on the highway. I couldn't face going into the bedrooms, as they were just a reminder to me how lonely my life had become. The room that Paul and Mary had slept in was now empty except for a few remnants they left behind. I walked in their room a few days after they left and sat on their bed and wept all day. I sat there with the dog at my side and cried from about six am when I got up to about nine P.M. when I finally walked out and closed the door behind me, thinking I will not open this door again until I can handle it better.

I had given all of Frank's clothes away except for a sweater and a handkerchief that he always carried in his back pocket. I put the sweater on and put the handkerchief in the pocket. I hoped it would make me feel closer to Frank, but instead it just made me feel even more lonely.

The phone would ring, and most times I would just sit and look at it, not wanting to talk to anyone. I really had nothing to say. I didn't want to hear how someone wanted to know how I was doing, because as far as I was concerned I wasn't doing.

The two buildings on the property were in need of so much work. I had started to try and repair both but it was beyond my expertise as I had no skills in the area of remodeling and repairs. The house had no floor in the living room or kitchen. The cupboards in the kitchen needed fixing. The walls needed painting, and any work that had been started was only half done, making things look even worse.

The office building was also in so much need of repairs. I had no idea how I was going to do any of it.

I would sit on the sofa night after night, watching the traffic go by on the highway. I couldn't face going into the bedrooms. One room had been where Paul and Mary had slept and now it was empty, with just a few remnants that they had left. The bedrooms were just a reminder of how empty my life had become.

The only thing I had left was the dog. He followed me everywhere I went. Sometimes I would put him in the car and we would just drive. I had nowhere to go, but it didn't matter; it was just the thought of getting away. It was almost like trying to run from all the loneliness and despair, but it followed me everywhere I went.

I didn't eat, really. I had no appetite. Anytime I thought that maybe I could get something down I would take a few bites and then sit and feed the rest to the dog. Once in a while I would open a can of chicken soup and would put some in a bowl for me and some in another bowl for the dog, and I would watch Chimo eat his food and then usually give him most of mine.

Eva would stop almost daily and tell me I had to pull myself together and get on with my life. It was as if she was talking another language, as I couldn't understand how I was going to do that.

I put the place up for sale while at the same time I tried to find a way to make the place look better without paying a fortune for repairs with money that I didn't have.

I was driving through Havelock and suddenly saw a man coming out of a building looking like he was a contractor, and I thought to myself that I should stop and ask him if he would come down to my place and give me an idea of what could be done.

I turned the car around and went back to where I had seen him. I walked up on the steps and a woman came out. The door was open, and I could see the gentleman that I had just seen a few moments before. I pointed to him and asked the woman, "Could you tell me if he is a contractor, and if he is could I speak to him?"

She turned and yelled into the house, "Hey Eddie, someone here wants to speak to you."

He looked over at me and then walked towards us. The woman continued to stand beside me. "I was wondering if you are a contractor, and if you would mind coming to my place to give me some advice on what I could do. I met the contractor from hell and my place is about to fall down around me. Even if you don't have the time to do any work, I would appreciate your advice."

"I'll have to drive him over," the woman jumped in before he answered.

He stood quietly for a moment, and then he said, "Here, write down you name and phone number, and I'll call you tomorrow and we can set up when I can come over. I don't need any more work, as I have enough here to keep me busy for a while." He handed me a small note pad from his pocket and a pencil.

I wrote my name and phone number like he requested. I handed the note pad back to him and said, "Thanks, I'll wait for your call."

A few days later I still hadn't heard from him, so I drove over to the building again. The door was closed this time, so I knocked on the door and it took a few minutes, and then he finally opened the door.

"Hi," I said, "You forgot to call me."

"Well, actually I was going to call you later today."

"Well, I'm here now, when do you think you will be able to come over and take a look?"

"Give me a few minutes, and I will come with you now." With that he turned and went back into the house, and I went back to the car to wait.

About ten minutes later he came out of the house and got into the car and we drove off. When we arrived at the property I took him into the office building first to look around. "I was wondering if it would be feasible to put a handicapped apartment here and then rent it out. I was hoping that maybe I could get government funding to do this."

Eddie looked around and then said, "I have worked on a few jobs that were government funded, and it takes forever to get some money out of them, and then they are always on your back about what you are doing. I don't really recommend it."

"Well I need to do something that I can make a living from."

"I don't think that is the way to do it."

"Well, let's go next door and see what you think."

We walked across the yard and into the house. Within a couple of minutes I had explained what I was trying to do to fix the place up, and he had given me a few pointers.

"Can I get you a cold drink or something? I have some ginger ale here from the east coast, would you like to try it?"

"Yes, I'll try it," he said as he sat down on the sofa while I went to the kitchen and prepared two glasses of ginger ale. I came back into the living room and sat down on a chair next to the sofa.

As we sipped on the beverage, Eddie told me how his mother had taken him to the doctor when he was just an infant and asked the doctor what she should do, as he was colicky. The doctor told his mother to just give him ginger ale and he'll be fine. The next time she took Eddie to the doctor to get checked, his weight had dropped to almost his birth weight and the doctor asked her what was happening. She told him that she was giving him just ginger ale. Eddie laughed as he told the story.

I sat there feeling relaxed and was enjoying the company as I listened to him tell me what he was doing at the house he was working on and who he was doing it for.

"So your wife works with you?"

"You mean Cathy that you met at my work? No, she's not my wife. She just likes to give people that impression. She would like us to have a relationship, but she's married and I'm not going to get involved."

I didn't say anything, but I thought that was pretty admirable.

"I lost my driver's license, and she drives me back and forth to work most days but sometimes I take a cab as well."

"I guess it must be hard to have to depend on other people in this area," I said.

Eddie shook his head yes as he finished his drink. "Well, I think I should leave."

A few days later Eddie phoned, and we just talked for a long time. He told me a bit more about his life, and then he talked about the renovation jobs that he had worked on and also about the job he was currently doing. He asked me where I go to have a drink.

I laughed and said, "I don't really drink. I don't go to bars, and I don't hang out in party places trying to pick someone up. That's just not my style. My best friend in this area is Eva who lives next door, and she is in her eighties. We go out once in a while for a coffee together, and she loves it if I drive up in front of her house and ask her to go for a drive. That is about the most excitement I get around here. I guess I sound really boring compared to what you are used to."

When we hung up I looked at the clock and saw that almost an hour had gone by.

He is such a nice guy, I thought to myself.

For the next few nights in a row he called and we talked, just getting to know each other. He seemed to have a good sense of humor, and I enjoyed listening to him. His voice was soft and easy to listen to.

It was the Thanksgiving weekend. Al and Jay came up for a couple of hours. I really enjoyed seeing them. We went to a restaurant and ate and talked and just enjoyed ourselves. I stood with tears in my eyes and watched them drive away to go back to Toronto. "I miss you guys so much," I whispered into the wind.

I sighed and walked back into the house. Chimo came over to me as I sat down on the sofa. He put his head on my lap, and I stroked his head as I brushed a tear away with my other hand. The silence of the house was deafening, and the loneliness was closing in on me.

"There is nothing like the sound of silence. It is the loneliest sound on earth, when you walk into a house and there is no one there to share your home or your life with," I said softly to Chimo, who lifted his head up to me, and I bend down and kissed the top of his head.

I got up of the sofa and cleaned up the glasses of pop that the kids had left on the coffee table. I washed the glasses and then I turned to Chimo and said, "Well that took a whole five minutes. What do you want to do now?" I put his leash on and we went outside and sat on the deck at the front of the house. We watched cars going by, and we continued to sit there until it got dark. Chimo starting getting anxious, and I realized he was probably hungry. So we went back into the house and I fed him.

The phone rang, and it was Eva saying she was going out with a friend and would be back later. I hung up feeling even lonelier, as my neighbors on the other side of me had gone to Toronto to see their kids for the weekend.

I picked up the phone and called Eddie. He answered on the second ring.

"Hi, it's just me," I said. "I was wondering what you are doing?"

"Well I was just finishing dinner. Cathy brought it over a little while ago."

"Sorry, I didn't mean to intrude," I said.

"No you're not intruding; she left and I just finished eating."

"Well, do you feel like some company? I feel like I need to get out of here for a while."

"Sure, come on over."

"Alright," I said. "I have to call a cab, as my car is not working. I've been having a lot of problems with it lately."

About an hour later I got out of the cab in front of Eddie's place. He met me in the driveway and then escorted me inside. It was a one bedroom apartment in a house on a quiet street in Campbellford. It was modestly furnished, and he said it was cold in the winter.

"Do you want to walk with me to a store close by, and we will pick up some pop or something as I have nothing in the house."

"Sure," I said.

We walked to a local store, and we were back in the apartment within fifteen minutes.

We both sat on the sofa and talked for a couple of hours.

"Well, I think I had better call a cab and go, as I left my dog at home and he is not used to me being gone." We kissed, and before I knew it the kisses were becoming more urgent. We made love, and it felt so good to be with someone. To have someone hold me and make me feel alive again.

It was around two o'clock in the morning when I called the cab and I went home. I walked into the house and bent down and gave Chimo a big hug and said, "I missed you."

I think he said he missed me too by the way he acted and jumped around. I took a shower and laid down on the sofa, and Chimo laid on the floor next to me. I think I finally dozed off around morning. When I woke up it was already eight am and the sun was shining brightly into the living room.

A few minutes after being up, Eva came to my front door and knocked. I saw it was her and beckoned her to come in.

"I came over last night when I got back around ten o'clock, but you weren't home. I just wanted to make sure that you are alright."

"Yes, I'm fine. I went to a friend's house just to get away," I said as I poured her and myself a coffee.

"Well I am going to go to Campbellford to pick up a few things in about another hour, do you want to come?"

"Sounds like a plan," I said.

"Alright, I'll be back to get you in about an hour."

While I waited for Eva to come back, I thought I would phone Eddie and see what he was up to for the day.

He answered on the second ring, and I noticed right away that he didn't sound good.

"Are you sick?"

"I think it might have been the dinner that Cathy brought over. I woke up like this."

"Maybe you're allergic to me," I said jokingly.

"I'm going to Campbellford. I'll stop by and bring you a coffee. I remember you have nothing in the house."

When Eva picked me up I asked her if she minded if we picked up coffee. I knew she wouldn't, so I got him a toasted bagel and coffee and dropped it off. "Call me later and let me know how you are doing."

Later that evening he called, and he sounded a bit better. We talked for a little while and then hung up.

The next day I started seriously going out and actively looking for work. It seemed that unless you knew someone in the area, you were not going to get a job. "Jobs are just too scarce in this area," one person told me.

A few weeks later I found a job through an acquaintance of Eddie's. I was to start the next Monday painting group homes. I would be subcontracting, so I hired a friend of mine Lilly to help me so we would be able to get through the jobs quickly.

We went to the first group home and had a couple of rooms to paint. Within a week we had finished and moved to the next group home.

There was a maintenance man who also worked in all the homes, and he would oversee what we were painting. He would also show up on the jobs and tell me what was expected to be done and what I could leave alone.

The fourth week into the job, Lilly and I were working in the basement of one of the group homes. It had been snowing outside, and when we arrived I could not park in the driveway due to the fact that the driveway had not been plowed. I parked on the next street that the street plow had already gone through, and Lilly and I walked over to the house. I had the key, and I let us in. We went into the basement and started getting ready for the day. We would often paint in the same room, but she would concentrate on what she was doing, and I would concentrate on what I was doing, and we would not talk much. So I guess this morning we were being quiet, too quiet that no one knew we were there. Around lunch time I said to Lilly, "Let's take a break and go to the car and have a lunch."

We laid everything down and covered the paint and went upstairs. There in the living room was the maintenance man and one of the counselors, making out on a sofa. They jumped up as we walked up the stairs that led directly into the living room where they were.

"Sorry," I said, "we didn't mean to intrude. We are just going to get some lunch." With that Lilly and I proceeded to leave the house.

As we got outside, Lilly started giggling and said, "I don't think they knew we were there."

"I'm sure they didn't know that we were there since, we parked a street away," I said as we walked to the car.

A few days later I got a phone call from the man who hired me to tell me that I was fired.

I asked him why, but I already knew the answer. I just wanted to see if I would be told the truth.

"Well, we have decided that the maintenance man should be able to paint the rest of the homes now. You got it started for him, and he can take over from here. Thanks for your help anyway. You can pick up your pay on Friday."

I hung up and phoned Lilly and told her the news. "That's alright, you can find a better job than that," she stated, trying to make me feel better.

This just put me back to job hunting again, and month after month of trying to find a job and not really getting anywhere. One day I was on the highway between two towns and my car died. I sat there for a few moments and wondered, am I ever going to be able to do this? I got out of the car, and I knew I had about three miles to walk. It was cold and windy, and I didn't have winter boots on because I didn't own any. I had been trying so hard to maintain bills that I didn't feel that I could afford to properly dress. My feet were freezing by the time I got to town.

I looked in my purse to see if I had enough money on me get a cup of coffee so I could warm up, but I was about thirty cents short. I walked from store to store, seeing if I could fill out an application to work. Some let me fill them out. Others just said they couldn't afford to hire anyone, especially in the winter time. After about two hours of walking around the town and going from store to store, I finally decided that I was too cold to do this anymore, and I made my way back to the car.

I couldn't afford to have it towed, and I couldn't afford to have anyone look at it, so I just prayed the whole way back to the car that it would start. When I got to the car, I was so cold that I thought my feet would fall off. I had cramps and pains in my feet and legs from the cold, and I was fighting the tears back. I thought, that's all I need to do is start crying, and I will have icicles frozen to my face.

When I got back to the car I just sat there trying to get my breath back. It had been a long walk, and I was exhausted. I took my key and put it in the ignition, but I was scared to turn the key. I sat there for a few more minutes, and then I tried to start the car. It started right away. I was shocked. "Thank you God," I said out loud as I turned the steering wheel and drove back towards the house.

Maintaining the bills had become a real chore. There was a propane stove in the house, but I couldn't afford to buy propane for it at that moment. I had priced the propane, and I knew that what I could afford to buy would only last me about two weeks, so I was trying to heat with hydro because the furnace in the office building was so old that the repairman said he could not repair it any more. The oil tank was so old that he said it would also have to be replaced. So I had a heater turned on low in the office building just so the pipes would not burst, and in the house I had it turned on to about sixty to try and keep warm, but it was still really chilly as this was an old house and no basement under it, so the floors got really cold.

I paid the phone bill and a few other things and managed to purchase some groceries for myself and Chimo, but I held onto the hydro bill, which was over four hundred dollars, thinking and praying that I would get a job and then I would pay it.

Christmas was getting closer, and the kids said that they were going to come up for the day. As much as I missed them and wanted to see them, I didn't want them to see me while I was still trying so hard to find work. I felt so useless at this point.

I felt like I was a big disappointment to them and myself. I had always wanted to make them proud of me, and there was nothing to be proud of.

I purchased some tiles for the floor of the house, and I was slowly putting them down every time I had nothing to do. I got a couple cans of paint, and I painted the kitchen cupboard and the place started to look a bit better. I had the place up for sale, and I just wanted the place to look good in hopes that it would sell quickly. Fixing up the house kept me busy and my mind occupied.

The hydro bill for that month finally arrived and was astronomical. It was over a thousand dollars for the house and the office now. In with the bill was a typed letter telling me that I had until a certain date to pay the bill or I was getting cut off. I sat for a long time with the letter in my hand and wondered, what am I going to do? I can't afford this, and I can't live here without heat.

I had no choice. I had to sell Frank's truck. So I sat the truck facing the highway and put a sign in the window. Within a couple of days the truck was sold, and I went and paid off the hydro bills for both buildings and purchased propane for the stove that I heated with it. I bought some groceries and paid a few other bills that had been collecting. When I finished I had enough to but a few small Christmas gifts and enough to get me through the next month's bills.

Eddie would stay at the house some nights, and other nights he would go home. When he stayed over he would have to turn off the phone, as he said that Cathy liked to call him at nights just to talk.

I thought that was a bit strange, since they worked all day together. One morning as he was getting ready for work I said, "How about I come and pick you up and drive you home to change, as I have to go to Campbellford today anyway?"

"No not today, I think I had better let Cathy drive me home, as her nose is getting out of joint because I am spending so much time with you and she hasn't driven me home in a while."

I felt my heart sink. I guess a questioning look must have been on my face. "Since I have to work with her, I need to keep her happy as well."

I knew what he had been telling me about her wanting to have a relationship with him, but he didn't want to because she was married, was not adding up. I pushed it to the back of my mind, as I had other things to worry about. Eddie was good to me and seemed nice enough when he was around. It's strange, but I had started out with this relationship with an open mind and heart, but I found that suddenly I was putting walls up that would never be knocked down.

Christmas day arrived, and the roads were bad with ice and snow. There was an icy rain falling as I sat watching the cars move slowly down the highway and decided to phone the kids and tell them not to come, as I didn't want to see them getting into an accident.

The rest of the day I spent putting the floor tiles down in the living room and kitchen, one tile at a time. I was exhausted at the end of the day, but it was starting to look a lot better. I turned the radio on and sat down with a cup of coffee and watched the snow gently falling outside. Everything was coated with the white fluffy snow, and the highway looked peaceful and quiet with only the occasional car going by.

It was in January when the kids finally made it up for a few hours. They looked surprised when they walked in and saw the place. I had all the floor tiles down except two, which I had kept for Al to do when he arrived. I just had a hard time to get them to fit, but I knew he could do it and he did.

We spent a few hours eating, talking, laughing, and having a good time. My heart sank as Jay stood up and said, "Well, I think we have to go. I need to be somewhere in a couple of hours."

This was always the hard part for me, to watch them all walk out and drive away. I would try to fight back the tears, but by the time the car rolled down the highway my eyes would be so blurry from tears that I couldn't see the car.

In February I decided that since I couldn't find a job I was going to teach myself how to make signs, and then I would open the sign company again. I went into the office building, and it was so extremely cold in there that I could see my breath in front of me. The computer didn't want to work at first, as it was too cold. I found a portable heater and got it turned on, and then I spent the next few hours looking over the sign stock and trying to familiarize myself with how to make signs.

Frank had tried to show me a few times but had said that he couldn't really teach me because he had taught himself, and I needed to do the same thing.

I sat looking at the computer and trying to remember how to turn it on and get into the sign-making program.

I first had to learn the computer. I knew nothing about computers. I knew nothing about the programs of making signs. I had watched Frank a few times, but he would do things so fast that for someone who knew nothing about computers it was just too confusing. "Help me, Frank," I said out loud. "You wanted a son to carry on the sign business for you. Will I do? I hope so. Guide me somehow, will you?"

I sat down in front of the computer and turned it on. With the heater blowing on me and the computer, it began to feel a bit warmer. I sat there for hours trying to figure out what I was seeing. I took some vinyl and put it through the cutter and tried to find a way to get it to cut out what I had typed into the computer. Eventually and very slowly I started to get it to work. When something would go right, I wasn't always sure how I did it, and I would try and do it again. Finally I thought I was starting to get the hang of it.

There was a flea market opening a few blocks away, and the owners just happened to be related to Lilly, who had been my painting helper. I asked her to tell them that I would make their sign for them and not charge them very much.

Within a few days I received a call, and they placed the order for the sign. Within another week the sign was made, and there was a picture in the local papers talking about the grand opening of the flea market, and they showed a picture of the owners standing in front of the sign I had just made.

It gave me a bit of confidence, so I started looking for other signs that needed to be made. I was surprised how many I did in the next two months. Every sign I did was a learning experience for me. I would pretend to whoever I was talking to that I knew all about sign work and that I could do any job they wanted. Then I would go back to the office and pray that I could do it. I would fight with the machine and myself until I got it right.

Eddie and I discussed the fact that maybe he should give up his apartment and move in with me. So in April we rented a moving van, and we moved all his things in. He didn't really have much furniture, so it was mostly boxes, clothes, and tools.

I went and took out a mortgage on the place so that I could try to fix the place up. The roof needed to be done on the office building, as it was leaking into the building. The house also needed a new roof. I replaced the ceiling tiles and put new flooring down in the office, and within a couple of months the place had totally changed in appearance. People would drive by and stop and tell me how nice the place looked compared to before. That was nice to hear even from strangers. It helped to give me more self-confidence.

I purchased a digital imagining machine, and I advertised in the local newspapers every week, trying to bring business in. I hired three people to work in the office, and things were starting to look up and business was improving.

People from everywhere stopped in to see the place and to put an order in for signs. I even got work from three major hospitals in Toronto to make surgery boards for them. During the first summer I had managed to fix the place up and get the business rolling.

The following spring Eddie was coming to an end of working on the house that he had been doing the renovations on, and we discussed him opening a welding shop at the end of the office building, as there was plenty of room, and since we were on the highway he would get a lot of exposure.

We purchased over forty thousand worth of equipment, and he set up shop. He was working hard at getting his business off the ground while at the same time I was still trying to get the sign business up to where I would actually be making a living. At this point everything I made was just going back into running the place such as stock, staff, bills, taxes, and now a mortgage on top of everything else.

Little did I know how much hydro would be once Eddie started welding. Suddenly the hydro bills for each month where averaging around eighteen hundred per month for just the office building, and I still had the hydro bill on the house as well. I made the comment one day that, "With what we are paying in hydro bills I could afford to be paying another mortgage."

In the summertime it was busy with cottagers, tourists, new businesses opening, and older businesses just renewing their signs.

One day I drove down the highway and was surprised to notice that I had actually done all the signs on the highway except for two within a few miles of two towns. I thought to myself, that's not bad for someone who didn't know anything about signs before I started.

Then one day I got a call from a lady in Hastings who had been in and had a sign made by me and had sat and waited for me to make the sign for her. We had talked while the sign was being made, and she had asked me what I did before I made signs, and I had told her that I did wall murals and paintings. So when she left she said she was going to have someone call me, a friend of hers who wanted a wall mural done on the side of a building.

The next day her friend Henry called and asked if he could come over and discuss what he was looking for. When we talked about what he was wanting, he said he had always wanted to do a mural on the side of a building, and he purchased a building in Hastings at an intersection and wanted to have something painted that represented the history of the town.

We talked about the age of the building and how it might need repair in the next few years, so I talked him into having a mural painted on a very durable sign board, and then we would install it on the side of the building. That way if the building ever needed repair then it could be taken down and put up again later.

I drew up a few sketches, and Henry finally accepted a sketch of a train station that had been in Hastings many years before, and then he gave me pictures of people some from more than a hundred years before and asked for me to work them into the painting.

Eddie helped to put the sign boards together and built a beautiful metal frame around it to get it a finished look as well as making it more sturdy.

I ran the sign shop with the help of my staff, while at the same time I worked on the mural under a large carport that was at the back of the office building. If customers came in then I would drop my paintbrushes and go inside to talk to the customers and help them decide what they needed on their sign, or just answer any questions that they might have.

In the evenings I would go out there after the office had closed for the day, and I would work until it got dark. Chimo would lay down out there and watch me. One day I noticed a movement out of the corner of my eye, and I looked over and saw that a young deer was at the fence of the back yard and Chimo had walked over, and they were nose to nose with each other. Then for the next week or so the deer would come to the fence almost every night around the same time to see Chimo. They seemed to become friends.

Sometimes nights after I quit painting I would go back into my office and turn the sign-making equipment back on and make signs until about two or three in the morning or until I got so tired that I couldn't do it anymore. The staff I had were great to help out with guidance, but they could not seem to grasp making signs on their own.

One Saturday morning I was working on the mural before the staff arrived, and I heard a car pull up out front. I walked around the building to see Henry stepping out of his car and then rush around to the passenger side of the car and help an older gentleman out of the vehicle. As I walked towards them, Henry looked over and called out, "Jenny, here is someone who wants to meet you."

I stepped up to them and produced my hand to the gentleman. "Hello," I said as we shook hands.

"Hello," he answered. "I hear you have painted me into your mural. I would really like to see that."

I looked over at Henry, and Henry jumped in and said, "Yes, this is the gentleman who is in uniform standing next to the car. He was in his twenties at that time. George is now ninety-five years old."

"Well I am thrilled to meet you. Please come around the building here, and you can see the painting." I walked in front of them back to the carport.

George looked thrilled as he surveyed the painting. "Wow, this is a lot of work."

"Yes, but I've enjoyed it. Art relaxes me. I turn the radio on, listen to music, and paint the hours away."

They stayed for about an hour and took some photos of me and George together in front of the mural.

"It has been an honor to meet you," he said as they started to leave.

"Trust me, it has been an honor for me to meet you." I said as I walked them back to the car. I stood there and waved to them as they drove off.

Almost three months later and the mural was finally complete. It had been a lot of hard work for me with many stiff necks, but I was pleased with the final product. Henry was very pleased with my work.

He got ahold of the newspapers and asked the local politicians to come out for a ribbon-cutting ceremony that he was holding, as he was donating the mural to the town of Hastings. I was thrilled.

Here I was, the person who had been so abused for so many years. What a different life I was now living.

Then when Frank died I was totally lost and thought I would not survive. Now here I was going to be honored as an artist.

I phoned and asked the kids if they could come, but they were all busy working so no one could make it. I talked to my sister, but I could tell that she was busy with the grandkids and she needed to be around for them. So as much as I wished for my family to be around, no one was going to be there. Well it doesn't matter, I told myself, trying to make myself feel better about no one being there. I worked hard to get here, and at least I was being recognized by Henry, even if he didn't know what I had been through to get to this day.

When I awoke on the day of the event, the day was cold, windy, and raining. I knew that people would be showing up around two P.M. and hoped that it would clear up by then. It seemed as the day went on the worse the weather got. It seemed to get more cold and windy as the day went on.

Eddie came with me to the ceremony. He wore hearing aids and was having a difficult time hearing what anyone was saying, making him uncomfortable; also, he didn't know anyone. I tried to make him feel a bit better by asking him if he wanted something to drink or eat, but he just shook his head no and stood there looking almost like he wanted to run. I felt really sorry for him.

In the painting there was a woman that I was asked to paint. Put her into the window of the train, Henry had said. Her husband worked on the train, and he was also painted into the mural in his railway attire, standing beside the train.

I was standing at the party being interviewed by a reporter when I saw an older woman walk in. Someone helped her to get seated comfortably on a few chairs that had been placed up against a wall. I watched her carefully and thought that she looked very familiar to me. The reporter was trying to get the story out of me on how I had put the mural together with all its history. I answered his questions, but I was fascinated by this older lady to the point that it was distracting me from everything else.

When I finished the interview, I went over to Henry and asked, "Is that the woman that I painted in the train window?"

Henry looked in the direction that I pointed and said, "Yes it is. Come with me and I will introduce you to her. She will want to meet you."

Henry made the introductions, and I sat down beside her and we talked for a few minutes. A man came over to her and asked if she wanted a drink, to which she replied, "Yes."

"That looks like the man I painted as the train conductor, he would be your husband?"

"Yes, that's right. You did an excellent job of painting us both from pictures that had to be at least fifty years old," she said, smiling.

"This has been such an honor to meet you and your husband," I said as I got up and moved across the room to speak to Eddie, as he was looking even more uncomfortable.

I explained excitedly who I had just met.

"Yes, I can see the resemblance to the painting."

Henry was there talking to a few people. I approached him and said, "Remember me?"

He smiled and said, "How could I forget such a beautiful lady?"

I laughed and said, "I heard you had eye problems."

About an hour later Henry spoke up and was asking if we would all move outside so that the mural could be unveiled.

I was so nervous as I stood there in the pouring rain, waiting to see the people's faces and to hear what they thought of the painting.

The cold wind blew as people huddled together under umbrellas, waiting for Henry to pull the cloth down that had been draped over the mural, waiting for this moment in the ceremony to unveil it.

Finally Henry took hold of a corner of the cloth and down it came with little effort. The people all clapped and stood and pointed out different things in the mural. It sounded like a positive response. I heard people saying, "Oh, I know that person." Or another person said, "Wow this is spectacular, the way the artist has been able to paint all of our history into one painting." Another person pointed someone out in the painting and said, "The artist has captured these people from photos that are up to a hundred years old or more." People were smiling as they slowly walked away, making their way back into the building where there was food waiting for them. I made my way back as well near the end of the crowd. I felt pleased at the response of the crowd.

Once inside people where milling around the food table and then off to look at photos that Henry had put up that he had taken of the mural when it was still being painted. Henry had also put up copies of the photos I had to work from, some of them over a hundred years old. People walked from photo to photo, making comments and learning about the history of the town.

I went and found Henry and thanked him for the showing and said that I had to go. I could see that Eddie was not enjoying himself, and I was feeling really bad for him to have to stand around when I could see he was wishing he was anywhere but there.

"I'm sorry that you have to leave. We'll talk soon," said Henry as someone tapped him on the shoulder to get his attention.

Once Eddie and I got into the car and as we started to pull away, I took one last look at the mural and thought, I've come a long way from the time that I had to hide my art work for fear of getting caught. I quietly wished again that my family had been there to share in something that meant so much to me. I had struggled so long to give them a reason to be proud of me. Maybe someday they can be as proud of me as I am of them.

CHAPTER EIGHT

The summers were always busy, but the winters were killers. It was like someone closed the door in October and didn't open it again until April. I had to make enough in the summers to pay off last winter's bills and also to pay the summers bills, and then enough to live off of in the winter. It wasn't happening.

It had become too expensive to maintain the bills on both buildings. Hydro to run the equipment in the sign shop as well as the welding shop averaged about fifteen hundred to eighteen hundred dollars a month, and the house hydro was about one hundred fifty to two hundred fifty dollars, depending on the time of year. Property taxes were over twenty-two hundred a year. Heat in the office and the house ran me about four hundred dollars a month each, and then I had the phones as well and still be able to put gas in the car and be able to eat.

After trying to get through three winters, I couldn't do it anymore, and I put the place back on the market for sale. I took another mortgage on the place to get me through the next winter, but it still wasn't enough.

I knew that if I didn't sell the place soon I would lose it, and the thoughts of that happening just made me sick. "I can't lose this place. It belonged to Frank, and I can't lose it."

There were days when the bills had to be paid, and I had no money to pay them. I would get in the car and go out and talk someone into buying a sign. I would continue to do this until I managed to get the bills or mortgage paid.

The stress of trying to make ends meet was taking its toll on me. I was so sacred that I would lose the place. I was tense all of the time, as I had it in the back of my mind always that I could not lose what Frank and I had worked so hard to save.

Most nights I couldn't sleep, as I would be so worried about how I was going to make ends meet. If I did fall asleep, I had a re-occurring dream that I was lost somewhere and I couldn't find my way. I would be in a building with no one around, and I couldn't find the door to get out. I would go up and down stairs and through many rooms, but there would never be an exit door. I would feel scared, and I would wake up with my heart beating fast, usually in a cold sweat and feeling totally exhausted.

Throughout, August, September, October, and November, every morning I would walk across from the house to the office and there beside the front door would be a big spider web. I never saw the spider. I would knock down the web and then continue to unlock the door and go inside. If I had things in my hands when I got to the door, I would go inside and put whatever I was holding down on my desk, and then I would go back outside and knock the web down.

This does not look good to have this web by the door, plus I never liked spiders anyway, I thought to myself.

Then one morning I was telling Eddie about this spider and how determined he was to have his house by this front door. Then it hit me. I had something in common with this spider, as he was trying so hard to hold onto his home, just like I was trying so hard to hold onto mine. I suddenly had empathy with this creature I had never seen. I had to admire how determined he was, as he was not allowing anyone to destroy his home.

If this spider is going to rebuild his house every time I knock it down, then I had to fight harder to hold onto mine.

I had a local business man named Mike come in and ask me about him purchasing the place. He wanted to start up a cardboard recycling business with his father and thought this would be a great place to do it, as it had the highway exposure.

Finally, a glimmer of light at the end of the tunnel, I thought to myself as I waited for him to talk to his father and his girlfriend about it.

Over the next two months Mike drove me crazy, as one week he was going to buy it and then the next he wasn't sure what he wanted to do. I didn't know if I was coming or going. I wasn't getting any other offers, so I had to hold onto hope with him.

Eddie and I were having problems at this time, and the stress of everything else happening and trying to make ends meet were not helping. We finally decided that if we did sell we would each go our own way.

Finally in the middle of November, the man decided he wanted the place but came and said he didn't have the money for the down payment right then but would give it to me by February. I felt like I didn't really have much choice but to let it go. At least I wasn't losing it, and when he would pay me in February I was only going to be getting enough to pay the mortgage and a small amount to walk away with, knowing that at least I did not lose the place.

I agreed to the deal and the paperwork was done. Mike decided he wanted the property right away, and I had less than two weeks to try and find a place to live, as well as Eddie had to find a place too.

We had all of the equipment that we had purchased, and no place to put it and no way of moving it. We held a sale on a Saturday and everything got sold at a fraction of the cost. Over forty thousand dollars worth of equipment went for around seven thousand dollars. Once I paid off some bills and the property taxes on the place, there was no money left.

Eddied found an apartment in town in a small house, and I rented a room off a customer named Murray who had come in and said he had a room to rent when he heard I was looking for a place to live.

The week before I was due to move out, I received a phone call from my son Paul. We talked for a few minutes, and I could tell something was wrong. Finally he said to me, "Mom, no one has told you that you have a very sick son."

I felt like my heart stopped, and I couldn't breathe at that point. I clutched the phone and asked, "What are you talking about?"

"Jay has cancer," he said, as I heard his voice breaking with emotion.

"What are you saying?"

"Mom, Jay has brain cancer."

I grabbed ahold of my desk as the room started spinning. Nothing in life had prepared me for this news. "You must be wrong."

"No, it's true. He found out about a year ago, but he didn't want you to know."

I was so stunned. I felt like someone had just drained all the life out of me. Paul apologized for telling me. "I felt you had the right to know, Mom."

We hung up, and I cried like a baby. I can face anything but not losing a child.

I can't accept this.

I walked around for the next few days in a haze. Nothing seemed real anymore. Here I was leaving the place that Frank had left me. This was where I was taught to believe in myself, where I was taught that I could achieve anything if I tried hard enough. In many ways, this was the place that I had grown. I had learned to believe in life here. Now here I was trying to comprehend that my son was ill. I felt like my life was ending.

Within a few days we moved out of the buildings. I had a few fireworks that been in the office for years, and as we walked out of the buildings for the last time I asked Eddie to stand with me and light the fireworks. This was my symbolic way of saying goodbye one last time.

The next few months were pure hell for me, and I found I cried any time no one was around. I couldn't adjust to anything. The room I was renting was not working out. I didn't trust the Murray that owned the house. I was not comfortable being in the house if he was home, and even less comfortable if he wasn't.

One night I sat in the kitchen of the house drinking a coffee when Murray walked in and put some pills on the table saying, "I think you need something to make you sleep; you don't look well.

I looked down at the pills, shocked, and said, "Thanks, but I'm fine. I don't believe in pills."

He picked them up and left the room without saying another word. A few minutes later I got up and went to the washroom that was off the kitchen. When I came back, he was in the kitchen standing by the stove.

"I'm going to make a can of soup, would you like some?"

"No thanks," I answered.

I sat back down at the table and sipped at my coffee as Murray made small talk as he stirred his pot of soup on the stove.

I started feeling dizzy and sick to my stomach. I sat there scared to get up, thinking that I would fall.

Murray didn't seem to notice and poured his soup in a bowl and came and sat down at the opposite end of the table and began eating.

"I think I must be tired," I said as I started to stand up. "I'm feeling dizzy and weak." I stood up and grabbed ahold of the table and stood there for a moment trying to gain my composure, and then I let go of the table and started to make my way back to the bathroom, but I found that I needed to hold onto the wall as I went. I staggered as I made it to the washroom, and the last thing I remember was putting my hand on the washroom door. Everything goes black after that.

THE WEB

The next morning I woke up in my bed, and I got up with a splitting headache and felt very ill and shaky.

From then on I had Chimo with me in the car, and we would sit in the parking lot of a local Foodland store that was open twenty-four hours a day.

When the dog and I got too cold, then I would drive around until the car got warmed up and then I would park again. I went to the room only to change and to feed the cats that I still had there, and then I would leave again. I didn't think about the next day or what lay ahead for me, as there was no future as far as I was concerned. I was just a robot at this stage, doing what I thought I should to get me through the next few minutes.

Christmas was getting closer, and I tried to see what the kids where doing for Christmas. Al didn't really want to do anything, as his wife's mother had just passed away a few months before. We met at a coffee shop in Toronto, and I told him I felt it was important that we be together at least one day for Christmas. I tried to fight back the tears as I said, "Please try to understand, you brother is sick. How do we know how many Christmas days we will have together?"

Al just got angry and said, "We don't want to celebrate Christmas. We intend to visit her mother's grave, and that is it."

He got up of his chair and started to walk towards the door, and I said to his back, "Listen Al, how are you going to feel if you don't have your brother around to celebrate Christmas with next year?"

Al continued on walking out the door. I walked him to his car. He turned and said, "Bye, Mom."

I drove for the next two hours with tears streaming down my face. As I pulled into the parking lot of Foodland to wait out the night again, I wondered why I was even bothering. Chimo laid across the front seat and put his head on my lap as if he knew that I was feeling.

I called Jay and asked for him to meet me at his house. When I arrived we sat in his living room, and I asked him straight out, "Do you have cancer?"

"Someone told you," he said, smiling.

"Jay, I'm your Mom, I have a right to know."

"I didn't want you to get stressed out about it, as that would just stress me out and I need to stay calm about all of this. I have it under control."

We talked a bit more about the cancer, and then we changed the subject. I stayed about an hour and then he had to leave to get to work.

I drove back to Foodland again. I sat there all night in a daze. I had begun coughing a few days before, and I was finding that every time I coughed I would lose my breath. Gasping for air, I would roll down the window and then the dog and I would get so cold that I would have to roll it back up again within a few minutes. Within the next few days I started running a fever and was chilled most of the time.

I started visiting Eddie, as he just lived a few blocks from the Foodland grocery store. He was nice enough to let me come in and get warm and even give me a hot drink.

Around ten P.M. I would leave and go back to the Foodland parking lot and wait out another night, coughing and feeling ill.

After about a week I went to the hospital and found I had pneumonia. The doctor put me on medication. I took the medication for about a week, but I continued to get worse. I was in terrible pain every time I coughed or even moved. The doctor did X-rays and found that I had cracked three ribs from my extreme coughing.

About a week later my cell phone rang, and it was a call from Paul saying that we would all get together at his apartment on Boxing Day. I felt a bit better knowing we would all be together, but still there was this pain so deep down inside that I thought would never stop hurting.

The day that I went to Paul's and Mary's for Christmas was really hard on me. My heart was breaking as I looked at Jay, wondering how many more Christmas days we had together. I tried to smile as the kids joked around.

Paul had cooked up an excellent meal, and I tried so hard to eat everything on my plate, but I wasn't used to eating much anymore. The conversation was light and happy as we all sat around the table enjoying the few hours we had together.

I knew that when I left there I would go back and sit in a parking lot with the dog and try to stay warm. The kids had no idea that I was living like this, and I had no intention of letting them find out. I felt like I was just one step away from being a bag lady on the streets of Toronto at this point. Once I couldn't afford gas in the car anymore, then I knew I was done, unless I could find a job before that happened.

After Christmas things just got a lot worse for me. I became even more ill with the pneumonia. I would gasp for air, rolling the car window down and trying to get the cold air to revive me. I knew that I couldn't keep living in the car.

I would still go and visit Eddie when I knew he was home. He had picked up a job working on one of his landlord's houses, and he was enjoying it. He also had worked out a deal with the landlord that he would do work in his apartment and he would get some money taken off the rent.

When Eddie realized how sick I was becoming, he asked if I wanted to move into the apartment with him. Not as a couple but just as friends. I took him up on his offer, as I couldn't see going on much longer the way I was. I was just too ill to carry on.

Eddie would get up and go to work, and I would put the dog in the car, and I would drive around most days. I had no idea what I was doing or where I was going. I looked for an apartment of my own, but everything I found was close to one thousand per month plus heat and hydro, and there was no way I could afford to pay that kind of rent on my own. I didn't even have a place that I could make signs out of, and even if I did I still would not make enough to cover those expenses. I would drive around each day, half-heartedly looking for a job, but I knew my chances were slim of finding one, especially this time of the year in this area. Plus I was really too sick to talk to anyone about being hired.

I went to the hospital and got put on more antibiotics, and within two weeks I needed more as I still wasn't getting better. Finally they started to work, and I started to become a bit more positive. I told myself that I had to be strong for my son, and I would have to be positive around him.

I asked Eddie if he minded if I sat up the sign computer and the cutter in the apartment. I was ready to start trying to get some sign work again. He agreed the only place in the apartment was the floor in the living room that was big enough to sit it up and still be out of the way. Then I spent the next few days on the road looking for sign work.

Within a week I had two big sign jobs to do. I was still a bit ill from the pneumonia but willing to push myself and becoming a bit more positive and getting back into the swing of things.

Within a month I had those jobs done, and I was working on some smaller jobs. My confidence was starting to slowly come back again.

I sat down one night and talked to Eddie about maybe us renting a bigger house together or even maybe buying one, as I couldn't find any cheaper rents and that I believed I could purchase a house and pay a mortgage cheaper than rent. He thought about it for a few days and then said we could start looking around to see what was out there.

I put a lot of my energy into looking for a rental house or a house to buy. I began to lean towards buying a house. I need the money from the sale of the other property to use as a down payment on another place. The time was coming when the down payment was to be paid to me.

I went to see the man who had purchased my place to remind him the money was coming due.

"I'm sorry Jenny, but it's not working out for me here, and I am going to be moving out."

"You must be joking," I said, never expecting to hear that. "You had me move out within a few days of you saying you wanted the place. I bent over backwards for you to make it easier for you. I had no place to go, and I have basically lived in my car only to find out now that you are taking off, and you've never paid a cent for this place."

"I don't have the money, and I am going to claim bankruptcy. You can have the place back again. I have painted the house and have done some other things around to help improve the place."

Within a few days of that conversation, he moved out, leaving the place with cardboard boxes everywhere. He and his father had tried to get a cardboard recycling business off the ground. Now I was stuck with bails of cardboard all over the place. Inside the office building there was a cardboard crushing machine that went from floor to ceiling.

At the same time I found a house that I thought I could maybe afford. I went to my mortgage holder on the old property and asked if they would consider holding another mortgage for me.

"We trust you and we will do it, but you need to come up with twenty-five percent of the purchase price."

"Well, I'll see what I can do," I said as I walked out of their office with a glimmer of hope.

From that moment on, I spent all of my waking hours trying to find as much sign work as possible. I worked night and day. I spoke to everyone I could think of to convince them that they needed a new sign or more signage. I also needed to get the money together to pay off the land transfer taxes, legal expenses, and other expenses. I was able to talk people into signs and other work that they needed done. Some wanted to wait, but I managed to convince them that they needed the work then. I put in long hours in hopes that it would pay off.

It seemed like no matter how much work I did, there was no way I was going to have enough to pay twenty-five percent of the asking price plus everything else.

I sat down with my real estate agent and asked him to go to the seller and see if he would be agreeable to hold the twenty-five percent in a small mortgage. I would give him letter of recommendation from people who knew me. I would do whatever he wanted. I pleaded.

"I don't know, Jenny, if he will do this. He rented the house out before and got burned with them not paying the rent. Then they destroyed the place. He might not trust anyone enough to hold a mortgage."

"Please try, or I won't be able to do this."

A few days later, my real estate agent came back and said the owner wanted to meet me. We arranged a meeting, and the day I went to see him I was so nervous knowing that my future depended on this man accepting to do this.

I entered into my real estate agent's office, and a tall gentleman stood up and shook hands with me.

"Jenny, it is so nice to meet you. I have heard a lot of nice things about you. I have also heard how hard you have struggled, and I just wanted to meet you first before making a decision."

"I appreciate that," I said, smiling, trying not to look to desperate or nervous.

We talked for a few minutes about what I intended to do for work. I re-assured him that I did not think it would be a problem to pay the mortgage.

Finally he stood up and said, "I am satisfied."

Two weeks later the paperwork was completed, and my lawyer handed me the keys to the house.

I unlocked the door and walked into my new home. It felt big and empty as I stood there looking around.

"Wow, I did it," I whispered into the air as I stood in the doorway of the kitchen.

I lucked out with this house, as it had a room at the front that I was able to convert into an office and set up my sign equipment and began immediately making signs so that I could pay for all the expenses of moving.

The purchasing of the house and what I went through to get it and then the move into the house seemed to take its toll on me. I found I was always tired, and most of the time and I felt like I was struggling to breathe. I had lost weight, and I was about eighty pounds at this point. No matter what I did or how much I ate, I couldn't gain weight. My clothes just seemed to hang on me. Everything I owned was too big. One morning I had my arms full of sign sup-plies and the phone rang. I walked towards the phone in my office, and I could feel my jeans slipping down over my hips and fall around my knees. Thank goodness there are no customers around, I thought to myself as I put everything that I was carrying down and pulled my jeans up before picking up the phone.

"Hello," I said into the phone.

"Hi Jenny, it's Donna. We have a small dog about an hour north of you that needs to be rescued. We don't have anyone that can go. Would you con-sider going and picking it up for us?"

"I'll speak to Eddie and let you know."

I told Eddie about the dog, and it took him about three minutes and he said, "Alright, when are we going?"

I phoned Donna back and let her know that we would be going the next day.

Eddie and I drove what seemed like an eternity. After about an hour driv-ing north, it just felt like wilderness to me, as there were miles of road and trees but few cars and houses.

"When do we hit civilization?" I asked Eddie.
He looked over and me and then burst out laughing.

I donated paintings to shelters that were doing fundraisers to raise money to support unwanted or abused animals. I knew what I had been through being abused, and I could only imagine what an animal must go through to be abused. I had spent a lot of my life feeling like I didn't belong or was unwanted, and I had so much empathy for what an animal must be put through if they had no home or were lonely and scared.

Without intending it to be, I found that my door was open to any animal in distress. Eddie is fantastic and has gone along with and supported me in my quest to help cats and dogs that are in need of help.

It has given me so much joy to watch a terrified animal suddenly know that they have nothing to fear and that someone cares about them. They actually become like a blossom opening up. They take on their own personality, and for the first time in their lives they experience a life without stress.

As we drove into a winding driveway surrounded by trees, I saw a woman walk out onto a deck of a house, and she carried a tiny white dog. As I neared the steps of the house I could see that the dog was shaking like a leaf.

The woman handed me the small bundle and said, "She should be fine, she just had a crap a few minutes ago."

"What's her name?" I asked.

"She doesn't have a name. She is about a year old and has been healthy up to now."

We drove away and I wrapped a blanket over this poor little dog. She was so terrified that my heart broke to see her suffering like this. I held her close and talked softly to her.

She shook the entire drive back to our house.

Eddie brought Chimo out of the house to meet her while I sat on the grass and stroked her head and still continued to talk to her. Chimo walked over to her and sniffed and then wagged his tail. I could feel her loosen up a bit, and she seemed to relax with him around.

We took her inside, and I put some food down for her and Chimo. Much to my surprise she had a hard time to stand up and eat. She was so weak. I then took her back outside to see if she needed to pee. She was unable to walk, and I just picked her up and hugged her and told her she was going to be alright.

"Eddie, I am not giving her up to anyone. I could never put her through this again."

Eddie agreed, and we tossed several names around and we decided on Miracle, as we both thought it was a miracle that she survived whatever she had been through.

Every day she came around a bit more. Her personality came out bit by bit. She loved Chimo, and she would pick up his leash and walk him through the house. He was happy to oblige her until he got tired, and then he would flop down on the floor and she would snuggle up next to him.

A couple of weeks later I decided that I was going to quit smoking. I decided I wanted to quit on a date I would remember. My son Al's birthday was coming up, and I thought that I would quit smoking on that day so I would always remember.

The night before Al's birthday, I smoked my last cigarette, and I must admit I truly enjoyed it. I laid my package of cigarettes and lighter down and whispered, "I'll make it without you."

A few days later I seemed to come down with a cold. I could feel it settling in my chest. I made an appointment with the doctor, who put me on antibiotics.

Every time I moved I would start coughing. I could feel even more weight falling off of me. Ten days later I was put on more antibiotics, and still I felt like I was continuing to get weaker each day. I had no energy, and I was finding it really hard to do any type of sign work. I knew I was getting sicker and sicker, but I didn't know how to stop it. I would cough until I couldn't breathe. My sides would hurt. I would sit and gasp for air.

When the next dose of antibiotics were done, the doctor put me on more, but it didn't seem to be working either. It was now three weeks of being sick, and I was becoming even weaker as each day passed. I felt like my legs couldn't hold me up most of the time.

I woke up one morning and thought that I was actually feeling a bit better. I had managed to sleep most of the night, which was unusual, since becoming ill I was not able to sleep due to problems breathing and coughing. So feeling a bit more refreshed I got up and walked to the bathroom, but within a few minutes I started coughing. I could not breathe, and I knew I was in trouble. With a lot of effort I made my way back to the bedroom where Eddie was asleep. I woke him up and said, "Please call me an ambulance. I can't breathe."

Eddie jumped out of the bed and ran to the phone. I sank to the bed and gasped for air.

Eddie hung up the phone and helped me down the stairs to wait for the ambulance. It only took a few minutes, but when you are fighting to breathe a few minutes seems like hours.

In the ambulance I continued to get worse, with my blood pressure raising and my oxygen level dropping. At the hospital I was told that I was dying and that I needed to be admitted immediately. They hooked me up to oxygen and intravenous. They were giving me steroids every couple of hours.

The next day the kids came to see me. I was so grateful to see their smiling faces. I told them I was not sure I was going to make it. I tried to tell them what I wanted them to have if I didn't make it.

Al said, "Mom, I would like it if you would come and live with me. Eddie is welcome to come to. You can have the basement of the house. You don't need to worry about anything."

"I appreciate that so much," I said, "but I think you need to talk to your wife. I would also need to sell my house."

I looked at Al and thought to myself how lucky I was to have my son offer this to me. I love him so much and I am so fortunate, I thought to myself.

The kids stayed for about an hour, and then they had to leave as Jay needed to get to work. They left, promising to stay in touch.

The hospital did what they called shocking my lungs every three hours for the next five days, which was painful as I was having a reaction to it. My hands and arms would swell up for a few hours and then the swelling would start to go down just in time to start all over again.

My sister and brother-in-law came to visit me. Everyone was acting positive, as if this was such a common cold. I wished I could feel as positive as they did.

Every time I would start coughing I would start choking on thick heavy phlegm. What a terrifying feeling. Not only could I not breathe, but I was choking as well. It seemed to take every ounce of my strength to cough, and I hard to fight so hard to get the phlegm up and many times it just did not want to come and would be stuck in my airways, cutting off my oxygen.

Every day I would try to get out of bed and walk around the room and then try to make my way down the hallway. It was just too much for me. I couldn't make it. There was a breathing therapist who was sent to me after the third or fourth day, and she was to help me try to regain some of my strength and help me walk down the hallway. I would get into the hallway totally out of breath, and then with her carrying my oxygen bottle she would walk beside me, checking out my oxygen level at the same time. I would make it only six or seven steps and she would say, "I think that's enough, Jenny. We had better get you back to your room."

"When can I go home?"

"Not until you are a bit stronger and your oxygen level is better," she replied.

Eddie was wonderful and slept at the hospital on the bed beside me every night. He would leave only to go home and feed Chimo and the cats, eat, shower, and change his clothes, and then he would be back at the hospital again. I was so very grateful for him being there with me and seeing me through it.

After the fifth day I was told they were sending me home and that I would still be on oxygen.

"How long will I be on oxygen?"

"I don't know, truthfully," the doctor replied. "I don't know if you will ever be off oxygen. You only have half of each lung. The bottom half of both lungs are dead, and only the top half is working. It is going to be up to you how well you do. We will have to wait and see."

"This is a scary thought, that I might not get off this oxygen."

"Yes, I'm sure it is. If you do get off the oxygen you will have a lot to face. Every time you get a cold you will probably get pneumonia, and there is a chance that you could die from a severe case. If you do survive you need to be aware that each time you get a cold it will weaken your lungs. You are going to continue to deteriorate. It is going to be up to you, how you accept this and live your life."

"At the moment I am just worried about going home and how I cope with that."

"What worries you about going home?"

"I'm worried about how am I going to make it up the stairs of my house, as I can't even walk across the floor here," I stated.

"Just take it one day at a time right now. Don't push yourself." The doctor got up and patted me on the shoulder, and then he walked out.

The nurse came into the room and gave me instructions on what I was to do and not do. She explained how the oxygen company would come to the house and set up everything for me. I would be sent home with a couple of bottles of oxygen that would keep me going until the other was set up.

Eddie helped me to get dressed. It seemed that everything I attempted to do just knocked the wind out of me. As we were getting ready to leave, my sister Isabell walked in the room.

"How did you know that I needed you?"

She just looked at me and said, "That's what sisters are for."

Eddie went ahead to get the car, and Isabel stayed with me and helped me to the lobby of the hospital.

I was so out of breath I felt like I was going to pass out. My legs shook with every step I took. It terrified me to know how weak I was. Eddie drove up at the front of the hospital, and Isabel helped me to get to the car and then helped me get inside. That was a long walk for me, and it just totally exhausted me.

When we arrived at the house, Eddie and Isabell helped me get into the house, taking slow steps and allowing me to stop and catch my breath every few steps. The oxygen company arrived about an hour after I got home. They set up all of the equipment and told me how to use it. Then they left, and a few minutes after Isabell left as well, leaving Eddie and me alone.

Eddie made dinner, and every once in a while he would come and check on me. If I started coughing he would come and stand beside me, knowing that I was going to be choking.

I knew it was going to be a long road ahead of me, but I was determined that I was not going to stay on oxygen. I hated the sound of the machine. Chimo would lay at my feet and sometimes come and put his head on my lap, as if he was trying to give me encouragement.

It was spring time, and Eddie helped me with the oxygen. He ran the hose through a window so that I could sit outside on the deck and listen to the birds sing, watch the squirrels, and just try to take my mind off what I was going through.

There was a local marina that I had been printing up registration numbers for boats that they sold. I had been doing it for a few years. They contacted me and asked if I was up to making the numbers for them still.

I said that I could, as I needed the money to pay for the medications, puffers, and even the oxygen that I was now on.

"I don't think you should be doing this. You're pushing yourself, and you need time to rest and get better," Eddie said as he guided my oxygen hose to the office.

"I don't have a choice," I said, trying to make my voice sound stronger than what it really was. I was so weak that I needed to sit down while I typed the numbers and letters into the computer and then getting the rolls of vinyl to cut the numbers to go on the boats. It was almost every day that they needed these, and even though it was hard on me to do it, it helped to make me even more determined that I was going to get better.

Day after day I would sit outside as soon as I got up and dressed. I would take a cup of coffee, and with Eddie's help with my oxygen line, and I would sit and listen to the birds.

There was a lilac bush at the front of the house that was coming into bloom, and it was full of buds with the heavy aromas drifting over to where I sat. I appreciated the smell so much. Even though I was on oxygen the smell of the lilacs was inspiring.

The town was building new sidewalks at the side of my house, and Eddie and I walked out the back door one morning to see how the work was progressing. We stood there in the driveway watching the construction crew coming and going. I turned and started to walk away to go around to the deck to sit down, but something made me look down, and there in the grass beside the busy sidewalk was a tiny robin, so small that he couldn't fly.

I bend down and scooped him up, and Eddie guided me around to the deck of the house. "I'll go and see if I can find a box to put him into," Eddied said as he walked away. A few minutes later he came back with a box in his hand. I looked in the box and saw that Eddie had already spread some grass on the bottom of the box to make it soft and warm for the little bird. I placed the bird gently into the box.

"Eddie, what should we feed him?"

"Well, we need to get some worms. Maybe we can phone the local vet and see what they recommend."

Eddied helped me back inside, and I went to the phone and made the call. They recommended corn meal mixed with water and to feed him with a syringe.

For the next couple of days I would spend my days sitting outside with the box near me. I would feed the bird about every half hour. We noticed that adult robins always seemed to be close in the trees watching what we were doing. My neighbor Helen and her husband would come to the fence separating our backyards, and they would ask how the bird was doing. Then one afternoon we were sitting under the trees with the little robin when a stray cat went through our yard. Several robins went chasing after the cat, making a lot of racket.

"Wow," I said to Eddie. "It looks like they are watching over us and this baby."

"I think you're right," Eddie replied.

Helen checked on us daily to see how the little bird was doing. Other neighbors started getting interested as well in what was happening. Every day they would come over and see how the little bird was doing. We all agreed that he looked healthy. He seemed to get more feathers every day, and he was growing. Some of the neighbors came over to bring worms and bugs that they found.

"This is so neat," I said to Eddie. "This little bird has become a neighborhood project."

That same afternoon Eddie helped me into the house to get something to eat for dinner. I left the baby bird in the box on a bench under a big shade tree in the back yard. As we stood in the kitchen, Eddie said, "Look, there is a robin sitting on the box."

Just as I walked over to the window to look I saw the bird jump down into the box. "I think it's feeding the baby," I exclaimed in amazement.

We stood there watching the bird fly away, and another bird landed on the box to do the same thing, it would sit for a moment on the side of the box and then jump in to feed the baby.

"That's amazing," I said.

After we ate, we went back outside, and I continued to feed the baby bird. There were berries in the box. "Eddie, did you feed this little one some berries?"

"No," Eddie replied.

"I guess they think he needs berries as well as worms."

A few more days went by, and then one morning I had just finished feeding the bird when all of a sudden he started fluttering his wings in the box. I sat back and watched him. He finally made his way up onto the edge of the box and teetered there while he looked around while he decided what he should do next.

I looked up into the tree overhead and saw that there were several robins sitting, watching, and chirping as if they were yelling out instructions.

Finally the baby robin spread his wings and flew to the ground. An adult robin instantly was on the ground with him.

Helen came out and was also watching in fascination what was happening. "Do you want to catch him?" she asked.

"No, not at all. I've done my job, and now it's their turn to teach him what he needs to know," I smiled.

For the rest of the day I sat listening to the birds in the trees, and sometimes I thought I could hear the sounds of a young bird chirping.

If that little bird as weak as he had been when we found him could survive, then I could too. He was my inspiration of hope and made me even more determined to fight and get strong again.

RE-CAPPING

SINCE THE ENDING OF THE BOOK

I did get off oxygen, and I don't let the fact that I only have half of each lung stop me.

I now jog and do sit-ups each day to try and build my lungs up and make them stronger.

I am now a grandmother of twins who are beautiful, and I adore them. Paul and his beautiful wife are fantastic parents, and you can feel the love when you walk into their house. They are both writers and have written a movie that is positive and inspiring.

Al and his gorgeous wife are now looking forward to the birth of their first child. Al works hard in construction, and his wife is a teacher. They have a beautiful home that is going to be blessed with the pitter patter of little feet.

Jay has beat cancer. He works as a doctor in Toronto and has opened a brain clinic to help people with brain injuries. Newly married this year, he is looking forward to a long, healthy life. His beautiful wife is a professional ballerina, and they are looking forward to a wonderful life together.

Needless to say I am so proud of each one of them to have come through what they did when they were growing up.

They have all moved on with their lives. It was a learning experience for all of us.

They are in contact with their father.

I don't ask any questions, and we never really discuss what took place.

It took me four years to write this book.

I would get to certain points, and then I would have to stop for months as I found that reliving it was hard to do.

I am hoping that this book will help give encouragement to other women who are in an abusive situation.

Things are changing, and hopefully there is more help out there now than there had been when I was in an abusive relationship.

I know that you feel alone, but don't feel ashamed to stretch out your hand and get help.

Believe in yourself.

They are talking about bullying in schools.

People are beginning to understand that it's wrong for one person to pick on another person. Well, an abuser is a bully.

FACTS

One in five Canadians suffer from a mental illness, impacting countless lives.

Because there is a stigma attached to the term mental illness, many people suffering from this disease will not seek help.

In Canada, 4 out of 5 people murdered are women by their spouses. In 1998, 67 women were murdered by their spouses or ex-spouses. That is 1-2 women per week.

In 6 out of 10 murders, police are already aware that there is a history of violence.

Wife battering carries into old age. Spousal homicide accounts for 30 percent of women murdered over the age of 65.

A minimum of one million children have witnessed their mothers being abused by their fathers, mothers often fearing for their lives.

In Canada, a man who beats or rapes his partner can remain in his home while the mother and children are removed to a shelter and often are bounced from one shelter to another.

In a 1993 survey, 295,000 abused women had no access to counseling or housing services.

In Canada 21 percent of women abused were assaulted during pregnancy, and many reported that the abuse began during a pregnancy when they are most vulnerable and relying on their partner for support.

In 1996, 48 percent of all violent crimes were committed by a male perpetrator against a female victim.

So, the age-old question, why do women stay in an abusive relationship?

Brainwashing: Many men will brainwash their partner into believing they are worthless.

Making the woman question her identity.

Making the woman believe that she is not a good wife or mother, eventually making her believe that she is not worthy of her family and husband.

He will work on her physiologically until she reaches her breaking point. With identity in crisis, and experiencing shame, and she will ask herself questions, such as:

"Who am I?"

"Where am I?"

"What do I do now?"

It is when a woman gets to this point that the husband now has total control over her on a daily basis, with his threats and other tactics.

Normally the abuser tries to keep the woman isolated as much as possible.

Often the woman does not get enough sleep, and sleep deprivation just adds to the fact that she does not think straight and make decisions independently.

In the late 1950's, the psychologist Robert Jay Layton studied former prisoners of the Korean and Chinese war camps, and he found that the prisoners had gone through a series of brain-washing techniques that consisted of assault of identity, guilt, self-betrayal, and breaking point.

In reality, there is not much difference between a woman who has been brainwashed by her abuser or the veteran who has been brainwashed by his captor.

Fear: Women have been murdered or severely abused when trying to leave a relationship. A woman may feel safer to stay where she is so she can keep an eye on him, rather than leave and be stalked and maybe killed.

Current reports find that there are about 19 million Canadians who had a current or former spouse in 2009. Out of the number, there are 2.9 percent who were victims of sexual or physical spousal assault during that year.

Stats Canada found that the number of domestic assaults has stabilized during the past five years, or the reports of these incidents has stabilized. In 1999, there were 7.4 cases reported abused during that year.

The psychological effects of abuse are low self-esteem, self-degradation, self-abuse, difficulty with relationships, acute anxiety, frequent crying, unusual or pronounced fear responses, chronic stress, phobias, flashbacks, insomnia, nightmares, passivity, memory loss, loss of concentration, and productivity.

The psychiatric effects are depression, suicidal thoughts, dissociation, post-traumatic stress disorder, eating disorders, adjustment disorder, depressed mood, and obsessive disorder.

BELIEVE in YOURSELF and YOUR DREAMS.